JAX'S GAME

A.E. CALDER

Cover by Ana Chabrand Design House

CONTENTS

ACKNOWLEDGMENTS

I cannot express enough my thankfulness and gratitude to those who have supported me with writing and producing a novel.

Myléne, my best friend since childhood, you cheered me on throughout the whole journey of writing. You encouraged me during the lows to keep writing and celebrated with me during the highs. I thank you for listening to me ramble on about all the ideas that made its way into this novel or didn't.

Madi, a good friend in my life, you helped me with formatting ideas and the plot that brought this thought into action. If it wasn't for you, this book wouldn't be the way it is. Thank you for allowing me to bounce ideas off of you and to keep this project alive.

My mother, who supported me through this whole project and believed in me since I began to write. Thank you so much for everything you do for me.

And finally, thank you to my beta readers who told how to bring the story alive further.

Writing a book isn't a solo action it's a team of inspiring and supportive people.

I love you all so dearly and thank you so much.

DEDICATION

I would love to dedicate this novel to my younger self who never believed she would write a book, let alone allow people to read it and make her dream come true. We did it, we accomplished it and we love it.

PROLOGUE

She sat on his bed, the fifth one out from the door. Harriet watched him pack what little belongings he had. She was silent, she didn't know what to say. Was she devastated? That was an understatement? Words couldn't express how she was feeling. Jax was leaving, and she didn't know if he would ever come back to her.

"Promise me you will find me once I get out of here?" she pleaded, eyes looking down to the concrete tile on the orphanage's floor.

The seventeen-year-old across from her, dark brown hair with dishevelled curls very much on display, looked at her. Jax nodded slowly, crouching down to her height. Her small yet gorgeous sapphire eyes connected with his pale blue ones.

"I promise," he whispered, cupping her cheeks and bringing them in for a kiss. Lovers but survivors, the two orphans held onto the only love they had ever known: their love for one another.

Jax was leaving. His biological father was taking him

back. The boy had been left to rot since he was born, as his mother never wanted him. Recently, his father found out about him and had decided to take him back from the orphanage. This was the only home that he had ever known. He was leaving her, and she didn't know what to say. Her red, tear-soaked eyes continued to watch him.

The brunette boy took her in when she appeared at the age of four, him seven. He taught her to not be scared, to look at the joy of life. Their relationship had progressed to young love.

Their plan had been simple. The moment he was eighteen and released from the government's hold, he would work, make money, and become her legal guardian. However, plans had changed, and he was no longer able to do that. Instead, he was going 'home' to his father, whom he just met, wherever home was now.

His father seemed to be a nice man, in his forties, married with two children. Harriet hadn't met him, but he seemed better than anything she could imagine from what Jax had told her. She was stuck here for another three years while he would be out there living his best life with a family. Harriet needed to be happy for him.

"I love you," she murmured, eyes dropping back to the grey concrete tile.

"I love you too, kitten," he kissed her cheek, hearing footsteps outside the room.

"Jaxon Irwin, your father is here to take you," the older woman, Betty, came in and gave him the terrible yet incredible news. A nun at the Catholic orphanage, she admired the two, watching them grow up to be such good *friends*.

"It was always supposed to be you who gets adopted, not

me," he said. Harriet got up, gave him a hug, holding him so close. Tears filled her eyes as she held him for the last time.

Jax held her, rocking them back and forth and placing a final kiss on her cheek. His hand clutched hers and began to let go slowly, dragging his fingers from her as he walked away.

"I will find you. I promise. I love you forever and a day."

She watched him walk out, her greatest love leaving her there in the rotten system. She didn't know where her future would take her. It was broken, therefore who knew where she would go in life.

He promised, though.

1

13 YEARS LATER...

L*ondon, England.*

Who would ever have imagined that she would end up in England? Leaving New Zealand was not even fathomable until now, but nevertheless, she was here.

"One year, you will be here only one year and then you can go back home," she whispered under her breath as she grabbed her bags and exited Heathrow. *"You're working for a year and then you will be home."* It was her silent mantra.

It was scary, leaving the island and her little town where her life consisted of surfing, partying, and working. Now, she was here for a job, working as a nanny to take a break from her life back home.

"All it is, is a break," she whispered again. Gathering herself and her luggage, she exited the baggage claim. *"Here goes nothing."*

Harriet looked around for a sign with her name on it. Her employer, Claudia, had told her that her driver would pick her up and take her to the manor. Her long, dyed silver hair was draped over her shoulder and glasses perched on her freckled nose. This she paired with grey sweats and a crew neck she had stolen from an ex.

Her blue eyes scanned the people waiting for their loved ones. Biting her lip, she walked around the pickup area.

Ms. Harriet Kensington

She spotted her name. Gathering herself one last time, she walked up to the sign that belonged to a tan individual. Italian descent, possibly? He had dark brown hair, close to black, with a toothy smile which made him seem more welcoming. A good boy in her eyes, the type of guy you would bring home to your mother.

"Hi, Harriet," she said, her Kiwi accent startling him.

"Hi, I'm Marco," he replied, hand out ready for a handshake. Definitely Italian, she noted with that gorgeous accent. "How was your flight?" he asked, leading her to the car. He took her luggage from her, explaining he wanted to take it off her hands.

"It was good. Long though," she sighed.

"How long?"

"I'm from New Zealand, so it was close to twenty-four hours."

Marco's eyes widened. "Holy. The longest flight I have done was ten hours, and I thought that was hell."

"Yeah, I get that. Thank God Mrs. Alderidge paid for my flight here, so I had the little cubicle thing where I was able to sleep. I don't know how I would have survived if I was just sitting," she exclaimed with a chuckle.

He laughed as they stopped in front of a black Jaguar SUV. She looked at her surroundings, which was an outside parking lot. The sun beamed down on her. It was hot, not crazy, but enough for her to be a little warm in her jumper and pants. June weather in England was completely different from New Zealand's June weather. It was good to have summer come early.

Marco opened the door for her, then climbed into the designer leather seats.

Here goes nothing, one year of work and travel, then she was back home, and everything would be fine. All the drama would cool down, she prayed.

Harriet wouldn't admit it, but she had left for a reason. A traumatic incident had happened to her, and she needed to leave the island to take a breather. She loved kids. Back at home, she worked as a social worker, so, to be a nanny for a five-year-old, and a two-year-old was exciting. What was more exciting was that they were in a good home. She didn't know if she could take another child from a tragic home. Too many stories, too many tears.

"Do you work for the Alderidge's?" she asked as the two of them headed for the Manor.

"Yes, I work as their chef. It's a wonderful home, old and possibly haunted, but it's beautiful. The couple is very kind. The husband I rarely see as he is a workaholic, but Claudia is quite nice. She works for Vogue in London, and he owns his own law firm, I think. The kids are sweethearts, very kind, and Ember, the daughter, has quite the personality. Caleb takes after his sister," he told her.

She smiled, "That is amazing. I am glad to soon be part of their lives."

HALF AN HOUR LATER, the car pulled up to a cobblestone building with a towering roof and small windows. A perfect garden of hedges and lush flowers surrounded it. They pulled up in front of the roundabout. A garage sat beside but detached from the mansion itself. She reckoned it was newer by how clean the stone was. There was a playground in the distance with a pond beside it. Very different from her flat back home, its size was probably the same as a bathroom in this place.

"Wow," she muttered to herself.

"I know, it took me a while to get used to it," Marco told her as he unloaded her bags. "Claudia will be out in a second."

An older woman came out with a younger dirty blonde one. The younger one was gorgeous and tall; five foot ten possibly. She was giant compared to Harriet's five-foot-four stature. The woman was slim, tiny and model-like with perfect doe eyes paired with long lashes, a petite nose, and a jaw-dropping smile. As she came closer, Harriet noticed her brown roots.

"Hi Harriet, I'm Claudia. It's amazing to meet you," the woman said. Her smile was perfect. She could attract anyone and make any man swoon. Her voice was light but warm and soothing. Claudia gave Harriet a hug. "Sandy will take your bags up to your room, and you can follow me. The kids are dying to meet you."

Sandy was older, in her sixties possibly, and quiet. She must be the housekeeper. The place kept getting posher every minute.

Harriet smiled, nodding to her new employer as she followed her into the house.

"My husband is away right now in Paris for work, so he

won't get to meet you till later." The two of them entered the house and were greeted with a modern yet traditional interior. It was all so neat and kept in pristine condition. A double staircase led upstairs, and beautiful sculptures and art lined the foyer.

"My husband's father collects art," she told her as they walked through the home. Harriet couldn't get over the collection he had, all different types and styles. Her passion for art made her yearn to study each piece and ask a million questions about the artists, but she kept it to herself.

"It's gorgeous. I wish I had studied art in university. All of this is just heaven for me."

The dirty blonde turned around to the silver haired lady. "Really? What did you study instead?"

"Social work, with a minor in English lit. Back in NZ, I was a social worker, working with kids from tragic homes."

Claudia gave her a shy smile. "That must've been hard."

"It was, but it was also nice to know they're no longer in those homes."

The pair entered the kitchen and Harriet spotted two kids at the breakfast bar. The room was timeless, with grey cabinets and the white walls featuring engraved designs and wooden framing. Quartz countertops and bright lighting from many windows allowed in the natural light. The door to the back garden was open, and the June weather invited her outside.

Claudia turned to the kids, beaming at her children. "This is Harriet, babes. She is the new nanny I was talking about."

Harriet walked up to them, greeting them.

The younger girl, who she assumed was Ember, had dark brown curls and hazel eyes. She sat there innocently with a blue dress on while she ate her snack of cheese and crackers. Caleb was the complete opposite from his sister with platinum blonde curls, blue eyes, and little freckles littered all over his face. He could possibly be the cutest kid she has ever seen.

The blue eyes of Caleb haunted her. For some odd reason, she recognized them as if she had seen them before. However, the silver-haired woman shook off that thought.

"Hi, I'm Ember," she said, shying away while Caleb began to make grabby hands for his mom.

"How's your snack, girly?" Harriet asked, giving the child a wide smile and a wink.

"Good," she mumbled, as she picked up a piece of cracker and cheese and handed it to Harriet.

"Thank you, Miss. Ember." Harriet took the food from her, eating it. "They are so cute," she exclaimed to Claudia.

Claudia nodded. "I know. This one," she began, messing Caleb's hair, "looks exactly like me, but his eyes are definitely his father's. Em is the spit and image of her daddy, but with my eyes."

"Now," she said, taking out two mugs. "Let's talk. Tea?"

Harriet nodded, thanking her.

"I recently got promoted, so I'll be working five days a week, eight to eight. I work at Vogue in London, so I won't be home till eight-thirty, nine. Weekends you have off. I travel a lot for work, and so does my husband. His schedule is extremely unpredictable. I never know when he will be home. I'm in the process of hiring a weekend nanny as well."

Harriet nodded, taking the cup of tea from her.

"Em goes to school, while Caleb doesn't. She goes to the private school up the road. Take the Jaguar. Her school starts around eight and pick up is at three. I wrote this all in the email I sent to you, but with me being a control freak, I will tell you everything again and again until you yell at me to stop." Claudia went on, explaining bed routines and Ember's schedule.

"Weekends, you are more than allowed to stay here. Your room is upstairs and across from Caleb's in the east wing. My husband and I are in the west, which is off limits. The Jaguar is all yours. Take it even on the weekends. Now that is all settled, welcome. Let me show you to your room."

Harriet thanked her. Everything seemed exciting. Taking care of kids should be a fine, easy job. Then on weekends, she could experience what the country had to offer.

Claudia held Caleb as they exited the room and headed back to the main hallway. She heard running footsteps and a small hand grabbing onto hers.

"You have drawings on your arm," the little girl said.

Harriet smiled. "Yes, I do."

"Can I colour them in?"

"Of course, you can," Harriet winked.

Her arm was covered in tattoos of her country's native flowers, plants, and birds. It was truly a work of art, and Harriet was quite proud of it.

"They are very pretty," Claudia said. "I wish I could do it, but I am afraid of needles and have a low pain tolerance even though I pushed two kids out."

"Yeah, I understand that."

Eventually, after walking for what seemed like forever, the two of them and the kids were in front of a set of double doors. Claudia opened them, and she was met with white walls and a king-size bed with an ottoman in front of it. The room was gorgeous with a white velvet bed frame, birch dresser, and side table. There was a walk-in closet and an ensuite; everything white and sleek. The one thing she couldn't get over was the view, looking out over the front gardens. It was absolutely divine.

"I'll let you settle in," Claudia said, exiting the room and closing the door.

2

Jax woke up, groaning a little over the buzzing of his phone. He reached out, a thick muscled and veiny arm coming in view as he brought the device to his ear.

"Hello?" he mumbled, looking around the room his eyes instantly falling to the naked blonde next to him.

"Hi Jax, it's Dorothy. I have two calls for you. One line is your wife. Something about a nanny arriving... and the other is Mr. Clifford," his assistant told him. A groan escaped his lips.

"Line two, please," he mumbled. Three seconds later, he heard the familiar voice.

"Hi, Jax. This is Shawn Clifford. We talked yesterday regarding the settlement to..." a small, deep groan escaped from his lips.

Jax got up, eyeing himself in the mirror and ignoring the small blonde next to him. Thick pecs and abs came in view in front of him, chest hair present and trailing down to his deep v line where he saw his prominent manhood. Proud of what he saw, he grabbed a pair of joggers and walked backed to the room, barely listening to what Mr. Clifford was talking about.

Ocean coloured eyes gazed at the skimpy female clothes on the ground. He grabbed the tiny clothes and threw them to the woman occupying his bed. Her eyes shot open, he told her to get a move on.

He got a dirty look from her. French girls were so stuck up.

"Yes, yes, the meeting is tomorrow about the settlement," he said, a deep voice echoing around the flat. Jax watched the woman leave his multi-million euro flat in downtown Paris. The man wanted this phone call to end, as he truly wasn't in the mood to talk about anything work-related. It also didn't help that he was nursing a nasty hangover.

"Well, Jax, unfortunately, we can't do it tomorrow. Today at two works?" Jax's eyes instantly opened, turning around to look at the clock in the kitchen. One p.m. that would be fine. Three coffees and a shot of whiskey would be enough to help him survive the meeting.

Continuing to walk through the house, he saw another woman on the couch. Groaning once again, he shook her awake.

The brunette's eyes opened, locking with his blue ones. Jax mouthed 'get the fuck out' before going back to the phone call.

"Yes, I will be there, Mr. Clifford. Thanks again for everything," he hung up and groaned, raking his fingers through his locks before making a coffee.

"Sabrina, Sarah, Sally, Serena-" he trailed on, trying to remember her name.

"Fleur," the girl snapped, grabbing her dress from the floor.

"Thanks for last night. You need to leave. Don't forget to sign." Jax turned his attention back to the espresso in front of him, downing the first one of the day and then slamming down a whiskey shot.

The girl left begrudgingly, signing the book at the door.

Two seconds later, his phone rang again.

"Seriously," he mumbled, taking the phone to his ear.

"Jax Alderidge speaking," he said, heading to the ensuite bathroom.

"Jax, it's Claudia. I have left twenty messages for you this morning. The nanny arrived today, and I expected you to be here."

'*Claudia. Fuck.*'

He hummed, taking out a suit from the closet and turning the shower on.

"Stuck in Paris. I won't be back yet. Give the kids kisses for me, I'll see you soon." Hanging up, he threw the phone onto the bed and stepped into his morning shower.

Claudia hired a new nanny. She actually did it. The question was, who was the nanny?

Jax prayed that it wasn't some grumpy old lady who screamed at his children.

3

Harriet quickly changed out of her travel wear, taking a quick shower and throwing on a pair of jeans and a cropped cardigan. Her silver hair was pulled up into a topknot while she gathered her belongings. Round tortoiseshell glasses perched on her nose, delicately framing her face. She went downstairs.

It was close to six at night. Her stomach grumbled as she was reminded of the fact that she hadn't eaten since her flight. Plane food never sat right in her, always making her either have nausea or a loss of appetite. She had the latter up until now.

The scent of Italian cooking hit her nose as she walked into the kitchen. The two kids played outside in the garden while Claudia spoke on the phone. Marco was busy, making dinner for the family. She waved at him and walked out into the back garden.

Ember held a bottle of bubbles, while Caleb thought the rocks and grass were far more intriguing than the sticky liquid dancing around him. Harriet smiled at that. Children always found a way to get dirty.

Claudia spotted her, waving and started walking away. Well, Harriet guessed nanny duty started now. Ember ran up to her. Her hands, sticky from the bubbles, clamped onto Harriet's arm and rubbed soap into her skin.

"I wanna have drawings on my arm," she said so innocently. Harriet giggled, poking her nose with her finger.

"Maybe one day," she winked.

"What's that?" She pointed to the bird on her inner arm.

"It's a tui, a native bird back where I am from. They have the most beautiful songs," she told her. "And this is Pohutukawa. It's our Christmas tree," she told her.

Ember shook her head. "No, Christmas trees are big and green, and have pokey things."

Harriet chuckled, "Very true."

Marco came out, a white apron on top of his black tee and jeans. His toothy smile - something she would never get over - shone as he watched the kids play. "Dinner!" he called out.

Ember ran in while Caleb stayed occupied with the grass. Harriet had to walk over and pick him up. His beady eyes instantly filled with tears until he saw it was Harriet who was holding him.

"Dinner, mister," she hummed as they walked in.

Claudia was nowhere to be seen. Ember sat at the dining table, babbling on about some imaginative game she came up with. She pointed out to Harriet where Caleb usually sat. Harriet fastened him in the booster chair, while his tiny chubby finger grabbed her shirt.

"Dinner, bub," she replied. He let go of her, eyebrows furrowing as she helped Marco dish out dinner.

"How long will you be here for? Are you leaving soon?" Ember asked. "We didn't have a long playdate."

Harriet giggled. "No, I am not leaving soon. Guess what?" she whispered.

"What?" Her eyes widened with curiosity.

"I am sleeping over...*forever*," she whispered.

Ember's mouth dropped open, "No way."

"Yes, way."

"Then you will have to be my new best friend," she said, taking her fork out and stabbing the pasta dish with it. Caleb was using his fingers, smearing tomato sauce all over his face, but his smile gleamed as he did it.

"Wow, me? Your best friend? I would be honoured," she gushed. Ember grinned, laughing and smiling. She was truly a happy child.

Once dinner was over, it was time for the kids to have their nightly bedtime bath. Gathering the two, they all headed upstairs together. Being her vocal self, Ember talked about school and painting a butterfly in class, which now was alive because she saw it in the park...kids and their wicked imagination. All Harriet could do was nod along.

Caleb was mostly silent, occasionally babbling and pointing at the things around them. He pointed to the duck in the bath and said, "duck". Then he went back to playing with his car, making "vroom" noises. Ember all the while, was still a Chatty Betty with Harriet, telling her all types of stories.

"My daddy has brown hair like me," she told her, grabbing her curls and scrubbing them with the shampoo. Harriet raised her eyebrows.

"Oh, really? Well, I love your curls," she said as she

rinsed the shampoo from her hair and applied the conditioner.

"Thank you. He has curly hair too, but it's all short now."

Harriet nodded along. "What's your daddy's name?"

"Daddy." Of course, it was, of course.

"When was the last time you saw him?" she asked, now washing the shampoo from Caleb's mop of curls.

"Ummm, I don't know," Ember shrugged and went back on to playing with her dolls.

To Harriet, this had been the easiest job in the world. The kids were compliant, easy-going and overall good. They were good at listening and doing what they were told to do. In all honesty, Harriet was having more fun than she thought she would and didn't see it as a job.

A few days later, Claudia was barely heard or seen, and Harriet began to feel bad for the kids. Their mom was nowhere to be found and who knew where their father was. However, she was truly settling into life in England. Things were becoming good.

Thursday night, the kids were in bed. It was nine p.m. when she heard the door open, and a British female voice mixed with a male accent; British but with a hint of something else.

Harriet didn't think much of it. In sweats and with her hair pulled back, she walked down the stairs heading to the kitchen. Her water bottle in hand which needed to be filled before she called it quits for the night. Quite frankly, she was fancying a cup of tea as well.

"You're never home," she heard Claudia sneer at the other person.

"I am working," she heard the male voice. His was harsher, deep, and his tone was rough. His accent was different, and Harriet couldn't quite put her finger on it. Nevertheless, she continued with her nightly routine.

"You haven't been home in two weeks, you missed Ember's dance recital." The yelling continued and things began to escalate.

"It's not like you are always at home. Working twelve-hour shifts and hired a nanny to do the hard work," the male voice piped back. "I am sorry I wasn't there, but I had to be in Paris for this deal. My work-"

"Your work shouldn't come before family."

"The same goes for you, Claudia," the male voice bit back.

Harriet walked into the kitchen, ignoring the couple fighting. She quickly filled her water bottle and planned to run back upstairs.

"Harriet," she heard Claudia say. It was stern. She was still riled up from the fight with her husband.

Turning around, Harriet looked at her and sent her a smile. "Just filling my bottle before going upstairs."

Claudia nodded, hand against her head and pushing her hair back out of exhaustion. "Oh, well, meet my husband, Jaxon." Harriet turned her attention to the male figure to her left.

'Jax.'

He was six foot two, with shorter dark brown hair than the last time she saw him, yet small curls could still be seen. Stubble adorned his face, but the eyes she remembered had lost the glimmer they used to hold. He was in a very expensive suit, black with a loosened tie. His face had matured and there was a rustic look to it. He definitely had the facial structure and look of a hard-working man, defined and strong.

It pained her, seeing him standing before her.

"Well, I'm going to bed." Claudia exited the room, done with whatever had just happened.

Jax had his eyes glued to the woman across from him. Harriet couldn't take her eyes off him. Was it love? Who knew, but most definitely, it felt like a stab to the heart.

"*Kitten*," he muttered the old nickname. She didn't know what to do, whether to run or stay, to cry or punch him or hug him.

"Hi," she muttered, breaking eye contact. "I'm just going-"

"You're the new nanny." He walked over to her. Harriet put the bottle down as he placed his hand on her cheek. She felt the roughness of his touch, soft hands no more. His eyes were sad, filled with burden and stress. The woman just wanted to hold him, but she couldn't.

He had fucked up. He didn't find her, and she had *tried* so hard to find him. Then it hit her, his last name was changed. Irwin to Alderidge...it would have been impossible to find him. Hiring a private investigator would have gotten too expensive for her broke self to deal with.

He stood before her now looking completely different. He was no longer the delinquent with a baby face and a head full of curls. He was older, mature, rough looking.

Harriet nodded. She still couldn't believe it.

"You never found me," she muttered, pulling away from his touch. He was offended by that action, but he understood. "You promised me."

"I wanted to, but I-"

"You got a life. A great life, with a wife, money, kids. Good on you," she replied.

"What about you?" he asked, puzzled as he tried to read her.

"I'm the product of the system, so not much. Work to live," she dismissed.

He nodded and tried to excuse his behaviour. "I wanted to find you, but I couldn't. I was stuck here. I had obligations. But that doesn't matter because *you* found *me*," he stressed those words.

"You're married and have kids," she paused and looked at him, shaking her head, "I know that look. Nothing can happen. I'm here to work for a year, then I'm going home. Who knows where I'll end up? Maybe I will go back to my job and life or not. I've always wanted to live in Canada or Australia..." she trailed off. Harriet felt uncomfortable that he was here in front of her, hinting that he wanted her. It was as if her past wanted to haunt her further.

"What do you do back home?" he tried to make conversation.

"Social work."

He sighed, giving her a sad smile and leaned his body against the counter across from her. "You've always worn your heart on your sleeve." Harriet let out a snort and turned away from him.

"I need to go to sleep. It's past midnight, Jax. Welcome home," she told him, bitterly, giving him a shy smile before turning back upstairs.

'This could not be real.'

Harriet looked at herself in the mirror, her eyes staring into her reflected image. Thirteen years later, he was here. He was here, married, rich, and with kids. What a perfect lifestyle he had, but she was different. Running from her past, which made her run away from her dreams. This woman's fuel was trauma, drama, and pity.

Taking a deep breath, she turned around, hastily wiping her tears and walking to the bed. She was here for a break, to run and forget. Why did her past have to appear when she least needed it?

Of course, it was a rough sleep.

He stood in the kitchen the next morning, leaning against the counter with a coffee in hand. The lawyer watched the British sunrise in front of him.

She was here. Claudia actually did hire her and not some old, grumpy lady. Harriet was here in the flesh, in front of him. A piece of him was nervous that she was back, and another was thrilled that his greatest love was here.

Jax couldn't believe it. His past creeping back up to him out of the blue, and God was he thankful...she was here. His love, his kitten, his life led him back here. He stared out through the wide windows to the rolling fields he had grown to love as his mind raced miles a minute with thoughts and opinions.

'What should I do now?'

Little does she know about his life, and vice versa. The pain, the loveless marriage, his work, and the multiple women that had made his bed warm. He felt shame for the last thirteen years.

"Morning," he heard. He turned around. His blue eyes made contact with her beautiful icy ones. She sent him a smile as he noticed his son on her hip.

Her silver hair was thrown into a messy ponytail, while round glasses framed her face, and her pyjamas covered her curvy body.

"Morning," he grumbled. Caleb was still asleep on her shoulder as she poured herself a cup of coffee. The minute he spoke, his son's eyes snapped open.

Little whimpers came from Caleb's mouth as he made grabby hands at his father. Jax set his coffee down, taking the small boy from Harriet's arms.

"Hi, mister," he said, kissing his cheeks and bouncing him. "How'd you sleep, kitten?" he asked.

Harriet sighed, turning around. "Don't call me that," she sternly said, taking her coffee and going to the fridge. She pulled out fruits and eggs, planning to make the kids breakfast.

Jax raised his eyebrows, putting his son in his chair before going back to the kitchen. "You didn't answer my question," he mumbled, his rough morning voice echoing the room. Jax took the eggs from her as he turned the stove on.

"I slept fine. How about you?" she asked, cutting strawberries.

"Couldn't sleep. This *beautiful* woman appeared in my house last night. All I could think about was her and the hundreds of questions I want to ask her," he responded as if it were nothing.

He spoke as if he was talking about the weather. It drove her mad as Jax seemed to not understand how serious this situation was.

Jax had feelings for her. However, he was married, and she was in no state of mind to date at that moment. The man couldn't treat his life as if it were a game where he could always win and sacrifice whatever he seemed fit. He had a marriage and kids to think about.

Ember walked into the kitchen, rubbing her eyes.

"Morning, Em!" Harriet sang, shaking off her thoughts and smiled at her. She kneeled as Ember ran into her arms. The curly haired girl - who looked just like Jax - grabbed her and held her. Her small brown eyes met her father's, and instantly Harriet was forgotten as the little girl ran to him.

Jax twirled her around, placing a wet kiss on her cheek.

"Daddy, you're home!" she exclaimed, giggling as he threw her in the air.

"Yes, I am! Planning to work from home for a little bit and help around with Harriet," he told her, looking over at Harriet whose eyes widened.

"You're working from home?" she asked, narrowing her eyes and sending him a look.

"Yeah, why not?" he shrugged and removed the eggs from the stove onto colourful plastic IKEA plates.

Harriet hummed, adding the fruit to plates and taking them to the kids; an orange plate in front of Caleb and a purple one in front of Ember.

Once they were busy eating, she turned around to Jax. "Jax, we...we need to talk. You're married, and I can see in your eyes that-," she tried to express her thoughts, but he took her arm and pulled her out of the room far from the kids' ears.

"I am broken without you," he snapped, his tone harsh as he ran his fingers through his hair. "You being here just shows me how my life isn't right without you. I am in a loveless marriage. I work too much and-"

She raised her eyebrows from his confession.

"I love my kids, don't get me wrong. I just-"

"Jax," she groaned, "I am not here to fuck up this family. If you're telling me that me being here is triggering you to make a bad decision, then I should leave. We are adults, let's handle this like adults."

He groaned even louder. "No, stay. I need you. Har, it's been you and me since the beginning. I'm worried about you," he said.

"*Me*?" she questioned not understanding where he was heading.

"You're running," he stressed. She shook her head.

"Go to work, don't hang around me. I know you. You put yourself into your work to distract yourself from your problems. I remember the supermarket job when you were in trouble with the law. I am the past. This," she said, looking around, "is your future. I need to be here for a year, to forget my past for a moment and my pain in order to accept my future. You should do the same." She turned around after her advisement, but he grabbed her arm again. His strong grip yanked her causing Harriet to look him straight into his eyes.

He glared at her as if he was trying to discover information about her. Harriet was turned on for a split second, her body sighing from his touch, but she couldn't allow that. Jax was married.

"What are you running from? You would *never* leave New Zealand." He glared at her, his words spitting out. "You're scared of change. You would *never* leave."

A loud snort escaped her lips as she gripped his hand and pulled it off.

"That's none of your business. You're my employer, not my friend," she responded, trying her best to end the argument. She walked back to the kitchen, leaving him there dumbfounded. It pained her to be blunt, but it was needed.

Jax let out a loud groan. '*Immature asshole*,' was all she could think. He was used to getting his way, having control and making people listen. The man was the king of manipulation and being the boss. It annoyed him, frustrated him to tell her to do something and she wouldn't do it.

'You're my employer, not my friend.'

It echoed in his mind. Shaking his head, he quickly ran his fingers through his dark curls. Two could play that game. If she wanted to play hard to get, he was more than willing to playing that game.

"Em, are you ready?" He heard her from the kitchen.

Sighing, but more like a groan, he walked back into the kitchen. He would never stop wanting to be with her. She was his, his person. Jax knew what he had to do then and there.

"I'm coming," he grabbed his jacket from the chair in the kitchen. The trench coat had sat there throughout the night, as he had dropped it when he came in from his flight before Claudia belittled him. The kids screamed, excitement lingered from their noises, but all he cared about was her. Harriet just groaned from his statement.

Ignoring him, she took Caleb's hand and headed out the grand front doors. Jax followed her to the black Jaguar SUV parked in front of the steps. Following her footsteps, he climbed into the passenger seat. Harriet was buckling in

Caleb, making sure he was all good before heading to the driver seat.

Not a single word was spoken between the two adults as she drove to the private school. The only noise heard was Caleb's babbles and the odd talk from Ember. However, the little girl truly wasn't a morning person. She was quiet, which was unlike her. The two talked to her, trying to spark a conversation, but not a single word was spoken between the two past lovers.

"Her name is Olivia," she babbled, playing with her doll, "and her favourite food is chocolate cake!" she exclaimed, shouting with excitement when she said, 'cake'. Caleb joined in, and absolute chaos erupted. Now Ember was awake, which earned a small chuckle from both the adults.

"Alright, silly goose, it's time to get out," Harriet said, pulling up to the brick building. Loud, sad noises came from the two munchkins, knowing that their fun was over.

SHE KEPT her composure during the drive home, not moving, and focused on the British roads. If she didn't utter a word, a conversation between them wouldn't start. For the next year she would focus on being a professional. After all, she wasn't prepared for her first love to waltz back into her life.

Instead, the deep rolling hills of the British countryside were what she focused on while driving. She noted that the sun was rising and shone on the bright grass. It was extremely similar to New Zealand; creepy almost how similar the scenery was.

"Harriet-"

"*Don't*," she sneered, interrupting whatever he was going

to say. Her grip went tighter on the wheel, and her jaw clenched. She instantly felt an ache from it. He shook his head.

"You know I am paying you," he quipped.

"And?" She raised her eyebrows, encouraging him to continue whatever he was going to say next. In her experience, it was either cocky, rude, stupid, or somewhat smart. At the moment, she felt it was going to be stupid.

"As your employer, you should be kind if you want to continue having a job."

Harriet let out a loud scoff, shaking her head in disappointment. Was this the best he could do? Threaten her? Harriet was absolutely shocked.

She quickly looked in the rear-view mirror. Caleb was still fast asleep. Once that was noted, she pulled the car over. Bodies leaned to the left as she quickly swerved the car to the side of the road. Her hands shifted the gear stick into park and turned to him.

"Outside now."

Harriet opened the door, closing it with bang. The SUV shook. With her arms crossed, she glared at him watching him walk around the SUV, taking his time.

"Don't you fucking dare bring my job into this. I am working for your wife, *not you*," she sneered, glaring at him while spitting each word out with such anger, he should've flinched.

"You aren't letting me talk," he fought back. "I sign your damn cheques so let me fucking talk, *Harriet*."

"Because all you want to do is fuck. I know you, Jax. You want to fuck. You don't want anything else from me besides to fuck me. Well, I am sorry, but under the employment contract that your wife wrote, there was a no 'fucking my husband' clause in the terms and conditions. So do not *honey* me or *Harriet* me or even fucking *kitten* me. I am working for your wife for one year. I need the money, and I need to get away from New Zealand. So, leave me alone and let me do my damn job and you do yours. Be a father, be a husband, and leave me the fuck alone!" Her blood was boiling, her voice was getting louder and louder as each word came from her plump lips.

Jax remained calm. He stood there, allowing her to release her anger. Her icy blue eyes shone with passion with every word spoken. Frantic gestures came from Harriet, while her honey, warm voice went off on something he couldn't care less about. In that moment, he simply admired her anger...she was even hot when she was mad. It went straight to his dick, her anger. Feeling it harden a little bit as she spat each word out. Eventually, her lips closed, their blue eyes connected, as he raised his eyebrows.

"You done?" he shrugged.

Her glare went hard. If looks could kill, she could commit homicide. "Well, yes," she muttered, hands on her hip.

"Good," he shrugged again. In one swift motion, his hand was plastered on her hip, pulling her in as he smashed her lips with his. Instantly, they moved together with such fire and passion, as if it was second nature to them. As if the last thirteen years were nothing, and they were both stupid teenagers again. Love and lust controlled their actions. His gripped weakened, hands moving up to her cheeks, cupping them as his lips dominated hers.

Harriet pulled away, looking blankly at him as if she were putting together a puzzle of what had just happened. Blinking aimlessly, she shook her head.

"What the fuck?" she whispered more to herself. He just smirked proudly.

Her eyes darted to the back seat of the black luxury SUV, where the child was most definitely still asleep. Thank God.

"Did I prove my point? We are-"

"No, you proved *my* point." Was all she said before running to the driver's seat and locking the car.

Jax chuckled, shaking his head and trying to open the car door. It didn't open. He tried again, more frantically this time. Again, nothing happened.

"For fuck's sake, Harriet, open the damn door," he yelled, trying to open the door again and banging on the window.

Harriet, being the badass she was, flipped him off, grabbed her phone and sent him a message.

New Message at 08:32

From Harriet Kensington:

Get your own ride, fucker.

"Fucking bitch," he mumbled, watching her drive away.

Where was he? Who the fuck knew? All he knew was that a woman had just left him in the dust, quite literally. That had never happened before. There was a cow, a red barn, and a few trees in the distance. Where was he?

Jax took out his phone, dialled his personal driver, and angerly spat out, "Beckett, we have a situation. I'm sending you my location right now."

PEACE RESIDED over the manor for about forty-five minutes. Caleb was helping Harriet make blueberry muffins. His small hands were playing with the batter, smushing it between his fingers and trying his best to eat it whenever her back was turned. However, Harriet caught him and gave him a sweet telling off.

"It's like play dough," he babbled. A small and youthful chuckle echoed in the kitchen. All Harriet did was swoon from the innocence and glanced at Sandy in the corner.

"I will clean up, I promise," she pledged.

"You better, Miss. Kensington. I just cleaned the kitchen." The old lady walked away briskly.

Caleb couldn't care less about anything at that moment besides playing with the muffin mix. The gooey and sticky substance was very much stuck to his tiny digits and in his hair. How it got there, who knew? But at least he was having fun. Harriet simply noted that after this, he needed a bath.

The blueberries were added to the mixture, and the pan was prepped and ready. She'd been told that she made the best blueberry muffins. However, chaos interrupted everything minutes later.

Who left their boss' husband in the middle of the road? Well, Harriet did. That woman surely had the guts to do that, and Jax was not the down and dirty guy like he was when they used to know each other.

He was a successful managing partner at his law firm. Where people did anything for him, practically kiss his feet. The man had a serious amount of bank in his pocket, a rocket of a wife, several cars, beautiful kids, and women at every corner. That man was used to being treated like a God. Therefore, to be left on the road by a woman who should've been kissing his feet and jumping into his arms was absolutely not what he was expecting.

"You really have a pair of fucking..." She heard it, the wrath coming from around the corridor. He was looking for Harriet.

She simply ignored his yelling and whining.

Putting the muffins into the oven, she closed the door gently. "Let's get you cleaned up," she mused, placing Caleb onto her hip she helped him clean his hands off. "Soap and water, scrub, scrub, scrub." Clumps of batter were still stuck in his platinum curls. She chuckled a little.

Jax entered the room, seeing the woman bent over the sink washing the sticky substance off his son's hands. It was picture perfect and warmed his heart. His anger was gone for a split second before it returned.

"You left me," he stated, arms crossed as he looked at her. Harriet rolled her eyes, taking the tea towel and helping Caleb dry his hands.

"Sandy, can you take Caleb upstairs to get the batter out of his hair. Mr. Alderidge and I need to talk about something from this morning regarding Em," she told the older woman.

Sandy sent Harriet a displeased look then complied and helped Caleb down the hall to the stairs. Harriet knew there was going to be a serious amount of swearing and yelling from them. She didn't want Caleb to witness that.

Once the little footsteps were no longer heard, he took a step closer.

"Don't kiss me," she replied, as she turned to the sink and started to wash the dishes.

Jax licked his lips, arms still crossed, muscles bulging. Harriet couldn't let that distract her.

"Shit, Claudia, we can't tell your wife-" she tried, instantly remembering that he was, in fact, *married.*

"We have an open marriage. She couldn't care less," he bit back, arms crossed as he watched her walk around the kitchen. It sort of made sense, Claudia didn't wear a ring and neither did he.

Harriet closed her eyes, letting go of the bowl and leaning on the counter.

"Breathe, one, two, three. Five types of dog breeds... dachshund, golden retriever-"

"What are you doing?" He asked. Harriet shushed him harshly.

"Poodle, beagle and pug. Four cities: Amsterdam, Auckland, London and Vancouver. Three..." she counted down and looked back at him.

"I left New Zealand for a break, to breathe, and to reassess my life. I had something traumatic happen, and I need time. You are not helping," she whispered, running her fingers through her hair.

He was quick, moving to her and wrapping his arms around her body. Holding her and rubbing her back. She didn't reject him or embrace him.

"I don't care about the business of your marriage," she whispered, "I just need to do my job." She pulled away and walked out of the kitchen to be with Caleb.

4

Jax met her when she was four, and he was seven. He watched from afar as a little girl came through the big black doors with a stuffed kitten in her hand. Fear was painted on her face as was a small frown and tears in her doe-like eyes. The seven-year-old watched the girl from the stairs as Ms. Betty Stevenson held her hand and explained to the small girl that this was her new home. The fear on her face was intense, but Jax couldn't relate.

He had been there since birth. She actually had a mother, and now she was here. He wondered what happened.

The brunette with tight curls and ocean eyes watched her as she walked past him, going up the stairs to her new room, the girls' ward for ages 5-10. Being the kindred soul he was, he gave her a small, gentle smile when she passed him, and she gave him one back. The small boy instantly knew that look. She wasn't happy, and she was more than just scared. It was as if she had just witnessed something terrible and unimaginable.

All he knew at that moment was that he wanted to protect her, hold her, and take care of her gentle soul.

HARRIET DIDN'T SEE Jax for the rest of the day. Fair enough, she wanted it, and now he listened. Finally, peace and quiet.

She continued her day as per usual, picking up Ember and driving her to her art class, then dance. Taking Caleb to a playdate and then picking them all up and taking them back home. Life as a nanny was constantly running after kids. Marco was in the kitchen, cooking up a storm as the kids ran around the halls playing hide and seek.

"The husband is home," Marco said, trying his best to gossip.

"Yes, I met him last night. Nice guy," Harriet responded, grabbing herself a glass from the cabinet and pouring herself a vodka soda. It was Friday, after all.

Marco pivoted, eyes wide open and curiosity spread on his face. "You met him, and you thought he was *nice*?" She slowly nodded. "He was an uptight asshole to me."

She nodded along. "I got that vibe too. I walked in on them fighting," she told him, a light chuckle mixed with the words, downing the drink quickly and chasing it with some water to cover the smell.

"Was it about the swinger parties, the whores, or the-"

"What?" she questioned, scrunching her eyebrows.

"Rumours spread. I think they have an open marriage, and he fucks anything that moves, and she probably does too. When you're that hot, you have the right too," he shrugged as he dished up the plates. "Dinner!"

She heard the running footsteps. "Tell me everything once they go to bed," she whispered to him.

DINNER WAS A SUCCESS. Caleb passed out as soon as he had food in his belly, and now Harriet was tucking in Ember.

"Tell me more about your mommy and daddy," Harriet asked, tucking the pink blanket into her sides.

The room was gorgeous, with pink wallpaper and dollhouses. She was spoiled, but Harriet couldn't care less. The little girl was the sweetest thing in the world with the most humbling heart. She smiled at her, tucking the curls behind her ears as her brown eyes filled with life looked at hers.

"Mhmm, my daddy is cool, and my mummy has a funny laugh."

"Do you miss daddy when he is gone a long time?"

"Mhmm, yeah!" Ember exclaimed. So innocent, she really didn't know what she was talking about. "But he always gives me extra kisses," she mused.

"Of course, he does," Harriet winked, tickling her belly. "Well, it's time to sleep, girlie," she told her, switching off the fairy lamp and kissing her small head.

"Nighty-night, Harry."

"Night, babe," she closed the door behind her and walked down the stairs to the kitchen.

"Claudia is in Madrid. Just got the call from her she won't be home for a week," Marco told Harriet, pushing the vodka to her.

Pouring herself a drink, she looked at Marco. "Well, I'm stuck with him then," she mumbled, sipping the burning liquid. "Tell me everything now."

"Mhmm," he hummed. "So, rumour has it they have an open marriage. People think they were arranged, or she got knocked up, and he had to marry her. Everyone thinks they literally did not want to marry, but they had to."

Harriet nodded along, letting him continue.

"Some say that he indulges himself in prostitutes, swinger parties, and alcohol. Whereas she indulges herself in swinger parties and 'work trips'. Whatever those entail. It's all a rumour, though, talk between employees."

Harriet nodded. "That's their business, I guess."

"Well, I am off. Got to head home. I will see you tomorrow."

Harriet waved him off and gathered her book to head to the living room for a light read. However, her best friend from home, Cameron, called her.

The two had known each other since they were in university. Cameron became an international aid worker and had been doing part-time work in the Ukraine, while Harriet stayed back in New Zealand to work as a social worker. Nevertheless, the two had been friends since the beginning of their post-secondary education. Cameron had been living in London for a few years now and took trips for work. However, she had just arrived back in the U.K. for a week. The two were making plans to see each other tomorrow.

Quick chit-chat was made, her talking about the lifestyle in the Ukraine and Harriet telling her the news about her "employer". As one guesses, Cameron was more than just shocked.

"So *Jax-Jax*?" she asked, eyes bulging through the screen. The brunette, who Harriet called her best friend, was in pure shock. The two met as soon as she was out of the system, so she had seen her friend go through the heartache of waiting for him. "You waited three years for him before you fucked off. You got married, and even then, you still waited for him."

"The marriage was security, needed money, and a house," Harriet responded with a roll of her eyes.

Kai... she really didn't want to think about him at that moment. However, halfway through their conversation, close to midnight the front door opened, and a very drunk large person entered the house. A grunt was heard and heavy footsteps. A bang echoed through the room. Harriet groaned.

"I have to go, Cam. Welcome back to the U.K., can't wait to see you tomorrow. The man of the hour is home," she said to her friend on the phone. The brunette nodded and left the call.

Pocketing her phone, Harriet walked to other room where she could hear banging. The grunts and objects falling were getting louder as she found him in the kitchen, pouring himself a large whiskey, and downing it quickly.

Leaning against the wall, arms crossed, she watched him talk to himself as he poured another drink. Words were coming out of his mouth, but they were not audible, just a bunch of mumbles.

"Jax," she muttered. He turned around, a guilty look on his face. "I think you have had enough. Let's get you up to bed."

He shook his head repeatedly. "No, no, no," he said, trying to go back to what he was doing.

Harriet took the bottle from him, placing it back in the cabinet and looked at him. He looked back at her, his eyes lost and mind elsewhere. "Let's get you washed up. You smell like cheap perfume, cigarette smoke, and booze," she told him, coming closer.

Her hand made contact with his shoulder, steadying him

from falling over. His hand crept up and wrapped around her waist, holding it. The man was heavy, she realized as he leaned on her for support.

"Ok," he muttered. He swung his arm around her neck as she grabbed his side, helping him up the spiral stairs to the master bedroom.

It was truly a workout to help him. The man was clumsy as hell. A vase was knocked over, then a painting, and he hit the wall too many times to count, but she couldn't care less. All she wanted was to put him to bed.

"I have loved you since I met you," he mumbled, head leaning on her shoulder as they walked down the hallway to the other wing.

Swallowing, she ignored him. He was drunk, and who knew where he had come from. He could've come from a brothel, a pub, or even a poker game. They were all possibilities, but she knew to never trust drunken words.

"I bet," she mumbled, finally finding the double doors to his room.

The room was grand, slick, and masculine, with black artifacts and a clean-cut, minimalistic, modern aesthetic. She put him down on the grey duvet, walking to the bathroom to fill the glass of water next to his bed.

Jax laid down, looking up to the white ceiling. Then, a burst of energy hit him, and he stood up, following Harriet to the bathroom and leaning against the doorway. She turned around, jumping a little and continued to walk past him. Jax simply watched her.

"Go to bed, drink the water, and I will-"

"I need a shower," he mumbled, pivoting and pulling his shirt off.

Harriet stayed still, his broad muscles in view, pecs

thicker than she thought and abs that made her want to kiss them. He was perfect, his chest hair short but still there and trailing down to his v-line. She could just imagine what laid there. Well, she had seen it once or twice, but that was in the past. Jax was built, more built than when they were teenagers. The vein in his neck was prominent and about to burst. All she wanted to do was apply teasing kisses up and down the area.

"Like what you see?" he hummed, fingers going down to the zipper of his jeans.

He was teasing her, pulling down the pants slowly. Boxers coming down with the pair of pants, and he was standing in front of her, butt naked, and all she could do was gawk.

His dick, proud and hard caught her eye. It was huge, thick, and long. A vein popped out and travelled down from the circumcised tip. Precum glistened at the tip, and she licked her lips, lust coming into her, but she couldn't. She couldn't do this. He was drunk. Whether the open marriage comment was true or not, he was drunk, and she would be taking advantage of him.

"No," she replied a moment later. He shrugged his shoulder.

"Your loss," he mumbled, going to the shower and turning it on.

She should've left, she should've turned around and let him go about his business. He had business to attend to... very clearly. A very stiff and beautiful type of business. However, she didn't move. She stood there.

"It's very warm, refreshing, kitten," he mused. Hands gliding in his hair and washing the stench of the day off of him.

His rough and thick fingers, which she imagined could do very dirty things, travelled down his chest and encountered his member. He gripped it, squeezed it, and a noise came from his lips. His other hand held the wall to provide support from his little rendezvous and sinful behaviour. He gripped harder, thumbing the tip, and a moan escaped his lips.

Jax was going to jerk off in front of her, she realized.

Still not moving, she watched him begin to pump himself. Grunts and moans escaped his lips as he pleasured himself.

"Harriet," he mumbled, eyes still focused on his own undoing.

She shook her head.

"Come," he sternly said, control laced in his voice.

She knew better, she truly did, but her heart was taken by this man. Her motives were clear but unclear at the same time. Pushing her sweatpants down and pulling the t-shirt off, she stood there naked as well.

Tattoos littered her skin, a name on her hip, and a bouquet of wildflowers on the other side of her ribs. Her tattoo sleeve was on full display as she let herself take delicate steps towards him.

He opened the glass shower door, allowing her to come in with him. She was perfect, curvy with full breasts. A small tummy and an ass that was the biggest he had ever seen. She was utter perfection. He noticed a scar right away. It was faint, but there. It ran across her lower stomach, a crescent shape. Jax thumbed it lightly, but she jerked away.

His hand gripped her hip instead, his tip coming in contact with her stomach. She was bare down there, whereas he had hair: trimmed and neat. Her eyes didn't break from his. Stuck to his ocean ones, she bit her lip.

"We can't have sex," she mumbled, breathing in his cologne, cedar and germanium. He nodded but took her hand from her side and placed it on the hardened member.

"Do it," he growled. Lust laced his voice, eyes dark and voice controlling. She took over the controlled movements, pumping him, and thumbing the tip. She squeezed and released then went on with jerking him off.

Jax laid his head on her shoulder, holding the wall with his hand and the other gripping her hip in order to keep his balance. Pleasure flooded his system as he groaned from every jerk from her.

"Good, kitten," he mumbled, kissing the side of her neck.

She continued, speeding up her actions until she felt his cock jerk, and she knew he was going to be done soon. Jax felt the normal wave of pleasure, the knot that needed to be released. One hand moving to her ass, he gripped it as she pushed forward. Member jerking in her hand, and all of a sudden, a white substance covered her digits, and the lust began to die down.

Harriet let go of his manhood, seeing it fall back down. She grabbed the soap off the side and quickly rubbed the dirty evidence from her hands. He just held her hips, head still on her shoulder and kissed it lightly.

"Thank you," he mumbled, trailing the kisses to her jawline and cheek. Trying to catch her lips, but she was wise enough to dodge it.

"We can't speak of this," she replied, exiting the shower.

"Stay with me tonight, please." He was in the shower still, the hot water falling on his head and running down his shoulder. His lip quivered and he leaned against the tile of the shower.

Harriet held her gaze to the floor, grabbing the towel from the corner, she wrapped it around herself. Biting her lip, she turned around. His gaze was locked on her.

"I can't," she sighed.

"You can," he growled louder, turning the shower off and walking straight to her.

Crashing his lips with hers again, he proceeded to push her against the wall. His hands were wandering, brushing in places that made shivers run through her body. The kiss was aggressive, teeth clinking together as he sucked her bottom lip.

His fingers slid down, brushing her labia and pushing hard against her clit. A cry released from her lips as he rubbed the area. Seconds later, he pulled away. The towel dropped, and her figure was once again naked in front of him. Swollen lips, arousal clear, and lust shined in her eyes.

Jax pushed her in front of the sink, helping her jump onto the counter. His lips captured hers, dominating the kiss as his tongue swirled around her mouth and sucked the reddened lips.

Hiking her leg onto his shoulder, he went down. Hand gripping her breast, squeezing and releasing, kneading it as cries escaped from her mouth.

"Quiet," he grunted. His lips now attaching themselves to her swollen nub.

Pink and glistening, her arousal was at its highest. He could taste it. Her wetness flooding her womanhood and letting her feel unbelievable pleasure. He parted her lips, flicking her clit with his tongue. Her sobs filled the room and it spurred him on. His own lust taking control and driving him to this point.

Fingers creeping up her thigh, he pushed them inside of her and moved them gently. Eventually, picking up the pace and making a 'come here' motion. It was sinful, but this was all he knew; fucking and destroying; his specialty.

He sucked her freshly swollen flesh, her hand catching his hair. Raking her fingers through the dishevelled locks as the other hand pushed on the mirror. She was uncomfortable sitting on the small flat spot on the sink, but she couldn't care less. Harriet was getting the orgasm of her dreams at the moment and her comfort was the last thing she was thinking of.

With every flick, push, and motion coming from him, she jerked and squeezed her eyes shut. Heavy breaths escaped her lips as well as desperate cries, pleading for him to continue.

"I'm coming," she muttered.

Jax helped her through the orgasm. The pulsing feeling controlling her body as the tension was relieved. He came back up, unhooking her leg from his shoulder. Fingers gripping her chin, he tilted it up.

"Stay with me," he purred, telling her again as trailed his fingers up her jaw and brushed her ear with his lips.

Harriet was a mess, heavy breaths escaping her lips as she tried to return to reality. Was this manipulation? She was stunned by what just occurred.

"Jax," she whimpered, letting him continue with the kisses. "I need to go to bed."

"With me," he muttered, kissing the side of her jaw.

"The kids-"

"Set an alarm."

She pulled away, getting up and grabbing her clothes off the floor and exiting the room. Jax was left there, naked and alone while she ran so fast down the hallways before she was in her room. Quickly closing the door behind her, she could finally breathe again.

Sliding down, she sat there. What had just happened? Stunned and unresponsive, she stared at a singular corner of her room.

'Jax...my Jax just ate me out. What, how, when? How did I let this happen?' she thought.

All she knew was that it was past midnight, and she was off tomorrow. The children would be left to their own devices and how could she let that happen? She had seen him with them. The man wasn't a terrible father, but he was distant. He didn't know the first rule of parenting.

Cameron lived in London. She was working there at the moment and Harriet promised her that she would meet her tomorrow for drinks. She could spend the day at the manor and then go to London for the night.

Getting up and continuing her night-time routine, Harriet finally got into bed. However, she was still wondering, 'What the fuck happened?'

A DOOR OPENED. Heavy footsteps sounded as the wooden floors creaked. Harriet was asleep on the right side of the bed, knocked out, and dreaming happy thoughts. It was close to morning, a little past four.

The bed shifted, a heavy weight came upon the bed as he climbed in, pulling the covers over them. Jax looked at her sleeping figure, fingers grazing her cheeks. Due to his weight, the mattress dipped down, making her roll closer to him. He embraced her and just looked at her. Gently, he placed a kiss on her forehead. Harriet shifted, pulling the blankets closer to her.

"Tell me everything," he whispered, tucking a piece of her silver hair behind her ears. "Why did you run?"

5

Her alarm blared. Eyes gently fluttering open, the sunlight hit her blue irises. The heat warmed her skin. She rubbed her eyes and rolled over to turn the alarm off. Seven in the morning, the sun was already too bright, the morning birds were too annoying. However, she had to accept it.

Getting up, she threw her long locks up into a messy bun and headed to the ensuite. The beautiful modern room with retro black and white tiles was calming as she turned the shower on. Looking at herself in the mirror, a very obvious hickey was visible on her collarbone.

"Fuck."

Sighing, she began to strip off her night clothes and then entered the warm water. Wetting her body, Harriet let her hands roam. He made her feel things she had never felt before. Even her ex-husband - soon to be ex-husband - never made her come that hard. Blushing from just the thought of Jax's mouth on her womanhood, she moaned.

Was it wrong? More than ever. But she craved for it again.

Her hands travelled, gripping her full breasts and kneading them. Harriet leaned back, hitting the tile of the walk-in shower. Biting her lip, she let herself relieve the pressure. Her fingers rubbed her pink nub while the other hand cupped her left breast.

Harriet moaned, trying to cover it by biting her lip. Her fingers then circled the sensitive area as they made their way to the opening of her pussy. Fingering herself, she allowed herself to try and relieve the pressure.

Minutes later, nothing happened.

"Fuck."

She needed him. Ending her shower, she groaned. Wrapping the towel around her curvy figure, she went back to the bedroom, making sure to grab makeup to cover that horrible purple mark.

Oddly enough, the left side of the bed was unmade. She must've had a rough sleep.

"MORNING."

She looked to her right as she entered the luxurious kitchen. Jax was sitting at the table, newspaper in hand and glasses perched on his nose. He looked perfect even in the morning.

"Morning," she grumbled, grabbing her coffee and walking out of the room.

"Where are you going, grumpy pants?" he asked sternly and with a smirk. He continued to sip his coffee.

She pivoted. Innocence was displayed on her face. "It's

my day off. My best friend is back in town, and I am planning to see her."

"What?" he mumbled, eyebrows scrunching, as lips pursed against each other.

"It is my day off," she said again, more slowly.

"You have days off?" Jax scoffed. Harriet groaned, rolling her eyes.

"Saturdays and Sundays...Claudia-"

"Didn't say shit. I have a meeting today. You need to stay here," he commanded, focusing on going back to the newspaper.

"Tough, I have plans." Harriet turned away, pouring herself a coffee.

"Harriet. Camille. Kensington," he barked. She shook her head, refusing to turn around.

"I will come back tomorrow. Ask Sandy to watch the kids or hire a weekend nanny." She walked to him, sitting down beside him with her mug in hand.

"No, I want you here," he argued.

"You want me here so you can fuck me. I will be back Sunday," she responded. He licked his lips and shook his head again. His gaze locked on the newspaper.

He was perfect even though his hair was not done yet and he wore sweats and a t-shirt.

"Possibly, but I also need childcare," he argued.

"How long is your meeting?"

"Two days," he fired back, no emotion, no movement.

"Fuck you," she mumbled, getting up and walking to the exit.

"You can't have the car," he yelled, trying his best to halt her movements.

"Thank god for public transport."

"Nice hickey, by the way!" He could hear her frustrated groans ringing through the house.

CAMERON PULLED up to the manor, her brunette hair pulled in a low bun as a sundress caressed her curvy figure.

She parked her 1998 green Jeep Wrangler at the doorstep as her best friend since college ran down the steps with a black tote. The top of the car was removed for the summer.

Harriet noticed the car and instantly groaned. It was like Russian roulette every time she got in. The car was seconds away from breaking down. Cameron had had it since she got her license and shipped it to England when she moved. But Harriet couldn't complain now.

"Drive and drive fast," she hastily said as she jumped into the car.

"What the fuck?" Cam asked, chuckling as she put the car into drive.

"Long fucking story, but Jax-"

"Oh, here we go...what did the asshole do?" she questioned, and Harriet let out a loud, frustrated groan. "Fuck me, tell me more," she mumbled and laughed right after that.

"That, that happened, but to me," Harriet mumbled. Cam's eyes shot to her, widening. "I jerked him off in the shower, and he ate me out on his bathroom sink." Harriet said it as if it were nothing.

"You aren't even divorced, and he is-"

"Don't mention it. I left for a reason and Jax might be the reason."

"I thought a woman hired you?" Harriet looked out to the country as they drove to the city.

"Yes, his wife," Harriet responded, and Cam just shook her head.

"You're fucking ridiculous."

"Open marriage." Harriet shrugged.

"Fuck. Just stop. I need help unpacking and then we can deal with all this fucking drama. He has kids, Harry! Kids, a wife, and a *very* nice house."

"He is also controlling as fuck, amazing at making me orgasm, and he is in a loveless marriage, plus he is Jax. My Jax. Jax from the orphanage," she fired back, trying to reason with her.

Cameron shook her head. "He never looked for you."

Harriet stayed quiet after that. She was right, he never did look for her. The girl waited and for whatever reason, destiny made her feel like a fool and then threw this at her. He was married with kids.

"Let's drink tonight and forget about this mess because I need one."

LONDON WAS MANY THINGS, but one word to describe it was big. *London was big.* Big city and a lot of people. Auckland was like this, but not as chaotic. Well, the traffic was similar, absolutely terrible and horrendous. However, Harriet was a homebody and lived in a little town now. It's crazy to think that everyone here has a life, a person, a lover, and a purpose. They all work, and they all feel emotions. It's so crazy to her.

"This is so different from home," she muttered.

"Jax is back," Cam mumbled.

"Jax isn't home."

"He once was," she reminded her friend.

JAX HEARD HER LEAVE, the door slamming. His hands gripped the rim of the sink, harder. He looked up at the mirror and released a loud sigh then a grunt. It was a stab to his heart, all of this. What was he thinking? Sending the nanny ad made by Harriet to Claudia. He didn't think she would hire her, but now look at them. Maybe, hiring the grumbly old lady was a better choice.

Did he really expect to 'pick up' things off from where they ended?

Thirteen years...he was a complete idiot. The woman was untraceable for years, not existing on the internet. He tried to find her, but it was as if she didn't want to be found. Until, out of the blue, she was there with all her social media linking back to years ago. Why did she just appear out of nowhere?

That was a month ago, stumbling upon her profile and better yet, finding an ad that would lead her here.

JAX SAT at his desk overlooking the city of London. Skyscrapers were all he saw, no interest with the intern on her hands and knees in front of him with his cock in her hands. He couldn't care less about anything besides busting a load and getting his work done.

His thoughts wandered around his mind. Every time he had sex, he thought about her. Not just during sex, but every moment of every day, he thought about her. Raking his fingers through the blonde's hair, he pushed it back as his focus returned to his computer screen.

No motion was coming from him, almost no pleasure from the woman as he typed Harriet's name into the search engine.

Harriet Kensington - Auckland, New Zealand

Seconds later, her social media came up. For years now he had tried to find her, but she was never there. He pressed the link, and her beautiful visage appeared. Her once dirty blonde hair was now silver, she had tattoos, and the same old freckles littered her skin. She had round tortoiseshell glasses and a large smile. Then he saw her body, breasts popping out of her sky-blue dress as she posed with her friends.

She was there, she was alive and God, she was beautiful. Pictures from years ago were posted. Why did a simple search lead him to her? It never did before.

Exiting that website, he saw an ad with her name in it.

Nanny available to hire:
Harriet Kensington, 28
Worked in childcare for 4+ years
Background: Social Work

Copying the link, he sent it to his wife. She had been looking for a nanny. Clicking back to her Instagram, he focused on the image of Harriet in her bikini holding her surfboard while the intern continued sucking and licking. In seconds, he came.

SHE HAD five missed phone calls from Jax that day, but she didn't realise until later that night. Harriet and Cameron went out for lunch with drinks, shopped a little, and did a bit of sightseeing before going back to her flat. Harriet was completely fine with crashing there for the night.

Upon entering, tipsy from the pub across the street, she finally saw all the notifications. Groaning, she walked off.

"Jax," she muttered to her friend, as she rolled her eyes and walked to the bathroom.

She pressed his name, seeing the screen light up as it rang. Two seconds later, he answered.

"Do you ever fucking answer your phone?" he growled. She could hear his heavy footsteps as he paced around the room.

"Depends on the person. I have been busy today," she told him, raking her fingers through her hair and grabbing the washcloth to remove her makeup.

"Answer your fucking phone, Harriet. I don't normally take care of the kids by myself. I don't know shit. I had to call my stepmother. My *stepmother*, Harriet. She is great with the kids, but I don't want to talk to her. You can't-"

"Talk to your wife. She is the one who hired me."

He huffed, groaned and grunted all at the same time. "You can't have-"

"Saturdays and Sundays, I am off. Hire a weekend nanny for fuck's sake."

"Fine," he snapped. "Also, why the fuck do you have mail from a lawyer?"

Frozen, she looked at herself in the mirror. What should she say?

"Don't open it."

"Already have." He hung up.

'What the fuck?'

She exited the bathroom and saw Cameron sitting on her couch, eating crisps, and drinking wine. Harriet was about to have a panic attack. Heavy breaths came as she grabbed the wall for support. She could feel her heart beating rapidly, hitting her chest. Anxiety flooded her veins as she took a step forward, almost falling. It was hard to breathe. Every breath she took was shaky. She gasped as the tears hit.

The lawyers sent her something, and Jax opened it. Her privacy was being invaded, and now he might know *everything.*

"I need to get home to...t-to the manor," she stumbled on her words.

Cameron turned around. "Are you ok?" She got up and walked to her, helping her stand and holding her shoulders.

"My lawyer mailed me something, and Jax opened it," she was dizzy, and her words were slurred.

"Oh shit."

"I am going to call a taxi. You can't drive me."

"Call Jax. He will pick you up." She shook her head. "Call him. The taxi fares will be too much."

JAX PULLED up to the brick building, sending a text to her phone that he was here. Harriet came out, frazzled, seeing the black Maserati GranTurismo. Not thinking, she climbed in.

"I can explain everything," she mumbled, looking at the dashboard. He looked over at her. She was shaking. "Kai is my ex-husband - soon to be ex-husband," she trembled. Jax nodded along as he put the car into drive. "We experienced something tragic, and it broke us. He was never the same. The lawyers must have sent me papers to sign or something." She looked over at him. "What did they send?"

To him, it made sense. How she wasn't traceable... different last name. She had a life after him and didn't want to be found. She had a life; he had a life. Crazy how fate works.

"I didn't open it. I was mad, so I said something stupid," he told her coldly.

Harriet shot her attention to him. "You did what?" she yelled.

"Now you can spill, Har." He turned his body to her, eyes peering into her, pleading for the truth. Harriet shook her head. "Why is there a male name tattooed on your hip? Why do you have a scar on your stomach? I need you to tell me," he stressed, voice pleading to her. This was pure manipulation; he was playing his stupid mind games with her to get her to spill her life story. The man was a control freak!

She continued to shake her head. "No, you don't get to do this manipulating, controlling mind trick on me," she scolded.

"What did Kai do to you?" he mumbled softly, placing the car in drive and signalling to get back on the road. He looked worried, anger was in his eyes, but she couldn't care less. "What happened to you, Kitten?" he whispered.

Jax was in a white button-down and blue jeans. His sleeves were rolled up as he sported a silver Rolex. The last few buttons of his shirt were undone, his chest hair was peeking through.

"No."

"I married a woman who isn't even attracted to men," he

replied. "I was young, and my father wanted someone good for me. The first blonde socialite he saw, he picked. I married her when I was twenty. We had two kids, but she only ever touched me for that. Instead, I have women I go to-"

"Stop talking, Jaxon," she interrupted, putting her hand up. He saw the tears in her eyes and watched her blink them away.

Jax knew this conversation was serious. He pulled over and placed the car into park as he turned his full attention to her.

"Are you going to kick me out?" she fired at him.

"Like what you did to me? Had to call my bloody driver to get me. No, I am better than that."

'Better than that? Jax, you're a complete asshole who needs to know everything and have control over everyone's life. The world is your own damn game!'

"Just drive. You ruined my sleepover."

"Have a sleepover with me," he retorted with a smirk going on his features. She rubbed her eyes and looked away.

"Just drive, please."

"I love you can't you see that?" he exclaimed, his voice getting louder as he ran his fingers through his now dishevelled hair.

She simply shook her head and looked at him with such pity. "You loved me. You loved the fifteen-year-old me. I am no longer her."

"I don't care. You're my kitten. Fate put us here today."

"Can we go home? I wanna go home," she muttered, crossing her arms as she leaned her head against the window.

"Ok, Kit."

THEY FINALLY ARRIVED HOME, but she didn't say anything to him. Instead, she took the envelope from Jax and went to her room. She had a bottle of red wine in her bag and *Bridget Jones' Diary* ready to play on the television. Tonight, was going to be a hard night.

Wiping her tears, she texted Cameron, saying she was ok. *Who was she? What was she doing here?* All she knew was that she was running and running fast.

Crewneck and underwear on her figure, she played her movie and cozied into bed. The warm duvet drowned her as she opened the bottle, bringing the whole thing to her lips. With one big breath, she opened the envelope and removed the documents.

Harriet read the words and tears flooded her eyes. Were they happy or sad tears? She didn't know. A knock sounded at her door.

'Jax, he is just trying to be kind.'

"Come in," she muttered, wiping the tears off quickly. Jax entered, dark and mysterious as per-usual. His chest was bare and saggy joggers were hanging from his hips. He had two glasses and a whiskey bottle in his other hand.

"Thought you would want company," he smiled, settling on the bed. "As a friend, of course."

'A friend, of course. The irony,' she screamed internally.

He poured himself a glass as he settled into the bed beside her. His foot grazed her leg as he got comfortable. She continued to watch the movie, bringing the bottle to her lips. With her cheeks, wet and puffy, he realised she had been crying. It pained him to know his kitten had been crying. It angered him that she wouldn't tell him anything. He was stuck to his own devices. She was hurt by this man, and it pained him.

Jax googled him, of course. *Kai Fitzgerald was a* construction worker, twenty-nine years of age. He had sandy blonde hair, long and pulled back most of the time. Kind, green eyes, but he was definitely not kind. Jax wanted to uncover this mystery.

"Let me read," he mumbled, hand out for her to pass the papers.

"It's nothing," she responded.

"Obviously, it's not nothing. You have been crying, Kit. Give them to me. If you need lawyers, I have the best. I'm a lawyer, for Christ's sake. Let me look at the papers. If you need money, I have shit loads-"

"I just need to leave New Zealand forever," she whispered. It was barely heard. "He took everything."

"Are you in debt?" he asked. Her focus was still on the television in front of her and the bottle of cheap wine.

"Always have been, always will," she uttered, focusing on the movie.

He sighed, taking her hand and holding it. "I promised you when we were kids that I would *always* take care of you, let me take care of this. I have too much money, Har. I can probably pay your debt ten times over."

"Don't. I just need to be by myself." Pursing her lips, she turned away from him, cuddling deeper into the blankets. The rerun of her favourite movie played in the background as she watched it. Jax had no interest. Instead, he watched her. He took the bottle from her and placed it on the side table. The silver-haired woman moved closer to him. He wrapped his thick, muscled arms around her, feeling her face on his chest as she snuggled deeper.

"Him and I are done though, the divorce has been finalised. He took everything, including my dignity."

"Stay with me then. Let me help. We had a plan, kitten."

Harriet heard those words. They comforted her slightly, but she knew what the plan was for this year.

"Goodnight, Jax," was all she muttered as she closed her eyes.

6

She felt something on her forehead, rough and firm. Blinking, she came to her senses. Coarse hair tickled her face. Harriet moved slightly. It was firm this pillow. Harriet looked around. She saw the open window and felt the morning summer breeze drift in. Rubbing her eyes, she tried to move. However, that didn't work. A strong arm held her down, but all she cared about at the moment was her need to pee. Badly.

'Jax.'

She moved her hands from holding his hips. However, she caught something instead. A firm object, proud and hard, hit her hand.

'Oh no, please no.'

"Jax," she mumbled, trying to squirm out from his arms.

He groaned. "Sleep, Kitten," he muttered, and his grip got tighter.

"Jax, I need to pee and you-"

"Pee then."

"I need to get up," she tried to fight, but his grip was too strong. His larger body had her pinned.

"Five more minutes," he muttered, and she groaned. Ducking her figure down she managed to slip out. Harriet ran to the bathroom quickly. She heard his groans of protest as she relieved her bladder and ran back to her bedroom.

He looked delicious - he always did - but at that moment, he was more gorgeous and edible. The sun hit his skin illuminating his best features. Strong pectorals and biceps were perfectly shaped as was his jawline. He loved her; this man loved her. If only they'd met earlier.

"Come back to bed," he mumbled, turning to his side and facing her. He patted the side of the bed, commanding her to come back. She hurried, jumping and pulling the blankets over her. He smiled with his eyes still closed.

Harriet wanted to kiss him, kiss every inch of him. Was she selfish for wanting that? Her lips brushed his and as if it was a force of habit, he allowed the kiss from her. His hands moved to her hip, pulling her front to his chest.

"Good morning, you," he smirked in the kiss as his hands travelled her body.

Harriet pushed her body to be on top of his as if it was second nature to be in control. Jax realised the power play as she straddled him. The kiss was full force, his lips dominating hers once again. Lips sloppy, sharing saliva, as his hands gripped her ass. Fuck, he loved her ass, so plush and large. Thick and round, it was curved perfectly for him.

Being the tease she was, she began to roll her hips lightly, grinding them on his manhood.

"Fuck, Harriet," he muttered into the kiss. He bit her lip lightly. A moan escaped her lips.

Her fingers stroked his biceps and caressed his cheeks as

she rolled her hips. He was putty in her hands, absolute putty, and she loved it. The power she had with just a few small actions was mind-blowing.

He ripped the crewneck over her head, lips attacking her right breast, nipping and sucking as his hand grabbed the other one. It was her turn to let go of the control and allow him to exert power over her.

"You're mine," he purred, the vibration of his words hitting her skin. She shivered, biting her lip, and rolling her head back.

His fingers slipped into her underwear, swiping the wetness of her pussy, and brought the juices back to his lips.

"Mine," he teased.

Fingers going back to the black lace, with his veins bulging, he ripped the pair in half.

"Fuck, Jax," she gasped. He smirked, kissing her lips quickly before lifting his hips up for her to remove his pants.

"Down," he growled. "I wanna fuck your mouth." His eyes were black and filled with lust. She bit her lip, a blush appearing on her pink cheeks. His blue eyes glared at her. She cowered further down.

Mighty and strong, his manhood was evident. The circumcised with the tip glistening with his seed. She licked her lips. It was huge. How the hell would it fit in her mouth?

"You will be ok. Take it slowly," he cooed, his hands grasping her chin and tilting it up to him. Harriet nodded.

Her small fingers gripped the shaft as she placed the tip in her mouth. She heard him hit his head against the bed frame. He panted and groaned deeply as she licked the tip of his member, her hands jerking the shaft as she sank her mouth deeper.

"Fuck, Harriet. Fuck, shit-" he rasped as she began bobbing her head.

Fumbling with his balls, she sloppily sucked his dick. Jax took his hands, grabbing chunks of her hair, and began moving her head in rhythm. His dick fucking her mouth. The further he went, the more the gag reflex began to cut in. He let go, allowing her to continue. She swirled her tongue around his shaft and then deep throated him.

Harriet made eye contact with him, and he was gone. He rubbed his eyes and then gripped the bedsheets. His Harriet was here right now, giving the best damn blowjob he'd ever had.

Using her hands and mouth, she quickened the pace, and he was done for. Moaning her name and grunting, he was so close. Her reddened lips became swollen from every motion, and he desperately wanted to kiss them again.

Three, two, one, he came. Shockwaves filled his body as he released his seed into her mouth. She swallowed and released her mouth with a popping sound. Wiping her lips, she looked at him with such innocence it drove him mad. The saltiness lingered on her tongue as she washed it down with some water.

Jax leaned over, capturing her lips with his.

"My little slut," he muttered, cupping her cheeks.

Instantly, Harriet pulled away. Jerking away from his affection, she got up. Unbelievable. Un-fucking-believable! This man had the audacity to say shit like that to her. Harriet walked to the bathroom and locked the door.

"Harriet," he called, getting up quickly and walking to the door. He tried to open it, pushing against the door. "Open the damn door. Tell me what happened," he tried again.

The woman opened the door, dressed in a robe now as she walked past him to the closet while grabbing clothes for the day.

"Harriet." He tried to grab her arm.

She turned around and looked him dead in the eye. "I am not your *fucking* slut," she sneered with such anger. "I am not something to fuck around with. So don't you go and treat me like an outlet or a prostitute. I have more dignity than that. So, fuck off, Jax."

"Let's talk about this. Some women like it when I call them-" he cupped her cheeks, and she shook her head.

"I am not *some* woman, Jax. I am me! This is wrong, so fucking wrong. We are not doing something right. I need to - I need to get another job," she muttered to herself, while she hastily grabbed her stuff and suitcase.

He gripped her arm and pulled her to him. "No, stay with me. Stay with me, Ember, and Caleb. Please. Do it for them. They love you."

Harriet bit her lip. "I will see you Monday. I need a break," she acknowledged. "Get out."

7

The coffee at this café was the best she had ever had. The bitterness was strong, but the sweetness that lingered on her palette, just made her smile. It was different, but a good different. It had been a week of ignoring him. Jax was nowhere to be seen, no noises at night, no evidence he was home. He must be back in Paris, she concluded.

Sunday, a week since the disaster, she sat in the local cafe in town. Swirling her spoon around her cup of coffee, she glanced out the window of the old building. The coffee bean and sandalwood smell filled her senses as she watched people walk by in the town centre. Tomorrow, she would be back at work. She didn't know whether she wanted to see Jax or to continue the way they were going - complete radio silence.

"Harriet!" she heard the name screamed from a young female voice. Turning around, her blue eyes captured the little hazel ones. Ember.

The small figure ran to her, enveloping her in a hug. She

rocked both of them back and forth as Harriet began to play with her hair.

"What are you doing here?" she asked, still playing with her curls.

"Brooklyn is taking us to get hot chocolate!" she exclaimed.

'Brooklyn?'

The silver-haired woman nodded, eyebrows puzzled as she tried to figure out who this woman was.

"She is our weekend nanny, but you're my best friend still," she smiled, giving her a kiss on the cheek.

"Aw, thank you. Well, maybe you should go back to her and get your hot chocolate, girlie," she winked.

"I am so sorry," a young brunette came up to her, Caleb's hand holding hers. She was tiny, thin, and model-like with big doe eyes and plump lips. Her figure was small, tiny breasts, and barely an ass to see. Everything Harriet was not.

"It's ok, I know them. I am Harriet." She put her hand out for her to shake it.

"Oh, you're the weekday nanny. It's great to finally meet you. The kids talk about you constantly."

"Of course, they do," she winked. Caleb started screaming, letting go of the brunette's hand to run to Harriet.

"Hi, baby," she kissed his cheeks, placing him on her hip. "When did you start working?"

"Yesterday was my first day. Mr. Alderidge is so nice and handsome," she exclaimed and smirked.

"Hmm, how old are you?"

"Twenty-one," she replied. Harriet hummed, letting the kids trace their fingers on her tattoos and touch her face.

"Well, I think it's time for you guys to go back to Brooklyn."

THAT NIGHT, Harriet entered the manor. Her black leather tote bag was on her shoulder. She opened the grand door, hearing laughter coming from the living room. It was a child's laughter, a squeal, and a deep chuckle.

'Jax.'

Placing her bag down on the floor, she walked towards the traditional white living room with panelling on the walls and its original fireplace. Jax was sitting on the sofa, both kids at his side as they watched a movie. It melted her heart to see the smiles on the kids' faces and Jax's eye candy of a grin. Harriet leaned against the archway, watching their laughs as he threw Caleb in the air, and Ember climbed on his shoulders.

"Harry!" Ember squealed as she made eye contact with the silver-haired woman. Her hair was a mess, possibly from all the ruckus that occurred. Ember jumped from the couch and ran to Harriet, grabbing her arm, and pulling her to the couch. She sat in the far corner as Caleb was still climbing all over his father.

Brooklyn entered the room, her small frame so much tinier than his. She sent her a small smile. "Bedtime, guys."

The two pouted but eventually went as they begged for Harriet to put them to bed. Jax told them to go with the other nanny. It was just them now.

He took a sip from the dark liquor next to him letting the burning liquid glide down his throat.

"How was Paris?" she questioned, getting up and walking to the little table in the corner. Harriet poured herself a glass of the dark poison.

"Fine," he muttered, clearing his throat, "just got back

tonight." Harriet hummed and sat back down on the couch, far away from him.

His blue eyes looked at her. She was wearing a pair of black jeans, a turtleneck, and a brown striped cardigan layered on top. Her silver hair was pulled back in a low bun and her makeup made her features pop: light eyeshadow, mascara, and her classic bold red lip. His suit was still on, his hair gelled back, and his light stubble was gone. He looked very professional, but still so sinful.

"Brooklyn seemed sweet, gonna fuck her too?" she sassed, not catching his eyes. Harriet took a sip from the brown liquid.

"No, not my type," he retorted back. Eyes locking on the fireplace.

"Fair enough," she muttered, getting up to go grab something to eat.

"Claudia is coming home tonight."

"Lucky you." And she left the room.

HARRIET POURED herself a glass of red wine. Then she leaned against the outside brick wall of the building as she watched the sunset. Her focus was locked on the beautiful scenery. How she wished to be high at the moment, the best way to relieve stress in her eyes. It was gorgeous. She loved watching the day end. The sunset behind the country fields. She placed the bottle down next to her.

"You look like you need a cigarette or a blunt," she heard the feminine voice.

Claudia came from behind her, walking out from the tobacco. Harriet chuckled, looking at the dirty blonde. She looked beautiful, dress pants and a button up, layered with gold jewellery. A very sexy feminine suit adorned her figure.

"I..." she tried to resist, "yes, I do."

Claudia handed her the packet, helping her light the cigarette as the two of them leaned against the building. Silence lingered.

"Jax has an inkling for you," the woman muttered, looking over to Harriet.

"Does he?" Harriet chuckled, smoking the cigarette and washing it down with the red liquid.

"Watch out, Harriet. We aren't a perfect family; he fucks anything that walks. Don't fall for it."

Shocked by her own boss' words, the silver-haired woman choked on air and looked back at Jax's wife. The woman held no emotion as she watched the world around her grow dark.

"I-"

"I see the way he looks at you. You guys know each other from somewhere." Emotionless words gilded from the blonde's mouth.

"Claudia-"

"Are you fucking my husband, Harriet?" She turned to look at her, gazing her eyes and raising an eyebrow.

Harriet blinked a few times. What the fuck?

"No," she mumbled, trying her best to not stumble over her words.

'Does a few blowjobs and the fact he ate me out in his bedroom count as fucking? If not, then, no, we haven't physically done the whole penis in vagina thing. It was just a small white lie... but that won't hurt.'

"He's probably fucking the weekend nanny. Little

brunette young thing, she is *irresistible*," Claudia mumbled to herself, blowing smoke from her lips. Harriet just watched her. The woman was truly an alpha female.

"Claudia," she mumbled, "I think this conversation needs to-"

"He was an orphan. Was in the system for seventeen years before his father adopted him out, not even knowing he had a son with some kiwi bimbo he met on his travels one year. My husband met a woman in the system, *Kitten*. I don't know her name, but when he sleeps, for the years we actually slept in the same bed, he mumbles that name in his sleep," she said, looking over at the Kiwi. "I know he is looking for her, and the minute he finds her he will leave us for her. She will *always* come first."

Harriet bit her lip and crushed out the cigarette. "Do you have weed?" she blurted, catching herself.

"Of course, I do. Give me a second."

Claudia left, going inside as Harriet took a seat in one of the outside couches. The outdoor electric fire was turned on. Her back was against the couch as she snuggled deeper with her glass of wine.

"Here," she handed her the blunt as the two sat and smoked the drug. "You're quite cool, makes me question what you are doing here?" Claudia asked, looking at Harriet. Her eyes looked at Harriet's curvy figure as she waited for an answer, eyeing her tits.

"Running," Harriet responded, fully relaxed as she let the addictive substance take control of her system.

"I feel that. There's a reason I work abroad so much. Running is the only exercise I am good at, besides sex." She winked at her, taking a drag from her own blunt. Harriet let out a small laugh.

"Of course. What are you running from?"

Claudia chuckled, shaking her head and biting her lip. "I am married to a man I do not love. I love my kids, but I hate this life, this house, him." Was it the drug talking or her trying to release her emotions? All Harriet could do was be supportive. Sometimes it was nice to have a direct conversation.

"Why not leave him?"

"Our families are linked in business. So, we just fuck other people," she mumbled.

"I am running away from a divorce. The asshole took everything from me. I can't go back to New Zealand."

"Then don't," she mumbled. "Where did you grow up in New Zealand?"

"Auckland, but I now, well, used to, live on a small surfing beach." Claudia nodded. The two of them were sitting next to each other, thighs touching as they watched the electric fire flicker. It was dark. Nothing else could be heard except the fireflies and the odd car.

Claudia's eyes flickered to Harriet's red lips, her hand came up, cupping her cheek, and tilting her face to her. The blunts were gone, finished, and the two of them were riding their highs together.

"You're beautiful," she mumbled, leaning down.

Their lips brushed against one another. Claudia hungrily attacked her lips as her hands trailed down to her hip, pushing their bodies to be flush against one another. Harriet caressed her face, kissing her hard.

Instantly, her rational thought came back. Harriet pulled away, flustered, and wiping her lips.

"We can't," she mumbled, getting up.

"You're her, the orphan." She said it as if there was hurt

in her voice. Claudia knew that moment that since she had been found, everything was going to be different.

"I am not her anymore." Harriet grabbed the bottle and walked away going back into the house.

When Harriet was out of earshot, Claudia mumbled, "That's why he wanted to hire you."

Walking to her room, she heard Jax on the phone in the office. The girl was drunk and high, two addictions that shouldn't be mixed. But the drugs provided her with increased confidence. Opening the large wooden doors, she walked in.

His suit jacket was hanging on the chair as he placed the phone back on the desk, typing away on the computer.

"Claudia, I am in no mood-" he looked up, and Harriet was there. "Hi," he smiled, closing the laptop.

Harriet walked to him, putting the bottle on his desk. She pulled the chair away from the desk and climbed onto him. Her ass made contact with his groin as she wrapped her arms around his neck. Instantly, his arms wrapped around her torso, holding her. Head against his chest, she closed her eyes.

"Who were you talking to?" she hummed.

"Work. What is the best way to say, 'thanks for working here for thirty years, but we need you to retire'?" he asked, running his fingers through her hair.

"Cake," she mumbled, voice muffled from his chest, "or cookies or like an edible arrangement."

A chuckle came from his lips, noticing her quietness. "Are you ok?" he mumbled, one hand holding her ass and the other one flicking pieces of her hair back. "You smell like weed, cigarettes, and alcohol," he grunted, kissing her forehead. His face scrunched up from a whiff of her musty stench. "You fucking stink," he groaned, grimacing.

"Shhhh," she mumbled, "I need to sleep."

"You're high and drunk. Where the fuck did you get...Claudia," he realized, grunting.

"She kissed me," she mumbled into his shirt. However, he couldn't hear it. All he knew was that her red lipstick was now smudging his white t-shirt.

"Let me get you to bed," he mumbled.

Jax got up, carrying her bridal style and walked out of his office. Claudia came around the corner and saw her husband holding Harriet in his arms. Harriet's soft features relaxed as she slept.

"You found her. How do you feel?" she retorted, tone passive aggressive.

Jax shook his head, ignoring his wife's antics. He walked up the stairs to head to his room; the two slept separately. Claudia followed him.

"You got the girl, Jax. You found her, congrats," she bellowed. Then stopped, dead serious face as she threatened, "If you fucking run away from your kids, I will kill you. Being a father comes first." Jax rolled his eyes.

"Night, Claudia."

Jax placed the sleeping beauty on his bed, slowly unbuttoning the cardigan. He removed her jeans and turtleneck. To cover her naked body, Jax helped her put on an old shirt. The name on her hip caught his eye, *Arlo*. He wondered who that was as he thumbed the cursive name. She stirred a little but went back to cuddling the grey duvet.

Jax unbuttoned his white-collared shirt then took it off. His abs were perfectly sculpted, and his chest was covered with hair. Once his pants were removed, he was left in his boxers. Throwing back the duvet, he got in, sinking into the mattress as he watched her sleep so peacefully. Her chest rose and fell slowly. Fuck, he was so in love with her.

"Goodnight, Kitten."

8

Halfway through the night, she suddenly woke. Nausea clouded her vision as she felt bile rising from her stomach. Hastily, she ran to the bathroom, spilling her guts out.

Jax woke up from the sudden movement. He heard the dry reaching. Instantly, he went into a panic and ran to the bathroom. He got on his knees and pulled her hair into a makeshift ponytail while he rubbed her back in comfort.

"It'll be ok," he cooed in her ear. Harriet continued to rid everything from her stomach. Cries began to escape from her lips. She felt absolutely ill. "This is what happens when you mix alcohol and weed Kit," he told her, soothing her and kissing her hair.

Harriet cried into the toilet, hating this feeling. "I know Jax," she cried. "This isn't my first time."

He nodded, letting her grasp her surroundings. She moved from the toilet and sat against the wall, while wiping her mouth.

"Not the first time?" he questioned; his voice low. The

anger was palpable, but he tried to not express that emotion. She nodded her head.

"Do you do heavy drugs?" he asked sternly, as if he was interrogating her.

"What?" she scoffed, pursing her lips.

"Answer me, Harriet," he insisted.

"Jax, I know my family line. My mother was a drug addict, and my father was a dealer. I know I have a line of-"

"Harriet," he snapped.

"No, I don't do hard drugs. Have I done them, sure-"

"You fucking idiot," he bellowed, raking his fingers through his hair as he sat across her.

"I am not an addict."

"Well, from the way you drink-"

"Says fucking you. Every time I see you, you are drinking. I don't do drugs, I smoke a cigarette here and there, and I do weed. That is all. Now I am going back to bed." She got up, hand splayed on the wall as she balanced herself and walked back to the bed.

"I care about you," he said, following her.

"I can take care of myself. I don't need you to protect me."

She roughly pulled the covers back, getting in, and turning her back from him.

"I want to. I once promised you," he humbly said, reaching out for her. However, she shrugged him off. "I love you," he muttered.

"Go to sleep, Jax."

Claudia was gone by the time she went downstairs. Caleb was on her hip, and Ember was chasing the rabbits out in the field.

"I need a date," she heard the raspy morning voice fill the room. His heavy steps echoed the room as he walked from the doorway to the breakfast table. Jax was shirtless, and sweats hung from his hips. It took everything inside of her to not stare.

Caleb was still fast asleep on her hip as she made breakfast for the kids. Her eyes darted to the clock, they had time before Ember needed to be at school.

"You have a wife for a reason," she replied, turning the kettle on and grabbing the cereal from the cabinet.

"Claudia is away this weekend. I need you to be my date. It is just a client event for work," he poured himself coffee from the French press and brought the steaming liquid to his lips.

"No."

"Yes. Name your price," he bargained. Turning around, she looked at him. What could she ask? Harriet thought for a moment before a wide smirk ran across from her face.

"Hmmm," she covered Caleb's ear, "no sex, and we end this," she whispered, eyebrows raised.

"That is a bad deal. How about I pay off your debt."

"Five hundred thousand dollars? Please, you can buy a house."

$500,000...Jax was shocked...tuition sure, but what else...drugs? The divorce...

"What's your account number?" He got up, took out his phone and called someone.

"Jax," she snapped, placing Caleb in his seat and

hurriedly, walked to him. "Jax!" she shouted as he entered the office and closed the door in her face. "Fuck."

She hurried back to the kitchen, serving up cereal and making herself tea before helping the kids get ready for school. He wouldn't dare, right? He physically wouldn't do this to her. It would be a relief to not deal with the debt anymore, but there was a line between what was kind and what was crazy.

He came back moments later. "You owe me a date."

'*No. No, no, no. He didn't.*'

"Jax...you didn't actually-"

"I did, call it an early birthday present. Now, Saturday, you and me...ok?"

"You paid off everything?" he nodded. "My divorce? Kai's fucking gambling, my therapy? My tuition? Everything? My mother's debt?" He nodded. "*The funeral*," she whispered to herself.

"The funeral?" he questioned, picking up her mumbled words. "Who died?" he whispered, grabbing her arm. Harriet yanked her arm sharply from his grasp.

Their eyes locked.

"Kids, time to go to school," she said, turning and walking off.

'*Who died? I wondered, then it hit me, the name on her hip, the scar on her stomach...*' Jax thought.

CALEB HAD A PLAYDATE THAT DAY, some kid named Louis from across the street. After dropping him off, she went back to the house. Sandy's vacuum and Marco's whistling as he prepared dinner could both be heard in the distance. What was she supposed to do now? The kids weren't there and no duties to attend. She smiled to herself, excited that she could finally have some 'me time'.

"Harriet," she heard, turning her attention to the voice. Jax was in the corner. He wore dress pants and a red button up that was undone with his chest hair poking out. She knew that look, say goodbye to "me time".

Harriet groaned at him, walking away. However, he was fast. Jax grabbed her forearm and pulled her to him. "My office, now," he ordered.

'Fuck.'

Harriet sat in the office on the big black leather couch in front of his desk. He was pacing back and forth, arms crossed as he tried to find the words to say to her.

"Who died?" he asked, deciding to jump the gun. His stare was hard and long, prying the truth from her eyes. Harriet scoffed. "I can't get this question out of my head. Who died, Kit?" He stressed further, hands on the desk as he leaned over.

"You don't ask someone that," she replied, shaking her head and trying to get up.

"Sit your fucking ass down," he pointed back to the seat, snapping at her. He walked over and grabbed her hands, kneeling down. "Tell me Harriet. I need to know. It isn't your ex as his name is Kai...a friend, an old lover "

"I lost my baby," she mumbled, cutting him off, "there, simple." He was still just looking in her eyes. Tears flooded hers as she mumbled those words. "You heard it, so now let me go. Don't fucking talk to-"

"Arlo," he mumbled, "your child?" She nodded. "What happened?"

"He-he didn't make it," she whispered. "I was happy,

really happy Jax. I loved my husband. I had a life, and I was having a baby. He didn't survive. I went crazy, and Kai too. We turned into our worst selves. I ran for a reason."

"I am sorry," he replied, kissing her forehead. "What happened?"

"He was born with a lung issue, and he died hours after he was born. I don't wanna talk about this, Jax. You win, I lost. We are different people."

"When did it happen?" He tried to dig further.

"Jax!" she snapped, harshly wiping her tears away. How dare he attack her like this? Jump on her and expect her to spill everything. "A year ago," she responded. He sat next to her, wrapping his arms around her, and pulling her in.

"It'll be ok, Kitten." he muttered.

'*She ran for a reason, and that reason was to heal. It all made sense now.*'

"I am sorry," he whispered.

He watched her exit the office. Who was Kai Fitzgerald? That was his next mission to figure who the hell this man was? He seemed shady. Harriet seemed like she was still hiding something. What was it? What were their real secrets? It was time to hire a private investigator.

9

There was a knock at her door. It was ten at night, and Harriet was in her bed, drinking tea, and reading a book with a random movie on in the background.

"Come in," she responded.

Jax came in, clad in his classic sleepwear of just sweats. His hair was dishevelled, curls evident, and droplets of water were sitting on it. He must've just had a shower.

She looked at him through her glasses as he sat down on the bed. His broad body was blocking her view of the television. Harriet could see every outline of his back muscles moving as he turned to look at her.

"I'm sorry about this morning," he muttered, blue eyes filled with pity. "It was highly inappropriate, and I shouldn't have forced information out of you." It was sweet and to the point.

"Now you know."

"Was it genetic?" he asked, getting up and moving to get in the bed. She moved over a little for his figure to fit in.

She shook her head 'no'. Jax nodded, closing his eyes,

and fidgeting to find a comfortable spot. Giving up, she continued with her book and movie.

"I'm going to leave Claudia," he mumbled into the pillow.

She simply ignored him. He was a stubborn guy, and once he made up his mind, he would always follow through with it. Nobody could change it. Jax was going to leave his wife, and the question was, was he leaving her for Harriet?

A DRESS WAS HANGING in her closet that morning, a gorgeous long black slip dress. Harriet thumbed the silk material, so smooth and soft. The price tag was still stuck to it. Her eyes widened, three thousand pounds!

"Shit," she mumbled. Jax really liked to have the best.

Ember walked into the room, wiping her tired eyes and holding her doll. She sat on Harriet's bed, watching the woman brush her teeth.

"These are really big underwear," Ember mumbled, holding up a pair of boxer briefs. Harriet looked over, eyes bulging.

'Where the fuck did she get those?'

Harriet stormed over to her, snatching the underwear from her hands. "Where were these?" she pressed.

"Under the bed, Harry," she responded, lying back and rolling in the unmade bed.

Harriet looked around, getting on her knees to look under. Sneaky, a pair of joggers were under the bed too. *Fucking, Jax.* It must've been when they... what a mistake! She showered quickly, placing her makeup on and grabbing her jeans and a band tee. Harriet walked out of the room; Ember hot on her heels as they headed downstairs.

Jax was in his office, and Caleb was seated on his lap, bouncing on his knee. She looked at him, the little one snuggled against his side in the dark academic styled room. Large wooden bookshelves filled to the brim with books, a dark desk, a red leather chair, and a black leather couch. Small windows were behind him as he typed away.

"When you stay over, clean your shit. Em found a pair of your boxers," she told him. He looked up innocently as Caleb gripped his grey tee harder. He must have just returned from a run as he had water droplets on his skin and sweat marks.

"A present for you, Kit," he winked.

"Jaxon. Clean your shit," she whispered the last bit, making sure no child could hear it.

"Hey," he said, holding his child to his chest and adjusted his sitting position, "my dad is coming over for a drink today. He wants to meet you." Jax closed the computer screen and got up.

"Oh? Does he now?" she cocked, crossing her arms and leaning against the doorway.

Jax came over, cupping her cheek and leaned down, placing a kiss on her forehead. "Yes, he wants to meet you. He's coming around one, put this one down for a nap, and then come downstairs. We are having a few whiskeys and cigars."

"Ok, well, um, I need to drive Em to school, so I-"

"Let me come," he smiled. His muscles were popping through his t-shirt, tight around his biceps, and outlining his pectorals. He was absolutely delicious.

"M'kay," she responded, grabbing her bag and keys.

"Let me drive," he winked as he grabbed the keys to the Jaguar; the Maserati didn't have the kids' seats. With a sigh, she gathered the children before following him outside to the black SUV.

"The dress is beautiful, thank you," she responded, watching him throw his keys in the air and catching them, earning giggles from the kids. Jax beamed, climbing into the car. Harriet placed the kids in their seats and walked to the passenger side.

"My stylist showed it to me, and I just thought of you. It would really accentuate your curves, Kit," he hummed as he drove around the round-a-bout and down the driveway to the main road. Even though she had been here a while, she still couldn't get over the scenery around her.

"Oh, will it?" she mused. His eyes were focused on the road. However, a little smirk spread on his features.

"Yes, black will look so good on you too. Specially with the hair," he told her, making circle gestures with his hands to her silver hair. Her roots were coming in, she noticed. However, that was an issue to deal with later.

"Thinking of going platinum," she mumbled, looking back to the countryside.

"Like beach blonde?" he scoffed.

"No, more like ash platinum. Bored of the silver," she responded.

"Oh, ok...will you ever go back to your natural colour?" he asked, biting his lip as he pulled up to the brick school, parking, and getting out.

"Maybe," she shrugged, helping Caleb out and putting him on her hip as the four of them headed to the entrance.

"Jaxon!" a female voice called posh and defined. It was

the sound of someone who definitely had the silver spoon in their mouth.

Harriet looked up to the broad male next to her, towering over her with his stature. His face scrunched up, a little wince escaping his lips. He knew her. Turning around, Harriet took an eye of the brunette in pink workout clothes. She was tiny and older looking, Botox was very present, and sunglasses were perched on her head. Her diamond ring was massive, shining bright as it captured the light rays.

"I have not seen you in forever. How are you?" she said, placing a hand on his bicep and squeezing it a little.

"Good. Yourself, Cherry?" his husky voice responded, but Harriet knew that look, he wanted to flee.

"Same old, same old. You should come over sometime," she continued to massage his arm, "have some coffee, the kids could play. My husband has been going on and on about how he wants to have a rematch in golf."

"Um, I-"

"Hi Cherry, I am Harriet. We could set up a playdate. I can give you my number, and we can sort out everything," she cut in. The woman looked over at her as if she had no clue who she was. "I am the nanny, by the way," Harriet added.

The woman with red lips and clumpy mascara, wearing some fancy brand of sweatpants, sent her a nod. "Well, I was thinking-"

"My schedule is crazy, Cherry. I rather fill the little free time I have with being at home with the kids. Harriet is more than happy," he responded, patting Harriet's back and shrugging off the woman's touch, "to set up a time that Hazel and Em can play."

"Fair, I will get my nanny to text you. I will just get your number from Claudia," she settled but was disgusted with the way it went.

Ember was gone. Harriet saw her hanging out with some boy as the two walked into the school. Harriet smiled as she shifted Caleb on her hip.

"Who is the boy?" she heard him say. Jax's eyes were focused on the brunette.

"A classmate. Now, I want a coffee, and we should get home." He shook his head, hand wrapping around her back and cupping her hip.

"Nah, let's go get you a coffee."

CALEB WAS MUNCHING on some chocolate pastry as Jax phoned someone from the table they were sitting at. Harriet waited patiently for her drink, hearing the anger laced in Jax's voice as he yelled at someone.

"Fix it, Wagner. I have met monkeys smarter than his fucking intern. Those idiots go around, and fuck shit up. Then, I am expected to clean it up and they go back to university after the summer is done. I can't fucking deal with this shit right now-"

Shaking her head, Harriet glared at Jax. "Go outside, your kid," she nudged him.

He sent her a hardened look, getting up and walking out the café, his voice echoing as he walked out.

"For Harriet, large cappuccino!" She got up, grabbing the coffee from the barista's hand. He was cute, tall and had green eyes with dirty blonde hair tied back into a bun. Her type, he looked just like Kai.

"Thank you," she responded. The barista nodded to her.

"I'm Felix. I've seen you around here, mostly on the weekends," he responded. Felix propped his elbows onto the counter, leaning over as he talked to her.

"Harriet."

"Australian?"

"Close," she chuckled, "I am from New Zealand." Felix hummed.

"Is that your husband?" he asked, testing the waters. Harriet laughed, shaking her head.

"No, my boss. I'm the nanny," she responded, sending him a smile.

The man nodded. "Well, Harriet, I would like to take you out sometime," he leaned closer in, and she could see the freckles scattering his pale skin.

"I would like that, Friday?" she asked, taking out her phone and handing it to him for his number.

"Sure," he smirked. Good boy, he seemed like a good boy; kind, raised by a nice mother, never had anything traumatic happen to him and was probably in university. Maybe it is time to date the good boy.

The door opened, a little bell ringing signalling Jax's reappearance.

"Harriet, we need to leave," she heard his voice behind him. "I need to get to the office."

"It was really nice chatting to ya, Felix. See you Friday," she smiled at him as she turned around. Caleb's hand in Jax's large one as he took their coffee from the table and walked out. She followed.

He didn't say a single word when they climbed into the vehicle. Tension was obvious, his hand gripping the steering wheel hard. Knuckles went white as he sped out the parking lot and onto the highway.

"Are you ok?" she asked. His jaw was clenched, eyes focused on the road.

"No, something happened at work, and it didn't help that my *nanny* was getting some asshole's number," he mumbled, speeding up more.

"What?" she mumbled, "I was just talking to him."

He scoffed, shaking his head. "You're whoring yourself around now, huh?" he responded, pulling up the house. "Unbelievable, Kit, absolutely unbelievable."

"What?" she spat. "You're fucking jealous. News flash, Jax, I am single, and I can fuck whoever I want to fuck," she whispered, trying to make sure Caleb didn't hear.

"Why won't you fuck me?" he whispered shouted, pulling the car up in front of the door.

"Cause you're married," she responded, getting out of the car, unbuckling Caleb and heading inside.

"That is gonna change," he scoffed, driving off.

SHE LAID in her bed that night. Was she elated? Harriet came to England to work and forget. However, her past decided to pop up once again and haunt her. Was she good at this job? Who knew? Maybe she should leave. Maybe she should go back. Maybe she should just forget everything.

The girl felt like she was stuck there, working while dealing with bullshit and drama she didn't want to deal with. Taking out her phone, she looked up jobs in London, waitressing, barista...retail...stripping? She scrolled through all the options. The woman had a degree in bloody social work and a minor in English. What could she do now with something that useless? The idea of going back into social work pained her. However, she did intern once at a publishing house. Possibly and most definitely, she could get a job there working in publishing. Googling more, she quickly edited her resume before sending it off to multiple companies. If she played her cards right, she could run away from Jax.

Pressing her name, she called Claudia, hoping she was up at this time.

"Hi Claudia," she said, getting up and walking to her window. Jax was pulling in with the SUV, the high beams hitting her eyes as he parked. His heavy figure walked into the house. His shoulders were rounded, and his body posture sluggish. The love she had for him was unimaginable, but she needed to focus on herself and her mental health at that moment. She also needed to not fuck this family up.

Claudia's words haunted her: *"I know he is looking for her, and the minute he finds her, he will leave us for her. She will always come first."*

Harriet couldn't let that happen. He had kids. She knew what it was like to grow up without a parent, and it pained her that he would do that to them. He was once an orphan too or did he forget that when his father took him from her?

"You can't tell Jax, but I think it'll be best if I leave. I will help find a replacement, but obviously, I am damaging to your marriage and family. Jax is saying things that he shouldn't say, and I fear I am pulling apart this family. My last day will be Friday. Brooklyn could start full time Monday until a replacement is found indefinitely. I am sure she would be happy with that."

"It is ok, Harriet. I wish you the best. I won't tell Jax." Was all Claudia said, then she hung up.

'You're running again, Harriet.' She heard her own voice echo in her brain.

'Running is the only thing I knew'.

The door opened, heavy footprints walking up to her. The world was dark outside her window. Her focus was on the scenery before her, the flower beds were no longer visible, and the trees were merely silhouettes.

The door to her room opened and the scent of heavy cologne entered the room. She sighed, feeling his lips collide with her neck, pressing aggressive nips, and sucking her flesh. Her hand held her phone, clutching it to her chest. Harriet rolled her head to the side, allowing him to have more access. Her body trembled as his hands curled around her hips and slipped into her shorts.

'Maybe one more time... or maybe not.'

"Jax-" she whispered, his stubble was back again and now was against her flesh. It was scratchy, dragging it up to her lips. His fingers dipped further down in her shorts as her mind grew filthy, imagining him running the prickly flesh against her thighs. The thought aroused her, her pussy clenching. He was overwhelming, ruining her rational thinking.

"Shhh, I need this. Tough day," he cooed, swiping the pad of his finger between her folds, capturing her wetness. Biting her lip, she let out a noise of pleasure; the phone dropped onto the floor.

"No," she shook her head.

"Yes," he groaned, cupping her pussy.

Her back was against his chest. She glided her hands on top of his bigger ones, eyes squinting. They glided down his arms to his hands, gripping them, and removing them from her core. Harriet leaned back to his chest, placing all her weight on him. Just maybe, maybe one more time.

"Take me," she mumbled. Jax smirked against her skin, hands roughly cupping her breasts.

Harriet turned around in his arms, tilting her face up to see his eyes on his six-foot-two structure. A smirk was plastered on his face. His hand graced her cheek, cupping it in his palm. He leaned down and pressed a sensual kiss on her plump pink lips.

Harriet nipped her bottom lip, allowing him to guide her to the bed with his lips. The kiss was sweet and slow. Hands gripped each other's flesh as he pushed her onto the bed. Harriet laid back, propping herself up on her elbows. She watched him stand there, biting his lip and pushing her legs open gently.

"Be quiet," he purred, bringing his index finger to his lips, shushing her. Harriet stayed quiet, watching him as he pulled off the grey t-shirt. Her breaths were heavy and deep, eyes raking his figure. His toned chest was on display. Hair and muscle were all she saw when she glanced him up and down.

Sculpted by the Gods themselves, Jax was perfect, everything a girl could dream; a body that could make anyone squirm from just looking. Harriet stayed still. He towered over her, his hands were beside her as he leaned down, eyes mere inches away.

"You're mine," he growled, leaning down and brushing his lips against her ear, teasing her. His words were intoxicating, making her back arch and shivers flow through her body. Jax was a sex dream come true, sinful and dark; Harriet submitted easily to him. His hands trailed up her thigh, squeezing the inner part as he littered delicate and teasing kisses on her jaw. Harriet felt his chest hair against her skin, tickling her, and earning light moans from her lips.

"All mine," he purred, licking her jaw. Harriet moaned, a sound of pleasure escaping as she concentrated on the touching.

His hand cupped her heat, sending jolts of pleasure throughout her body.

"Jax!" she gasped as he pulled down her sleep shorts in one swift motion. He smirked, capturing her lips, biting and nipping her bottom lip. They fought for dominance with the harsh kisses exchanged as he began to circle the pad of his thumb on her clit. His eyes were locked on hers, eyesight intact as he played with her dripping cunt.

Moans and gasps left her lips. His facial expressions didn't change, just a frown, and orbs looking into her blue irises. It was as if he was concentrating on her, a job that needed to be fulfilled. His cock hardened, seeing her in absolute pure bliss with pleasure overflowing. Harriet bit her lip and arched her back. Jax simply admired her.

All of a sudden, he removed his hand from her pink nub, bringing them to his lips and slowly sucking the juices off. Fuck, he was hot.

"Why-"

"Do you have a condom?" he asked, running his fingers through his hair and standing up.

"Um," she racked her brain, looking around the room.

"I need a condom, Har. I can't do this without-"

"Drawer next to my bed, next to my," she paused then mumbled, "vibrator." He nodded, walking around the bed to the bedside table, pulling it open, and seeing the red device. Smirking, he quickly grabbed the foil package.

"Vibrator...?" he was full blown smirking and biting his lips.

"Don't get any ideas, Irwin," she mumbled the last name he hasn't heard for a while. It slipped out.

'Irwin...she used to call me Irwin all the time and for her to slip that name...'

A wave of nostalgia hit, good memories of them rolling around in the sheets at such a young age, and experiencing their firsts...well, her first. He lost his virginity long before she did to him.

"I haven't heard that in forever," he mumbled, "but don't call me that." Harriet mumbled a sorry.

The last name was dead to him, dying the moment he left that orphanage. It was a reminder of his past. Jax didn't want to associate himself with his mother. She was nothing to him. She was just the carrier, nothing more.

He quickly shook off those thoughts and began to unbutton his pants. Harriet got up onto her knees, crawling over to him.

"Let me," she whispered. Her delicate fingers began to get to work. With his towering height, her on her knees on the bed, she almost was the same height as him...almost.

He leaned down, capturing her lips as her fingers delicately palmed his manhood through his boxers. Rolling his head back, he took a breather before roughly kissing her once again. His jeans were pushed down, and she managed to free his hardened cock, stroking it with her small hands, their lips attacking each other again. The foil package was still in his hand. He broke away and ripped it open with his teeth.

"Get rid of the bra," he growled.

She pulled the t-shirt bra over her head, letting her

breasts fall and be exposed to the air. Her nipples hardened. His tongue glided over his lips when saw the perfectly round flesh. Rolling the condom on, he grabbed her hips roughly and flipped Harriet over to her hands and knees.

"Stay," he grunted as he pushed her head down onto the bed. Harriet yelped - caught off guard - but nevertheless, enjoyed the roughness coming from him. His fingers held her down, raking them through the silver strands of hair.

Her ass was perfect in the air, round and plump. Jax bit his lip as his other hand caressed the cheek, so soft, juicy and big. A cry escaped her lips as he applied a spank to the flesh. A reddened handprint appeared as he applied it again. Every slap, she jerked forward a little bit.

His cock was hard and ready. He lined his member up to her hole, thrusting in, and instantly feeling the tightness and warmth of her cunt. Jax pulled her hair as he pounded into her womanhood.

"Jax," she cried.

He let go of her hair, trailing his hands up her side and to her hips, gripping them as he thrust in and out of her. Harriet took the opportunity to muster the strength to move, so her back was flush against his chest.

His hands wrapped around her abdomen as her head rolled back onto his shoulder. He smiled, kissing her cheek hastily before fingering her clit. Her moans were getting louder, his grunts too, as the sound of slapping skin filled the room.

"You're fucking mine," he growled, nipping at the side of her neck, sucking and hoping marks would appear.

"Mhmm, I am nobody's," she mused. Instantly, he pulled out from her words, grasping her jaw, he turned her face to his.

"*You're fucking mine*," he growled again, but she shook her head. His hand clasped her throat, slapping her pussy. A sob escaped her lips. "Harriet."

She turned around in his grip, so their chests were flush against one another. Her hands clasped his cheeks, pulling their lips together. His hands were gripping her ass as she pulled Jax on top of her. They fell backwards onto the bed with him on top. Harriet's legs wrapped around his ass, rolling them, so she was on top now.

"No," she purred, winking. He was on his back, sprawled out on the mattress. She slowly moved her body, hands on his chest, as she lifted herself to sink on to his cock.

She was in control now. Her hands glided up to his chest to his shoulder, leaning on them, light breaths hitting his skin. Jax's hands were holding her ass as she began to ride his cock, rocking her hips with the pace she desired.

"Look who is mine now," she mocked. Jax growled but secretly enjoyed her taking control.

"No, that is not how it works, Kitten," he teased, wrapping his arms back around her and rolled them over.

The two of them were filled with arousal and lust. The sinful desire for one another was all they cared about, selfish enough to fill each other's need.

Boom!

A crash happened. The two let out a small chuckle as they realised that they had just fell off the bed.

"Fuck," she mumbled, the back of her head hitting the ground.

"Kit, fuck, are you ok?" he asked, quickly rubbing his hand over the part she hit. Harriet smiled and quickly kissed him again. Jax slipped inside of her as he began to slam his hips against her wet, hot core. Her hand clasped the duvet from the bed, the corner falling off the mattress and threw it over their bodies.

He was rubbing her clit as their lips attached to one another.

"Who owns you, Kitten?" he rasped, kissing her jawline as she felt the knot inside her stomach build.

"Me, I own myself," she screamed as she felt it coming closer and closer. He smirked against her lips. He pulled out of her, moving her small figure, throwing her on the edge of the bed. Her stomach was against the mattress edge as he bore all his weight on his knees.

He fucked her from behind. Then he tried again, "You're mine."

She shook her head, gripping the mattress from all the pleasure as he slammed his member in and out of her wet pussy.

"Fuck!" She was screaming and crying at the same time. "Faster," she begged.

"Mhmm, who owns you, Kitten?" he murmured.

"You, Jax. You fucking-"

He picked up the pace, thrusting as fast as he could, holding her hips. With grunts, the two experienced the shockwaves of an orgasm rushing through them. Curse words fell from their lips as they reached their highs. Him jerking inside of her as her core shattered with pleasure. By far, the best orgasm in the world.

Jax helped her back onto the bed. The duvet was on the ground and the room was a mess from their rendezvous. He picked up the duvet and placed it over her naked body. They laid beside one another, trying their best to catch their breaths. The room was filled with heavy heaving as they regained the strength to get up or move. Her body was quaking still, shaking, nerves on overdrive as she tried to calm her senses. Jax smirked because this was all from him. His handiwork and skill. His hand reached out, fingers gliding down her cheek, sweetly touching her skin. It travelled further, over her exposed hip.

The condom, filled with his seed was still wrapped around his cock which was slowly becoming flaccid.

"You ok?" he asked, still naked and perfect. Sweat covered his shoulder, and with the moonlight, she could see the glistening of it.

"Yeah," she mumbled, sending him a smile. "I can't come on Saturday anymore," she said, hesitant with her words and worried with how he would respond.

Jax blinked and scoffed as he shook his head. "Bullshit," he mumbled, walking to the ensuite and grabbing a wet, small washcloth. While there, he ripped off the condom, tying the end, and throwing it in the garbage.

"I have a..." she raked her mind for an excuse, "a thing."

Amused by her words, he walked back with the cloth. "A thing?" he cocked an eyebrow as he washed the sweat off her face and removed her makeup. He was taking care of her. He was actually doing aftercare as her pussy tried to recover from what just happened. She was definitely going to be sore tomorrow.

"Yes," she responded with confidence.

"No, you have a thing," he began as he slowly climbed in the bed and kissed her forehead. "You have a thing with *me*," he mused as he littered kisses along her wet flesh.

"Jax," she mumbled, pulling away from his affection. "I am serious. Something important has come up," she responded.

Still not taking 'no' for an answer, he let out a dry chuckle. "What is so important?" he grumbled.

"It's personal," she avoided.

"Personal? I just fucking-"

"Drop it, Jax," she snapped, turning her back to him as she pulled the duvet closer to her body.

"No," he responded.

"For fuck's sake, you really don't know what personal space is and privacy. I am not your fucking whore, Jax. I am the nanny. I am the help! I am *Harriet*. I don't need to tell you everything, the reasons why, and how or whatever. So, drop it, I don't ask what you did in Paris. I don't ask about your marriage or about the several interns you fucked. That shit is private. Whatever I am doing Saturday night, it is private. So please, drop it." Raging at him, she got up from the bed and went to the bathroom.

"Where are you going?" he yelled.

"To fucking get away from you because you are being entirely inappropriate right now!" she shouted over her shoulder.

"Fine, be a fucking bitch, Harriet!" he screamed at her as he got out of the bed and grabbed his underwear. Jax threw it on and grabbed the rest of his clothes off the floor before heading out the door. He made sure to slam the door.

CLAUDIA, wrapped in a robe, looked out her hotel window and placed her phone on the counter. Harriet wasn't so stupid after all. The blonde was close to firing her. She couldn't care less that her husband was sleeping around even when she was pregnant but doing it in their house… that was a big no. The two of them were idiots.

One rule she had. Don't fuck other people in the house. Jax knew that. There may be no 'actual' proof that they are doing it when the kids are sleep. If Jax was as bright as he said he was, he would have a hotel booked. But he was on his own high horse, thinking he could break every rule. He couldn't.

Claudia was glad that Harriet realised how this would be a conflict of interest. Don't bring the kids into this, don't let the personal life affect the business. She tsked her tongue and walked over to her laptop to finish her work.

Harriet was smarter than she thought. Fuck somewhere else, not in the damn house. There was the other thing…she knew Jax would leave everything for Harriet and Harriet knew that. She was making a wise choice.

10

Sandy was cleaning Harriet's bedroom, removing the sheets to get washed, and vacuuming the area. She came upon the ripped foil on the ground and the used condom in the garbage. The older lady smirked. She called her employer to let her know that her theories were correct: *Harriet and her husband were not only having an affair...but in the house.*

Idiots.

FRIDAY CAME AROUND, her last day here and then there was the interview on Saturday. For one, she was quite excited that her resume was accepted. She had an interview booked at The AVA House the next day. It was a prestigious publishing firm located in London as well as New York City, Vancouver, and Auckland. If she was accepted, she could live in any of those locations or go home. It was exciting, she could admit to herself.

With a smile, she walked down the staircase. The classic screaming of Jax from his office and the squeals of children's laughter echoed through the walls. Were they up? Questioning the commotion, she quickly ran down the stairs and turned to the kitchen. Claudia was cooking up a storm. She laughed and smiled at her daughter, who was drawing a picture and munching on a piece of toast.

"Morning," she said, nodding to the silver-haired woman. Harriet sent a kind smile to the woman as she walked around to say good morning to the kids. "Pack up your stuff, I expect you to be gone by noon."

It was harsh, no emotion as she looked over and sent her a scowl. Harriet scrunched her eyebrows, biting her lip as her eyes widened.

"What? I know today-"

"You're fired," she declared, looking at the woman across from her.

Eyes blinking rapidly, Harriet choked. "What?"

"Pack your shit and leave," she said again, anger laced in her voice. "Do I need to spell it out?" she quipped, raising an eyebrow with her hands on her hips.

"Claudia-"

"It is Mrs. Alderidge. *Missus* Alderidge to you," she interrupted, dropping the spatula to the side. She walked over to the younger woman. "You should've thought twice before you *fucked* my husband in my house," she spat with a whisper, "get out!"

Harriet backed up and quickly turned around, running up the stairs. Tears flooded her vision. The embarrassment she felt at that moment! She was absolutely mortified, ashamed, and felt downright dirty. What had just happened? The woman had turned vile even evil. Harriet had been fired because she fucked her boss' husband. She should've seen it coming.

'But he told me it was an open marriage...'

Grabbing her shit, she threw it into her bag. Wiping the tears away, she mustered up the strength to leave as fast as she could. She called a cab and exited without a single goodbye. She was a homewrecker. Harriet couldn't believe it. She had fallen for his trap, and she *had* ruined everything. It was all her fault. If she hadn't done this, it could've been ok.

Harriet called Cameron, asking her friend if it was ok for her to sleep on her couch tonight. Not asking why, the brunette agreed but expected her to spill the details as soon as she arrived.

Pulling her suitcase down the stairs, she raced out of the house. Jax's booming voice could be heard outside as she saw the black taxi pull up. Taking one last look at the manor, she got in.

Harriet was good at running. The only thing she was good at was running.

11

Jax hung up the phone, voice hoarse from the commotion that just occurred. Could people just listen for once and follow orders? Things would be way better if they did. He ran his fingers through his dishevelled curls as he pushed away from the desk. He needed his Kitten at that moment. He needed Harriet. The stress that came from this job was unimaginable and definitely not what he signed up for. But nevertheless, he got paid well, and he genuinely enjoyed what he did.

Huffing, he followed the children's laughter. Jax figured that she would be with them. A grin was plastered on his face. He was excited to see her beautiful face and to be with her goddess-like nature. But he was confronted with something else. Claudia was dancing in the kitchen as his kids were shoving pancakes in their mouths.

"Claud," he mumbled, his frown appearing, and his excitement long gone. "Have you seen Harriet?" he inquired, crossing his arms making his bicep bulge.

"Oh, I fired her," she shrugged and turned her attention

back to the kids. She said it as if it were nothing, as if she was just mentioning something that was no big deal. However, *this* was a big deal.

Jax's scowl grew. "*You did what?*" he seethed through his teeth, shaking his head, and running his fingers through his curls as he paced the room.

"Yes, she was causing a disruption-"

"She is," he was bursting with anger as he turned to her, "she is fucking mine to deal with. Did you think maybe we should've talked about this first?"

Claudia got up, grabbed his arm and pulled him into the other room. Jax was a bomb ready to explode, huffing and puffing.

"We have a family to raise-"

"Claudia, you're mad at me because I fucking filed for a divorce."

"Do you really think that we would end, and she would fall for you all over again. That you two would get married and have babies. Even live happily ever after?" she mused, raising her eyebrows at him. Her hands were on her hips, glaring at him. "She is different than that. The woman is broken and ready to run at any time. When I gave her an out, she ran. Today was supposed to be her last day. She was going to leave *you*. She got a job in the city or something. I just fired her as it made me feel good-"

"No, you're lying. She would never have kept that from me," he sneered, rubbing his face. "She was mine. We are-"

"She left you."

"Why did you fire her?"

"She fucked you and fucked you in *our* house, so I fired her. Also, you have kids to parent. I know you, Jax, you are ready to up and leave us. That can't happen. Brooklyn will fill in for the meanwhile."

"You're an absolute bitch. You always have been, and now you have *destroyed* me," he roared, voice deep and loud as it bounced around the house.

"Be quiet, will you? You're going to scare the kids-"

"You took away my happiness!" He shoved his finger into her chest as he bellowed the words.

Claudia wasn't scared of the words rolling off his lips. She was used to his quick anger. She didn't even flitch when he began to yell.

"No, she was going to leave. Jax don't fall for the broken ones because they will *always* leave you. She left you and she ran. Good luck finding her. She won't want to be found."

Jax didn't want to believe it, shaking his head repeatedly he spat vile words at her, "You bitch. I will fucking take everything away from you. I will make sure of it."

Claudia was unaffected by them. With a shrug, she simply muttered, "Try and see how that goes."

12

Harriet got out of the cab with a tear-soaked face. She handed the driver cash as she spotted the red brick building where her friend lived. The driver sent her a small, sad smile after he noticed the blotchiness of her face.

"I hope you feel better," he said to her in an Indian accent.

"Thank you," she mumbled, rolling the suitcase to the front doors.

Cameron raced out, slamming into Harriet's body. Quickly hugging the woman as she rocked Harriet back and forth, shushing her. Harriet cried softly.

"What happened?" she asked, cupping her cheeks and wiping the tears away.

Through her sobs, Cameron tried to understand her mumbles. "I got fired for fucking Jax. His wife found-"

"Oh my God. One that sucks. And two, you should've known better," she chuckled, rubbing her back and guiding her into the building.

"I think it'll be better for all of us. He was just too

controlling and manipulating. I think I am better without him," she cried as the two of them walked up the stairs to the old apartment.

The building was older, therefore no elevator. There was creaking stairs and thin walls, the perks of the living in such an old place. Cameron's apartment was newer looking, but still held the personality of the original architecture. With the original brick walls still showing, the kitchen was modern mixed with a dignified past. The whole apartment held an eclectic theme, retro and funky. The kitchen was a sage green, and the bathroom was white with black dotted wallpaper. It was very fun, the whole interior. Gold frames and trim mixed with wooden floors that creaked and a toilet that plugged at least once a week. Nevertheless, the place held its own personality and mind.

"Let's drink," Cameron responded. Music to her ears, Harriet smiled and laughed.

"You know me too well," she replied as her friend threw her arm over her shoulder.

The two of them sat on Cameron's couch, tequila in the middle as they did shots at four in the afternoon. Junk food covered the table as they drank their feelings and laughed about the old times. Who knows how many drinks she had? She lost count after five.

"Let's recap, girl," Cam said. "Why did you leave New Zealand?"

Harriet sighed. "To leave drama."

"What was your one rule when you got to England?"

"To not fall in love," she mumbled, knowing where this was going.

Her best friend raised an eyebrow and a drink to her. "And how did that work?"

Harriet groaned loudly. "You know," she rolled her eyes, "you know I have loved him since the very moment he entered my life and still loved him when he left."

"You're fucked, girl," Cam muttered, sipping her drink.

Harriet groaned. "New chapter time, I have an interview tomorrow with The AVA House...for a junior editor position. It's exciting. I loved working for Samantha Way in NZ."

"Well," Cameron began, pouring two more shots, "let's just hope your new boss isn't someone from your past, married with kids, extremely hot, or all three," she joked.

Harriet laughed. "Yes, let's hope. I feel like my life has turned into some stupid, mediocre, rom-com. He has so many issues and a complicated marriage. I had to leave," she explained then sighed. "He isn't my soulmate or anything, I think. He is *just* an old friend from my past. To a new chapter," she cheered as the two of them clinked their glasses and downed the burning liquor.

Her phone rang for the millionth time, groaning she pressed decline to Jax's call. However, persistent Jax, sent her a text.

New Message at 18:32

From Jax:

Just tell me you're safe, at least.

Groaning, she replied.

Yes, I am safe. Wish you the best.

Short and simple, 'wish you the best' simply means, 'fuck off, get lost'. Harriet prayed he would get the hint.

You're running again, Harriet. Tell me where you are, and I can grab you. It is ok. You're not fired. Ignore fucking Claudia. We are divorcing for a reason Kit. Just please, let me get you wherever you are, and we can forget about this.

Goodbye, Jax.

I made a promise all those years ago. I promised to find you, to protect you, to be with you.

Promises are a joke when they come from you. You promised to be loyal to your wife when you said your vows. Goodbye, Jax. Don't contact me ever again.

Downing another shot, she smiled at her friend.

'Asshole.'

Then she texted the nice barista, simply saying, 'it's not you, it's me. I have to cancel, sorry.'

THE SKYSCRAPER LOOKED huge as she stood in front of it. She squinted due to the sun in her eyes and saw the large letters "The AVA House". A little breath left her lips, a new start.

'Don't fuck it up.'

She collected herself and walked inside the modern and grand building. Her hands slid over her dress pants to rid the sweat on her palms and fixing the wrinkles. Business attire graced her figure; she made sure she dressed appropriately for the occasion: tattoos hidden under the brown sweater, tucked into her pants. Her silver hair was pulled into a sleek low bun as her glasses were perched on her freckled nose, makeup perfect and glowing. She threw her black leather tote bag over her shoulder and let out a final huff.

Harriet walked up to the receptionist with black hair, in her early 20's, fake lashes, and tattoos scattered on her arms. She had several piercings, her ears were stretched, and her nose had a golden hoop piercing.

'Thank god, I won't be judged.'

It made her feel better that the company wasn't as conservative as she had thought. The silver-haired damsel felt that she could be herself. The art scattered on her skin could be expressed without being unprofessional, frowned upon, or judged. It was a good start already.

Harriet smiled at the woman, looking at the quartz wall behind her with gold letters spelling the company's name.

"Hi, I have an interview with Viola Robinson," Harriet told the woman.

"Perfect, Harriet?" the woman asked, typing away on the silver Mac computer. Harriet nodded. "She will be right down. Good luck and if you need anything, holler. The name is Kate." Kate smiled at her, giving her one wink before glancing back down to her work. Friendly, she was friendly.

The elevator doors opened, and clicking heels were heard. A woman in her thirties appeared. She had bleach blonde hair in a straight bob and an elongated face, paired with a bold red lip. She had a slip skirt on, and a white turtleneck oversized sweater tucked in.

"Harriet, this way," she smiled at her, turning back to the elevator. "I read over your resume. You seem like a perfect candidate for our junior editor position. We would be pleased to have you, now tell me more about yourself."

The elevator dinged as the two walked out onto the 23rd floor. Harriet followed her steps and admired the grand windows. Her eyes were instantly drawn to the view of the city. Viola turned left, going down a hallway where they entered an office. She nodded to a seat, signalling for Harriet to sit on the black chair. Viola was across from her, crossing her legs, and then she gave Harriet her full attention.

The view was beautiful. Frosted glass doors and grand windows overlooked London. It had an industrial interior, black framing, red brick walls, and teakwood desks. Where there weren't brick walls, a dark teal blue covered the wall and plants littered the room. It was quite homey, she thought.

"Well, I am from Auckland, New Zealand. I interned for Samantha Way in my bachelor-"

Viola stopped her there, hand up. "I know. I read your resume. Now, tell me something I haven't read. Something that I don't know, and that is *you*." Harriet widened her eyes as she was definitely caught off guard by her. Viola shrugged her shoulders and then gestured for her to continue with her response, nodding her head towards Harriet.

"I love to read, name a classic, and I have read it. I wrote an essay about my experience in the system as an orphan, and how broken it was and still is. I was granted a full scholarship to complete my master's degree. However, I turned it down to become a nanny. I love kids, my degree is in social work, and I have seen horrible things in that line of work. I love to read. I love books. I interned for Samantha Way, and it was an amazing experience, and it made me want to fall in love with literature all over again," she responded. Viola nodded, still not impressed by her response.

"If you could publish a book written by you, what genre and what would it be about?"

"Romance of course, that is why I applied as an editor here. I would write about two orphans falling in love with one another in the system. Holding onto each other as the only love they knew were theirs in their corrupted lives. He leaves her, and she finds him again. However, their paths were different. The difficulties in their lives as they try to fall in love again thirteen years later."

Harriet was shocked by the words that came out of her mouth. It has been only one day since she departed from Jax. But his holy body and smirking face were still plastered in her mind, tattooed permanently in her consciousness. She wanted to forgive and forget, but she didn't feel like either of them did something wrong. They just wanted to love one another. Then it hit her, she would never not love him. Shaking herself from that thought, she focused back on the interview.

Viola hummed with a smile. "I do love a good romance; it is my job after all." Then, she went all serious once again. "You say you were an orphan?" she questioned, leaning farther back in her chair, arms crossed as she watched over Harriet's every movement.

"Yes."

"By chance, is this an autobiography?" she inquired. Harriet eyed her, the perfect red manicure and her thin figure. Viola analysed her; Harriet noticed. It was as if she was looking for one small flaw in order to say an upfront 'no' to Harriet.

"Unfortunately, no. I was an orphan, but I wish I had a

connection like the two people in my story," Harriet firmly said, the white lie rolling off her lips.

"I like you. You're fiery, passionate, and intelligent. At AVA, that's what we want, someone with passion and a love for literature. But also with an attitude of pushing your ideas forward, craving for your own success. Call it competitive, but that is what makes our people so strong. Why did you want to leave social work?"

Harriet pursed her lips then the truth escaped. "I thought I could help those in the system. I wanted to help them so that they could have a different experience than I did, a better one rather than being left in the system to rot. However, I can't change the system. I saw things I wish I had never witnessed. Instead of healing my past and moving forward, I was still letting it haunt me."

The woman nodded, emotionless still. Her facial features didn't change from the beginning, firm face and eyes analysing everything coming from her mouth. "See you Monday, Harriet. Mr. Astor would be pleased to meet you. Welcome to the team," the woman said to her, getting up and stretching out her hand. Harriet gladly took it, shook it, and thanked her for the opportunity.

She got the job. A small smirk came to her face as she left the building.

Jaxon sat in his office, overlooking the city of London. The almost empty scotch bottle was next to him, as he downed the burnt liquor. There was a high possibility that he was experiencing the five stages of grief as he reminisced about Harriet. She was gone and nowhere to be found.

The first stage of grief was denial. He experienced that when Claudia told him the words: "*When I gave her an out, she ran. Today was supposed to be her last day. She was going to leave you.*" He didn't believe her words as he truly believed she would never run from him as he was Jax, her Jax, first love and, in his opinion, soulmate. However, he needed to accept her disappearance, yet he was Jax, so he would fight to get her back.

Part of the denial was that he truly believed that Claudia was lying. If Harriet did actually leave, he expected her to be back that night.

It had been hours since she left that morning. It was now eleven at night on Friday, and the news of Harriet leaving was still echoing in his brain. He didn't believe it. She would never leave him ever! Jax truly believed that they were destined for one another that this was just a freak out on her behalf, and she would be back.

He sat at the kitchen table, on his third or quite possibly, his fourth scotch as he waited for her return. He had been there since eight o'clock, waiting patiently for her blue eyes and curvy body to be back where it belonged, with him. He played the words over and over in his head.

She was going to come back. She had too. Harriet would realise that she had made a mistake, and she would come back to him. However, when the clock hit twelve, then one, Claudia came downstairs.

"She isn't coming back, Jax," she told him, arms crossed, standing in front of the table.

His head hung, looking down at his empty glass. He refused to accept the truth.

"No, she will come back. She is just upset. She'll come back. My phone will ring any minute now and she will ask me to come get her, and it will be all good. She isn't gone," he mumbled, wetting his lips with his tongue and filling the glass once again.

"Jax, she is gone."

"You're wrong, Claud. You're always wrong. She is coming back. And if I have to wait here and dwell on every word I said to her, I will, but she'll come back."

Claudia sighed, "Go to bed, Jax. Call her in the morning if you're so desperate."

HE CRAVED A CIGAR. The burnt yet sweet taste hitting the back of his tongue mixed with the scotch could ease the pain, the anger that now was taking over. Taking a deep breath, he turned his chair around, focusing on his computer and the papers in front of him. It was a tempted distraction from a specific silver-haired damsel that he would sacrifice everything for. Jaw knew he needed to finish filing this divorce so he could be with her.

Who knew divorce was hard? Who knew that separating funds and property would absolutely do his head in? Claudia had shares in everything and separating everything without losing a lot of money was hard. He needed a drink, a very strong one.

However, he couldn't care less about that. All he wanted at that moment was her. Harriet needed to come back home to him, *now*. Yet, it was hard to find someone who didn't want to be found.

'Where would she go first?'

He thought to himself. The girl was new to this country barely knowing anyone here except Cameron, her roommate and good friend from New Zealand. Harriet was staying with Jax until Claudia kicked her out, therefore, she didn't have time to find a place for the night. Either she was staying at a hotel (not possible due to her funds), or she was with Cameron.

He got up abruptly from his desk, ran his fingers through his curls before he yanked his suit jacket off the chair and headed out the office doors. She had to be with Cameron, yet the problem was, he didn't know which unit was hers.

"Cancel all my meetings today and clear everything from my schedule, Dorothy. I have something personal to attend to," he told his personal assistant as he began making a beeline for the elevator.

He heard her make a call to the valet, asking them to bring his car up. She then began to cancel everything for the day.

Jax rode down the elevator to the main floor, exiting the building. The Maserati pulled up and the valet handed him his keys. Sure, it was the morning, but where else would she be? She had no other job. It was a Saturday and her only friend was Cameron. She *had* to be at her place.

With a huff, he placed the car in drive as he sped down the street. He couldn't care less about getting a speeding ticket at that moment, he just needed to find her. Harriet didn't want to be found, but Jax was one to never follow the rules. She was playing a game of hide and seek, and Jax always won at games.

The old brick building came into view as he pulled over. He did a quick fix to his jacket and walked to the doors.

112...Lincoln Roberts....113... Ally Fisher... he kept looking at the names...223 Cameron Harrington, bingo. Ringing the intercom, he waited. His foot bounced as he looked around the shady street, seeing people walking, homeless begging, and a few crack addicts wandering around. He was slightly uncomfortable. Call it privilege.

No answer, he tried again. Seconds later, nothing.

"Fuck!" he grunted, banging his hand against the wall. What is he supposed to do now, wait it out? Jax let out a loud groan, fingers pulling his curls, making the hair gel crack. His hair was now dishevelled and a pure mess. His small mental breakdown in the street caught a few people's attention.

"What are you fucking looking at?" he growled, walking back to his luxury car and speeding off once again.

CLUB MUSIC PLAYED as the two girls did shots in a booth. They were each other's own personal cheerleaders as they encouraged one another on with who could drink the most. The blue lighting covered the room as the music blared, making the two of them yell over the music in order to hear.

"I can't believe I got it!" Harriet screamed at the brunette across from her. Cameron signalled the bartender for another round.

"Was the interviewer male?" She cocked an eyebrow, leaning back as she smirked at the girl.

"A woman, and she just asked me if I could write a book about anything, what it would be?" Harriet responded.

"What was your response?"

"I kind of blurted about Jax and I, but that is ok. I am in

the middle of getting over everything! Call it coping with my trauma," Harriet responded with a chuckle, but her friend just shook her head. "I just need to get away from the drama. I am twenty-eight, I am divorced, and my debt supposedly has been paid off, but it's time for me to have fun, get stupid tattoos, meet men, and work!" she yelled, thanking the bartender for the drinks. The two clinked them again and chugged them back.

"Whatever you say, girlfriend. Speaking of working, I am leaving London to head back to the Ukraine in two days, so I am wondering if you would want to house sit?"

She felt a weight was lifted off of her, she didn't need to go scour to go find a place anymore and worry about funds. "I would be honoured! I will have a place to stay, thank you."

Another hour went by, as drinks were shared, and the two girls laughed at each other. As they enjoyed their twenties that night, they made stupid plans and drank endlessly.

"I didn't order this," Harriet mumbled to the bartender when he handed her a fruity drink.

"I know, but he did," the waitress told her, pointing to the man in the corner.

Fuck he was gorgeous. Late thirties, early forties possibly, with dark brown hair that flowed back and a subtle beard. He had smaller eyes and a smirk plastered on his face. Strong jawline and facial features were on display as he winked at her and raised his glass to her.

"Go!" Cameron mouthed. Harriet laughed as she got up, leaving the fruity drink and heading to the mysterious man. She was in for a real treat.

She smoothed down her leather skirt and adjusted the lingerie top, making sure everything looked just right. Her silver hair was half up and down with a smoky look and a classic red lip. Tattoos on display, she pulled out the barstool and sat down next to Mr. Tall, Dark and Handsome.

"Romeo," he nodded to her. Italian, she thought as soon as she heard the accent.

"Harriet," she responded with a small smirk, "buy me a drink. I don't drink those fruity things." She turned her chair to face him and leaned on her elbow against the bar table.

"Ah, ok. What-"

"A scotch, please," she turned to the bartender and told him. The man next to her was in awe, watching her as she displayed such dominating energy. She wasn't the normal kind of woman he dealt with. She didn't need a man to live, and he was intrigued.

Harriet downed the drink, wiping the last droplets from her lips and biting her bottom lip.

"I have never seen a lady-"

"Are you intimidated?" She leaned over and whispered. He smirked.

"No, intrigued. Now, Harriet, tell me about yourself."

13

Harriet woke up with a pounding in her head. Groaning, she wiped her eyes and began to open them. Instantly, she noticed that she wasn't in Cam's flat. Harriet was puzzled. Then she felt a very heavy arm wrapped around her waist.

'What the fuck happened last night?'

Looking around, she noticed the tan male next to her. Mason, Matthew...Mat...Matteo. Fuck. Delicately, she tried to remove the strong grip around her waist. His grunts of annoyance alarmed her. She needed to be swift and sneaky. Harriet tried again, prying the arm from her body carefully. It was a success. The male rolled away from her. She took one last glance at the man as she quickly grabbed her clothes off the ground and headed straight to the door.

It was an expensive apartment, dark and mysterious, like him. However, the sex hadn't been the best. She couldn't care less about him when she left.

Where was she? Opening her phone, she saw another hundred calls from Jax. A groan rolled off her tongue as she began to flaunt her walk of shame to the tube. Looking around the busy street, Harriet stopped when she saw a hair studio. Lux London in bold gold lettering. With a smirk, she opened the door.

"Hi, can you do a walk-in? I need to get rid of this." She motioned to the silver. The man smirked.

"Of course, sweetie. You look like you had a remarkably interesting night," he mused, looking her up and down. Gay, most definitely, Harriet pieced together. Laughing with him, she followed the brunette. He was older and covered in floral tattoos and had multiple piercings, including his nose.

She sat in the salon chair, looking at her dishevelled appearance in the mirror. Rough didn't cover what she looked like. It looked as if she had been to hell and back. The man introduced himself, Toby. He owned the salon.

Toby tried to help remove the knot of an updo she had. The aftermath of sex and partying.

"What are we thinking?" he asked as he raked his fingers through her long locks. "The silver is gorgeous and very well done. Absolutely no breakage! How long have you been dying your hair?" he admired.

"Nine years, but I am ready a change," she stated. "I am naturally a blonde, but I need a colour that is like 'fuck you, you don't own me.' But I also work an office job, so I can't do colour."

He hummed. "A man?"

She laughed. "Yes, sir."

"And he is attracted to...?"

"Blondes," she flatly replied. The man pursed his lips, humming.

"How do you feel going, brunette? We can do a darker root with some ash lowlights and add some bangs."

"Let's do it."

HARRIET FELT LIKE A MILLION BUCKS. She thanked Toby for the gorgeous hair. It felt good to have something different. It was truly the first step to freedom. Toby wanted to hear everything about what triggered this new look, and of course, Harriet obliged and told the tedious tale of Jax. Toby was in pure shock, responding with 'oh honey, yes, you totally need a 'fuck you' hairstyle', which made her smile.

Pleased with how the day turned out and awfully glad the silver was finally out, she headed to her next appointment. The brunette was in desperate need of some retail therapy.

14

The day came. Harriet stood in front of the tall glass skyscraper from the past Saturday. Today was the day where she began to work there. It was a new beginning to a new chapter. Harriet saw it as more of an "unproblematic" work environment, which was what she needed. With a jump in her step, she entered.

The woman from Saturday was back at her desk, talking to a man in a grey suit. His hair was longer, dark sandy blonde, close to brown, and combed back. His voice was deep – obviously British – as he leaned over to talk to the receptionist.

The tattooed woman looked over and saw Harriet in a red polka dot wrap skirt with a white turtleneck sweater tucked in. Harriet had her new brunette hair pulled into a low bun and had paired her look with chunky gold jewellery. Meeting Kate's eyes, she gripped harder onto her bag and took a deep breath. Her feet began to walk closer to where the two figures were.

"Hi, Harriet. Here's your new pass, and Viola will come

down in a minute to give you the full tour," Kate smiled, red lipstick complementing her white teeth and overall aesthetic of black hair, tattoos, and chic business wear.

"Thank you," Harriet grinned.

The male, roughly six-foot-one, turned around to face Harriet. He was older, late thirties, with light stubble, and gorgeous earthy green eyes. He had a boyish look to him and most definitely was a gentleman.

"You're new?" he asked, leaning against the counter as he turned his attention to Harriet.

"Yes, it's very exciting," Harriet beamed, pushing her glasses up her nose.

"Atticus Astor," he smirked, locking eyes.

"Harriet Kensington," she nodded to him. Atticus Astor, he owned the company. More handsome in person, he seemed like the type of guy to bring home to your mother.

"Pleasure to meet you. Welcome to the AVA House. What's your position?"

"Junior editor." He nodded, smile still shining just as bright.

"Well, welcome. Hope to see you around," he beamed, placing his hand on her shoulder squeezing it lightly before walking away. His touch lingered, so comforting, soft and gentle. It was as if she craved for it more. In all honesty, she couldn't deny how handsome he was.

The girl prayed that she wouldn't have a 'Jax situation' all over again. However, her gaze lingered on his figure as it sauntered to the elevator. She couldn't deny the fluttery feeling in her stomach.

"Harriet!" Viola's clicking heels came into earshot as the brunette turned around, spotting the platinum bob.

The floor was beautiful. It held an industrial vibe yet

glamorous feel to it. Crystal chandeliers, brick walls, and black podiums were holding the place up. Viola showed her the 23rd floor where Harriet would be working. She had a cubicle in the corner by the window that overlooked London. In her eyes, she felt spoiled. There was even a brand-new Mac computer on her desk. It was perfect, and the recent brunette was in heaven.

"Make yourself at home. You will need to read few manuscripts a week and edit them. Once they are done, send them off to the senior editor and repeat the process. We are a family. You're part of the romance team. Everything we do is in the romance genre. This floor is a fix of erotic and contemporary works. Mr. Astor will probably pop down here once or twice a week. He is an extremely sweet man," she continued her introduction as they got into the elevator.

Viola scanned her key card and pressed the thirtieth-floor button. "We are going to the top now, Mr. Astor works up here. I am not sure if he is in today, but we can see," she mused as they went up.

Harriet sent her a smile, holding her bag close to her still as the elevator dinged. The two of them walked off, Viola waving to the receptionist.

"Hi Chloe."

There he was again standing and talking to a red-haired woman at the desk. He was smiling with a Cheshire cat grin as he laughed along. From his body position, he seemed very invested with what the woman was saying, eyes glimmering with each word rolling off her lips. He seemed sweet, kind and casual. Harriet didn't know what the feeling was, but she just wanted to be held by him or simply be near the tall man. As if there was a magnetic force between them, making her want to be in his presence.

"Mr. Astor," Viola beamed, all preppy and smiley. Gross, it was as if she was trying to impress him, woo him even as if Viola had a crush on him. Harriet internally grimaced.

'So, this was my new boss. Holy fuck...'

The man turned around instantly locking his green eyes with her sapphire orbs. The smile was back, but bigger than when he was talking to the red-haired woman. What was this feeling she was experiencing? Butterflies in her stomach? A small tint flustered on her cheeks as she looked at the man across from her.

"This is Harriet Kensington. She is new. Junior Editor with contemporary and erotic romance," Viola introduced.

He walked over shaking Harriet's hand. It sent sparks up her arm, and her breath halted. "We met downstairs. How is it going, Harriet?"

Loss of words she had to quickly gain back her focus. "Wonderful. It is an amazing, gorgeous building. I have my desk right next to the window overlooking London, and I am at a loss of words," she rambled on, eyes gleaming. Her smile was large as she made grand gestures with her hands.

"I am glad. New Zealand, huh? Your accent?" he asked, licking his lips and crossing his arms. She eyed his suit, noticing a few top buttons were undone, and he had no tie.

Shocked by his accuracy she smirked. "Yes, usually people think Australian. You're the first, congrats," she chuckled.

"You Kiwis and Aussies get offended if we say the other, so I had to learn. Viola," he looked to the older woman, "leave her with me, I will finish the introduction tour."

Viola jerked back a little, shocked. "Oh, sure! I will see you later then, Harriet," she nodded to the brunette. Harriet smiled.

"Come to my office," he quipped, nudging his head to the grand two doors, wooden and high. She followed him as he opened and closed them.

The office was massive, a table with different amber coloured hard liquor bottles and a bookcase behind his wooden desk. He walked around to his desk. A French press was located on a cart beside it.

"Coffee?" Atticus questioned, taking out a mug from the bottom cabinet of the bookcase.

"Please."

"Have a seat," he said as he poured the drinks. "Milk, sugar?"

"Just black, please."

Atticus sat down, handing her the mug of the steaming liquid. He leaned back on his black leather chair, crossing his legs. Then their eyes locked.

"Have you worked in publishing before?" Atticus asked, cocking an eyebrow.

"Yeah, I did an internship during university." He nodded, taking a sip and still admiring her. Harriet looked behind his head, seeing the different books homing his bookshelf – classic romances. He was a hopeless romantic she connected.

He hummed, noticing her looking at the books. "Romance is my favourite genre. A bit of a hopeless roman tic, I am. What about you?"

Harriet's smile grew. "Romance, definitely. I used to read the classics in my school library growing up, waiting for the day when I experience my own great love-"

"Did you?" he interrupted, taking a sip from the mug again. "Have your great love?"

She thought, darting her attention away from his wide

green eyes. Did she have her great love? Her Romeo, Mr. Darcy or Heathcliff?

"When I was fifteen, I thought I did," she eventually responded.

Atticus slowly nodded his head humming, "High school, love?"

"Something like that," Harriet mumbled. Atticus was still simply admiring her.

"What made you go into publishing? Work for my company?"

'Was this an interrogation?'

Harriet pursed her lips and let out a sigh. "Do you want the brutally honest answer or a sugar-coated answer?" she chuckled, sipping her coffee.

A smirk grew on his face, head tilting to the side and eyes narrowing, analysing her. "I like you. You're authentic. Give me the brutally honest answer, hit me with it," he quipped, smirk still evident, yet he was biting his lip now.

"Do I still get to keep my job after I spill? Promise me," Harriet joked, rolling her eyes. It was playful, flirty even.

"Yes, of course. I am sitting here, looking at you, a New Zealander who is in London, working a job where your degree has nothing to do with it. You worked one other publishing job in your life, and it makes me question, why are you in publishing?" he stated, studying her. Then he added, "I looked up your file after we met this morning."

Harriet blinked absentmindedly as she choked on air, shocked of how well he read her. "Would you believe it if I said I am running away from my ex-employer and his crazy wife, where-" she narrowed her eyes, pausing her words. Maybe it wasn't time to explain her bullshit. "I want a career that helps make someone's dreams come true, allowing their book come to life while doing something I love...reading," she smiled.

Atticus placed his coffee mug down on the dark mahogany desk, leaning over towards her this time. "Very," he paused, searching for an answer, "convincing and original. One day, I will get the true reason why you want to work here," he winked.

"Why are you in publishing?" she asked this time, leaning back and admiring him with a smirk plastered on her face.

"I like making dreams come true, and I like books," he mimicked, sending her a boyish grin yet a flirtatious stare.

"How," she began but paused and began to mock him, "convincing and original. You know what Mr. Astor-"

"Atticus, call me Atticus."

"*Atticus,*" the name was perfect as it rolled of her lips, "one day I will hear the real reason of why you're in publishing."

"Touché, Ms. Kensington."

She winked at her boss. Then it hit, what the fuck was she doing? She was really doing the whole 'I am sex on wheels, get with me' look and vibe. This was her boss! Harriet could do it to Jax all she wanted and possibly, since she experienced that, she might have all the ego in the world. However, she was sitting across a multimillionaire who owns multiple publishing companies, had more money than her and oversees her job. Was she that intoxicating and naive? Was she being Jax, trying to get what she wants with just a wink and a little cleavage?

'*Unacceptable!*'

He slid a piece of paper to her, his name in bold with a

number on it. "I like you, Harriet. Here is my number, we should go for drinks-"

"You're my boss," she blurted, dusting off her shirt and taking a deep breath.

"As friends, Harriet. I like you *platonically*. You're new to London, you need a friend, and I think there is a story behind you, and you look...fun," he told her. "And I want fun."

"Are you flirting with me Mr. Astor?" she sassed, cocking an eyebrow and narrowing her eyes.

"Let your imagination soar, Harriet. I am a hopeless romantic. However, no, I am simply being friendly."

"Ok," she nodded, getting up. "I should go and do work. Thank you, Atticus. See you around."

"Tonight, Harriet. The Ivy, let me drive you after work."

"Ok."

What the fuck did she just get herself into? Another date – platonic date, as he stated – with a *very handsome gentleman*.

WORDS. All day she read were words. One might complain, but Harriet could not care less. She was stuck in the stories, the imaginative world of strapping men and sex. Biting her lip, she sat at her desk, reading and marking with a pen as she went.

It was pure erotica, what she was reading. Her thighs clenched together as she read what was happening in a particular scene. She could get used to this, getting paid to ready raunchy stories; the woman was in heaven!

"Harriet," she heard the sweet yet deep voice. Looking

up, she saw him with his boyish grin leaning against the black podium by the elevator. Atticus watched her as she nibbled away at her pen and focused her attention on whatever character she was reading.

"Hi." She looked up for the first time that day. There was no one left in the office, the bright sky was long gone, and now the night life was beginning to entwine on the streets of London. His classic smile was given to her with his hands in his pockets. The CEO was devilishly handsome, boyish with kind looking eyes, his slicked back hair and wide grin. It would make any girl swoon. He wasn't Jax. He was the type of guy to marry for love, make you orgasm ten times in the row before him and not fuck you, instead make love. He was the guy she dreamed of having since a little girl. Kai wasn't even him.

"It's eight o'clock. Let me wine and dine you, take you for some good food and delicious wine." He pushed off the podium and walked to her.

What was she doing? Her heart was beating fast, telling her to go for it, but her mind was telling her this would be a mistake. But she was young and naive and couldn't care less. Harriet was in London to make mistakes. What could she lose?

"Seafood," she looked up, pen still between her teeth. Her grin was cheesy and flirtatious, but she couldn't care less. "I want seafood."

"Sure." The way he said, letting roll of his lips like honey. She melted.

Atticus nodded to the exit, signalling her to come. Hastily, she grabbed her stuff, throwing her bag over her shoulder. Harriet quickly followed him.

The elevator ride was silent, the two looking straight

ahead. He was perfect, a prince charming to her. The ding was heard, and the two were out.

An Audi A7 was in front of the skyscraper, black exterior and interior. He opened the passenger door for her, helping her in before going to the other side.

'Come to London they said. Leave your boring life and come to London, where rich men will fall at your feet and wine and dine you to the extreme.' She was definitely on cloud nine.

"Where are we going?" she inquired, looking at him with wide eyes and a flirty smile. His perfect face and bright green eyes were looking at the road in Downtown London, his smile still prominent. Was this a fuck you to Jax, a rebound? Or was this the man of her dreams?

"You will see. It's a steak and seafood place. I know the owner and he has by far has the best wine in the world, besides Antonio's. It is a little Italian restaurant out of London."

Red wine that sounded amazing. Good red wine, the sweet yet tangy flavour that could soothe any problem. The smoothest of liquids glide down your throat. Red wine and gin really were better than an orgasm.

"You know the way to my heart," she mused.

"You like wine?"

"Do I like wine? Is the pope Catholic?" she joked. He laughed, a deep mellow laugh as he threw his head back.

The two of them pulled up to the restaurant. The car was placed in park, and Atticus got out, walking to the other side of the car. He opened the door for her, holding his hand out as she grabbed it. What a gentleman! It made her insides flutter further. The man was sent down by God himself, and he knew more about her than anyone else in the world.

Atticus wanted to get to know *her*, which made her feel absolutely thrilled.

Yet the downside of this hit her mind. Fuck, he was her boss. Classic Harriet, fucking everything up that was good in her life. *She could lose her job*. However, young and naive, she was.

"Thank you," she nodded to him. Atticus placed his hand on her lower back, guiding her to the entrance.

The restaurant was beautiful, dim lights and jazz music. Plants hung on the wall and the paint was a navy blue with gold accents. It was gorgeous, somewhere she could see Atticus spending his time at. But all she cared about was wine at the moment.

"Mr. Astor, pleasure to see you again, come this way," the host said. Atticus had his hand still on her lower back, guiding her to where the host was taking them: a private booth with black curtains. The two sat as the host pulled the curtains closed.

She questioned whether or not Atticus was getting in her pants, but as he told her that morning, he was simply just trying to be a friend, a warm welcome to his company.

"Red wine, huh? Merlot, Shiraz, Cab Sav, Pinot Noir or Carignan? Pick your poison," he listed, sitting across from her. His suit jacket was now off as he sent her a grin.

"Oh, you pick. I just drink," she responded with a light chuckle.

"French Pinot Noir wine made in Burgundy," he winked, telling the waiter.

"Oooo, sounds exotic," she responded. He chuckled.

"So, Harriet, you owe me a story," he recalled.

A light scoff came from her lips. "I need multiple glasses for that," she retorted.

"Mhmm, I see. Let's get you a few drinks then.

Harriet laughed in favour with that idea. Then her phone went off.

New Message at 20:25

From Jax:

Talk to me, please. I miss you, and I love you. Where are you? You're making me worried. Do you need cash? Kitten, I am at a loss for words and overwhelmed with worry. I need to know that you are ok or else I am going to find you. Answer me, please.

"Someone important?" Atticus asked, watching the waiter come with their bottle of wine, popping it and pouring the red liquid into their glasses.

"Far from it." Shutting the phone off, she flipped it looking back at the man across from her. Harriet cupped her own cheeks, elbows on the table as she looked at him.

"Favourite classic?" he quipped.

She hummed, pursing her lips. Taking a small sip of her red wine, she thought. "I have no idea, Pride and Prejudice probably," she shrugged. "They are just stories. Love in classics doesn't *actually* exist."

"How so?"

"Been around the block too many times. Been in love, got my heart broken, been married, got divorced. Love doesn't exist. We need to stop teaching young girls that love in books and movies is real because it isn't. Their expectations are high, and they go searching for it to just find out it was all fake. The only good thing that comes out of two people being together is sex. And sex is my greatest love."

Atticus raised his eyebrows, nodding along as she ranted. "Seems like someone got their heartbroken," he joked.

"Seems like someone got manipulated by the male species thinking that they love them," she fired back. "Enough about me-"

"No, you're intriguing. I want to know your story."

"To write a book about me and publish it?" she mocked him, winking.

"If it's a good enough story and I feel like it is, quite possibly. Tell me about your family?" Atticus topped her glass up as a bunch of appetizers came out. Eyes bulging, her mouth watered. It looked amazing.

"No family, I am an orphan. Father was a drug dealer and is in prison. Mother was stupid enough to die from a drug overdose."

"It even gets more interesting!" he exclaimed, then gave her a solemn look. "I am sorry, by the way." She shrugged, picking at the food. "Ok, you were married. What happened?"

"Are you psychoanalyzing me? I feel like I am getting interrogated."

"Possibly, now talk."

"Umm, married too young. I was nineteen we loved each other and was happy until shit hit the fan and we were unhappy. I just got out of the system after... after the boy I love got adopted out. No money, nothing and Kai saved me," she told him.

It shocked Atticus the fact that Harriet talked about her past as if it was no big deal, but when you experience it, and it was your normal, one might do that. Her life was full, and to the extreme, however she was a survivor, and he admired that. The woman across from him was the most intriguing person he had ever met. He craved to know more. It was as if she was a good novel that he was slowly reading, revealing the torturous story line and plots twists of the characters life. The man was in awe.

"I have two younger sisters. The oldest of them is thirty-five but my parents believe she is the perfect daughter. Married, two kids, white picket fence, whereas I am a workaholic and single. No marriage, no kids and enough money to support a family. Made my company from nothing and all they care about is when I am gonna get some girl pregnant," Atticus ranted, raising his glass up for cheers.

"That sucks. Marriage is overrated after all. I just fucked one up. Actually, it was always fucked, but I somehow screwed it more."

"I'm so sorry."

"It's fine. Not my marriage; someone else's."

Atticus' eyes bulged, a light chuckle coming from his thin lips. "Do tell. Don't spare all the nasty details."

"We need multiple shots before I explain that one," she muttered, then chuckled.

"Waiter!" he yelled. She laughed, enjoying every moment with this man.

Atticus was perfect. She couldn't get over it. A man of her dreams, and after three rounds of shots, she began.

"I fell in love with a boy when I was thirteen. He was three years older. Did everything with him. He was a troublemaker, got involved with the law. We were in the same orphanage too. I grew up with him, fell in love with him, lost my virginity, et cetera. When he was seventeen, he got adopted out and left me. He promised to come back and get me, so we could be together. Didn't happen. So, I moved on with my life, broken-hearted and hoping one day he would save me again. Thirteen years later, I run away from New Zealand and got a job as a nanny in London. My boss was his wife, and I let my heart get in the way, and we had a small affair. However, she was lesbian, and the marriage was arranged and an open marriage, well I think it is, but I got fired by her. She found out, and now I am here."

Atticus was lost of words, blinking rapidly as he took all this hot gossip in. "Fuck. You really have lived a million lives," he eventually mumbled with a light chuckle.

"More like lost in this life than anything."

"You should write a book about that, but they end up together," he shrugged.

"That would most definitely be the ultimate fuck you. However, I am not a writer. I dyed my hair brown because I was blonde, and he loves blondes. I want to get a tattoo, but-" she pulled up her sleeve, "I don't know what else to get."

He reached over to graze his fingers with the ink. "Those are beautiful. New Zealand birds and plants?" She nodded, pleased to know he recognized it.

"Now, tell me your fails and commotions in life," she cocked, sipping her wine and peering at him.

Atticus chuckled. "I think you won with your disasters, but ok."

After a series of several more drinks, delectable food and delightful company. Atticus picked up the bill after her several protests.

"It's getting late," she said, "I have work tomorrow."

Atticus smirked. "Let me call you an Uber, or you can come back to my place for a drink."

"I think it'll be best for the both of us if I go home. Thank you though, Atticus. It's good to have another friend in this new city. I had a great time," she explained walking outside with him.

He grinned, halting in front of her. "Anytime, love."

15

The two of them were outside the restaurant now, facing one another. The breeze hit her skin, making her shiver slightly.

"Here, take my jacket," Atticus said, shrugging off his suit jacket.

"No, it's all good, Atticus. My cab is almost here. Keep your jacket," she hummed. He sent her a smile, hand on her lower back once again. It felt good, like home, when it sat there.

Grinning at him widely, she got on her tippy toes and pressed a kiss to his cheek. It felt right doing it, even if she just met him that day.

Atticus smiled, thanking her.

The Hackney Carriage pulled up at the restaurant. Atticus took a few steps towards the cab, opening the door for her. Her heart swooned from such a small gesture. She couldn't get over his gentleman mannerisms.

"Goodnight, Atticus. Thank you for the dinner and

drinks. I'll see you tomorrow," she said to him, walking towards the car.

"My pleasure. Hope we are friends now, Harriet," he told her whole heartily as he placed his hand on her shoulder. He leaned down to her, kissing her cheek. "Goodnight, text me when you get home, please."

She nodded, getting in. Atticus closed the door, handing the driver some cash. With a final wave, he watched the car drive away.

Harriet had a new friend, and she was so pleased with how the night went.

Minutes later, the cab pulled up to the brick apartment. Cameron was back in the Ukraine, so she had the studio apartment to herself. Harriet was so much happier now that she had her own space and time rather than living with other people.

Getting out, she thanked the driver and walked to the building.

"Harriet," she heard the deep voice. This couldn't be happening.

Turning around, she was met with Jax in all his glory. Stubble long gone, all shaved off and hair perfectly in its curls with no product. He had jeans and a t-shirt on with a light cardigan. Harriet spotted the black sports car behind him.

'Here comes a fight.'

"Hi," she muttered, stumbling on her feet as she went to the door, fishing out her keys.

"You're drunk," he flatly told her, hand clasping her hip as he helped her steady herself. She tried to shrug his grip off, but he held her tighter.

"So? You're not m'boss," she slurred, opening the door

and walking to the stairs. Jax followed heavy footsteps echoing. "Just tipsy, Jax."

"Yes, I know, but you're coming home at one a.m., drunk in Downtown London. You're a woman too," he stressed, spitting each word.

"Don't tell me what to do. That I shouldn't drink because I come from a line of addicts, blah, blah, blah. Fuck off, Jax," she yelled, walking up the old wooden stairs to the second level.

Unlocking the door, Harriet went in and instantly began pulling her clothes off. Jax entered the flat.

"I told you to leave," she grumbled, going to the bathroom and taking off her makeup.

He leaned against the door frame. "You haven't answered my calls."

Furrowing her eyebrows, she looked at him. "Has it occurred to you that I don't want to talk?" she roughly grabbed her pyjamas from the unmade bed. "Little privacy, please?"

"It's not like-"

"Jaxon!" He begrudgingly turned around as she changed quickly, bumping shoulders with his as she exited the bathroom into the studio apartment. "You need to leave. I need sleep because I have work tomorrow."

"You have a job?" he asked, crossing his arms, biceps flexing even from such a small motion.

"Yes. Publishing house, junior editor. Pays the bills."

"What publishing house?"

"The AVA House," she told him pouring herself a glass of water.

"Atticus Astor. He is a client of mine. Nice guy, rich and has a thing for young women."

"Wouldn't know, I am a junior editor. Haven't met the big boss."

"Hmm, who were you drinking with?" he questioned as she pulled the covers back from her bed.

"Friends from work, Jaxon. Now I need to go to bed," she told him. "That's your cue to leave."

"Can we go out for lunch sometime this week?" he requested, standing in front of the unmade bed.

"Jax, you really can't let me go, can you?" she mumbled, running her fingers through her hair, tugging the strands.

"You're the love of my life, Harriet."

She sighed, "Don't say that. We are merely people who used to know each other."

His face scrunched up. "Not even friends?"

"You need to earn that title, Jax. Friends don't fuck, friends don't do what we are going, Jax. So, earn the damn title and do something nice for a change," she spat at him, exhausted from this conversation. Dropping the covers, she walked to the door, opening it for him. "Leave."

"Lunch, tomorrow, please. I will pick you up. I won't leave till you agree," he bargained.

He was persistent, a fly on the wall and a dog begging for her. There was one way to end this conversation, to get him to leave and for her to finally put an end to this.

"Fine, now leave, Jax."

Harriet was late. She slept through her alarm, and now she was running in heels across the street to the skyscraper while muttering swear words under her breath.

"Late, Ms. Kensington?" Atticus walked up next to her, locking his Audi with a coffee in his hand. Harriet groaned.

"Someone decided to give me shooters all night," she sassed, rolling her eyes.

"Mhmm, I wonder who that person was. I have to give them a stern talking to as my star employee was late."

"Yeah, they are a *really* bad influence," she mocked. They walked into the grand building, pressing the elevator button.

"They sound like it. Anyway, lunch today?" he asked, sipping the coffee and looking straightforward.

"As much as I would like to have bottomless mimosas with you, I have to have a dreaded lunch with my affair man," she groaned.

"Oh, that is going to be horrid. I pity you. Cancel on him," he chuckled, nudging her shoulder.

"He will track and hunt me down. May as well just get it done and move on. Anyway, coffee after work?" she pipped, the doors opening to her floor. He agreed, sending her one last classic smile.

Harriet sat down, ready to begin her day of work. Instantly, three people appeared at her desk.

"I am Cordelia. That's Daniel and Rebecca," the blonde said.

"Harriet," she replied, eyes focused on her computer, typing an email up.

"We heard Mr. Astor asked you to stay in his office. What was he like?" Cordelia asked.

"Is he sweet? He is obviously handsome," Rebecca piped in.

"What happened?" Daniel finally responded.

Harriet tore her eyes from the screen, looking at her co-workers. "He just welcomed me. It was sweet and sincere." The three of them were not pleased with her answer.

"He is looking for a wife."

"Good on him. That is his business. I must get back to work. Nice to meet you all," she beamed.

The office gossips, Harriet noted.

TWELVE O'CLOCK HIT and she groaned. This will be painful, she knew it. Harriet grabbed her handbag and smoothed her dress down quickly before she headed out. The Maserati was parked outside. Jax, in all his glory was sitting in it, tapping his fingers on the steering wheel to the beat of the music playing. Harriet exited the building, walking to the car, dreading this lunch. His attention was spiked from her opening the passenger door.

"Hi, Kitten. Your hair..." he purred. It hit her, the love and adoration he had for her. Her heart leaped a little, and a small smile appeared. He felt like home. His fingers came to play with the one strand that lined her face. She pulled away.

"Hi, Jax."

He drove the car out of the entrance area, the engine loud as he sped down the street. The man had planned on taking her to his favourite soup and sandwich place. He knew her down to earth spirit would love it.

Jax was wearing his classic suit, navy with a black tie and white collar. He was always so edible, looking like a full meal while driving and changing gears. His muscles bulged with every shift of the gear stick, gripping harder on the wheel with his other hand.

"Claudia and I are separated. She is living in a house down the street from us. Two nannies and the kids go back and forth," he told her, calmly and looking over to see her reaction. Harriet didn't have one.

"Are you happier?" she asked.

"So far, yes, but I want us to have a future," he murmured, pursing his lips.

"Jax," she began, "I won't deny there is a piece of me that yearns for you too, that when I lie in bed at night, I think of you, of us and what we could be. You have so much unfinished business, and I am trying to find a place in the world where I belong. I am not going back to New Zealand; my mental health wouldn't survive. I love my job here. I love London. Who knows where I will go, but I need to find myself before I can be with someone." The words came out of her mouth, the truth and emotions all at once, and it felt good to finally let it go. To speak the unspoken words. "We have a past, but who knows if we have a future. I am fucked up. You had a family to have Christmas and birthdays with and a dad who loves you. I have no one. All I have are false promises and a broken yet mended heart. I need to figure out what I want from life."

"I know, Kit, and you deserve the world. I want to be there for everything. I will give up my life-"

"You have kids, Jax. Kids! If Arlo survived and I was sitting here with you, and you were in my position, Arlo would always come first. You need to do that with Em and Caleb."

"Jane Austen, Charlotte Bronte, Margaret Mitchell...the list goes on. You're a hopeless romantic-'

"Love is dead, Jaxon."

"Love is everywhere. You love me," he growled, parked at

the restaurant. Jax leaned over, lips gently brushing hers as they connected, the softest kiss he had ever given her. Slow and full of love, he showed her. Harriet fell hard all over again. Was he manipulative, good with words or simply the love of her life? She didn't know, yet the kiss was everything she needed at that moment.

"No, I *loved* you," she mumbled against his lips as she pulled away. "I loved the idea of us when I was thirteen to fifteen. I am twenty-eight now, covered in tattoos and scars that have yet to heal-"

"Harriet," he tried.

"I told someone who I really wanted to have lunch with today that I couldn't because I needed to end this for real. We are done, Jax. We will never be good for one another. We are the past, who knows what is in our future-"

"Us, Harriet. We are the future. Can't you get that in that pretty little brain of yours? We are like every classic novel. We are the future!" he yelled at her.

Harriet pressed her lips together and spat, "Drive me back." She pulled out her phone, sending a text to Atticus asking if he could pick up lunch for her. Her fingers wiped her tears away.

Jaxon growled, displeased with this meeting, as he put the car back in drive. His knuckles were white from gripping the wheel. Tension filled the car.

"I hate you as much as I love you right now," he hissed.

"You can't let me go."

"No, because-"

"We aren't soulmates, Jaxon. We were teenage lovers!"

"Get out, *now*," he cursed as he pulled up to the building. "Get out before I do something I will regret." She stayed put.

"Tell me you will never call me again. Delete my number," she commanded.

"You know I can't do that-"

"Jaxon," she sneered. "Let. Me. Go."

"You're going to regret this, Harriet."

"No, I won't," she got out of the car. "Promise me."

His eyes just locked hers, jaw shut, and tension filled. "I love you." Then he was gone.

QUICKLY FIXING HER MAKEUP, she headed into the building and going straight to her desk. On it, a sandwich sat with a cappuccino and a note.

Hope it wasn't too awful.

-A

She smiled sitting back down and quickly finishing the sandwich before going back to work. So kind, so generous. However, a piece of her yearned for Jax. She missed him, she wouldn't admit it, but she did. Yet, the other piece of her reminded herself that he wasn't good for her.

Hours later, multiple meetings and one manuscript a third of the way edited, the day was over. The elevator dinged, and the man with the dark sandy hair and boyish smile stepped out. Multiple people stopped him for a chat, but his eyes always seemed to find Harriet's. With a light blush, she packed her stuff up.

"There is this really amazing coffee place by my flat. They roast their own beans and everything. I would love to take you," he told her, leaning against her desk as she finished packing up.

THE COFFEE SHOP WAS GORGEOUS, brick and industrial with yellow accents and vintage furniture. It truly screamed Harriet when she walked in. In awe, his hand was on her lower back, touch lingering. Atticus leaned over to whisper in her ear.

"Cappuccino?" he asked husky yet soft. His voice vibrated making her quake. She nodded finding a place for them to sit.

Minutes later, the sandy-haired man came back all smiley as he handed her a coffee and a little pastry. Thanking him, the two settled in chit chat.

"What happened with..."

"Jax?" she asked, taking a sip.

"Yeah..." he trailed off, eyebrows furrowing, "what's his last name again?"

"Alderidge," Harriet responded, pulling apart her pastry.

Atticus' eyes widened, choking on the hot liquid. He quickly shook it off and took a deep breath.

"Jaxon Alderidge? Married to Claudia...two kids? Ember and Caleb? Owns Alderidge Law? That man has screwed half of London, Harriet. It is well known, he screws any woman he sets his eyes on," he told her. It felt as if he was shaming her. She felt shamed and sexualised by Atticus. His gentlemanliness was gone in that moment.

"How would I have known that Atticus?" she defended, voice hoarse and offended.

"I am just letting you know. That man is trouble. What happened today?"

"He tried to get me back, but-"

"He is a member at a prostitution house, and he hosts swinger parties. He and Claudia used to go to them all the time. He is the definition of a man whore."

"How-"

"I was one of his best friends. We met when I worked at a media company in my twenties, and his dad was their lawyer. Jax was still in law school. I was the best man at his wedding."

"Oh," she mumbled.

"What happened today, Harriet? Did you-"

"We didn't have sex if that is what you're implying. He took me for lunch, tried to woo me back, and I said no. Told him to drive me back. Nothing happened. Why should you care, though?" she spat.

"Because I am your friend. You deserve the world, Harriet," he cooed, reaching for her hand. She allowed him to take it, squeezing it before letting it go.

Pursing her lips, she took a deep breath. "Thank you."

"I have to ask you something, I have a publishing event to go to on Friday. I'm wondering if you could be my plus one. Its black tie event, I will get you a dress-"

She stopped him. "I have one, no worries. I would love to come." Harriet smiled at him.

Pleased with her words, the two continued with their little coffee 'date'.

16

Harriet had a black dress; she swore she had packed it. The event was in three hours, and now she didn't have a dress. Atticus would be here soon, and she was frantic looking for this dress. The silky slip black dress that Jax got her for his event a week ago. She needed it right now, and it was nowhere to be found. She must have left it.

"Fuck," she cursed, fishing out her phone. The brunette dialled that number she dreaded to call.

"Hello," his rough and deep voice rang through. "Harriet, did you-"

"Did I leave that black dress at your place?" she asked in a rush, clothes flying everywhere in the studio apartment as she looked for it. Her luggage was sprawled on the bed, clothes all over the floor.

"Yes."

"I have an event tonight. I need it, Jax. I don't have a dress and-"

"Atticus is taking you to his publishing event?" he questioned.

"Yes, and I am in dire need of a dress. Can you drop it off?"

"So, you *do* know Atticus?" he hummed, amused.

"Jax."

"See you soon." The line went dead.

A heavy breath left her lips. Jax had the dress, and he was coming over now. Pressing her lips together, she walked over to the bathroom to begin her hair and makeup. Curls and light makeup, she looked at herself and smirked. Feeling like a million bucks, she just needed Jax to arrive with her dress.

"You look good." She jumped, turning around and seeing him in all his glory, black suit and hair perfectly done. No smirk, nothing, just him holding the dress on the hanger as he peered at her. "Why did you dye your hair?"

"Felt like something different, had the silver for a few years now," Harriet dismissed, walking to him.

His ocean eyes were clear, no lust, no desire, just pure perfection and adoration that he had for her. Biting her lip, she withheld herself. The feeling she had when she was around Jax was undefinable. No words could be explained as she looked at his broad figure. Maybe it was the little alcohol she consumed while she got ready, but it couldn't be.

She only sported a silk robe, the fabric teasing her as she was only naked underneath. Her nipples hardened from it. Harriet placed her hand on his cheek. The electricity flowed from her fingertips, coursing throughout her body as their eyes held one another. His free hand clasped itself around her waist. She loves him, she realized.

Harriet got on her tippy toes, lips brushing against one another. Jax dropped the dress and wrapped both hands around her waist. It was gentle at first, but the lust filled them both. Seconds later, teeth were clicking together, lips franticly moving as the two moved to the bed. His fingers travelled, untying the robe hastily. It dropped to the floor, and she was left naked and to his exposure.

Jax pulled away and let his finger trace the tattoos on her arm and down her navel to her scar. She shuttered at his touch. His lips nipped at her collarbone, licking and biting as he let it roam her upper body. A moan left her mouth as his lips attacked her.

"Jax," she panted.

"I'm here, baby," he cooed in her ear, "always here, never leaving."

The back of her knees hit the mattress. She fell, her back hitting the mattress as her thighs clenched together. His eyes raked her body. The curvature of her breasts, her hips and little belly, but he couldn't care less. Harriet was perfect in his eyes. He didn't care that she was a size ten. She was gorgeous.

"Come here," she murmured, making a come here motion with her two fingers. A little smile covered his face as he lowered down to kiss her.

Her fingers pushed back his suit jacket, letting it fall to the floor, then undid his buttons. Jax loosened his tie, removing it and pushing his shirt off. Abs and defined pecs caught her eye as her fingers played with his chest hair, pulling and tugging.

"Harriet," he growled. Jax kissed her hip, making his way down to her pussy. His cock was throbbing, hardening from the soft touches she did.

He got up. Her legs were spread, and her pussy was dripping right in front of him. Gliding his tongue over his lips, the lust took control. His calloused hands threw her legs over each of his shoulders, gripping her hips and pulling her to the edge of the bed. Instantly, his tongue was on her clit, licking and teasing her.

Harriet was a mess, moans and curse words spilled out of her mouth. His fingers were on the folds of her vagina, opening them as he made out with her wetness, sucking on her clit. He bit down and instantly her back was arched.

"Jaxon! Fucking hell, you fucking-"

"Shush it. I can stop when I want, Harriet," he growled. The vibrations from his lips talking pulsed through her womanhood, making her orgasm come closer. His tongue flicked, and her feet pointed, heels digging into his back. He couldn't care less.

The shockwaves went through her as she came hard minutes later. He didn't give her a long to ride out her orgasm before he had her flipped to on her knees, facing him. Her eyes were lined perfectly with his clothed manhood. Jax removed his dress pants and boxers. His harden cock was right in front her eyes.

"Suck."

She opened her mouth, and he helped guide his cock into her mouth. It was his turn to let out sounds of pleasure. His hands gathered her long locks into a makeshift ponytail as her hands grasped his shaft. Then, he began to fuck her mouth, deepening each time, hips thrusting. Slobber rolled down her chin as they did such an unholy act.

"Take it, Kitten, take it all," he grunted.

With tears in her eyes, she looked up and made eye contact with him through her lashes. Harriet swirled her tongue around and jerked his shaft. Even with this roughness, she enjoyed it.

The man came, the saltiness hit her tongue. Swallowing,

she looked up. Jax noticed how swollen and reddened her lips were. His thumb swiped away her tears, then her lips, pushing them down as he entered his digit into her mouth. She sucked it, gracefully.

"Such a good girl," he praised, dropping her hair and removing his finger from her mouth.

Jax climbed on the bed, on his knees as he began to kiss her again. He gripped her cheek and explored her mouth with his tongue.

Moans left their lips as the two of them kissed. He pushed her, back hitting the bed. Jax got up and grabbed his tie.

" Are you ok?" he asked, kneeling on the bed, leaning towards her.

"Yes," she muttered, hands playing with his chest hair as he began to tie her wrists.

"Safe word?"

"Purple."

He sent her a nod.

Harriet laid back as he tied her wrists to the bed frame, tightening them and pinning them down. Bondage, it clicked. How new for her. Light bondage, actually. Heavy breaths filled the room. She couldn't deny she was anxious. Jax wouldn't hurt her. She knew that, but this is a whole new level of intimacy.

Jax got up and left Harriet there, strapped to the bed as she looked up to the ceiling. What did she get herself into? Atticus' words echoed her mind, '*He has screwed half of London*'...was she just a number? A milestone, an accomplishment or a challenge? Was this all part of his game? He wanted to control her, and he was close to it.

'*Fuck.*'

His heavy footsteps came back. The mattress dipped as a ripping noise was heard. She couldn't see. Her wrists were tied. Jax rolled on a condom to his hardened cock and patted her legs. His lips began to apply subtle kisses to her inner thigh. Her shallow moans were heard and all he could do was smirk.

His hands travelled up her body, grabbing her breasts in his hands, cupping them as he massaged them. Twisting her nipples between his fingers, pinching them as his kissing travelled up.

Then, his face was above hers. They felt each other breaths as he hooked her leg around his waist, thrusting all the way in with one motion.

"Fuck!" she screamed, back arching. He kissed her jaw then the sweet spot behind her ear. Her eyes rolled back as he began to roughly fuck her. Her fingers gripped harder around the tie as he thrusted his pelvis towards her, grazing her g-spot.

"Be quiet. I didn't say to speak, Kitten," he purred by her ear which sent a shiver through her body. Jax griped her hips hard as he fucked with so much anger yet love.

Gasping, she tried to hold every moan inside of her. His fingers began to circle her clit then rub vigorously. Her back arched, but he pushed her body back down.

Then suddenly, he pulled out. He grabbed her hips, flipped her over with her ass in the air. Her hands grasped the bed frame, holding it with every fibre as he fucked her pussy again from behind her.

A slap was applied to her ass, and she jerked forward as he rammed his hips inside of her. He moaned and groaned as she did too.

"Such a good girl, Kitten. You make me *so* happy," he praised her.

Moaning, she rolled her head back as the pleasure began to be unbearable but wonderful. The sound of slapping skin could be heard a mile away as their noises of pleasure filled the room as well. The bed was shaking, headboard hitting the wall. They were fucking, absolutely fucking, and she *loved* it. She was in love with this roughness.

He flipped her around again, wrists pinned as he fucked her some more. His ocean eyes connected with her sapphire.

"I think I am in love with you," she muttered through her teeth, eyes closed as she felt the knot building up. The words just flew out of her mouth without any consciousness.

Jax heard them loud and clear, and instantly he undid the tie. Letting her hands wrap around his neck. He held her, the roughness calming down as he then began to roll his hips. Her legs were hooked around his waist, heels digging into his plump butt as he grabbed the sheets.

"Jax-" she tried to signal her closeness.

"Me too, Kitten," he purred.

The two of them came together, their breaths aligned as he pumped his seed inside the condom. Her orgasm shattered throughout her body. Their curse words mixed as they rumbled them, riding their orgasms out together.

He rolled over beside her, catching his breath while she got up. Her eyes instantly seeing her reflection in the mirror.

"Atticus will be here soon. I need to redo everything cause I look-"

"You look like you just got fucked hard," he replied with a smirk. She rolled her eyes and walked past the mirror.

"Jaxon!"

He snickered when she looked closer at her appearance.

Her hair once curled and gorgeous, was now absolutely sex hair heaven. It was frizzy and everywhere, plus her makeup was all smeared.

"You owe me!" she grumbled.

"Duly noted, Ms. Kensington."

Rushing around the room, she hastily got ready as Jax just pulled his suit back on. He threaded his fingers through his hair, and he was ready to roll. Men, ugh!

"Tell Atticus to not come. I will drive you," he commented as he watched her fix her hair.

"What?"

"I am invited too. I am the company's lawyer after all," he flatly said. She turned around and looked at him blankly.

"You're going to be-"

"Yes."

"Well, I am Atticus' plus one, so I can't cancel on him," she responded. Jax chuckled. "What's so funny?"

"Atticus is definitely trying to wife you down, Kitten," he whispered as he applied soft kisses to her jaw, hand snaking around her waist again. "However, he is going to lose this game," he growled in her ear, touch lingering on her hips. "I always win the chase. You are my trophy."

She tried to push him off of her, but his grip hardened.

"No, we are friends."

"Sure, but you're *mine*," he growled, nipping her skin. "Go back to blonde."

Harriet looked at the clock that was above the bathroom door. "First off, no I like this colour and second off Atticus is going to be here in five minutes. Get out, Jax!" Her hands slapped his back, pushing him to the door.

"Fine, see you tonight, Ms. Kensington," he told her with a roll of his eyes. Jax kissed her on her lips once more before leaving the house.

'Fuck, what the hell just happened?'

17

"Hello?" Atticus called into the room. His voice echoing throughout the small studio apartment. Harriet was still in the bathroom spraying hairspray for the final touch.

"Coming!" she exclaimed. Her hair was pulled back into a low pony. The easiest way to fix sex hair. The curls were evident, and makeup still light. She paired it with her black slip dress and strappy heels. Giving herself one final look, she walked out and sent a light smile to the man in her flat.

Atticus was awestruck. She looked gorgeous. Heaven right in front of him. Red lips that he desired to kiss that night and a slight smirk on her face that he wanted to get rid of. Atticus looked her up and down biting his lip as he watched the woman across from him. Harriet could quite possibly be the woman he was going to love forever. His eventual triumph in life.

"Ready, Mr. Astor?" she quipped, hand out and ready for him to take. He took it, kissing it lightly before hooking it around his arm.

"Follow me, Ms. Kensington."

The Audi was parked in front of the red brick building looking sleek and sexy. The nightlife was loud on a Friday night in London, cars honked, and people yelled. Harriet smiled slightly, thinking of the city's story. Everyone had a life here, a story to be lived. Their arms were still linked as he opened the passenger door to the car. She thanked him as she got in.

THEY ARRIVED at an older concrete building with pillars and a roundabout. Like something out of the movies. A fountain was in the middle as cars and limousines of grand brands parked around it. Brands that she could never afford. Audis, Aston Martins, Maseratis, and Range Rovers, the list goes on. People sporting fine clothing came out of their vehicles with their snobby faces. This was truly a lifestyle she was not yet comfortable with, but she could get used to it, possibly.

The door opened. A man dressed finely helped her out of the car. He gave her a warm smile as her heels hit the red carpet. Atticus' voice was in the background as he handed his keys to the valet. He came around sending her a smile as his hand found its way once again to the bottom of her back. The touch was lower than normal making her shudder from the contact. His hand was planted at the beginning of the curvature of her ass. It was a light touch, not groping or cupping, just a light nudge. Harriet just ignored it. It could have been a friendly touch rather than a flirtatious touch.

"This way, love," Atticus told her, leaning over and whispering in her ear. It made her shiver as his voice vibrated through her body. She nodded, following him through the grand entrance. She could hear the band, the tapping of heels, and light chatter from the polite weather talk.

They entered together into the grand ballroom. Instantly she saw people dressed in elegant clothing, black and white, with expensive smiles and tastes. Their hair was done to the pristine and lives that are deemed to be flawless, yet they probably all have a skeleton in their closet as most rich people do. Words couldn't express how she felt when she walked into this event. The two of them were on a balcony that surrounded the area, two staircases in front of them diverging from one another as it led down to the middle where the party took place. Everything was old, sandstone and pillars, but nevertheless gorgeous. She felt like a duchess at the ball about to meet her prince charming.

"Let's get a drink," Atticus offered as they went down the staircase, her hand gliding down the railing to the dance floor.

Her eyes took one final look around the room before being diverted back to the bar. She recognised the ocean eyes she used to call home in the distance. Jax looked handsome as ever in the black suit he wore earlier on, clean shaven, and hair styled. Harriet could not keep her eyes off of him. Images of earlier flashed through her mind as he stood talking to some men with a champagne flute in hand. His smile was grand, and laughter rolled off his lips. Harriet had to hide her smirk. He truly was a God. The God of sex, power and dominance.

Harriet glanced over at him, biting her lip lightly, but her attention was taken elsewhere. Her figure, embellishing her black dress, was next to the bar, eyes now focused on Atticus as he came back with two drinks in hand. She didn't even notice he left for a moment.

"Gin and tonic for the lady," he winked at her, handing over the drink. Atticus stood in front of her and blocking her perfect view of Mr. Dark and Handsome.

"Thank you," she smiled at him. Harriet angled her face to her right, looking over Atticus' shoulder and locking eyes with Jax's once again. The man nodded towards her, smirking and tilting his drink towards her. She didn't respond in any way, just gawked.

The tension was high. She noticed it right away. The sexual tension was overwhelming as she lusted on that man. It was intoxicating to be around him; she was instantly wet. Her thighs clenched together. Jax noticed, sending a wink and a smirk. She felt like she was riding a good high in his presence, nothing bad happening in her world.

Her daydream was broken by the gentleman in front of her, her prince charming of the night. Hopefully, her night wouldn't end with a shoe left behind at the ball.

"I have a few people I want you to meet tonight, Harriet," Atticus leaned over and whispered in her ear. His hand was on her hip, cupping it, yet her eyes were still set on Jax's metres away.

He led the way to the company she had to endure for the night. Jax was now out of her eyesight as the two of them began to make their rounds. Atticus introduced his date to several of his clients, all romance authors with the odd sci-fi or mystery. She laughed alongside him, cracking jokes and trying to be the best date for the night. Harriet needed to leave an impression on his clients, and she was good at that.

Jax clenched his jaw as he watched her. He had to focus back on the man next to him talking about business or something else. His voice was blocked as Jax watched his girl laugh at some other man's jokes. It angered him even more as he saw another man's hand, Atticus' hand, on her hip. Harriet was his.

The job as being a CEO's date for the night was to be at his side all night, and she was doing her job well. It was once again, Atticus and her standing beside one another. His touch was still felt, his hand wrapped around and sat on her hip. Jax glared harder. Every single time Atticus touched her a little more, cupping her flesh or smiling at her, he had to control himself from starting a fight. The woman was his and his only.

"I forgot," Atticus muttered. "I have something for you," he gleamed.

They diverted their company away from the several clients and walked to the corner of the room. She sent him a smile, curious of the intention behind his words.

A man came up next to Atticus, a worker for that night. He was dressed in a suit, older looking and plump. In his hands, there was a velvet blue box. It was big, long and flat. Harriet let out a breath, shocked as Atticus took the box from the man.

"I thought that since you are by far more gorgeous than a goddess herself, a woman like you needs," he flipped open the case and a necklace filled with diamonds, grand and the total opposite of Harriet's style, "a necklace, diamonds." It was glamorous but too much glamour for her. The woman was more of casual chic, vintage or retro girl. Glitz and glamour were not her go to style.

Nevertheless, she smiled at Atticus' present.

Jax saw everything, putting the champagne flute down onto a table, adjusting his view to see what it was. He noticed what was in the box and internally scoffed. Harriet would absolutely hate that. With a smirk on his face, he sauntered over to where Atticus was, jaw clenched and hands balled up, knuckles turning white as he proceeded to where his Kitten was standing.

"Wow, it's beautiful, Atticus. I c-can't," she stammered, rapidly blinking as she took in the shine of the diamonds hitting the light.

"Please, a present from a friend. Turn around now," he told her with a curt nod.

Harriet turned around, eyes locking with Jax, who was closer than ever. He took the look as a plea for help.

Their eyes were locked as she felt the coldness of the silver and diamonds hit her neck. It sent a shiver through her body. She gasped lightly feeling his hands brush her neck. Jax crossed his arms, watching her with his jaw clenched, an ache beginning to spread, making him realize how hard he was gritting his teeth.

Once the clasped was done up, she turned around, smiling softly as Atticus grinned proudly.

"There, you look beautiful," Atticus gushed, taking a step back to fully look at her. "Gorgeous, beautiful. You're-"

'That was my Kitten, my woman and nobody could possess my girl. She was mine. He had no right to do such a thing.' Jax was fuming. He took it as a claiming motive. Giving his girl diamonds to claim her.

"Atticus Astor," he was interrupted by Jax, as he appeared in front of them. The two of them turned around to see him.

"Jax Alderidge," Atticus mimicked his tone, stern, curt and slightly aggressive, but nonetheless semi-polite and business-like.

Harriet looked between them as their expressions changed. Jax's still held anger, while Atticus' smile fell, and a frown appeared. Harriet was standing next to Atticus. She felt his hand back on her lower back.

'Bad move, Atticus, unbelievably bad move.'

Hell was about to break loose. She knew it. The action was unwise from Atticus. He was picking a fight in Jax's eyes.

"Harriet, we should-"

"She isn't going anywhere with you, *Jax*," Atticus sneered at him, spitting his name as if he was mocking him. Harriet's eye glanced between them repeatedly. She knew a fight was about to occur.

"Let the lady speak for herself," Jax bit back.

"This is *my* event. She needs to meet *my* clients right now."

With a groan, she mumbled, "I need another drink." Then quickly ridding herself to go to the bar. However, once her back was turned, suddenly, chaos erupted.

"She was *my* nanny before she was *your* employee!" Jax seethed, finger jabbing into Atticus' chest. His voice got louder by the second. She heard him over the band.

"The woman left for a reason, eh, Jax? You're a fucking-"

"No, you can't say shit. She is not someone you can woo with your gentleman ways in order to wife her up. We know all about your play of the game!"

"Rich coming from you. Harriet is most definitely just a tally or name on the chart in your *book*. She is just a distrac tion! All part of your game of what benefits you the most! She will never love a man like you-"

Out of nowhere, a fist was thrown. Harriet quickly downed the shot and ran to where the fight was happening. Everyone was silent as they watched two men of high power and status belittle one another in order to prove who was the better alpha, better lover. Any sane woman would leave the situation, but their reputation was on the line and about to be ruined in mere seconds. Harriet took a grip of Jax's firm bicep, pulling him back from Atticus. She held him, and he knew her touch the second she placed her hand on him.

"She is the love my life, so don't-" Jax began to spit at the man.

"Jaxon!" Harriet growled through her teeth, turning him to her. "People are watching," she mumbled for him, quiet, warning him. He bit his lip, looking at her sapphire eyes, his ocean ones lost in anger. Pulling his arm out of her grip abruptly, he turned back to the sandy-haired man.

Atticus' face was all bloody as he held his nose. Pain shooting through his body, but he couldn't care less. He needed to win this fight.

"You're fucking my *nanny*, aren't you?" he scoffed. "Un-fucking-believable, Atticus. It was always a competition between us since we were mates. Look how that turned out! She is mine, always has been and always will, so fuck off!" he spat at the publisher.

Harriet groaned, "Enough! I am nobody's. I am my own independent person, so you can all fuck yourselves!" Both men looked at her. "Grow the fuck up, both of you." With a shake of her head, she turned to Jax. "Jaxon," she tried again. However, her voice lacked its normal honey-like and warm, it held a warning tone to it. She yanked his arm in order to get him to look at her.

He turned around, eyes capturing hers. Harriet couldn't believe it, the embarrassment washed through her as she looked around the room, everyone's eyes were on her. A flash of a camera, mumbles and gossip began to spread. Taking a deep breath, she let go of Jax's arm.

"Go home, Jax. You fucked everything up tonight," she

whispered with a shake of her head. "Go home before your reputation is ruined. We all know how much you care about that."

Atticus looked at her, and with a scoff, he said, "He is the biggest womaniser, Harriet. He will woo you till he beds you, then-"

"Stay out of this, Atticus. It isn't your mess to clean up. It is mine." Jax held his eyes on her. She scoffed at his speechlessness.

Harriet locked eyes with Jax's, and with a loud sigh, she told him, "You know, I was just beginning to let you back into my life, but you went around and fucked shit up like you normally do. This is a work function, and now everyone knows about us, which will be horrendous for your image. I hide, I run, and you know that. So, go home before I run, and you do more damage." Jax looked at her for a second, then grumbled as he walked away, heavy footsteps echoing the silent room.

Atticus, who now had a tissue in his hand, dabbing away the blood gave her a look of pure pity. Once Jax was out of the room, he took a step forward to her.

"Don't," she whispered yelled, placing her hand out to stop him from coming close to her.

Harriet pivoted looking around once again as tears filled her eyes. Everyone was watching her, and she knew by tomorrow she was going to be on the front page of the tabloids. She gave a firm glare to everyone in room before she walked away, confidence dripping off of her. A walk of shame, no, a walk of 'fuck you' to everyone.

Her heels hit the cobblestone of the outside world, wrapping her arms around her body as she shivered from the cold summer night. The slip dress providing no heat as she stood outside. In fact, it was best at cycling cold air under the fabric.

"I need a cigarette," she mumbled to herself, taking her shoes off and beginning to walk to the nearest convenience store she could find.

With every step, the wind blew harder and the chill set into her bones. Nevertheless, she kept walking, holding her body tighter, prying what little heat she had from the cold air. Like any city, she heard catcalls while she walked the streets. Being herself, Harriet flipped them off before walking away.

Tears were in her eyes, sniffling as she wiped them away roughly. How fucking embarrassing that was, and now everyone knew about her private life. Everyone knew that she was some form of pawn between the men; a competition of conquering her.

"Harriet!" She turned around to the sweet male voice.

Atticus was running towards her. His hair was dishevelled, and heavy breaths escaped his lips from the jog. Harriet stayed put, not having the energy to deal with all this bullshit. His face was still screwed up, dried blood on his upper life, but no longer gushing red.

"Please, listen to me," he tried. He kept his hands to himself for once.

"Speak," she mumbled, ready to be done with the night. Her arms wrapped themselves around her body.

"I'm sorry that was poorly handled. He didn't-"

"Don't apologize for Jax. I will deal with him."

"Well, I am sorry for my actions too. I could've handled him far more maturely, but he makes my blood boil, love. Life is a game to him, Harriet. You're a game, and once he wins, he will let you go in order to go gamble in the next game. I can't stand the way he talks about you, and it hurts me to see you have to deal with him. I didn't realise he would be here tonight, but he will find any excuse to have a fight."

"How is your nose?" she asked, ignoring his words. Her back hit the side of the building, leaning against it.

"Eh, fine. Not the first time I got punched probably won't be the last. How are you though? You look like you've had better days-"

"I'm in a dire need of a cigarette and a whiskey shot," she joked.

"Come, follow me," he told her, nodding his head up the street. Harried followed, pushing off the building, heels in hand, as she began to walk. Atticus noticed them. "Really?"

"I grew up in New Zealand. I drive and walk barefoot. Doesn't bother me, plus these heels are hell."

He laughed, continuing with their way up the road to the convenience store. Seconds later, they came in front of it and lucky for them, it was next to a liquor store.

"I buy the whiskey. You get the cigarettes," he told her with a wink.

The two of them sat on a park bench, sharing a cigarette and drinking from the bottle wrapped in a brown bag. Silence filled the park except their talking. It was well past eleven at night, the park was dead. The darkness filled the area except the lamppost next to them, dimly lighting the area.

"You know, where I am from, we call convenience stores dairies," she stated, blowing smoke out.

"Dairies?" he chuckled, looking at her bewildered.

"Dairies. There is a diary up the road, so grab be a box of smokes."

"Huh, why?"

"Fuck knows," she chuckled, sipping the whiskey and handing it to him. "Jax loves to get into fights. When we were younger, he would beat up kids for even looking at him the wrong way. We went to school together, and he threatened every guy there, so I never dated until I was thirteen, and he was sixteen, and shit happened."

"You were thirteen?"

"Yeah, it sounds creepy now, but at the time it felt normal. I loved him since I was eight, and for him to stop fucking around for a second and realise that he loved me. It was every thirteen-year old's dream; an older man you admire looking at you more than a friend. However, he hasn't changed, has he? Fighting, controlling, fucking anything that walks but I still-"

"Love him?" he replied.

"Yeah, I do," she mumbled, taking a swig of the liquor again. "Men suck, sorry, mate."

Atticus chuckled, "He is a really good lawyer though. That is why I hired him."

"I bet he is. With all that fiery passion...I literally don't know what I am doing with my life. The only thing I am good at is fucking shit up," she mumbled.

"I am thirty-seven, and I still don't know what I am doing with my life."

The two of them laughed.

"You're going to go to him, aren't you? I lost, didn't I?" Atticus asked, peering into her eyes. Harriet took a deep breath, trying to find the words.

"We were always friends, Atticus. I may love him but doesn't mean we are right for each other. He needs to do a lot of self-work before he deals with my crazy ass. I need to do a lot of self-work too. I have demons, and so does him. Jax shows how fucked up he is, whereas I hide it." Atticus nodded, tearing his eyes from her and looking ahead.

Harriet nudged his shoulder with hers. "There is someone out there for you, Atticus. Just trust the universe, ok?" She got up, taking her hair out of the pony and letting it flow on her back.

"Will I see you at work Monday?" Atticus asked.

"Yes, you will," she chuckled, "I am not running quite yet, plus I need the cash if I am going to run."

"So, I am paying you to eventually run?" he pipped.

"Quite possibly. Goodnight, Atticus, thank you for the pep talk, whiskey, and cigarettes," she told him, turning around and taking a step before turning her head back to him. "Your great love is out there. Just be patient. The universe works in mysterious ways."

18

Her phone woke her up that morning. The repeated alerts and noises were coming from the device as notifications exploded her phone. Harriet groaned, picking it up and looking at it. The bright screen hit her eyes as she squinted.

11:21

30 New Messages from Jax Alderidge

45 Missed Calls from Jax Alderidge

She groaned again. What does that man want at this time in the morning? The intercom went off. The buzzing echoed through Cameron's flat. Harriet took the pillow and covered her ears with it, grumbling from the noise. The buzzing stopped for a second before it started again. Begrudgingly, she got up, wincing from a headache as she pressed the button.

"Let me in, Harriet," Jax's voice came through, firm and stern.

She groaned louder, buzzing him in and unlocking the door. Harriet walked to the kitchen, getting the coffee machine ready for her morning coffee and go to hangover cure.

The door opened and closed with a loud bang.

"For fuck's sake, I am nursing a hangover. Be quiet, Jax."

He ignored her, grumbling. "Have you seen your phone?" he asked.

"*Morning, Harriet. How are you?*" she mocked, making her coffee. "*I am doing absolutely terrible, as someone disrupted my sleep.*" The machine's noise was loud, covering his talking. Jax crossed his arms as he waited. Once she was done, she took the mug to her lips. He asked again.

"Have you seen the tabloids or your phone?" he barked, running his fingers through his hair.

"Nope, just woke up from your banging and screaming," she told him, walking to the counter and sitting on the stool.

"I fucked up, Harriet," he mumbled, fingers in his hair as he began to pace.

"No shit," she chuckled, remembering last night.

"Seriously, have you-"

"No, I have not, Jax. What happened in the tabloids-"

He shoved his phone in her hand, and instantly, she was met with:

Jax Alderidge and Atticus Astor Fight at Publishing Event Over a Mysterious Woman
Written by: Genevieve Gusta

Jax Alderidge, CEO and lawyer at Alderidge Law, and Atticus

Astor, CEO of the AVA House, got into a fight last Friday night over a woman known to be named Harriet Kensington. Alderidge, 31, married to Claudia Hughes, 29, have been having troubles lately in their marriage, an outside source has said, and that Kensington worked for them for a few weeks before being fired for having an affair with Alderidge. Now, she is working for Astor, which employees believe the two are having a relationship. The New Zealand editor has yet to say anything on the subject, but Alderidge has made it clear that the two have been an item for a while as he quoted....

"I haven't said shit, Harriet," he cursed, pacing back and forth.

"Last night, you screamed shit. Look at this picture. I look horrible," she grimaced at the picture, eyeing the snapshot of her. The picture was Harriet breaking up the fight. "Oh, I don't look too hot-"

"Please don't run over this," he interrupted her.

"Don't be daft. I am not going to run. It's just not every day you are plastered on the paper and told you're a whore. I can't go to work without being looked as if I am this woman whoring herself to her bosses, fuck me-"

"Work for me."

"Jaxon, this will be a big thing if I quit my job and start working for the man I am screwing."

"What are you going to do then?" he asked. The man was anxious, pacing the room with stuttering words and fidgety actions. He was irrational at this moment, driven by stress and anxiety.

He had an empire, one of the most prominent law firms, and people trusted him. Everyone honestly believed he had this wonderful life with a wife and kids, and now it was ruined. Whose fault was that?

Harriet sighed, taking a sip of her coffee and getting up to walk to him. She took both hands into hers and looked at his beautiful blue eyes. Instantly, she felt as though she was at home.

"Deep breath," she mumbled. His eyes looked at hers, yet his mind was elsewhere.

"Claudia-"

"Shhh." Harriet hushed him, bringing his hands to her lips, kissing them delicately. He was dressed in casual clothes, sweats, and a t-shirt. He most definitely just rolled out of bed.

He leaned into her touch letting himself gain back his calmness. With deep breaths, he kept his eye contact with her. Jax knew that the public now knew everything from this article. They knew his life was a hoax and that it was all just a show. He never loved Claudia, and their life was not so perfect after all.

"Everyone knows, Harriet," he mumbled, flipping their connected hands and placing a kiss on the back of her hand. "My dad is just," he let out a groan, "he is mad."

"Jax, you need to keep in mind that you did bring this on, and I tried to warn you-"

"I know," he mumbled. He leaned towards her, connecting their foreheads as their lips brushed against each other's.

Jax noticed the necklace on her bedside table, the one Atticus gave to her last night.

"What are you going to do with it?" he said, nodding to it

"The necklace? Just put it in my jewellery box and never wear it again," she responded. Jax nodded.

“I saw it and was like ‘she hates, it so not Harriet’,” he told her.

“It doesn’t matter. I am thankful that Atticus got me a gift.” He hummed, kissing her lips again. “Get rid of it.”

“Jaxon,” she warned.

“You’re mine, Kit. It was a possessive act, claiming property.”

“I am not property, now just kiss me, you fool,” she teased, dismissing his words.

Her hands dropped, holding his hip as he pushed her against the wall. Her legs hooked around his body as he held her against the brick. His fingers landed on her stomach, circling the bare skin before hiking her shirt up, exposing her nakedness to him. No bra, he threw the shirt off of her and connected his lips with her breast, sucking the flesh. Harriet’s head threw back, hitting it against the wall. Pain seared through her, but she couldn’t care less.

Jax’s hands gripped her breasts, kneading them as he placed little kisses with a mix of suction to each one. Marks were definitely going to be present after. Her fingers were raking through his hair, tugging it.

“Be mine,” he growled against her naked flesh. “Be my girlfriend.”

Harriet pulled away, unhooking her legs from him and feet hitting the floor again.

“What?” she whispered.

Jax caressed her cheeks, looking into her blue eyes. “Be my girlfriend,” he said again with love laced in his voice.

“I heard you, but what about Claudia and-“

“Claudia and I were barely even friends. We were more like co-workers raising the kids.”

“The kids, Jax! They think-“

He silenced her, still caressing her flesh and drawing circles on her shoulders. "I have a flat in Downtown, live there, with me."

"The house?"

"I only go there when I have the kids for the week. They are at their mum's right now. Live with me, be with me," he pleaded.

"It'll just be me then? No other women, no prostitutes or swinger parties?" she asked, eyes narrowing as she tried to make sense of what this relationship could be like.

"Swinger parties? Who told you-"

"It's a rumour I heard. Jax." Harriet took her shirt off the floor and throwing it back on before grabbing his hands. "You need to be honest with me."

"I...I've been to a few, hosted maybe a few. Kitten, for the last thirteen years, I have been lost, and I didn't know what to do. You make everything seem clear, my mind is no longer foggy, and I know what I want with life. I want *you*. I want to marry *you*, have children with *you,* to be with *you*," he mumbled, taking her cheeks in his hands and kissing her again. "I want us."

Harriet wanted that too, she could admit. She wanted Jax for the rest of her life, but there were so many things that he had yet to figure out. Jax was about to be divorced, and he had kids, things she never thought she would have to deal with.

"How would we do this?"

"Baby steps? Move in "

"Moving in isn't baby steps, Jax! I need to stay here for the month to house sit for Cam and once that is done, possibly we can. Claudia hates me. That needs to be cleared. You need to deal with your divorce-"

"Doesn't mean-"

"Don't interrupt me, Jax. You're the type of person who goes all in at once and I am not. Baby steps, ok? I am not going to move in with you and suddenly be your girlfriend."

"So, what are you saying? You don't want to be together?" He narrowed his eyes and ran his fingers through his hair offended by her words.

"No, Jax. What I mean is woo me. Take me on a date!"

He jerked back, almost offended. "We have fucked though."

Harriet groaned, "Oh my God, you're a child. Have you ever tried to impress a woman before?"

He chuckled, "No. I'm use to just looking at them and they are all over me."

Harriet groaned again, "Take me on a date before I spread my legs open for you, ok?"

"Anything for you, Kitten," he mumbled, kissing her lips again. "Get dressed, shower and we are going for breakfast...*a date*?" he told her, tapping her on the butt before going to the kitchen. "However, we could always shower together..." he trailed off, raising an eyebrow.

"Jax," she sternly said.

"Fine!"

Harriet wandered off to the bathroom, making sure to sway her hips. She turned on the shower and stripped down. Her eyes glanced over her figure when she looked at herself in the mirror. The curves that led down to her ass, the plumpness and fullness of her breasts, perfect size to cup and roll within Jax's palm. Her attention turned to the background, where she could see Jax leaning against the counter, biting his lip as he watched her through the reflection. Sighing, she mumbled a few curse words before making a "come here" motion to him through the mirror.

Jax pushed off the counter, bundling the hem of his shirt before pulling it over his body. He watched her as she let the water fall over her figure, touching every corner of her flesh. His cock twitched, watching her scrub soap all over herself. Instantly, he pulled down his sweats, hungry cock exposed, hardened and ready to destroy her. Harriet was being a tease, in his opinion, and she needed to be dealt with.

She felt his arm wrapping around her stomach and pulling her back against his chest. His cock poked her ass, and she felt it, the neediness, the hunger, the lust. Everything he desired at that moment was her.

"Jax..." she warned as he applied wet kisses against her neck.

"We are going on a date. I just want my dessert first," he hummed. Her head rolled back, hitting his shoulder, exposing her neck more to his pleasure.

He sucked, nipped, and kissed her jugular as his fingers travelled down her naval and to her pussy. Thumbing the nub, whines began to roll off her tongue. Jax smirked, loving how he had absolute control over her in moments like this. The control, the power, he enjoyed every moment of it.

He played with her pink flesh, fingers lapping over the most sensitive part of her body. Her hands gripped his bicep, holding it as if her life depended on it. Jax pulled his lips away, watching his handiwork as the purple bruise began to show. Proudly smirking, he placed an urgent kiss on her lips, sucking her bottom lip

Harriet groaned as his fingers went further down, playing with her wetness as he entered one finger. His thumb was still at her clit, adding pleasure to her existence.

"Jax," she rasped. A second finger entered, then a third and suddenly, he pulled out of her.

"Down," he growled, taking his hardened cock in his hands, pumping it.

She turned around her hand grabbing his waist as she went down. Her hand adjusted, so she was gripping his hip as he lined his cock with her mouth. His hands gripped her hair, pulling it back as he watched her take his cock. Moans were rolling off his lips as her tongue swirled around the base as she made her way to the tip, licking and sucking.

Jax groaned, gripping her hair tighter as he pushed her closer to his cock. Harriet choked, deep throating the hard cock as the tip hit the back of her throat. Jax was gone, eyes rolling back as he began to move her head back and forth. Her mouth was full-blown fucking his cock, and he was there for the view. Watching as tears hit her eyes, and her lips were now reddened and swollen. It just turned him on further.

Moments later, he pulled her up, manoeuvring her so that her chest was plastered against the wall. Her breasts were smashed against the tile as he pinned her wrists above her head. Harriet felt the wet tile against her cheek as he began to massage her ass in his hands.

"I want to come inside you," he growled, licking her neck and sucking the other side now. He pulled back for a moment, admiring the darkened spots on her neck now.

"Condom, Jax," she muttered against the tile.

"Are you on birth control?"

"Yes."

"Then we are fine. I've always used a condom," he told her as he parted her ass cheeks.

He placed himself perfectly behind her as his one hand

went up to hold down her wrists while the other held her one cheek to the side for a perfect angle. Thrusting his manhood inside of her, he heard her sob as he gave no warning. He went all for it without even giving her moments to get use to his grand size. Smirking, he held her as he began to fuck her from behind.

"Fuck," he grunted, pushing his hips farther and letting her wetness touch every bit of his cock.

She muttered her own sounds of pleasure. Under her breath, she muttered a wide variety of swear words.

Harriet was gone, whimpering with every jerk and thrust. Her legs were like jelly, and the only thing holding her there was him. Otherwise, she would have collapsed from the pleasure. Jax fucks, Harriet realized. He doesn't make love and smother her and give her all the kindness and care in the world. Jax was a primal animal, and he fucked like one, and all he wanted to do was fuck and fuck hard and rough. She enjoyed it, the roughness and sinfulness from him, but sometimes the little piece of her wanted more. More affection, love and care.

"You're mine," he growled in his ear, "all mine. My pussy to play with," he teased, letting her wrists go and holding her hips. "Tell me, who do you belong to?"

Harriet whined as he gripped her hips harder, potentially leaving a bruise. Her arms fell from the pinned position to her palms splayed on the tiled wall.

"Do you belong to Atticus? Can he fuck you like this? Make you feel like this? Make you come like this?" he growled.

Harriet simply shook her head, panting and rasping with every pound of his hips. She could feel his breath on her neck and hear the slapping of skin. Then, she felt a loud slap, the pinkness appearing on her ass as she felt the vibration of pain and pleasure.

"Who do you belong to?"

"Jax," she pleaded.

"Tell me." He pulled out, flipping her so that her back was now against the tiles. He gripped her neck, tilting her chin up. His eyes caught hers as he slammed himself back into her soaking pussy. "Who. Do. You-"

"You!" Harriet sobbed as his hands pinched her nipples. "I am yours," she rasped.

Jax liked that answer, letting go of his grip and letting his softness shine. He wrapped his arms around her. Harriet's head hit his shoulder. He held her as he rode out his orgasm, letting the shockwaves go through his system. Jerking it all inside her, he panted, holding the wall as he rode it off.

Taking a deep breath, he looked at her. Harriet didn't have her orgasm; he pumped his load inside her without even realizing he didn't please her enough. She squealed, feeling him going down and wrapping her one leg over his shoulder and his tongue instantly at her womanhood.

Jax could taste the saltiness of his own seed mixed with the sweetness of her arousal. It drove him wild, the taste, the view of it dripping out of her pussy and down her thigh. He growled as he parted her lips and swiped his tongue against her folds and nub.

Harriet splayed her hands against the tiled wall, panting and moaning as he flicked his tongue over her clit. Soon enough, she rode her own high as Jax bit down and sucked on her nub, the pulling feeling as the clenching and vibrating happened within her walls. The orgasm splinted her system as moans rolled off her lips.

"Fuck," she screamed, raking her fingers through his curls.

Jax removed her leg, coming up and planting a firm kiss to her lips.

"Breakfast?" he mused with a small smirk.

"Yes, please," she grinned. He turned the shower off, watching as she pushed herself off the wall and took a step. Instantly, she fell due to the mind-blowing sex she had just endured. Jax caught her, chuckling.

"Woah there, Kit."

"My legs are jelly," she mumbled, holding the wall as she tried to walk again.

"I'm not surprised," he laughed as he wrapped a towel around her. She kissed his lips quickly before getting ready.

THE TWO OF them sat in a cute café, laughing at his inappropriate jokes as she took sip of her morning coffee and bites of her omelette. Jax was still his teenage self, she learnt, carefree and a jokester, while still being a little humble when he chose to be. Harriet missed him, and she was happy that she had him back.

"I remember I was six, and you stood up for me..."

Harriet was six, and he was nine when her stuffed animal got stolen by one of the boys at the orphanage, Marcus. He was eleven years old, but Jax was still bigger than him. Jax was upstairs doing homework for school, and Harriet was in the living room, holding her kitten while watching a movie. Marcus, being the child and bully he was, thought it would be funny to take away the stuffed animal and hide it from the little girl with pigtails.

Harriet exploded; tears flooded her eyes as the blonde-haired boy laughed at her. Two other boys were part of this disaster, all laughing at her and calling her a baby. The red, teary eyed angel screamed as she made grabby hands to have the kitten back. She was, after all, only six and desperately wanted the stuffed animal back.

Jax instantly recognized the cries of his little girl. Anger rippled through him and worry as well. Why was she crying? Who hurt her? What happened, what was wrong? Questions flooded his brain as he dropped his pencil, rushing down the stairs to her. His ocean eyes recognised her sitting on her knees and crying hot tears. He sat next to her holding her close to his body as the little one cried her heart out. Jax whispered to her, asking her what happened. Mumbled words were said through the tears. Anger, more anger flooded through him as he looked up and glared at the kid.

"Give. It. Back," he growled. The boys laughed, but Jax surely wasn't having it. "I said, give it back. It is not nice to take toys away," Jax yelled. The boys continued the laugh and point fingers at her. Childish, the boys were, but they hurt her and nobody in Jax's existence could hurt his girl.

"Come on, Jaxon. She is a girl and a baby," Marcus taunted, and Jax raised his eyebrows. He got up, kissing her head and mumbled sweet words. Stomping, with fists clenched, he went to the boy. "Be mature and give her the toy back. She is six." The boy shook his head.

"What are you going to do about it, Irwin?" Jax rolled his eyes, winding his fist up and hitting him square in the jaw.

Harriet got her kitten back, but Jax was most definitely in trouble. She didn't see him for a few days after that. The girl didn't understand why, as he was standing up for her. Harriet saw him a few days later, bruised up with a black eye. He went straight to her

when she came down for breakfast, the kitten in hand and pigtails messy with her pyjamas still on. Jax held her, kissing her head and asked if she was ok.
"You're hurt," she mumbled, but he shushed her gently.
"It's ok, Kitten," he told her, not realizing the nickname rolling off his lips.

"That is how the nickname came," she realized. Jax shrugged.

"You were addicted to that stuffed animal. It only seemed fit."

Harriet nodded, remembering the times when they were young and before the world destroyed them. Her phone went off, looking down she saw Atticus' text.

New Message at 11:23

From Atticus:

Have you seen the tabloids?

Yes.

Are you ok?

Yes.

Have you talked to Jax?

Yes.

"Who?" Jax nodded to the phone.

"Atticus. He asked if I saw the tabloids," she muttered, turning her phone over and paying attention back to him.

"Let's go to Paris," he said, smirking.

"What?"

"Paris. I want to take you to Paris. Wine and dine you... city of love," he informed with a smirk and a wink. "You deserve the world, Kit."

Paris sounded amazing. To go to the city of love and to be with Jax. A piece of her wanted to do this, to give him a chance to prove himself, yet the other part said no, don't do it.

"When?" she asked.

"I have the kids on Monday, so the following week."

"Weekend only. I have a job."

19

Monday was hell. Her name had been splattered on the front page of every newspaper or tabloid in London, and now everyone knew about her, Jax and Atticus and their odd relationship. Harriet truly felt that her life was some sort of drama series. It shocked her really that her whole life was one drama after another. She was at the point where she was close to fucking off to New York.

Honestly, she didn't care about being professional anymore. If your bedroom life was being publicized for all to see, one wouldn't really care anymore. Monday, she arrived in orange and blue plaid pants with a graphic tee tucked in, tattoos on display, red lip and hair in a high ponytail. However, the minute the elevator dial hit the twenty-third floor and the ding rang through, she looked up to see everyone in the office looking at her. Viola was patiently waiting in front of the elevator.

"Kensington! My office, now," Viola sneered, arms crossed in her pencil skirt and short blonde hair. Oh fuck, she was in trouble.

Ignoring the obvious stares, Harriet grabbed her bag closer and followed the thin woman to her office. What wrath would she endure? Would she lose her job? She won't. Atticus would never let that happen.

The door slammed behind her as Viola walked around to her chair at her desk.

"Sit."

Harriet slowly sat down on the couch, leg bouncing anxiously. Viola was an easily angered woman. She knew some yelling would occur soon. Harriet grew anxious as she stared at her. The brunette woman hadn't even had her morning coffee. Therefore, she was in no mood to deal with this bullshit.

"Jax Alderidge is our lawyer. Atticus Astor is *your* boss. I wake up Saturday morning to your face, my boss and lawyer on the *Metro* newspaper, delivered to my house. *I read it.* I had a lot of faith in you but turns out you are troublesome. I can't fire you or else I will get fired. However, you have been an embarrassment to this company. You decide to make a scene at our public event, ridiculous! In front of all our clients, Ms. Kensington!"

"Viola-"

"Harriet," she spat, telling her to shut up.

"I lied to you..." Harriet began. Viola raised her eyebrows at her. "When you asked me if I could write a book about anything, and I talked about two orphans. You asked if it was more of an autobiography than a fiction story. Well, Jax and I were two orphans who fell in love when we were teens. I have known him my whole life. I am sorry about the scene, I tried to control it, but Jax has an anger issue and Atticus-"

"Mr. Astor?"

"Yes, Mr. Astor just poked the bear. I am sorry if you want me to resign, I can-"

"Shut up. You're my best editor, so shut up. This is a warning, Harriet...if I ever see you again causing a scene, I will fire you. However, you have been moved, believe it or not. Mr. Astor asked for you to be his personal assistant. Pack up your cubicle and go up to the thirtieth floor. Here is your new key card," she told her, sliding over the card.

Harriet stared wide eyed...Atticus moved her to his own personal assistant. Was that a promotion or not?

"Thank you," she mumbled, getting up and heading out the door.

"Harriet?" She turned around. "Write it."

Harriet raised her eyebrows, confused. "What?"

"Write the book about you and Mr. Alderidge. Send the manuscript to me and I will publish it. There is more to the story than you say. It'll make a great romance novel."

"Thank you, Viola. However, I am a reader not a writer."

"Never say never. Now get out of my office," she said sternly, attention back to the Mac computer in front of her.

Harriet sighed, gathering herself in the hallway. She was about to walk out into the main area where everyone will be eyeing her packing up her stuff, but one thought she had was, why did Atticus move her?

She took out her phone typing a text to him.

New Message at 9:17

To Atticus:

I just got some questionable news. I am moved from junior editor to your personal assistant. Why?

Yes, though it would be better for you to be on my level working beside me due to the chaos that just occurred. You're smart. You deserve a better job. Plus, a lot of my clients enjoyed your company on Friday.

So... it's a promotion?

Yes. You get to travel with me, be my so-called work wife, go to events, etc. Carrie left me this week to go on maternity leave.

Harriet closed her phone, shaking her head as she turned the corner. Eyes all looked up to her, and she rolled her eyes. Gossip whores...

Only being there for a short while, she didn't have much besides several manuscripts and a coffee mug. In all honesty, there was nothing that belonged to her. Therefore, she turned around and walked to the elevator, making sure it was more of a "fuck you" walk rather than a walk of shame.

The key card worked, and the door opened to the top floor. It was modern and cutting edge with dark colours and wooden walls, yet still had the old brick. It was different from the romance level which held more of an industrial finishing.

"Harriet!" Chloe, she remembered her name smiled at her when she walked through. "Welcome to the family. Mr. Astor is in a meeting so I will give you the rundown."

The blonde walked around in her professional royal blue dress with her hair in a French twist. Instantly, the brunette felt underdressed. This was the big guns; this was the professional side where she will be taking calls from offices in New York and meeting with people across the world. She was going be working a business job and that scared her.

"So, this will be your office right next to Mr. Astor," Chloe told her.

Harriet had an office next to him, her own office. The two of them walked in. Harriet had her own view of the city, her own desk and two computers. Holy shit, it truly was a promotion. There was a kettle and French press with a whiskey bottle on a table. There was a closed door across from the desk.

"It goes into Mr. Astor's office. He usually keeps it open, but he is on a phone call right now. Decorate the room how you want, welcome!" She exited the room and Harriet was left there to her own devices and her own thoughts.

The cabinets were a dark colour, close to black, with an elegant feel to them. Between the two cabinets, a bookshelf was there with a few plants and books. Harriet instantly wanted to fill it with her favourite classics and plants...she could just imagine a hanging plant sitting there. Her desk was in front of it, dark wood with gold finishing. It was beautiful with a large Mac on the desk and a MacBook Pro next to it. Two computers! Fuck, she was in heaven. The only question was, what was the pay?

Harriet wanted to add paintings and a rug. There was so much to do. She had never had her own office before.

"Enjoying it?" She heard the deep yet soothing voice. Harriet turned around, seeing Atticus leaning against the door.

"Yes, thank you. I hope I don't disappoint you," she replied as she looked at the view of London.

"Here, an office warming present," he told her, handing her a box.

"Atticus, thank you, but I hope you didn't do this in order

to impress me?" she mumbled, taking the box and opening it.

"No. You have a lot of potential, but people don't give you the opportunity to show it." His arms were crossed, and he wore a black suit jacket with a black button-up underneath, the last few buttons undone. He was handsome, classy and trendy...she knew this job wouldn't feel like a job, but more of a hobby. She would have fun. The only thing she needed to do now was put the line between their relationship. They were merely friends.

"Oh my God," she muttered, taking out the books. Classics, they were classics but first edition. They must have cost a lot. "Atticus. I can't-"

"Say thank you and put them on the bookshelf, love. I expect this place to be colourful and fun. Here is my corporate credit card, buy whatever you want for this. I genuinely believe you will be working here for a long time."

Then he was gone.

Fuck. The first thing she wanted was a sky-blue chair and a plant.

JAX CAME AROUND SIX P.M., driving up in his classic black Maserati with a bouquet of wildflowers in the passenger seat. The kids were with the nanny, and he was taking her out for dinner.

"Do you want something for dinner. About to order some takeout," Atticus appeared at the doorway with his phone in hand as he scrolled through the options.

Harriet looked up from her computer, looking at the

time. "Shit, I can't. Jax is picking me up," she told him, getting up and grabbing her black tote. "Also, what is the dress code? I feel a little underdressed..."

"Oh, um... I don't care. If you are coming to a meeting, dress professional but otherwise I don't care. Our calendars are synced now, so you will know when you need to dress well."

"Perfect, well, goodnight. Don't stay too late, and thanks again for the promotion," she said, rushing her words.

He nodded her way as she exited the room.

Harriet pulled open the car door, getting in and applying a much-needed kiss to Jax's lips. He was still dressed in his work attire, but his jacket was long gone, and his button-up was remarkably close to being unbutton.

"Good evening to you," he chuckled, as he gave her the flowers.

"Wildflowers...you-"

"You love wildflowers. I used to find you in the field picking them when we were little and outside at the manor, you did the same thing. They are from home; I hope you like it."

"Like it, Jax? Jax, I love it!" she exclaimed. "Thank you!"

He smiled at her, placing his hand on her thigh as he drove her to the restaurant that was in Canary Wharf, right by the river.

"I got promoted today," she broke the silence. He noticed how her smile was wider and toothier.

"Really? To what?"

"Personal assistant. I am basically Atticus' second half in work. I control *almost everything.*"

His jaw clenched, a frown appeared, and his face hardened. "He is grooming you," Jax said. Her smile fell, looking at him. No facial expression was noticed as he looked at the road.

"You're not happy?" she mumbled, eyebrows furrowing and pressing her lips together.

"He is grooming you, Kitten. Bribing you-"

Harriet had enough. "No, Jax! Honestly, not everyone wants to get into my pants. We are friends. Work friends, friends from work. Friends. Only Friends. I get my own office, two computers, my own coffee machine, phone. Be fucking happy for me," she defended, aggravated by his words.

He didn't say anything for minutes.

"Honestly, if you want us to work, you need to be my advocate. You need to be happy for me. Jax, babe, you honestly need to stop with this whole competitiveness with Atticus, it's not sexy. I picked you, chose you, love you. *So, stop it.*"

They pulled up to the restaurant, the valet ready to take the keys.

He turned to her, taking her hand and looking in her eyes. "I know, and I thank you. I am sorry," he told her. She squeezed his hand.

"Now feed me."

THE DINNER WAS WONDERFUL, good wine and food. Laughs were shared, and stories were told. It felt good. She honestly felt good. Now, they were standing outside as his car pulled up for them.

"I want to ask you to come back with me, but-"

She shrugged. "Ok, I can take the Jaguar to work. I have a parking pass *now that I have been promoted*," Harriet mocked. "Just need to get my clothes for tomorrow at my place."

Jax eyes shifted to her, a smile growing. "That's no problem," he quickly said. He kissed her, pulling her close as the car waited in front of them. "Fuck, I love you."

THE MANOR WAS STILL as gorgeous since the last time she saw it. The lights were on as Jax drove up the gravel driveway. A little piece of her was excited to be back, to see the kids. They would be in bed as it was after eleven at night, but it was good to be back. Harriet felt like she was back home, like things were going back to *normal.*

"It's still beautiful," she told Jax as he went around the roundabout and parked.

"It will always catch your eye, come here."

They entered the house. Everything was all the same. Untouched from the last time she was there, everything was the same, except Claudia didn't live there anymore. Jax went to the kitchen, she followed as he grabbed two glasses and a bottle of wine.

"I want to move," he told her as the two them went to the living room. "But my father will kill me if I sell the place. I want to move to a townhouse in London. It will just easier."

"It's beautiful, but it's huge," she responded.

The two of them sat. He was in the corner of the couch with her back against his chest. His arm was wrapped around her as he took a sip.

"Exactly," he responded. "I might sell the flat and buy a townhouse, but Claudia lives up the road. She wants us to be close for the school, but I want to be in the city." His lips began to attach to her neck, peppering kisses.

"Divorce and kids…tough decisions, Jax," she muttered as he sucked the perfect spot making her moan. "But I love this place."

Jax took the two glasses of alcohol and placed them on the table in front of them. He pushed her back, straddling her on the couch as his lips attacked hers. Lust filled them as his hands began to trail up her naked flesh under her shirt. Jax kissed her jawline as he cupped her breasts under her shirt.

Kneading them with his hands, her fingers began to unbutton his shirt. He threw it off as she took off her tee and bra then her trousers and underwear followed. Jax admired her nakedness, hands grazing her body, tickling her skin. Goosebumps were felt as she shivered from his touch. His calloused fingers traced the tattoos on her body as he pushed her legs apart.

His lips began to litter small kisses up her thigh before attaching to her clit. Harriet moaned, fingers grasping his hair as he licked and sucked her pussy. Every stroke with his tongue, her back arched as she let out a breathy moan.

"Be quiet, Kitten," he told her, pushing her stomach back down. "Kids are asleep."

Jax went back to lapping his tongue and applying pressure to her clit. His fingers parted her lips as they circled her hole. One finger entered, she huffed and groaned, releasing his name from her lips.

His second finger went in as he began to finger her,

making a 'come here' motion as he sucked and licked her nub.

"Daddy," a little voice was heard.

Instantly, Jax pulled away from her cunt, throwing a blanket over her naked body before looking up to see Ember standing in the archway with her blanket in hand. Jax got up, wiping his hands on his suit pants. He went to his daughter.

"Hi, Em, you, ok?" He asked, leaning down and taking her into his arms.

Harriet held the blanket close to her naked body as a petrified look splattered her face. She was just caught by his daughter like a cheap whore.

"I heard noises, and I came down and.... Harriet!" Ember mumbled, eyes glancing around the room and spotting Harriet. She let go of her daddy as she ran to Harriet on the couch. "What are you doing here? Mummy told me that you were on vacation for an *exceptionally* long time and that you wouldn't be back in a long time. Has it been a long time?" She jumped on the couch and went to go sit on her lap.

Harriet pulled the blanket up further. "First, *exceptionally*? That's a very long word. Two, yeah, it has been," she told her. Ember's hands went to her arms, tracing over the tattoos.

"I have been doing a lot of reading with Daddy, but why are you naked?" she asked, hands now squishing her face. Harriet looked behind her, seeing Jax with his arms crossed over his broad naked chest and a smug face plastered.

"Harriet just took a shower, and she didn't have any clothes. So, the blanket is what she is using until I get her some clothes," Jax said. Harriet choked on her laughter, a stupid excuse. He was so bad at lying.

"But why were you between her legs-"

"Daddy and Harriet were cuddling, sweetheart. We love each other, so we were cuddling."

Ember scrunched her eyebrows. "Can we cuddle? I love you too." It was innocent, but Jax had enough.

"Bedtime!" He walked over to Ember and picking her up and throwing her over his shoulders. Ember's little giggles filled the room as he went back upstairs to put her back to bed. "I'll be back in a minute," he told her over his shoulder.

Shit, she was just caught by his kid, yet her pussy was still throbbing. She should feel ashamed, and she was.

Harriet grabbed the glass of wine, downing it as she waited for Jax to come back. Ten minutes later, he rounded the corner in all his glory, looking absolutely delicious.

"Where were we?" he smirked, pulling the blanket off her body and pushing her legs apart as he went back down to her clit.

"Jax," she laughed, cupping his face and pulling him up to her face. He kissed her quickly and looked at her through his lashes.

"We should probably do this upstairs in your bedroom. I really don't want Em or Caleb to come down and see us fucking. They do not need to see that," she advised.

He pursed his lips, kissing her lips once more before picking her up bridal style. Harriet squealed as he kissed her and began walking her up to his bedroom. The blanket was thrown over her as he headed to his bedroom.

Harriet truly forgot how much of a trek it was to go to Jax's bedroom, but eventually, she was there. He opened the double doors, closing them with a kick before throwing her on the bed.

While the two of them fucked, Harriet tried her best to

not be as loud in order to not have an Ember situation happen again. Thankfully, there was no disruptions.

"I love you, goodnight," she muttered, the sheets drowning her body as she kissed his nose.

"I love you more," he mumbled, wrapping his arms around her.

20

Harriet felt light kisses being placed on her stomach. Still asleep, she moaned, thinking it was all a dream. Shifting lightly, she felt a rough hand push her down. The kisses began to go closer and closer to the most sensitive spot on her body. Harriet squirmed a little, eyes beginning to flutter open.

She was met with Jax, clean-shaven and naked between her legs as he began to kiss her clit. Letting him do his thing, she pushed her head into the pillow as her hands wrapped around his neck, playing with his dishevelled hair.

"Morning, handsome," she muttered while he took her clit in his mouth.

He smirked against it, humming. The vibrations were sent through her body, making her tug his hair more.

"Too rough, Kitten. Be gentle," he hummed.

She scoffed, "You call that rough?"

Soon enough she was orgasming. The feeling of being on cloud nine, as the fiery pulsation began to shatter through her body. His lips attached to hers once again as the two lazily made out.

"That is one way to be woken up," she mused as he rubbed circles on her back.

"I hope you enjoyed it. You could have this," he kissed her again, "all the time if you move in with me," he kissed her again. Her hands were holding his cheeks as his were wrapped around her waist. They laid in bed, taking each other in, crazy in love as the morning sunlight hit their bodies.

"The kids?" she asked as he kissed her again.

"Nanny," he whispered as he began to straddle her again, kissing her jaw.

"Oh, what time is it?"

"Eight," he hummed.

She pushed him off her, getting up as fast as she can and running to the bathroom.

"What the fuck-"

"Jax, I have work in an hour!" she yelled as she turned the shower on.

He groaned, throwing his head back on the pillow. He heard her shower for a few seconds before it turned off, and Harriet was running around the room getting dressed and putting makeup on.

She walked out of the bathroom with a toothbrush in mouth and dressed in baggy dress pants that have been cuffed and an oversized burnt orange turtleneck jumper. Her hair was extremely dishevelled as she tried to control it, throwing it back into a low braid as she quickly did her makeup.

"Love you, I am out!" Harriet yelled about to leave the room.

"Kiss, Kitten," he yelled back all pouty, tapping his cheek.

Harriet groaned, kissing his lips and cheek quickly before rushing down the stairs, grabbing her tote bag and her clothes that were all over the floor in the living room. The Jaguar's keys were hung up in his office. She hastily grabbed them before exiting.

"NICE RIDE, MS. KENSINGTON," she was pulled up to the building, handing the keys to the valet. Atticus was leaned against the wall with a cigarette in hand.

"Give me one. I haven't eaten today," she groaned. He handed her one as she joined him.

"Order something then. A cigarette isn't enough," he told her off. She groaned again.

"I will."

"Jax's car?" he hinted, nudging his head to the luxury SUV. Harriet hummed. "How was your night?" Atticus asked, spiking a conversation.

"Imagine being walked in by a toddler when you're about to orgasm. That was my night," she joked, dropping the cigarette butt and stomping on it. "How was your night?"

"That would be embarrassing. I did not have a toddler walk in on me. I just worked, boring as hell, trying to make a deal with this company. Anyway, you have a bunch of packages that came in."

The two of them entered the building, heading up to the top floor and parting. The minute she walked into her office, boxes of stuff that she ordered were there. Excitement flooded her veins as she began to unpack everything.

"ATTICUS," she knocked on the archway as he typed away on his computer. He turned around, spinning in his chair.

"Hey, next week I need Friday off and the following Monday. Is that ok? If not, that is completely fine!"

"Mhmm," he turned back to his computer, pulling up his calendar. "I can move the meeting with Everston to Thursday, and if that is ok, you're good to go. Going anywhere exciting?"

"Paris! Jax wants to take me there," she beamed, walking into his office window and looking out.

"Oh, fun! Jax and you are quite serious then, huh?" he implied, arms crossed.

"Yeah, I would say so."

"Be careful." Atticus got up, walking up to her. Harriet was still looking out the window as Atticus walked next to her. His hand went up to play with the wisps of hair that fell against her temples. "Paris is his fuck city," he warned. "His bitch."

Harriet turned to him, puzzled face as she narrowed her eyes.

"What do you mean?"

"Paris is one of the reasons we ended out friendship," he told her.

"What is in Paris, Atticus?" she asked sternly, crossing her arms as she gave him a concerned look.

"His bachelor pad."

"So?" she mumbled quietly, a little confused by his words.

"Beware."

"I love him, Atticus. He would never hurt me on purpose,

and if he does, I can stand up for myself and kick him in the crotch."

"I understand you don't reciprocate the fondness I have for you, Harriet, but he will break your heart. That is Jax. And when he does, call me because I will help put you back together," he warned her as he poured himself a whiskey and handed one to her.

She took a sip and shook her head. "You're wrong."

"Am I? We will see. I am one phone call away, love."

HARRIET IGNORED every warning from Atticus. She made the conclusion that he was jealous of Jax. Atticus still very much had feelings for her, but he needed to let that go as she was with Jax. Jax was the love of her life, and she wouldn't admit it, but she was growing to the idea of being with him forever. He was kind when he chose to be, the controlling part could use some work, but overall, she was extremely happy.

Paris was tomorrow. It had been over a week since he warned her, but Paris was tomorrow, and she was excited. The bubbly feeling was in her stomach as she began to throw things into her suitcase. Lingerie... hell ya, swimsuits, maybe, but she was packed for everything. Atticus' warning for Paris didn't faze her...he had a bachelor pad in London, too...what was wrong with a bachelor pad?

In her mind, it must've been a grand studio apartment or a one-bedroom place. It wasn't kid-friendly and had endless booze, cigars and sport games. That is what a bachelor pad held, right? Like a mancave, but expensive.

Anyway, he was picking her up at seven in the morning, and she honestly believed that their weekend would be a mix of great sex, food, wine and sites. What made her most excited was the museums. Sex was great, but historical art... she was jumping.

That night she barely slept, every hour waking up and looking at the clock. Couldn't the morning come sooner? The woman was getting antsy...counting down the seconds till the trip. She asked Jax to stay over that night, but he told her that he had a late-night meeting that he didn't want to bother her with. Harriet shrugged it off and slept alone.

Seven a.m. hit and she jumped up, pulling on her cutest "Paris" look. She had the most adorable little yellow polka dot wrap dress, paired with chunky silver jewellery and a bold red lip. Her hair was pulled in a low messy bun as she put the absolute essentials into her suitcase.

"Don't you look adorable," Jax smirked, opening the door with two coffees and pastries. She kissed him on the lips, taking the coffee from him.

"Aren't you the best boyfriend," she responded, closing her suitcase.

Boyfriend... it bounced in his mind. She was *his*. He was her boyfriend. A little flutter travelled through his body. He was so close to accomplishing his dream. The divorce was messy, but once that was done, he was free to finally make her his officially. To see her with a diamond on her finger and his last name would be a dream come true. To see Harriet swollen and round with his baby inside of her made it even more exciting. However, the divorce needed to be finalised first.

"Ready to go? Beckett is outside," he told her, grabbing her suitcase as she took her classic black tote bag.

He was right. Beckett, his driver, was outside with the black Range Rover Sport. One of the many cars he owned that she had never seen. Harriet took a sip of the coffee, scrunching her face...Bailey's?

"Did you booze this coffee up?" she asked as she climbed in.

Jax was wearing a black t-shirt that made his biceps bulge and blue jeans, one of his more casual outfits. Simple guy really with his hair flowing freely and the curls untamed. It was her favourite hairstyle he could wear, besides when her fingers raked through it as he ate her out. She bit her lip from that thought. Paris tonight would be a blast, sensational...insatiable. She just knew it. She knew that tonight she would be all his to play with. Harriet smirked internally as she sipped her boozed-up coffee, letting the filthy thoughts swim in her mind.

"Yes, it's party time, Kit," he winked as she leaned into him in the car. His arm wrapped around her shoulders, pulling her closer as he applied a firm kiss to her forehead.

"Jax," she chuckled, rolling her eyes, "it is seven a.m.!"

He shrugged, capturing her lips once again. "It is five o'clock somewhere!"

THEY ARRIVED IN PARIS. Jax had a private jet... she didn't realise that part. He played it off that it was the company's and that his dad purchased it, but Harriet couldn't get over the fact it was a private jet. Jax tried to get her to have airplane sex, but Harriet wanted to preserve some form of dignity with the workers and the fact that it was eight a.m. Jax told her it was never too early to have sex.

He had a car pick them up at the airport, an Audi A8 that took them to his place. So far, Paris was beautiful, old and definitely a place of love. She could just imagine the coffee dates that they were going to experience and the walks around the city. Harriet felt loved for the first time really loved, the way Jax showed affection made her so happy. Sex, love, affection, she felt as if she was in a dream.

It had the classic Parisian architecture, old and sandstone. It was gorgeous, the building. The car parked, getting their bags to the flat as Jax took her hand, twirling her around outside the building.

"Do you want to change, or do you want to go grab something to eat and drink?" he asked her.

Food did sound amazing coffee even better. "Let's go for an adventure," she mumbled, kissing his lips and entwining their hands.

The two of them walked down the street, swinging their arms as she glanced around the city. Harriet couldn't get over how many little cafés there were, how everyone was out there drinking, eating and smoking.

"I could live here," she laughed.

"Really?"

"Drinking and eating all day is a dream. I could be French...smoking too, sign me up! Plus," she leaned into his ear, "French people make great lovers." He laughed, pulling her for a kiss as he led her to a coffee shop.

The two of them sat, looking out to the Seine River. He gave her a menu as he ordered two cappuccinos in French. Harriet knew Jax was sexy, but French rolling off his lips was something else. Jax noticed how her smile has yet to dampen. It was still wide and gorgeous. Her eyes sparkled. Harriet was in pure heaven.

"You speak French?" she asked as the waiter walked away.

With a chuckle, Jax nodded. "Yes, I took it in high school. The girls were hot in that class, so a few of us took it."

"Really, how old were you?" Harriet questioned, still couldn't get over it.

"Fifteen, it was before us, Kit. It comes in handy now with work."

She hummed with a shake of her head as he thanked the waiter handing them their coffees.

"You speak French…I can't believe it," she rambled on.

Jax laughed, leaning into her side and whispering, "Do you want me to speak French to you when we *faire l'amour*?"

Harriet pretended to fan her face as she batted her eyelashes. "Yes please, Monsieur Alderidge. Make sweet, sweet love to me in French." The two of them erupted in a fit of giggles.

Jax's head rolled back as a deep laugh came from his belly, which made her swoon even more. His laugh was the cure to anything.

"I could get used to you trying to speak French."

"Absolutely not gonna happen, sir," she winked.

"So, Paris?" he changed the topic of conversation.

"Gorgeous! I can't get over this, babe. Like, I-"

"We can come here every weekend if you want," he mused, taking her hand and applying a kiss to the back of it.

She smiled from the action, butterflies still fluttering in her stomach as she took out a pack of cigarettes, lighting the dart and drank her coffee. Now, she truly felt French.

"You smoke?" he hummed, narrowing his eyes to the addiction.

"Once in a while…want one?" she asked, thanking the waiter as he brought them their food.

"More of a cigar guy," he responded as he began to eat. He placed a grape in her mouth.

"I haven't asked," she began, "how is the divorce?"

He groaned. "I didn't realize how entwined everything is, between our estates and money, assets and the company. Plus, Claudia is being a real bitch. Custody is figured out, but it's the finances that a truly fucking us. I own the manor, the flat in London and here, the New York penthouse, but she wants all this shit. Like sure, take your car, but the manor is mine, the flats are mine. Plus, somehow, she has shares in the company. The lawyers and I agree that we are just going to pay her out," he grumbled.

"How much?"

"She wants fifty-million. I am going to give her twenty."

Harriet's eyes bulged, choking when she heard those numbers. "Shit." She knew Jax had money, but how much money does he have? He paid her debt like it was slapping down a twenty. Twenty million pounds? She couldn't believe it.

"That's before I pay her spousal support every month," he added.

"How much?"

"I don't know yet. She wants to leech me. Anyway, don't worry about it. I have the money, so it doesn't matter."

"How are the kids taking it?"

He shrugged. "Um, fairly good as we have always been kind of like this. The only thing different is that I am home more because I have a week with them. Em loves it, more time with daddy, and Caleb is too young to understand. We kind of raised them so that they kind of knew we didn't love each other, which is awful to say."

"Well, I am glad that they are ok with it."

"When you got divorced, what happened?"

"It was a mutual decision, really," she sighed, "like we were just depressed. But he didn't tell me how much money he owed, and I didn't know to who and that scared me. Kai was amazing until he fucked with the wrong guys. He always had a gambling issue, but I didn't know how big of an issue it was until the divorce," she explained.

"How much debt was he in?"

"When he told me 600,000 NZ dollars. I paid some of it off, and he did too. At the end, when I met you, I had 500,000 dollars still in debt. That included my tuition fees and lawyer bills, as well as my mother's debt. I am very thankful that you paid it off, so thank you."

"Is he still in debt?"

Harriet shrugged and sighed, "I ask that question every day. It is his issue, not mine."

THE DAY WAS SPENT WALKING around the old city, going into shops and eating. It was quite blissful. Harriet felt the happiest she had felt ever, and Jax finally felt his own happiness being with her.

Paris at night was gorgeous, with the streetlamps and musicians playing in the streets. Harriet held onto Jax's hand, and the other held his bicep as they walked home, both a little drunk from the expensive yet delicious wine they just had.

"I can't get over it," she mumbled, holding him closer as they continued down the streets.

The only downside of the Paris trip was the smell of cigarettes in the air, but she was used to it. Everyone smokes here, except Jax. Jax had yet to have a cigarette.

"It is almost as pretty as you."

She groaned and rolled her eyes. "How original."

"Hey, I am just stating a fact."

The Eiffel Tower was lit in the distance, its lights brightening up her view as she walked along the riverside.

"Hey, Kit," Jax began as they both looked at the distant tower. Harriet hummed. "I fell for you. Like Eiffel for you," he snickered, "you get it?"

Harriet groaned, "Very funny, mister."

"What? It is true," he retorted, smirking.

"Let's get home."

EVENTUALLY, they arrived to the flat. Jax nodded to the doorman, as they entered the elevator. It was redone, normally flats in Paris didn't have an elevator, but everything was completely renovated. Grand entrance with a chandelier and red carpet.

It opened and she was met with his so called, 'bachelor pad'. It wasn't as dark and scary as she thought. Mid-century modern, but there were more greys and wood colours rather than dark colours. It wasn't a studio apartment, at least one bedroom, but it was quite open. Sliding doors into the master bedroom and the kitchen was just outside with the living room.

"Welcome," he said as he walked to the master bedroom. She followed.

Harriet took it back. The bedroom was very dark. Black accent wall with a king-size teakwood bed frame with black sheets alongside two bedside tables. It was smaller than his bedroom at the manor but still grand, nonetheless. Then there was a door to the ensuite, which fulfilled the whole mid-century modern theme, but the tiled walls were black. It was most definitely a bachelor pad.

Their luggage was beside the bed. She sat down on the silk comforter as Jax threw himself on the bed, groaning from how much food he ate. Harriet laughed.

In front of her was an exceptionally large drawers and a closet next to it. She ignored it as she laid back, so their heads were next to each other.

"I am so full," he groaned.

"Tell me about it," she added, closing her eyes and ready to sleep.

Jax got up from the bed, pulling his shirt off. Harriet sat up, admiring his perfectly sculpted abs covered in chest hair. He nodded to her, and she took it as a hint. Her fingers twirled the ribbon that held her dress together.

"Off, Kitten," he purred, hands beside her as he placed a kiss on her lips.

She nodded at him, pulling the tie as it came undone. Her breasts were exposed as the dress pooled at her side. Jax placed his hands on her upper leg, attaching his lips with hers. He pulled away, taking her hand and helping her up.

He nodded to her underwear. Harriet hooked her fingers with the waistband and brought the thong down. Jax bit his lip, watching her the whole time.

"Beautiful," he muttered, seeing her nakedness.

Jax pivoted, walking to the Chester draws, pulling it open and taking something out. Harriet gasped. He held a vibrator in his hand. The man sauntered back in, kissing her jawline and sucking it. He pressed the button, and the vibration was heard in the room. It touched her leg, sending a shiver through her body as she felt it going higher up. She grasped his bicep as it slowly inched closer to her heat.

Harriet shuddered, her pussy clutching from the vibrations filling her system. Jax kept eye contact, inching it closer and closer. He removed once it hit a few centimetres away from her clit. She gasped for air when it was removed. However, Jax had other plans. The device began to circle her nipple. She trembled again. Little breaths releasing from her lips as it travelled down her stomach.

Jax eventually placed it on her heat, teasing her as it pulsated. He applied it and then removed it. Edging her every second it was there.

"Jax," she mumbled, he smirked showing the smallest facial expression for the first time. "Don't tease," she warned. Her hand was still holding his thick bicep still, gripping it as he played with her.

"I am in control, Kitten, not you," he whispered in her ear, "you are mine."

The vibration went back. He pressed it to the perfect place. Harriet moaned, gripping his bicep harder. He turned it off, throwing it on the bed.

He pinched her nipples between his fingers then caught her lips, teeth clinking as they desperately kissed one another. That man was like oxygen. She needed him. She craved him. Harriet realised that she was more addicted to him than she thought.

Jax placed his hands on her shoulder, pushing her down so that she was sitting on the bed. She looked up through her lashes, innocence washing off of her. He was done. His hardened cock was throbbing. He needed her. The lust took over, the sinful thoughts travelled in his mind as he imagined what the night held for them.

"Are you going to behave?" he asked politely, finger tilting her chin up. "Answer me."

"Yes, sir," she responded. Jax smirked from her response, dropping her chin as his fingers quickly undid his belt, pushing his jeans and boxers done.

"Be a good girl and suck it just the way I like it," he cooed.

Harriet kept eye contact as her hand wrapped around his thick member, the girth felt larger every time she touched it. The prominent vein that travelled up the shaft as she took the circumcised cock to her lips. She began to kitten lick it, eyes still in contact as she licked up the member.

Jax released a moan from his lips, hands in her hair. He played with it as he watched her at work. She was beautiful, he couldn't deny it, and she was his. Biting his lip, he continued to watch her, admiring her handiwork.

Harriet took everything in, hands gripping his hips as she sucked, tongue swirling around as she took everything in. One hand began to jerk his shaft while her mouth swirled the tip, sucking and licking. Jax groaned loudly.

"That's it. Take it, Kitten," he cooed, hand grasping her chin. "Take it all in. Choke," he growled. Every word coming from his lips just turned her on, even more. The growling and roughness just edged her and made her pussy drip more.

And like a good girl, she did follow his commands. She deep throated him like her life depended on it. Gagging as it hit the back of her mouth, salvia dripping down her chin as she blinked away tears.

He pulled out, the salvia trail leading to her lips from his tip. Slobbery mess, running down her chin. It was a sight for sore eyes and Jax enjoyed every second of it.

"Good girl," he smirked, as he pushed her hair back in comfort. Flutters went up in her stomach, she enjoyed it, the roughness and darkness. Harriet was never one to be like this, but she enjoyed it. She enjoyed every moment and the slutiness from their actions.

Jax went back to the drawers, pulling out bondage cuffs. He walked to her; facial expression unreadable as they locked eyes. She swallowed, knowing exactly what was about to occur. She was going to be tied up and destroyed, and a piece of her was excited.

"Purple," he nodded to her.

"Yes. Jax-"

"Are you ok?" he asked, dropping the cuffs on the bed and cupping her cheeks. He kissed her, making sure everything was ok.

"Yes," she muttered. He nodded to her words, picking the cuffs back up.

"Get on the bed, Harriet."

She complied, lying down on her back as he walked around. He took her wrist, placing the cuff on and tightening it. Harriet didn't realise that on the wooden frame of the bed there were D-rings, and he had clipped the cuffs to that. She watched him as he went to the other side of the bed, doing the same thing.

Harriet sighed, looking up at the ceiling and mentally preparing herself for what was about to happen. Jax was kinky as fuck.

Her leg was pulled. The cuff now wrapped around her ankle, as he attached them to the end of the bed. Then he did the same thing to her right leg. The vibrator was back in his hand as he brought the device up her calf and thigh.

She clenched her teeth and core, feeling the vibration in every part of her body but needing it most on her pussy that moment.

"Jax-"

"Patience," he growled, eye connected. "Harriet, let me do my thing."

"Yes," she mumbled, he gave her a look. "Yes, sir."

Jax climbed on the bed, bringing the device closer and closer till it was on her nub. Harriet clenched her muscles as she sucked in a breath. There was something different about when someone else used a vibrator on you rather than yourself. It had a greater affect, turned you on even more.

His fingers parted her folds, dragging the device up and down her womanhood. He pushed it in for a second and pulled out. Harriet let little breaths out, quiet moans as she watched him. He did it again, pushing the device a little further inside her, but his thumb began to circle around her clit. Harriet gripped the cuffs, feeling the absolute pleasure coming from him. She couldn't believe, she absolutely was overwhelmed from pleasure.

Jax turned off the device throwing it to the side as he licked from the pink hole up. She clenched everything again, noises echoing the room as she fought against the restraints. He sucked her nub, pushing her body onto the silky black sheets.

His member was throbbing. He felt it. He needed to be inside her. Therefore, he pulled away, pinching the nub as he watched her expression. Her eyes bugled, as she cried out. His teeth grazed her clit before he pulled away, lining himself with her entrance.

He captured her lips, as he thrusted in. Harriet sobbed as he filled her up. Her fingers gripped the cuffs harder, knuckles turning white as she clenched everything in her body. Her jaw was tight as he pushed himself farther up. The pleasure and pain shot through her system as she arched her back.

"Stay still," he groaned.

He pressed her hips down again, thrusting a few times. His own sounds of pleasures came out but were much quieter than hers.

"This isn't working," he muttered more to himself, pulling out and releasing the ankle and wrists cuffs. He flipped her body so that her ass was facing him. He hooked her wrists again.

Jax took her ass, parting the cheeks before slamming his hips back into her. His cock filled everything inside her. Harriet groaned, as he began to fuck her from behind.

It was all new, she would admit. She didn't know whether she enjoyed it or not. His fingers attached themselves to her clit, playing as he fucked her.

He knew she was close with the clenching and gripping harder of the cuffs. Therefore, he leaned towards her ear. "Come, baby."

She was gone, the pulsing taking over as the fire burned through her. The knot was undone as the shockwaves took over her whole body. Harriet was tired and burnt out.

Jax wasn't far behind her, letting his orgasm ripple through and fill her up. He slowed his motions, pulling out of her. The juices fell out of her cunt and down her legs. He bit his lip at that view, a sight for sore eyes.

Harriet was breathing heavily, whole body shaking. He craved and wanted to turn the vibrator on again and press it to the clit. However, she was completely done. Shaking and collapsing...absolutely and utterly fucked.

Jax undid the cuffs letting her fall on the bed. She laid still, taking deep breaths as she regained her focus. Jax kissed her lips, holding her as she came back to reality.

"You're ok," he shushed, playing with her hair as he pulled her so that she was flushed against his chest.

Harriet hummed in response.

"What did you think?" he asked, pushing her hair out of her face so he could see it.

Harriet turned over, locking her icy blue eyes with his ocean eyes. The ones she loved so much.

"You fuck, Jax. You don't make love," she said between her heavy breaths, trying her best to catch her breath.

It did pain him, a stab in the heart when she whispered those words. He chose to ignore them, kissing her lips again.

"I know. Let me draw you a bath and clean you up."

She shook her head. "No, I want to sleep."

Harriet moved her body so that she was now under the covers, facing away from him. She didn't know what she felt at that moment. The girl knew that he wanted to do more than what he did tonight, and that made her worry with what would happen tomorrow. She was in his fuck pad. His bachelor pad of fucking and that made a shiver go through her body.

21

Jax trailed his fingers along her shoulder, circling the tattoos on her arm and leading to the curvature of her ass. Harriet shuttered from his touch and brought the duvet over herself, knocking his finger off.

"Stop, Jax."

He sighed, getting up and walking to the shower. He stopped at the mirror, admiring himself. His perfect abs, chest hair leading down to his prominent v-line, he smirked when he saw his hardened cock, ready for another round. His smirk fell to a frown as Harriet wasn't up yet. Well, she was, but she clearly wasn't in the mood.

His hand gripped the dial, turning the shower on as he watched himself in the mirror. He felt his stubble, noting he needed to shave and planned to do it after the shower. The hot water hit his hard back, muscles tensing as he raked his fingers through his brunette curls.

His cock hardened further, the throbbing shooting through his system. The pre-cum on display and in need to be dealt with. He gripped his boner and imagined Harriet's sweet red lips around her. Sucking, licking and fucking as he jerked off. His hand splayed against the tiled wall as he imagined such a filthy thing occurring.

"You can't go a day without fucking, huh?" His eyes shot up to see her leaning against the doorway, arms crossed as she watched him. Harriet had a blank expression, eyebrows raised as she shook her head, sighing. She had sweats and cropped tank on. He noticed how she wasn't wearing a bra. Her hardened nipples were poking through the white tank.

"Obviously there is something wrong with that tone of voice," he muttered, dropping his member, the mood clearly ruined.

She pushed off the doorway and headed out the room. He shrugged, letting her take a breather until he heard a door slamming.

"Harriet!" he called, no answer, and he tried again. She left. His fist hit the wall as he yelled.

HARRIET WALKED AROUND that Paris morning – Saturday at eight a.m., barely anyone was on the local streets. She didn't exactly know what happened last night: she was tied and fucked. The thought made her shutter. Atticus was right. The bachelor pad wasn't what she thought it was and who knew what other *toys* were housed there or, better yet, who he brought there. She shuttered from just the thought.

Jax had done unspeakable things there, she concluded. He brought women there to fuck, to destroy and to degrade. Harriet stopped in her steps, connecting the dots together. Jax was in Paris for weeks on end, telling Claudia it was a work trip. Was it really a work trip, or was it a sex trip?

Harriet couldn't believe it. She was brought to his fuck pad so she could be tied and destroyed like a whore at his own leisure. This can't happen. She was only on day two of the trip, but was she just a number? Just a fuck to him?

What she knew at that moment was that she needed a bottomless mimosa and a large coffee with Baileys. She deserved it after a night like that. Sitting down at the closest café, she ordered just that. Well, just baileys and coffee, as well as breakfast.

She needed to confide in someone, she needed to talk to someone about what just happened, therefore she called Cameron.

"He did what?" she exclaimed over the phone line.

"I am in public. I can't say it any louder."

"That kinky motherfucker. How do you feel?" she asked.

"I don't know. Sore. I just feel cheap and a whore. Like I was a little into it, but then it clicked that that was his fuck pad. He brought me to his fuck pad."

She heard her friend grimace, "Yeah, maybe tell him to sell when you guys get serious. Make clear boundaries. If you aren't into that, then tell him. You like sex, Har, I know you, but how far would you go is the question."

"*Harriet!*" She looked up, seeing Jax. He was in athletic shorts and a fitted tee, running. "I have been running around the area, trying to find you."

"I have to go, Cam. Love you."

Harriet looked up to her boyfriend as he crossed his arms and gave her a glare. "Can we talk more in private?"

"I am having breakfast if you want to join," she told him. He nodded, sitting next to her and signally the waiter down.

French rolled off his lips as he ordered his meal, and it made her swoon just a little. He turned his attention to her.

"What are you drinking?"

"Baileys and coffee," she hummed.

"You're mad. If you have an issue with me jerking-"

"I don't care if you pleasure yourself, Jax," she whispered yelled, hoping no one could hear their scandalous conversation.

"Then why are you mad?"

"You... last night, you just...I have never done stuff like that before," she tried to explain. "There were toys...you tied me-"

"If you had an issue with anything, you should've told me," he growled, offended by her words. "There's a safe word for a reason, Harriet."

"Jax, you were a completely different person! I couldn't talk. It was all yes, sir and shit. I tried, and you were in this mindset. I thought if I let you have your fun, I might enjoy it, but-"

"You didn't enjoy it," he huffed, taking her coffee and sipping.

"Stop interrupting me, and that is my coffee!" she grumbled, yanking the mug from his hand. "I enjoyed some of the other stuff, not really. What was the most unsettling was that it was there already. That means you have brought women there, and it makes me feel cheap."

His face dropped, eyes glancing down before he took her hands in his. His eyes connected with hers again. "You're not cheap. You're worth more than life itself. I have stuff at my apartment in London as well. I don't have a good excuse but know that you aren't cheap. I love you."

"You have stuff in London too?" she hissed.

"Yes," he responded with a shrug. "Harriet, before you, I had a lot of sex. I don't understand what is wrong with that."

Harriet groaned, rubbing her face with her hands. "Jax, you don't understand-"

"Then make me understand!" he pleaded, yelling.

She shushed him quickly. "I was promised a romantic weekend away with my man. Then after a wonderful day, I came to the flat where it was a literal sex dungeon. I feel like I am just a plaything."

"You're not though, you're my Kitten."

She nodded, drinking her coffee as the waiter brought his food over. Jax thanked him as he began to eat.

"I was thinking we could do some shopping today. Champs-Élysées is amazing. I want to take you there. It's shopping, but I thought you'd enjoy it. We could then go to the gardens."

"Sure," she muttered with a grumble. The man still didn't understand.

JAX KNEW HARRIET WAS DISTANT. She wasn't herself. They held hands, but it felt like she was absent even though she was present. He knew something wasn't sitting right with her and needed her to tell him, but they were in public. Jax shrugged it off, holding her hand as they entered *Chanel*. He wanted to buy her something, something nice.

He thumbed the material, taking bags off the shelves, but she shook her head. Harriet left the minute he turned around, walking up the road to a little shop that was more her. It was her turn to look at everything, thumbing the materials over the dresses and skirts. She pulled them off the shelf and took them to the changing room.

Jax groaned, knowing she left the designer shop. He

picked up a bag, the *Classic Handbag* and purchased it. Jax could just imagine her using this for work rather than the black leather tote that was close to being broken.

He tracked her phone, seeing she was just up the road. Harriet stood, looking at herself in the mirror with the suit on. It was beautiful, pastel blue colour. He leaned against the wall, crossing his arms as he watched her.

"You have this in yellow too?" she asked.

"Oui."

"I'll take it as well."

Harriet turned around, spotting Jax, and she gave him a small smile. "Nice suit," he nodded to it.

"Thank you. I need more professional clothes according to Atticus, and this is the closest I will get."

He chuckled, walking up to the register.

"Don't you dare pay, Jax!"

Simply smirking, he inserted his card. Harriet came out and rolled her eyes, taking the bag from the lady.

"*Chanel*?"

"A promotion present for you."

"Oh, Jax, that is too much. Thank you. I can't take presents like that," she told them as he grabbed her hand once again to go down the street.

BESIDES THE OBVIOUS tension between the two, the day was still beautiful and enjoyable. They went to the Luxembourg Gardens, and Harriet couldn't get over all the flowers and the architecture. Like any classic Parisians, they had coffee and wine. Now they were back at the flat.

It was just after ten at night when they entered. Jax

made a beeline to the shower as he felt gross. The man was still in his athletic gear from that morning. While Harriet took her time to come in. She didn't notice the first time she came in, but right by the door, there was a table with a book on it.

She placed her bags down, making her way to it. It was velvet red with "Guestbook" in gold cursive. Harriet wondered whether this was his guestbook from the wedding or if he rented this place out, curious, she opened it. Instantly she was met with female names and dates repeatedly.

"Holy fuck," she mumbled, hand coming over her mouth. She flipped the pages, dates going back ten years ago. Hundreds of names, female names. "*It's his fuck diary*," she muttered to herself.

She couldn't believe it. Harriet slammed the diary shut. Was she just a number in the book? A pawn in his game? Harriet took the book with her, marching to the bedroom. Jax was in the shower with some music on, hearing his light humming.

Harriet needed the truth and she needed it now. Throwing the book on the bed, she opened the dresser... sex toy after sex toy were there. Ropes, cuffs, vibrators, butt plugs, floggers...you name it, he had it. Her mouth was wide as she looked at everything. The closet was filled with boxes titled with female's names on them. Again, she ripped off the tops seeing sex shit once again. Holy fuck.

This was unbelievable. Ok, he has had partners, but she honestly thought they had something that she wasn't just in a pawn in his game of sex. Harriet picked up the red velvet book, opening the door to see Jax naked and wet under the shower.

Ignoring the flutter in her stomach every time she saw him, she dropped the book on the tile floor. Jax jumped.

"Holy shit, Harriet! You scared me."

"You are a fucking sadist motherfucker," she swore, every word biting with such anger.

Jax narrowed his eyes. "Harriet, where is this coming from, Kitten?"

"Don't fucking Kitten me. W*e are done*."

Jax turned the shower off, grabbing the towel as he followed her to the bedroom. "At least let's talk first!" he yelled, tripping over the book on the floor. When his eyes caught sight of the velvet book on the floor, a curse word was whispered under his breath. She found it.

"Boxes and boxes of sex toys," she exclaimed, throwing the boxes onto the ground from the closet. "The most sadistic shit, whips, and butt plugs that are bigger than your fucking cock! I am not interested, but according to that fuck diary, thousands of women are."

Harriet turned around, running her fingers through her hair and down her face. Jax noticed tears falling down her cheeks, glistening from the light. He knew he had a lot of explaining to do, but she didn't want to hear it. Jax tried to reach out to her, but she was seeing red. All she could do was seethe and yell as she tried to explain how wrong this situation was.

"Tell me, Jax, be fucking honest with me. How many women have you brought here and fucked? How many?" she spat, crossing her arms across her chest.

"Harriet, let's just talk-" he whispered, trying to calm her down.

"No, how many? More than fifty from this guest book

alone, hundred, two hundred. No, I am thinking it's close to a thousand. So, tell me how many women?"

"I don't know," he mumbled softly. "I don't know," he said louder this time with more confidence.

"Am I just a number?" she whispered, voice breaking from that thought. He shook his head repeatedly, trying to soothe her. Harriet moved away from his touch.

"No, you're not. How many times do I need to tell you that I love you-" he tried again.

"I am going home. I don't know if it has even crossed your mind how I feel about this, but you told me a romantic weekend away, to wine and dine me and be a lover. Instead, you took me to your *fuck* pad. I am pawn, I am fucking pawn in your chess game, and I am done playing and being sacrificed. We are done, whatever we had doesn't exist because you are too horny and fucked up to understand what real love is. I am leaving."

Jax shook his head. "*Harriet*, come back."

She dodged his grip, grabbing her stuff from around the room. Jax threw clothes onto his body, following her outside the door. She ran down the several flights of stairs as Jax ran after her. Harriet got outside, hailing down a cab as he took hold of her hand, pulling her to face him.

"Don't give up on us."

"I gave up on us a long time ago. Don't trust a cheater, especially one who is married and hasn't called you in 13 years. Don't trust someone who has a fuck pad. I should've known better, should've looked at the red flags, but no, I was too naive, hoping we could have what we once had, but I don't ever think we had love *ever*. Goodbye, Jaxon," she spat.

Her arm reached for the door of the cab, opening it as she threw her stuff to the other side of the car. Harriet sat herself down, seeing him still in front of her. Jax knew what he had to do, what he had to do to haunt her in order to get her back.

Just when she was about to close the door on him, he told her, “I hired you not Claudia.”

22

"Fuck!" he yelled as he watched her drive off. Harriet showed no mercy when she closed the door. The love of his life was gone once again, and he knew it was his fault *again*. What do you tell the woman who found your diary of 'arrangements', past endeavours and conquers? He swore on the road. He should've known better, he should've come early and get things ready and hide all of this, hide the evidence, but he knew she would've found out one way or another.

Jax couldn't be blamed for having a past. She had a past too. However, he realized that bringing the love of your life to the place where you fuck, and ditch wasn't exactly right. Now, he stood there feeling ashamed.

He knew that if he hid this for any longer, their relationship couldn't have been salvaged. He could fix this. Jax needed to fix this. Once again, he was at fault because of his stupid actions.

Jax walked back into the flat. The smell of cigarettes and her woody yet floral scent lingered even though she has only been there for a few days. The lawyer felt as if the world was against him, as every chance of happiness he had, it slipped through his fingers. Whose fault was that?

In conclusion, he needed to get rid of everything. Remove every drunken mistake and so-called evidence of any past lover. Paris was going to be *their* place, but he fucked up that too. Jax wanted to erase the weekend and restart it. He should've rented or even bought a new place. What was he thinking of bringing her *here*?

Jax swore and yelled. Once he was back inside, he took out a trash bag that had every device from the flat. Every sex toy, every object that had ever touched other women now gone. Harriet was going to be his wife, his lover, best friend and partner in life. This life he once had needed to go, and it needed to go now.

He took out his phone the screen brightening up as he pressed his realtor's number. Three rings later...

"J'ai besoin de vendre."

(I need to sell)

Jax was back in London by the end of the day. He called his cleaner asking them to get rid of everything in the Paris flat. To make it sellable and less like a sex dungeon.

23

"I *hired you not Claudia."*

It echoed in her mind. What did that mean? She gave him one final look as she shrugged the comment off, closing the door of the cab and telling them to take her to the airport. Harriet quickly booked the next flight to London as she drove off.

The names haunted her like an old tattoo. Was she overreacting? She didn't know, but she did know that she was hurt. It felt as if he was holding this secret from her and that he felt it was ok for her to be brought to his den of pleasures!

With that, Harriet left Paris not regretting her decision.

By Monday, she had a hundred missed calls from Jax and hundreds of texts from him. Harriet ignored him. He truly wasn't worth it. That man had a lot of baggage, and she was in no state of mind to deal with it at that moment. He needed to deal with his bullshit before they became something.

She wanted to be with him. Fuck, that was her only wish. Harriet wanted to be with forever and not because he had money or he knew how to give her the best orgasms, but the feeling they had together was what she wanted. He loved her, and he proved that to her. Harriet agreed she over-reacted a tad bit, but Jax needed to know that what happened was not ok. She wasn't his pawn. She was his queen, and she needed to be treated like one.

Atticus was sitting at his desk, legs crossed and resting on the surface as he had his morning coffee. Like every morning, the man genuinely believes the littles things make the most difference. Therefore, watching the view and drinking his coffee really made him smile. Until Harriet knocked.

Atticus spun around seeing the brunette that he loved so much as a friend. He gave her a puzzled look.

"What are you doing here? You're supposed to be in Paris!" he exclaimed, brows knitted.

Harriet groaned, walking over to the whiskey and pouring herself one even though it was nine in the morning. "You were right," she acknowledged, sitting down on the chair in front of desk. "Paris just made things clear."

"It is his bachelor pad," he advised, shrugging.

"You should've told me that it was his fuck pad. His den of pleasures...his sadistic enterprise. He has a guestbook of names of women who have bedded him!"

Atticus made a face. "I knew that. What was the last date?"

She scrunched her eyebrows. "You knew and didn't tell me!" she scolded.

"I warned you, though. At the publishing event I said to Jax about you being a tally in his book. That's the book, Harriet. Now tell me the last date."

She pursed her lips, sighing. "I actually didn't look."

He sighed, taking his feet off the wooden desk and leaned over to her. "I don't like him, but he is a different person around you. That is his past. You can't blame someone for their past, Harriet. You have demons, I have demons, and he brought you there to have a romantic weekend away. It didn't help that he had a room of pain. Make boundaries, love," Atticus lectured her.

She sighed. He did make a clear point. "You're right, I should give him the benefit of the doubt."

Atticus nodded her way. "Still don't like him very much." Harriet rolled her eyes as he took a drink from the coffee. "Arrogant son of a bitch. We were once good friends. There was four of us, Jax, Sebastian, Christopher and me."

"How did you meet again?" she asked, turning to him.

"I worked for a media company as soon as I got out of school. His dad was their lawyer, met Jax at a charity event that my boss at the time hosted every year. He was still in law school. When I found about his way of life, we got into a fight, and now we are just business partners."

"And who are the other two?"

"Sebastian, CEO of Prescott Enterprises and Industries in New York City. Great guy, fabulous humour and can be quite smug. I met him through Christopher Everston, CEO of Everston Media and Records and also in NYC. I worked with Chris because I am in publishing, and he is in media. Jax is the lawyer for them both. All great mates. Jax is still in contact with them."

Harriet hummed, thanking him as she exited the office. She sat down on the sky-blue chair, looking at her phone sitting on the wooden desk. Without thinking, she picked up the phone and clicked his name.

“I am sorry,” she muttered over the phone.

He picked up on the first ring. Jax got up from his desk, shutting the door to his office as he sat back down in his leather chair, turning it, so it looks out onto the London city view. His sigh ringed through, raking his fingers through his hair.

“It was my fault. I didn’t think, and that was a stupid and an immature excuse. There is a side of me that I never talked to you about, and I am sorry, so don’t apologize for your actions because I don’t know what I would have done if I was in your shoes. Kit, I love you, and I want to come clean with my past. I thought this through-”

“Dinner tonight?” she asked quietly.

“Please, my place.”

BECKETT WAS THERE when she came out of the building. He was leaned against the black Range Rover Sport as the sun began to set. He was younger, early twenties, yet he held that mature look to him, like Jax. His hair was short and had a little quiff, sandy blonde and hazel eyes. He was clean shaven and was dressed in a suit.

“Evening, Ms. Kensington,” he said, opening the door for her.

Harriet sat in the back of the luxury vehicle, letting out a loud breath as she looked out the window. She had seen Paris, what would his London flat look like... sex dungeon part two? Harriet pushed those thoughts aside. If this were to work, she needed to trust him. She needed to trust Jax, but he needed to come clean for that to happen.

Beckett got into the front of the car, driving out from the

entrance of the AVA House and down the London street. It couldn't be too far, as he said it was in the heart of downtown.

"We are here, Miss." Beckett got out, opening the door and taking her hand again. It was an older building. She could spot the chandelier...just like Paris with a bellboy and serious amount of security. A grand foyer welcomed her as she followed Beckett through the entrance.

He pressed the last level... he had a penthouse, she connected. Seconds later, the doors opened and in front of her was a grand and open penthouse. Beckett nodded to her as she exited. The doors closed before, and she was met with a most delicious smell ever...garlic...herbs. Who is making this, and what are they cooking?

It was modern with giant windows overlooking the river and the London Eye. She was in shock, as she looked around. It was white with dark furnishing, open layout and extravagant. A living room was in front of her, few steps going down with a flat screen TV and a fireplace with a chandelier hanging above it. Right next to the living room, there was a glass railing staircase going upstairs.

"In the kitchen!" She heard his deep, rough voice, which made a small smile crept onto her face. His voice was like home.

It came from her left, and she followed. There he was, dark, tall, and handsome in the kitchen. His classic sharp suit wasn't on, but instead a grey tee that outlined his pectoral muscles paired with blue jeans. He had a tea towel draped over his shoulder as he poured water from the pot into the sink.

The large kitchen was a chef's dream, black modern cabinets and white quartz countertops. It was beautiful and screamed Jax. However, she couldn't get over the city view.

"Hi," she said, walking to him, "I made Beckett stop to get wine." She held up the bottle of Merlot.

He turned around, rubbing his hands on the tea towel as he placed his palms on the counter, leaning on them and looking at her. She smiled, sitting on the barstool.

"Thank you, but I have plenty of wine."

"Just add it to the collection," she told him, placing the bottle next to her.

Jax was humming a tune, something she had never seen before. There was a skip in his step too. He grabbed two white wine glasses and a bottle, popping it and pouring it.

"I didn't know you can cook."

"I am full of surprises, *baby*," he winked. Jax went to turn music on, old hits from the 80s. She rolled her eyes from his dancing. "Pasta All'Arrabbiata for the lady," he sang.

"You're in a good mood," she chuckled.

"You called me back, thought I lost you."

"Jax..."

"Yes, I know we do need to talk. Let's eat first!"

Jax served the two of them food, sitting next to her at the counter. She moaned in approval with his cocking, and he simply said, 'I told you so'.

"I'm selling the Paris flat. Everything is in the past, Kitten. We are the future," he interrupted the silence as he took the glass of wine in his hand.

"You're selling it? Jax, I-"

"No, I needed to get rid of it. It was the chapter I need to forget. I shouldn't have taken you there. I should have rented somewhere else, and I am sorry," he said to her, words filled with emotions.

Jax got up, walking to the other side of the kitchen where a folder with a bunch of files were in it. He placed it in front of Harriet.

He let out a heavy breath, hands on his hips as he glared down at the brown paper folder. Papers were coming out of all ends, hundreds of papers.

"Non-disclosure agreements, Kit," he began, sitting back down and opening them. Harriet took few out, some of the names she recognised from the guest book. "I needed to preserve this image for my father. Nuclear family, bullshit. I never loved Claudia, and you know that, so I dove myself into the company of other women. However, they needed to sign one of these first so they wouldn't go telling the media. This was my life, but not anymore." He pulled the top one out. "Last one, dated months ago."

"Jax, even if they are dated months ago, you have hundreds of women signatures. Therefore, you could go back to them anytime."

"I know, and I haven't. Since that night in my kitchen when I saw you for the first since I left. I swore off anyone else. I want *you*, not...them," he told her, pushing the files away.

"Paris-"

"Paris was a *sex dungeon*," he rolled his eyes at his choice of words with a grimace. "It was my mancave. I don't know what else to call it, Kit. The boxes were for hygiene purpose, the ones we used were new. I was sad and lost, sex was an output. The guestbook was a pride thing, I felt like I accomplished something with those names."

"Power thing...*pawns*," she mumbled, looking away.

"No-"

"Yes, Jax. Women are pawns in your life. You use them

for your advantage: sexual pleasure, control, power and pain. I am not a pawn in your chess game. I am not something to throw away when you're done, I am not a sacrifice, and I am not a name for your stupid book-"

"I never asked you to be," his voice was louder. It boomed over her quiet tone. He took offence from her words. "Sorry," he mumbled.

"Be in my shoes for a second. How would you feel if I had a book of names, conquests, a flat of pain, and NDAs in folder? You would feel a little cheap," she whispered, taking his hand.

"I am sorry, Kit. I am sorry you think like that, but in my chess game, you're the queen. My queen, baby," he whispered, kissing her hand. "You control me, baby, just like that chess piece."

"Ok," she mumbled. "We need to talk about boundaries."

"Go ahead," he nodded her way, taking a sip on his wine.

"You're a fucking sadist-"

"Prefer dominant, Kitten."

"Light bondage is fine. Those cuffy things...no thank you. I was fine with the tie, but being strapped down, not my thing, Jax," she stressed to him.

"Duly noted."

"The vibrator I can handle. No whips, no flogs, and I might grow into butt plugs, but don't get too excited... I said might." His eyes widened but then narrowed as he raised his eyebrow. "No promises."

He began to kiss up her arm, looking up as she tried to discuss terms with him. He hummed as he kissed her shoulder, trailing down to her collarbone. Harriet sighed from his teasing actions; the man couldn't be serious for a minute.

"Jaxon," she mumbled, running her fingers through his

hair, going down to his chin and tilting his chin up. "I am not done with my terms."

Jax sat back up on the barstool, waiting for her to continue.

"You fuck me. You don't make love to me," she mumbled, tilting his chin up as she stood up. She towered over him as he sat. Their lips connected, Harriet nibbling his bottom lip. "So, make love to me," she whispered against them. "Show me how much you love me."

His arms wrapped around her frame, letting their lips dance, touching and sucking; letting the salvia exchange as they kissed. It wasn't forced or hungry like normal instead, she could feel the love coming from him.

Harriet grabbed his hand, pulling him up. His arms were around her again, lips together as they kissed. Jax hooked their fingers together, pulling her to the bedroom upstairs. She laughed as he mumbled 'hurry up'.

He was now running down the hall and up the stairs, pulling her with him until he opened the master bedroom doors. She didn't have time to even look around the room before his lips were on hers again. Jax gripped the edge of his shirt and pulled it up above his head before cupping her cheeks again, kissing her plump lips. He felt good, she felt the love ... the two of them could surely work together.

The two swiftly pulled off their clothes. Harriet leaned back, lying on the bed as he towered on top of her. Jax placed his hands next to her head as their lips met, kissing hard. She wrapped her legs around his body, heels digging into his hard ass as he grinds his throbbing cock on her pussy.

"Jax," she mumbled, pulling away from the kiss.

"I know," he chuckled, trying to get use to this slowness.

He pushed himself inside of her, thrusting and rocking

his hips slowly, making sure to hit the perfect spot inside of her. Her arms were around his neck, making him have eye contact with her as they kissed. The two of them felt the love between them, moaning every time he entered and brushed against the g-spot. Her fingers pulled the little hairs at the bottom of his neck as the two of them *made love* for the first time.

Harriet enjoyed it, she felt like it was the best present he could ever give to her. He was submitting to her, even if he didn't know it. He was compelling to her needs and fulfilling her desires even though it was so foreign and unlike him.

"I love you," she mumbled in the kiss. He smirked, pulling her bottom lip with his teeth and attacking her lips again with his own.

"I love you more, Kit."

Jax's hand cupped her cheeks, his thigh brushed her side as he flipped them so that she was on top now. Harriet gasped as she sank down. He held her hips as she rolled her hips and rode him.

It was a sight for sore eyes watching her as she took control, circling her hips as she rocked on his cock. The two of them were moaning, groaning, using every swear in the dictionary as they tried this new form of territory. He was her high. She was his drug, his heroine, and he prayed he would never have to go into withdrawal ever again. Harriet was perfect.

Her hands splayed on his chest as she moved her whole body in the perfect rhythm, taking deep breaths as his cologne filled her senses. The two of them were in pure bliss.

Jax came not long after, shooting his seed inside of her, holding her hips down as much as he could so she could take everything. The sex was slow but worth it...every second was like the edge to his own death. The pleasure slow and unbearable. He enjoyed it.

"That wasn't bad," she mumbled, falling beside him.

"Your turn, Kitten," he purred, kissing her cheek as he went down.

Like muscle memory, she wrapped her legs around his head as he pushed her folds apart, licking from her ass up to her clit.

"One day, I am going to fuck this ass," he growled licking it as he entered a finger inside of her vagina.

His tongue was back, attacking her clit, sucking and flicking his tongue against her stimulus. Harriet rolled her head back, gripping onto the navy sheets, eyes closed as she clenched her teeth together.

She was close. He continued and minutes later, she had the classic fire burning in her lower stomach as she came. Her fingers gripped his curls, pushing his head down on her pussy while her vaginal walls pulsated. Everything went tense, then relaxed. Jax came up, locking his lips with hers.

"I love you," he breathed.

24

The two of them sat in the bathtub her back flush against his chest as she leaned back capturing his lips. Jax's arm was on the tub's edge, fingers in the water as he flicked the water around. He admired her, every piece of her, as he took his fingers and dripped water on her bare skin. His eyes glancing over her naked body that was covered by the water. Her tattoos were bold against her pale skin. He traced over them...every single one of them. Jax traced the letters on her hip. She jerked a little, shivers flowing through her system.

"Jax," she muttered, rolling her head back further on his shoulder. Her cheek was touching his neck as he continued to touch her bare skin, especially dragging his fingertip over the faint scar on her lower stomach.

"What happened? You barely told me," he whispered. Harriet sighed, closing her eyes.

"Um, he was born and passed away hours later, Jax." Harriet hated talking about it. It's been over a year, but it still felt like yesterday when she heard the news.

She was at work sitting at her desk, when the soaring pain came through. Harriet thought it was Braxton Hicks at first as she was too early to go into labour. However, when her water broke, instantly, she feared everything. Harriet was twenty-eight weeks along with her pregnancy. Therefore, the baby would be premature.
She got up, the water pooling down on the ground as she tried to find her phone to speed dial, Kai. The pain seared through her, the contractions weren't close together...twenty minutes or so, but she was still internally freaking out.
The social worker drove herself to the hospital. It wasn't too far – ten minutes or so. She thanked God that a contraction didn't hit while she was driving. Who knew where Kai was? That man was always on another planet, but she was close to giving birth, and he couldn't pick up the damn phone.
Harriet told the nurse once she raced into the ER, "I am in labour." However, once settled and in the bed, the doctors told her that she was too early to deliver. No shit, Sherlock.
The contractions were now ten minutes apart, and the doctors had no choice but to deliver her baby boy. He was too early. Therefore, they chose to do a C-section.

"I was awake the whole time," she told Jax. He continued to show interest as he drew circles on her skin. Goosebumps rose from his fingering as she talked. "Kai didn't answer my messages, so he wasn't there. A nurse held my hand as I felt my stomach opening. I had an epidural, so no pain, but I could feel it. He didn't cry when he came out, and that was alarming for the doctors," her voice was emotionless.

Something is wrong," she muttered all breathy looking up the nurse as she focused on what was behind the screen. She knew, the mother deep inside her knew something was not right. Harriet looked around the operation room, seeing the blue scrubs and silver tools. Her baby was out. She could feel the emptiness inside of her. He didn't cry. She heard the shushed muttering as a doctor took her baby to another room.

"Where is he going?" she panicked, grabbing the nurse's hand and squeezing it. "Tell me, tell me what is happening? Where is my baby?" Harriet began to scream, tears rolling down her face as her wrath became undone.

"Mrs. Fitzgerald, you need to stay still. Everything will be ok. You are ok," the female doctor told her.

"I may be ok but is he ok?" she screamed through her teeth.

Harriet looked at the nurse next to her, seeing her eyes. Something was definitely wrong. Her baby was almost blue when she caught a glimpse of him bundled in a blanket as a new doctor left with him. Something was wrong, and no one told her.

"He had RDS, respiratory distress syndrome. He lasted the night before he passed away. Kai finally came when I was all stitched up and got the news about his diagnosis. We cried together, and he held my hand. Once the doctors left the room, he wasn't the same. Distant, cold, and almost evil, it pained me. All I needed at that moment was my husband."

Jax grunted as he wrapped his arms around her pulling closer to him. "He seems like a dick."

"He once was my prince charming, Jax."

Jax drew circles on her stomach, thoughts circling his head, questions that he wanted to ask her. Harriet grew quiet, wiping the tears from her cheeks as she nuzzled closer to him.

"What was the kids' birth like?"

Jax sighed, "I don't know. I wasn't there. I was in-"

"Paris?" she cocked, he grunted.

"No, New York, Kit. I was starting up an office there when Em was born and working part time there and here when Caleb came. Paris wasn't just my funhouse. I worked there too. I am setting up an office there right now."

Harriet hummed, "Did you have sex with Claudia? You two could've afforded help with doctors."

"We had sex. It was horrible. She isn't into men, so it was awkward. I told her we could get help with the doctors, but she didn't want it to be a thing with the media if they found out. I told her we could play it off as fertility issues, but no, she wanted to do it the natural way. So, we did and look, we have two perfect babies."

"Who is Sebastian and Chris?" she questioned.

His finger halted from drawing circles on her wet flesh.

"My best mates in New York City. Sebastian is a big partier, sex driven and cocky as hell. Hilarious guy, genius, *complete genius*. He started his company from nothing and great with money and numbers. You would grab a drink with him and have no idea that he is a billionaire, playboy, genius dickhead. Chris is the opposite, quite reserved and quiet if that makes sense. He runs a media company. Great guy, a woman's dream, sort of like Atticus."

"You must be in New York a lot."

"Used to be a lot, but they come to London for business often. You should meet them. They are a lot of fun," he whispered, kissing her hair. "How did you know about them?"

"Atticus."

"They are good friends with him too," he purred, kissing her cheek.

Harriet turned around, the water hitting higher up as she

moved to sit across from him. Jax grabbed her ankle, pulling her to her and kissing up her leg. She squealed.

"Jax," she warned.

"Not doing anything, Kitten," he whispered, going back to kissing up her leg.

Jax moved, crawling across the large bath and capturing her lips. Her hands wrapped around his neck, pulling him closer.

The two kissed, letting their emotions take a hold of them, exchanging salvia as their needy hands glided over each other's body.

She was taken by him. Absolutely in love with him and he was too.

25

Harriet laid in bed that night. Jax's arm draped across her figure as he snored lightly by her ear. Her eyes glanced at the clock. It was just past three in the morning. For the first time since the two started their relationship again, she found that he was truly being honest. It felt good. However, there were words echoing in her mind that she hadn't brought up to him.

"I hired you not Claudia."

What does that mean? She remembered specifically that her interview was with Claudia. Claudia was the one she was in contact with, so what did he mean that he hired her? Was it part of that manipulation play he does to try, and mind fuck her?

Harriet stirred a little, a heavy breath escaping her lips as she tried to get comfortable in the grand king-sized bed. Her eyes focused on the bright lights of the city through the giant windows. Jax was asleep, next to her. She felt his chest and leg hair tickling her smooth flesh. His leg was wrapped firmly around her, making her stuck in his hold. She could feel his little breaths on the back of her neck as he snored gently. Harriet could get use to this.

"Jax," she mumbled. He didn't move in the slightest. Trying again, Harriet gripped his arm, trying to pry off his hold. "Jax."

"Go to sleep, Kitten," he mumbled, gripping her harder and snuggling deeper into her.

"Jax," she whispered.

"Yes," he mumbled. His eyes were still closed, but he was now partly awake.

"I need to ask you a question."

"Shoot."

She turned around in his grasp. The tip of her nose was now touching his. His eyes opened, and instantly she was met with his ocean orbs, the greens and blues clouding his iris. She felt his touch on her hip as he tried to keep his eyes open, yet sleep was winning.

"You mentioned that you hired me, but that doesn't make sense. I was contacted by Claudia."

His fingers played with her hair, pushing the strands behind her ear as he tried to find his words. "Claudia was in contact with you, Kit, but I was the one who sent her your ad," he told her, kissing her cheek then setting his hand back on her hip. "Go to sleep, Kit, it's really late and I know you will think yourself to death."

She scrunched her eyebrows, narrowing her eyes at him. "Why didn't *you* contact me?" Harriet was confused. Did Jax try to reach out for her? Jax quite possibly did try and find her, but Harriet was too stubborn to notice.

"I was scared that you wouldn't accept it. It's been thirteen years, Kit. I was so scared that I would contact you and you had a whole life or that you wouldn't accept the job offer because of me. I was scared you would run if it was me. I thought you would be mad that it had been thirteen years I didn't know that you were actually hired until that night in the kitchen. There were others she was looking at."

She nodded, kissing his lips. "So, you did try and find me? Like you promised," she mumbled. Jax nodded, biting his lip. "You let me think that you were this man who..." she trailed off.

"Yes."

"Why?"

"I didn't want to scare you off. It sounds stupid now, Kit, but you're easily frightened," he told her. "Now sleep, please."

"You actually-"

"Kitten, there hasn't been a day that has gone by which I haven't thought of you. Sleep now."

Harriet didn't let it go. "Jax, just tell me everything, please."

He sighed, propping himself on his elbows and clearing his throat. She turned to face him, watching him with eager eyes.

"I stalked you for years. Well, I tried, you were non-existent on the internet. Then when you told me you married that fucker, it made sense. I was searching for Harriet Kensington not Harriet Fitzgerald. You blame me for not fulfilling my promise, but you *must* know there were so many factors. I feared about disinheritance if I left Claudia or my parents found out I didn't want to attain their standards when it came to life," he mumbled, running a finger through his hair.

Harriet reached out, hand on his pectoral, tracing circles on the firm muscle.

"This year, I searched for you. I hoped that you were on the internet. And there you were, plain as day. I couldn't care less about their thoughts anymore. Disinheritance my ass. Money is nothing compared to love. I wanted to hire you, I saw your ad and I didn't want to say shit because you are a runner. I thought you would get spooked thinking I was so stalker, so I sent it to Claudia, hoping she would hire you," he stressed, turning his head and smiling.

"Kiss me," she mumbled.

"Gladly," he hummed, pressing a sensual kiss filled with love on her plump lips. "Sleep now, Kitten."

"Don't keep stuff away from me anymore, ok?"

"Would never dream of it."

"THERE'S A DELIVERY FOR YOU, Ms. Kensington," Kate said to her as she walked into the building.

Harriet placed her sunglasses on her head. She was dressed in army green pants and a black tee tucked in paired with the new Chanel bag that Jax got her when they were in Paris. Her hair was down as she walked up to the reception table.

"See you upstairs," Atticus said to her as he entered the elevator.

The two of them just came back from a business lunch, where they just struck a deal with a small graphic design company. Harriet noticed the grand bouquet of wildflowers on the desk. There was a note attached to the bouquet. She flipped it open. Instantly, a grin formed across her face.

Kit,

Happy Thursday, my love.
Just reminding you that I love you.
I will see you at 5.
With love,
Jax

Red began to appear on her cheeks as she read the note. Since the two of them came clean with their secrets, he made her heart flutter even more. Jax was trying to be a good boyfriend, to love her wholeheartedly rather than try to control her. Harriet was proud of him. Jax was trying his best to not act on his normal instincts. He truly was becoming her prince charming.

"Thanks, Kate. Send them up to my office," she told the receptionist.

Harriet continued up to her office, waving at her co-workers as she closed her office door. Atticus sat in her sky-blue chair, legs crossed on her desk, giving her his classic boyish smile. She placed her bag on the chair in the corner, walking around and pouring herself a coffee.

"You have mail," he told her.

"Just place it on the table, Atticus. Coffee?" She pointed to her desk while her other hand held up the coffee pot.

"I'm good. Jax got you flowers?" he questioned.

"Yes, he is truly trying and you can't judge him. He is trying his best to be a good boyfriend," she explained, sitting down on the mustard yellow couch in front of her desk.

"I know."

Harriet grabbed the letter on her desk, flipping it over to read the return address. Her heart dropped. It was from the correctional facility back in Auckland. Her father was trying to contact her.

Anxiety hit her. Why would her deadbeat of a father try and contact her? She was confused. The woman met him once when she finally had access to her file at eighteen. Harriet wanted to see where she came from, and the minute she walked out of that prison, she swore to never talk to him again. He was the definition of trash and an asshole.

At that moment, she made her decision, he simply wanted money. Harriet wasn't even going to bother with opening the letter up. Deep in her heart, Harriet knew that if she read it, she would be in a terrible mood for the rest of the day.

Atticus watched her as she thumbed the envelope. His phone then rang, "Gotta take this," he told her, exiting the room to his office.

Harriet shook her head, swears rolling off her tongue. Simply even holding the beat-up envelope was putting her in a terrible mood. So, her decision was made. Hastily, she threw the paper into a draw in her desk.

HARRIET SAW Jax leaning against a brand-new white Range Rover Sport, round sunglasses were perched on his nose as he embellished his classic, immaculate suit. Jax was biting his lip, watching her as she walked out. Every time he saw her, his cock ached for her touch, for her warmth and love. He craved her every waking minute.

"New ride, mister?" she cocked, kissing him briefly before he pushed the car keys into her hand.

"*Your* new ride," he remarked with a smirk.

Harriet stood there dumbfounded, eyebrows scrunching

as she revised his words. "My new ride?" she asked, slowly, unsure what of his words meant.

He nodded, opening the door for the passenger side and getting in. "Yes, now drive it, baby." Jax gave her a wink as he got into the passenger seat.

Harriet giggled, running to the driver side and getting it quickly. She was met with buttons and a screen, everything that was so different to her shitty Honda back in New Zealand.

Jax laughed, "You turn the dial to go into drive. It is automatic, Kit. Just drive it, ok?"

Harriet panicked a little, trying to adjust her seat and mirrors. "Jax, this car costs more than my salary. I am freaking out a little. I don't know how-"

"If you crash, I'll buy you another one. Now, drive, Kitten." He told her with a chuckle.

Eventually, she placed her foot on the gas and showed her boyfriend how to really drive. Jax navigated her down the roads of London. She still wasn't in complete knowledge of where everything was. They were headed back to his flat for the night.

Harriet enjoyed every second when she drove the luxury vehicle. Jax, who sat beside her, chuckled at everything she did. For one, she would press down the pedal to go faster, speeding close to fifty miles, then freaking out and breaking quickly. It made Jax kiss the dashboard once or twice, but he couldn't care less.

They drove down the driveway to the underground garage, him signalling her where to park. It was right next to the black Maserati he owned and the Jaguar. She parked the SUV, getting out and running to her boyfriend. Jax wrapped his arms around her smaller figure, holding her as she littered kisses across his face.

"I love you. As much as I love the car, you shouldn't-"

"Shhh, you're the love of my life. I want to buy gifts for you," he told her, grabbing her hand as they made their way to the elevator. "I think it's time we eat. Wine and dine you, huh?" He winked as the elevator doors closed.

"You know me too well," she hummed back at him.

They entered the penthouse. Harriet headed to the master bedroom to change out of her work clothes into something more comfortable. Jax followed her up the stairs to the bedroom. The broad man leaned against the archway of the walk-in-closet, seeing her dressed in her undergarments as she eyed herself in the mirror. Harriet did a twirl, watching her body judging it as if she was ashamed of her own skin.

Sometimes, she had moments like this. She would glare herself down and wish that she was smaller and thinner. That the scar on her stomach wasn't present and that her little belly wasn't there or that her thighs were smaller.

"You're beautiful." The voice echoed the room, making her jump. She was in her own little world, and Jax brought her back to reality.

He took long strides to her, standing behind her in the mirror. His larger hands placed themselves on her hips as their eyes met in the mirror. Her body felt the calloused pads of his fingers. Her lover bent his head and began to litter light kisses to her flesh.

Jax kissed every part of her body, focusing on the parts she was not too fond of. His lips brushed her stretch marks and scars, giving extra love to them.

"I love every piece of you, Kit. Don't ever think you aren't enough. You're more than enough," he mumbled against her flesh.

Harriet nodded, watching him love her as if she was the only thing left in the world. His hands dropped down, cupping her womanhood as he went back to applying kisses on her naked flesh.

"Jax," she hummed, leaning back against his chest, head rolled back on his upper chest. Harriet pressed a kiss on his jaw.

He was much taller than her, towering over her with his six-foot-two stature compared to her five-foot-four. Moments like this made it clear how much more height he had on her. Her head hit his collarbone if she was lucky. Otherwise, it'll be his pecs. It made her chuckle internally.

"Move in with me," he whispered as if he was testing the waters. "Cameron is coming home in a week, and you need a place to stay-"

"On one condition, I will go to the manor with you on the days you have the kids. I won't be your secret," she told him.

Jax bit his lip and nodded. "Yes."

"Then, I'll move in with you, handsome," she told him.

Harriet turned around in his hold, looking up to meet his ocean eyes. Jax instantly placed a hungry kiss on her plump lips, letting them explore. They were in need of much atten tion. It made him burst with fulfilment. His Kitten was finally moving in with him.

Jax's fingers ran down the curvature of her spine and to her ass, holding it as they kissed.

"Get dressed, Kit. I'm making dinner," he told her, breaking the kiss and applying a few taps to her bum.

Harriet gave him a cheeky smile, pressing her lips to his

jawline once again as her fingers played with the buttons on his shirt. "What if I want my dessert first?" she purred with a smirk.

"Don't tempt me, Kit," he cautioned sternly. Harriet shook her head as she continued to express her brattiness. "Harriet!" He took her hands in his, spinning her around, so she was out from his grasp. "Clothes, now!"

Jax eyed his closet, the grand masculine room filled with immaculate suits, all clean and sharp hanging in all their glory. There was a dresser draw with all kinds of watches housed in it. He sat on the bench that was in the middle of the room, unclasping his watch as he dressed in his comfier attire. Harriet was long gone. She was in the bathroom removing her makeup.

His lover came in with baggy sweats and her university jumper. She watched him as he strutted around the room changing.

"Like what you see?" he cooed, pure innocence dripping from his words. He stood in front of her as she placed her small hands on his bare chest.

She fingered his unclothed body, the broad shoulders and firm abs, running her fingers down the hard muscle. Jax shivered from her touch as he looked down to her fingers. She admired how well he took care of himself. He constantly went to the gym, ate healthy and overall was in good health. Sometimes, it hurts her to look at him then to look at herself. She wasn't thin, no flat stomach or washboard abs. Her body was purely real. To see him like that either triggered her to be aroused or lowered her self-esteem. Nevertheless, she pushed through her negative thoughts.

Jax took her fingers from his chest, bringing them to his lips and kissing them. He dropped them lightly, placing them at her waist as he turned back to the racks of clothes. Harriet eyed him as he took a pair of sweats and tight grey t-shirt from his dresser, throwing them on effortlessly.

"Dinner time, love," he told her, now dressed in sweats that hung on his hips. Harriet bit her lip when she saw the perfect outline of his muscles with the fitted tee. "Stop gawking," he told her with a roll of his eyes.

"I am not gawking! I am *admiring*," she countered. He chuckled, walking out of the bedroom with her hot on his heels.

"Same thing, isn't it?" he chuckled, taking out pots and pans for dinner.

"No, gawking is like being pervy, Jax."

"And you're not pervy?" He joked with a wink as he walked to the fridge to grab ingredients.

"Oh my God, really? No, I am not pervy, thank you very much," she dismissed, popping a bottle of wine for them to share.

Jax set to work with cooking a meal for the two of them. Harriet didn't even bother to help because the woman was a terrible cook. If she were to touch it, the food would quite possibly end up on fire. She watched him walk around, looking absolutely dashing. The man was cooking up a storm for their meal tonight while sipping the white wine she poured herself.

It was past seven, she was on her third glass of wine that night, and the London sky was beginning to darken.

"I got a letter today," she told him. Jax raised his eyebrows at her, continuing chopping peppers. "From my father."

Jax looked up at her, setting the knife down as he placed his uttermost attention on her. Her voice was shaky, he noticed when she told him those words. "What did he want?"

"I didn't open it. I met that man once, and I swore I would never talk to him again. He is simply a sperm donor to me, not my father. I am guessing he probably wants money. He thinks that he could win his case if he had a good lawyer, so he wants money. Frank has been chasing me down for years, guilting me to send him cash. I just can't believe he found out where I work and sent a letter there."

Jax nodded. "Do you want him to be released?" he questioned, going back to his dinner preparation.

"No. He killed my mother. He deserves to rot in hell," she mumbled.

Jax instantly looked up. Harriet had never talked about her mother before, therefore for her to mumble those words, he was intrigued.

"Tell me more."

"My mother? She had the most beautiful strawberry blonde hair and the kindest soul. Her smile could light up the world. She used to read to me every night in bed. Even though drugs consumed her, she made sure I was educated and knew basic human morals. Unfortunately, she loved drugs more than me. My father used to come around to drop off a package of who knows, he would try to talk to me, but I was more interested in my books. He killed her," she told him. "I will make sure he rots in prison for the rest of his life."

He nodded, dishing up the meal, handing it to her and walking around the counter so he could sit with her.

"If you want to go back to."

"No, New Zealand has nothing for me. I want to stay

here. You're my home, Jax," she whispered, playing with his curls as she began to eat. "This is my new life now."

"Tomorrow," he began minutes later, "I have a family lunch and I want you to come."

Harriet looked up from her meal, eyes bulging. "Really?"

"My brothers will be there, dad, and step mum. We try to have lunch together once a week, but I haven't gone since you came back to me."

Harriet listened to him. He wanted her to meet his family for the first time. The question was, what did he expect from this meeting? His father, Adrian, had money, a shitload of it, and it was all old money. That meant that Jax's brothers, Nolan and Euan, came from that line too. They possibly didn't know the hardship of her life or understand it. Her fears were that they wouldn't accept her or understand her. There is also the fact that she was the one that broke Jax's marriage. It was either going to go great or absolutely dreadful.

"Sure," she responded with a fake smile, "it'll be good to meet them. I will text a quick note to Atticus, asking if I am able to have the day off tomorrow."

Jax's face lightened up, a wide smile plastered as he nodded to her response. He was pleased to know that she genuinely wanted to meet them, the people who he now called his family.

"I also have something to give to you," he told her.

Jax reached behind him, grabbing his wallet from his pocket and pulling out two bank cards: a black, thick credit and a debit, both bolded with 'Private Welfare'. Harriet intuitively knew what this meant. He was giving her access to his accounts.

"I want you to have access to my accounts," he firmly stated pushing the cards across the quartz counter to her.

"Jax, I have my own job. I make my own money. I can take care of myself," she told him. "I may not be able to afford such a grand life, but I can afford a reasonable life," Harriet solemnly said to him eyes glancing over the numbers and digits. How much money was in that account? Most definitely more than hers, she concluded. It made her anxious to have that power in her hand. However, this was the way Jax was. This was his way of making a step in a direction to forever.

"I know," he muttered, "but just take them in case of something. For instance, I asked you to buy food for the house or something regarding the kids. Just take them, do it for me," he pleaded, pushing the cards back at her.

Harriet let out a loud huff and then looked at her lover with blue eyes. "Fine," she stated, "if it makes you feel better, then I will take them."

Jax sent her a wide grin, placing a firm kiss on her cheek before going on to talk about his day.

"Now eat up. We have a long night ahead," he purred, sending her a wink.

26

Harriet sat on the edge navy blue sheets, looking in front of her where Jax pulled his shirt off. She dragged her fingers across his perfectly sculpted body as he leaned over and pressed his lips against her. Her fingers felt the smoothness of his chest mixed with the roughness of his chest hair.

"I want to try something with you," he whispered in her ear as he began to kiss down her neck.

Harriet's eyes enlarged, looking at him blankly. She slowly nodded, unsure to what exactly she was agreeing to now. Jax had his hands on each side of her, leaning towards her as he placed a kiss to her cheek.

"I need you to say something. Use your words, Kit."

"Ok," she muttered, barely hearable.

A small smirk came across his face as he exited the room to the closet. Harriet sat there, breathing slowly. She was unsure of what he could mean by it. Jax was gone for a few seconds before returning. In his hands were a blue butt plug, a vibrator and one of his ties.

It clicked immediately. Jax was going to try something sexual on her. He placed the items on the dresser by the bed. Humming to himself as he got it ready.

"Undress," he commanded.

Harriet stood up, taking the jumper off her body and shimming down the grey sweatpants. Jax was still turned away from her as he grabbed a bottle of lube from the draw. Harriet swallowed, waiting to see what her night entailed.

She sat naked on the bed; hair draped down on her shoulder as she waited patiently. Jax pivoted, no emotion of his face as he eyed her up. He took a few steps to the bathroom, then came back with a hair band. Harriet sat, eye to eye, with his clothed crotch as his fingers raked her hair into a ponytail. He yanked a little, pulling her head to the side, testing it.

"Are you ok?" He asked, looking down at her.

His fingers dragged across her left nipple, teasing her, then grabbed her breast.

"Yes," she responded. Because of her response, Jax pinched her nipple between his fingers. Harriet gasped, taking note that her response was wrong. "Yes, sir," she muttered again.

Pleased with her answer, Jax dropped his hand.

"Safe word?"

"Purple."

He turned around, grabbing the grey tie on the wooden dresser. Harriet sat still, watching him as he took her wrists in his hands, tying them together. He tugged a little, making her jerk towards him.

Jax kissed them before pushing her so that she was lying on the bed. Her back arched on the soft sheets. He pushed her arms up, pinning her wrists, then proceeded to apply light kisses down her body, nipping and sucking her skin.

Harriet released loud moans, but that ended soon. Jax shushed her. His mouth attached itself on her breast, sucking it as his fingers teased her clit. Harriet tried to keep her hands down as he played with her. However, the pleasure was too much and with the next rub and lick, her arms swung and now wrapped around his neck.

Jax instantaneously dropped his attention from her clit and breast, shoving her wrists back up above her head. "Stay, Kitten. Be a good girl," he growled.

Harriet gasped from his rough move, letting out a loud yelp as he pushed her wrists into the mattress, roughly.

"If you're not going to be good and keep it there, I will bring the cuffs out," he threatened, words spitting from his lips.

She nodded slowly, biting her lip, as he went back down to his work. His hands cupped her inner thigh, spreading them open. Light kisses were placed traveling up, one by one, getting closer to her heat. She clenched her walls, needing him to come closer and closer to her core. Her thighs clenched together, but Jax quickly pulled them apart.

"Kit," he warned, looking up from his handiwork to connect their eyes.

"I know to behave," she mumbled.

She knew the game. Harriet couldn't be needy, or else Jax would walk away and leave her there in her own despair. Patience was the key to success.

Jax, once pleased with her response, licked her swollen pink flesh, biting his lip as he came up. Harriet was heavily breathing as he licked his lips.

"Flip," he demanded, "hands and knees, now."

Harriet did what she was told. Ass was in the air as she leaned down on her pinned wrists. Jax, being kind for a second, placed a pillow by her head. Harriet thanked him softly as she got comfortable.

Jax applied a slap across her cheek. The pain vibrated through her system. Another was placed again, the sound echoing the room. Harriet jerked forward.

"This ass," he sternly said, grabbing her cheek roughly, "is mine. I can do whatever I want to this ass." He applied another spank to her ass. Harriet cried, gripping the pillow harder as he applied the pleasurable pain to her body. Ever so slowly, she began to fall in love with his rough side.

His eyes watched as the pale flesh turned a soft red. Smirking, he gripped both her cheeks, pulling them apart as he spat on her pink button. His finger rubbed her asshole, circling it and teasing it, while the other hand kept the cheeks spread apart.

"I am going to destroy it one day."

Harriet swallowed, scared of what that could entail. She gripped the pillow tighter, cheek plastered against the navy.

Jax grabbed the lube on the dresser, squirting some in his hand before placing his attention back to her hole. His fingers rubbed and entered slowly. Harriet gasped.

"Good?" he questioned.

"Yes, sir," she muttered. Jax smirked as her words went straight to his cock, making it twitch. He groaned from it.

He felt the hardening in his joggers, the ache and throb it had for her. It *always* ached for her. It needed to be taken care of, and it needed to be done now. Jax fingered her anus, rubbing her clit at the same time.

Harriet cried, which was music to his ears. He played with her pink button, hoping to expand it enough for the butt plug to go in. Eventually, he was pleased with its behaviour and grabbed the device.

"This is gonna hurt for a second. Ok, Kit?" he told her.

Harriet replied with words, feeling him grip her cheeks, adding more of the water-based lube to her sensitive parts. Then, suddenly, she felt the plug go in, spreading every part of her walls as he pushed it in. The pain was what she noticed first, shooting through her whole body before the pleasure came.

"How are you doing?" he questioned, admiring his own handiwork to her ass.

"Good," she responded, but it was still a mumbled sentence.

"This is for your own pleasure, ok? It will feel really good," he told her, pressing a kiss to her ass cheek.

Harriet didn't respond, instead just hummed. Jax pulled down his joggers, letting them pool by his feet as he stepped out of them. His hand gripped his hardened cock, the pre-cum glistening as he gave it a few pumps before kneeling on the bed. His cock had perfect view to her pussy, however he didn't want to take her that way. He wrapped his arms around her hips, bringing her up so that she was flushed against his chest. Harriet didn't think he would do that. It came to her as a shock.

She gasped as he slid his hands down her navel. There was a poking at her ass, his hardened cock needy as he applied his own love to her. Her head rolled back, contacting his shoulder and leaning back into his hold.

"I fucking love you," he growled.

His hands wrapped to her front, sitting at her lower abdomen. Hand pressed against her heat; his fingers parted her folds as they found their way inside of her. Pushing in, he began to pump his digits just the way she liked it, while his thumb circled her clit. Moans rolled off her lips, which helped his cock's hardening.

She was close. He knew it. Jax pulled his fingers away and adjusted her so that his cock had access to her entrance. Once lined up perfectly, he pushed himself in, his member filling her cavity. Her wetness covered his cock, as he grazed her g-spot. Harriet groaned. He continued to push it, his tip of his cock hitting her cervix. He was so large. Every time they fucked, it took a while before she was used to his size again.

She threw her tied wrists behind her head, hooking around Jax's head, holding herself there while he pumped from behind. His trusts were hard, skin slapping and hitting every perfect spot inside her. Harriet wouldn't admit it, but the plug made things feel completely better. It made her feel the pleasure ten times more. The brushing of his cock against her walls with the butt plug in made her just want to come right there and then. It made her scream internally with every hard thrust of his pelvis. The woman felt like she was riding a good high, her mind in another reality.

Jax, still pumping inside of her, reached over and grabbed the black vibrator next to them. He turned the device on instantly placing it to her clit. Harriet jerked forward as the jolts of vibrations shot through her whole body.

The woman was full blown panting at that point, getting so close to her end with every pump from him and shot of vibration from the device.

"Jax," she mumbled trying to let him know of her close undoing. Her head was still on his shoulder as she let the sinful noises roll off her lips. Her back was flushed with his chest, feeling his hard pecks against her soft skin. The chest hairs tickling her back as he pumped.

"Me too, Kit," he whispered back.

Seconds later, the knot filled her body. The need to release all the tension was dire at that moment. The coil needed to be unravelled as he turned the vibration on higher. The mixture of all that, the plug, his cock and that device, she was a goner.

Harriet began to shake, gripping onto the tie. Her hands were still wrapped around his neck. The fiery passion at the pit of her stomach was recognisable when the pulsing began. She came hard and long, riding her orgasm with his dick inside of her.

She panted. Twenty-seconds later she was done. The woman needed to lie down and catch her breath. Jax felt it, the end of the pulsing walls and quaking body. He took her arms and unwrapped them, turned off the vibrator and threw it to the side. His hands grabbed her waist, pushing her back down onto her hands and knees.

He proceeded to fuck her, slapping her cheeks once again as he picked up his speed. He went harder and faster, feeling his own need to let the tension go. Harriet was jerked back and forth as he pushed harder with his hips.

Jax came, seed spreading inside of her as he released every bit of himself. He came and came hard, holding her hips so that he could get every piece in her. The two of them released heavy pants and moans as they finished up.

He pulled out as she fell onto her stomach. Both bodies were drenched in sweat as he got off the bed. Jax ran his fingers through his hair as he walked around the bed to her figure. Harriet was now on her back as she caught her breath.

"Are you ok?" he asked as he placed his hand on her shoulder.

"Yes," she muttered. Jax smiled, leaning down and placing a kiss on her lips.

"I need to remove..." he stated, pointing to her womanhood.

"Right."

Jax opened her legs grasping the blue device and pulling it out gently. He watched as her asshole expanded, then shrank the minute the device was moved.

He placed the sex toy on the dresser, then went back to his lover untying her wrists and placed a kiss onto her reddened lips.

"I love you," he muttered, pushing the little strands of hair away from her face.

"I love you more," she whispered.

Jax proceeded to get a wet cloth wiping her legs while placing kisses on her thigh. She giggled as he sat between her legs, raking her fingers through his dishevelled curls.

It's crazy to think that her man was into some kinky shit, but then he was the sweetest person to her and her only. It made her smile that he could be this soft when he could also be so controlling and harsh. Nevertheless, he was hers and the word 'love' was not enough to describe the affection and adoration she had for him, and he had for her.

27

The two of them took a bath together. Harriet splashed bubbles at Jax, which resulted in him warning her to stop. She chuckled as he growled each time which followed by his classic, "If you do that again, you will regret it, Kit." She didn't listen. Jax dove at her placing wet kisses and nipping her skin while tickling her.

Harriet sat in her sweats in his walk-in closet, watching him walk around choosing his suit for the next day. Jax was a full course meal, and she couldn't get over it. His bottom half covered, but his top part was on display. Harriet could never get over his god like body. Simply watching him made her drool.

"So, tell me about your dad and step-mum. You haven't told me anything, Jax."

Jax sighed, picking out a grey suit and studying it in front of him. "My dad is a nice man, fifty-nine years old with three boys. He still works, but he works for me, which causes a lot of chaos. He's kind, intelligent and a good lawyer. What else do you want me to say?" he told her, still studying the suit in front of him.

"Your step-mother?"

"Dorothea, we call her Dory. She met my dad when she was twenty, and he was twenty-eight. Came from money, never worked a day in her life. All she does is host parties and go for brunch. She is stuck up but can be lovely when she chooses too."

Harriet tried again, "Brothers?"

"Nolan is younger, twenty-two, and in university for business. Euan is twenty-five and is working as a sports med doctor," he explained, turning around and kissing her lips.

"Ok. They don't sound at all stuck up and spoiled," she retorted, getting up and making her way to the bathroom.

"Kit, it's the life I am in it now. You can't-"

"I know. It is just hard to hear stuff like that or watch your life. I remember I had days where I couldn't feed myself, and I had to choose to pay my overdue rent rather than my weekly worth of groceries. I love you, Jax. It is just hard for me to get used to all of this," she told him, grabbing the duvet and getting into bed.

She quickly checked her phone, seeing the 'ok' for tomorrow from Atticus.

"Kit, I am sorry. Fuck, I should've come to you earlier," he rambled, pulling his hair as he paced. "I should've fucking found you when you were eighteen, but no I had to deal with my family bullshit. I can't believe, fuck," he mumbled. Jax looked at her, "I am sorry you had to go through with that. That isn't fair. We're together now and I am going to take care of you."

"Don't hate yourself. I love you. Come to bed."

He nodded, going to the left side and pulling back the

sheets. Her head was on his chest as he wrapped his arms around her. Their breaths were in sync as they whispered goodnight to one another and mumbled, 'I love you'.

HARRIET WOKE up with a huge amount of anxiety. There was only one other time that she has met with a significant other's family and that was Kai's. Kai's mother, Edith, was the sweetest woman on earth and eventually took the mother role in her life; the two of them were still in contact to this day. In her gut, she truly didn't know how today would go. There was one thing for sure, and that is that Jax and his kids loved her. It doesn't matter what his family thought of her when she had Jax's small family.

His arm was draped over her waist, hand landing right under her breast. Harriet's eyes glanced over her surroundings, seeing the light rays coming in from the large window. Jax was fast asleep, his breaths hitting the back of her neck as his shoulders rose and fell. Moments like this, she felt the happiest. Harriet was in her lover's arms and waking up within his embrace was the best feeling.

Harriet turned in his arms, seeing his closed eyes. She trailed her finger down his chiselled face, sharp jawline, defined cheekbones and light stubble. Harriet was in her complete state of bliss at that moment.

"You're staring," he muttered, digging his head deeper into the pillow.

"Admiring, babe," she corrected, placing a kiss on his nose. Jax smiled, his eyes still closed while his hand moved to her hip.

He was perfect, absolutely perfect. She remembered

when they were younger he had a more boyish look to him, softer facial features and longer hair. Now everything was different. Her fingers dragged down, across his jawline to his collarbone. Jax then began to rub circles on her hip, eyes still closed.

"What time are we going over to your parents?" she whispered.

"Noon, I think. Go back to sleep," he mumbled.

Harriet placed one more kiss on his lips before getting up and walking to the bathroom. Jax opened one eye. He watched her naked figure walk away, eyeing her ass swaying. The man smirked as she headed to the bathroom.

The shower turned on, and Jax was up flinging the duvet off as he walked to her. She was naked in the bathroom. Her hair was in a bun as she washed herself. His hand grasped the handle pulling it open and getting in.

Harriet moaned as she felt his kisses up her back and neck. Light stubble scratched her as they kissed. His hands were wrapped around her waist, giving love to her flesh.

"Good morning," she mumbled.

"Mornin'," he mumbled on her skin.

"Jax, no funny business," she warned, grabbing the soap off the shelf.

"I know."

"Jax..."

THE TWO OF them were in his car driving down the country road to his parent's house. Her leg was bouncing, looking out the window as she tried to distract herself from her own anxiety. Harriet had a massive fear that his family wouldn't accept her, and that was terrifying. Her other fear was that Adrian, Jax's dad set up his marriage, and now she was the reason why it ended. Adrian, in his head, thought she was a homewrecker. It would be hard to change his mind.

Jax noticed her anxiety. His lover was quiet and jumpy. Every time he said something, she would jerk from his words as if she was in a completely different world. His hand grasped her thigh while his other one had hold of the wheel, trying his best to calm her down.

"It will be fine, Kit."

Harriet nodded, turning her attention back to the British countryside. However, she peeked over, seeing him dressed in his grey suit, cufflinks on and a white button up under it; sharp, curt and business-like as per normal. There were little tuffs of his chest hair poking out from the few buttons that were undone. Harriet smirked from his classic look, all masculine and handsome. His hair was gelled back, widow's peak on display as he drove. Jax looked absolutely edible at the moment, he always looked edible.

"Pull over," she commanded sternly.

Jax looked over to her, eyes narrow and eyebrows scrunched. "What?" he chuckled.

"I said pull over."

"Why?" he trailed off. Harriet took the edge of her blush slip dress, sliding it up and exposing her upper thigh. It was paired with a beige cardigan on top. Jax noticed her actions, quickly diverting his attention back to the road.

"Harriet, what game are you playing at?" he mumbled, looking between her and the road.

"Pull over, and I am going to fuck you," she said flatly.

Seconds later, he pulled over the Maserati, placing it in park. Harriet's actions were fast; seatbelt undone faster than him pulling over. She locked the doors and undid the window a slight bit.

Jax was stunned watching her as she prepared the area for car sex. Car sex! That was one thing he had definitely not done before. He felt dumb sitting there not knowing what to do.

"Move your seat back."

Jax pushed his seat back as she climbed over the black console in the car. She straddled him, wrapping her arms around his neck before brushing her lips against his.

"Are we really going to have car sex?" he mumbled, between pecks of her lips.

"Yes," she said flatly, "you look *so* good in that suit." Her tongue gliding up his neck and jaw. Jax let out an awkward chuckle as she got to work.

Harriet's fingers undid his zipper, pushing his boxers down, and pulling his cock out. He hissed from the expose as her hand began to pump it. Jax gripped the door and leather seat as he let out light breaths. This was messy and far dirtier than he would like.

The man was a sex manic! But this was not on his 'to do' list. He had more elegance and etiquette than that, he believed. Harriet had a different state of mind when it came to the deed. She just whipped his cock out like nobody's business and was down for a little car sex on the side of the highway! Call her the sex manic!

Harriet pushed herself up, hand gripping the top handle as she bundled up her dress. Her panties were moved to the side, and she pushed herself onto his cock. A hiss escaped his lips when he felt her arousal, hips beginning to rock as she fucked him. Jax grasped her hips, trying to help her with a pace. The position was awkward. She either kept hitting her head on the ceiling, or her back would hit the wheel. It didn't help that he had the smallest car in the world.

"Why the windows-"

"Condensation," she muttered between a moan as she rocked herself harder on him, bouncing and trying her best not to hurt herself.

Jax just watched her with wide eyes as she went at it there and then. It shocked him, but he was enjoying every moment.

"I see you've done this before..." he trailed on.

"Multiple times," she responded, kissing him as she quickened her pace.

Minutes later, the two of them reached their highs. He gripped her hips harder as he pushed her down while his orgasm rang through his body.

The car was filled with their moans and groans. The two of them unravelled the tension held in their bodies.

"I just had car sex," he mumbled to himself as she climbed back over to her side on the car. She made it look so easy. The two fucked and she was back in the passenger seat. Jax tucked his cock back his boxers and zipped his trousers up. The man quickly gave himself a quick check in the rear-view mirror, spitting in his hands to fix his dishevelled hair.

"I just fucked you in my car. I am truly a teenage boy," he muttered.

"You really never fucked someone in the car before?" she asked, astonished. The man had done way more sexual shit than her, and he had yet to screw in a car.

"No, I am a proper man. A bed, bath, shower, just anywhere that isn't in the car," he rambled as he drove off again.

"So, if I were to ask you to have sex with me in a club's bathroom, would you?" she chuckled.

Jax grimaced as they headed back on route to his parent's house. "Absolutely not," he grumbled.

"You are really not that fun," she mumbled with a shake of her head, chuckling.

"*Baby*, I am the definition of fun," he teased, winking.

She hummed, rolling her eyes.

"When did you have car sex then?" he asked, looking over.

"I was a bit of a whore in high school. The minute I turned sixteen-"

"Don't. Stop there. I don't want to hear that," he growled, his foot pressing more on the gas.

"You asked," she told him innocently. "My honeymoon lasted for three minutes and thirty-four seconds," she rambled, "Kai and I got married in the town hall and then had sex in his shitty Holden Ute from 1990s. That fucking car's stink still sticks with me to this day, please tell me your honeymoon was better," she grimaced.

"Greece. Three weeks in the sunshine. However, we were fucking other women the whole time and barely uttered a word to one another."

"You win."

"And three minutes and-"

"Yes, that man couldn't last long," she responded. The two of them laughed.

THEY ARRIVED at his family home, and the word 'exquisite' didn't do it justice. It was cobblestone and castle-like, with towers and pointed roofs. There were wide windows and grand gardens. British and gorgeous with the best flora around it. Harriet was in awe. England just kept getting better.

"So, you lived here?" she questioned as he parked beside the multitude of luxury vehicles; black Mercedes AMG, white Audi Q6, black Jaguar SUV and a neon green Aston Martin. She was completely shocked with the line of expensive, high luxury vehicles.

"For a year then I went to Oxford for university," he told her as he backed up into the parking space.

"*You went to Oxford?* How come I didn't know that?" she questioned; mouth open as he parked the car on the gravel road.

"Never came up I guess."

"*Oxford*," she hummed, still not believing it. Jax, her Jax who hated school growing up, went to Oxford. A snicker escaped.

The two of them exited the vehicle, meeting up and holding hands.

She walked up the few stairs in her heeled chunky black Chelsea boots. Jax opened the large wooden door. Upon entering, a double stairway was in front of her, chandelier with crystals hovering above her and beautiful artwork lining the walls. It felt like a museum, the old and new mixing together, but still priceless and beautiful.

Jax didn't pay attention to anything, pulling her to the right archway and walking through the hallway. Harriet was hauled by him, but she didn't pay attention of where she was going. Instead, she stared at all the artwork that lined the walls and decorative wallpaper. The inside was purely romanticism with white and gold finishing, chandeliers with crystals and feministic furniture. It was much lighter than the dark exterior.

"Dad, Dory?" Jax called out. Three Australian Shepherds ran up to them, all different colours and patterns.

One of them, the tan and white, jumped on her and kissed her all over.

"Down, Luna," Jax said, pushing her down. "That was Luna. Lola is the blue and white one, and Leo is black and white," he told her. The two of them started playing with the dogs, getting wet kisses.

"Jaxon Fletcher?" a female London British accent was heard. Harriet looked up from on her knees, petting the dogs to find an older woman with greying black hair in a bob and thick framed black glasses.

"Dory." Jax walked up to her, give her a quick embrace before diverting his conversation back to his girlfriend.

The woman was nursing a martini and wore a white dress. She had minimal makeup, but bright red lips. This must be his stepmother.

"Where's dad?" Jax asked, kissing her cheeks before going back to stand next to Harriet, taking her hand.

"Poker game in the mancave," she responded. The greying woman shifted her attention to the brunette. "Hi, sweetheart, you must be Harriet," she smiled.

"It's nice to meet you," Harriet replied so sweetly.

"Likewise," is all she muttered before turning her attention back to her stepson, "Nolan and Euan are playing poker with your father. Get yourself a whiskey and join. I am in the sunroom if Harriet wants to join." Then she turned away.

"She hates me," she muttered, taking Jax's bicep in her hand.

"No, she doesn't. Come on, let me introduce you to everyone," he told her and placed a firm kiss on her cheek.

Once again, greeted with another sparkling chandelier, black and white retro tiles paired with the classic curved spiral staircase. She couldn't get over it, the glitz and glam of his lifestyle.

'He lived here after he left. Going for afternoon tea and dinner parties. He probably had a horse.'

No, he definitely didn't have a horse. If he did, she would have lost it.

The two continued down the long hallway. However, Harriet stopped in her tracks when she saw the particular boyish smile that she fell in love with. The picture must've been taken months after he moved here, his mop of curly brown hair and gleaming yet sad smile. It was maybe a few shorts weeks after he left her, and the sparkle that once was in his eyes was long gone in that moment. He was lost without her, and it was clearly shown in the picture.

"I was seventeen. Two months after I arrived," he told her, looking up to the picture.

"The boy I fell in love with," she muttered to herself as she touched the photo. "You were such a cute boy, all smiley and those dimples," she awed.

"You saying I am not cute anymore?" he says, acting all offended yet joking around with her. She chuckled from his words and began to walk down the darkened hallway. Doors upon doors were being seen.

"You're always cute to me," she winked, pulling him for a quick kiss, "and sexy," she pecked him again, "and I will absolutely love you forever and a day," she pecked him again.

Harriet walked into the entertainment room. Deep red walls and with minimal lighting.

She spotted three figures hovering over a table full of cards and cigar smoke filled the room. The three men sat around the table, chattering amongst one another as they smoked and played.

There was an older man, greying hair that was long and curly with a beard and a wrinkled face; his father, she clicked. The two other men were much younger than Jax. One had chestnut brown hair, clean shaven with a baby face while the other one had darker brown hair, not as dark as Jax, but darker than the other guy. He had more of a chiselled face with light stubble and shorter hair. All three of them wore a suit, an awfully expensive suit. It was if this life had a dress code: look your best, look expensive and always hold some type of addictive merchandise in your hand.

The three men looked up to where Jax and Harriet were. Their faces rapidly began to gleam as they noticed Jax.

"Jax!" the chestnut hair said, "and unknown woman..."

'Oh, did he forget to mention me?'

Harriet watched her surroundings as the three men looked at her. Jax didn't mention her, and that hurt slightly.

His hand was still placed on her lower back as he began to talk. "This is Harriet, my girlfriend." The three of them slowly nodded. "Adrian, my dad, the one with darker hair is Euan, and that asshole is Nolan".

"The lady Jax left Claudia for..." Nolan muttered, nodding his head slowly examining her.

'Ouch!'

"Nolan," his father warned. Harriet stood there awkwardly, looking back up at Jax for some type of help.

"Hi, Harriet. Pleasure to meet you. Euan," the darker-haired man turned his chair around dropping his cards on the red velvet and shook her hand.

"Are we playing poker?" she asked.

Euan nodded. "Yes, we are. Do you play?"

She chuckled lightly. "Yes, I do. I *always* win. Played throughout college, kept me alive - the cash from the game. I ran my own-"

"Harriet," Jax warned. Her eyes bulged, looking at him weirdly.

Euan was the older brother, more down to earth and a sports doctor. The man seemed sweet. The room was still filled with cigar smoke, which made her insides churn and crave for the smoky flavour. This was not a good place for someone who is trying to quit to smoke.

Euan laughed it off. "I see. Well, we should play sometime, Harriet." He nodded her way.

Jax looked between the two and leaned towards her, lips by her ear as he whispered, "Go join Dory in the sunroom." Harriet gave him a look.

"I thought I could play," she mumbled.

Jax sighed, running his fingers through his hair.

"Poker here is more of the male game, next time, Kit."

She scoffed lightly and tu'rned away.

'Unbelievable!

"It's a pleasure to meet you all," she said, giving them a firm nod. However, the males ignored her.

"Come join a game, Jax. We need to beat this bastard, won the last three times," Euan said, nodding to Nolan.

Jax chuckled then leaned into Harriet again. "I love you, go have some drinks with Dory. I'm going to have a game." He placed a kiss to her cheek before pulling out the abandoned chair.

Harriet nodded, watching as Jax took a cigar from his father and sitting down the velvet round table.

'Well, fuck. Where the fuck was the sunroom?'

She turned around, walking out of the mancave and started wandering. Harriet met Dory in the living room, the sunroom must be there. She wandered back through the empty halls, trying her best to remember where she came from.

Harriet heard British laughter echoing a room as she walked towards it. She was met with Dory and another older woman across from her. She had blonde hair and a sweet smile. Her attire was much like Dory; elegant, sparkly and expensive.

"Hi," she muttered as she walked in.

Dory, still nursing a martini, turned her attention behind her, spotting the brunette. The unknown woman was tiny. Her hair was pulled into a French twist, the greying obvious. Dory was more into the blacks and whites, while this other woman had beige and soft pink tones covering her body.

The two of them looked up to her, unimpressed looks on their faces. "Harriet, meet Cynthia, Claudia's mother. Cynthia, meet the woman who ruined your daughter's marriage," she stated flatly. Harriet was gobsmacked. The introduction was ruthless and evil. Cynthia raised her eyebrows at her, studying her as if she was some outlander. The look of disgust on Cynthia's face was something she had never seen before. It made her more than uncomfortable as if she was spitting on her with her eyes. Taking a deep breath, Harriet sat down on the couch.

The sunroom was gorgeous. It was made of glass. She could see the back garden and the lake. It was an art piece itself, the view. She could sit here and watch it for hours.

"You are covered in tattoos," Dory finally spoke with disgust when Harriet pulled down her cardigan. The summer heat was getting to her. The woman spat each word with pure villainy.

"I am," Harriet replied.

"I believe tattoos make you look trashy, cheap. I cannot have that associated with the family name."

"Guess I am trash then," she replied, sending her a smirk and a glare. Turning her attention away from the witch stepmother and making eye contact with Cynthia. She also held a long glare.

"How long have you and Jax been together?" she asked flatly, figuring out if there was an affair.

"Two months. I think."

"So, you two got together when my daughter and him were still together?"

"I-"

The two of them laughed together as they looked at Harriet. All she could think was, it was time to abandon ship and right now.

"My stepson brought you back. Claiming you're the one and that Claudia and he are over. You broke their marriage. What do you even do for a living besides breaking families up?" Dory asked, leaning against the couch, perching herself as she studied the young woman.

Harriet blinked a few times. She was a witch, created by the devil himself. "I work as a personal assistant at a publishing house. The AVA House, to be precise," she exclaimed.

"Atticus, what a gentleman? That man is truly edible. I would most definitely lick ice cream off him," Dory smirked, biting her lip and doing a little shimmy. Then she went back to her witch-like self. "What do your parents do for a living?" she interrogated.

Harriet took a breath. "I never had parents."

"Aw, you're an orphan. How sweet," she chuckled. "Jax must love the broken ones, something to fix. I am guessing you don't come from money." Harriet shook her head. Dory leaned closer to her, eyes glaring into hers as her voice became low, stern. "Our family is about reputation, Harriet. The months you have been with Jax has truly *fucked* this family up. Magazines! Papers! Divorce! If you want to be accepted, drop the white trash act and grow up."

Harriet sat there with her mouth open. "Excuse me?" she whispered yelled. "I don't know who you think you are, but I am not *trash or cheap or a whore*, if that is what you're implying. I am a woman. I come from a low income background, but I am not here to ruin your family image if that is what you're asking. I am not here to screw Jax for cash or fame. I love him so please keep your comments to yourself," she berated at her.

Dory sipped her martini, raising her eyebrows. "Are you done?" Harriet stayed quiet. "Leave my fucking sight."

Harriet got up, pulling her cardigan back on as she walked out of the sunroom. She turned around, looking at the two women. With a smirk to her lips, she mouthed 'cunt' to Dory.

The brunette walked around the manor. There were doors upon doors that lead to who knows what. She stopped, climbing the stairs and sitting on them. Harriet looked around her. This wasn't her, this life. It was too much, too much drama, pressure and toxicity.

Jax appeared through the archway, hands in his suit

pockets as he looked at her. There was a sad smile on his face when he saw her all alone.

"Did you win?" she asked about the poker game.

Jax ignored her. "You called my stepmother a cunt?" he asked firmly, arms crossed, and a single eyebrow cocked. He didn't take a step close to her, stayed six feet away as he gave her this look, a look she has never seen before. It was anger but held concern. He acted all offended by her words. "Don't call her a cunt, *Harriet.*"

Jax called her by her first name, and that stung. He truly was mad at her that moment.

"Jax, she called me white trash!" she argued back.

"With an attitude like that-"

"Don't, honestly don't," she mumbled, getting up and walking towards him. "I am your girlfriend, not your intern or fuck buddy. You need to stick up for me. This life is something I could never perfect. Sitting here in a manor, watching women feed off gossip and drama while men drink and fuck other women who aren't their wives...this isn't a good life. Jax, they *changed* you." She shook her head, jabbing her finger into his chest. Jax felt a firm glare at her as she whispered a curse word under her breath and walked towards the door.

"Where are you going?" he asked, grabbing her wrist.

"I am going to have a cigarette," she muttered, pulling his hand off her.

A PIECE of her hated this, the glam, the glitz and snootiness of this lifestyle around her. It would take years for her to get used to this life, but she could never be a woman who enjoyed it. She'd rather go surfing and hiking than stay in some five-star hotel with all you could drink and eat for a week. Jax was a man who liked people being a service to him, while she was brought up to be the service.

Harriet was outside, sitting on the steps that led into the castle home. Huffing and puffing the smoke, she watched the sunshine. The bright rays hitting the forest and rolling hills of the British countryside, it made her think. The things you sacrifice for love, they say or rather, the things you do for love. She loved him. She truly did.

Harriet lit the cigarette as she dragged the smoke through her lungs. A figure came and sat next to her, hands on his knees as he mumbled, "Give me one." Jax, she instantly recognized the voice. Harriet handed him the box of cigarettes, helping him light it as they watched outside.

"You said you don't smoke."

"I used to. I am sorry. I should've-"

"It's ok," she smiled at him.

The two of them smoked the cigarettes, silence settling for a minute before he talked. "I want to spend the rest of my life with you," he mumbled.

Harriet looked over to him. "Then do it," she whispered.

"I keep fucking shit up, don't I?" he mumbled.

She looked over, his hair dishevelled now, and with a solemn face he looked outward. The cigarette was between her fingers, but with her free hand she placed it on his cheek turning his gaze to her.

"I love you."

He smiled, nuzzling into her hand and pressing a kiss to her palm. "I didn't know Cynthia would be here."

"It is ok."

The two of them entered the house, hearing the chatter from the dining room. Jax grabbed her hand as she wrapped her other one around his bicep. She leaned into him as they turned the corner towards the dining room. Everyone sat drinks in hand as food littered the table.

Jax pulled the chair out for her in the far end, away from Dory. He sat beside Harriet. Instantly, he fell into the normal talk with his brothers. Harriet stayed quiet, not knowing what to say. Adrian was at the head of the table, the two of them at the end.

Minutes, it had been minutes, and no one had uttered a word to her. She tried to join the conversation. However, nobody seemed to care of her presence.

"Sorry, I am late!" Claudia exclaimed as she hurried into the room, kissing her mother's cheek and Dory before sitting directly across from Harriet and Jax. "Hi," she mumbled looking at the brunette, stunned to see her there. Harriet replied with a warm smile.

Jax gave a look to his lover, noticing her discomfort. Harriet hadn't seen Claudia since she fired her multiple weeks ago. His hand came and rest on Harriet's thigh. She felt his hardened grip of assurance then proceeded to go back to his conversation.

"Since everyone is here, let's eat!" Adrian exclaimed.

Jax dished her something up, different meats and salads, but Claudia held a glare to her the whole time.

"Claud," Jax mumbled, making her to break the glare from Harriet.

"The kids are with the nanny if that is what you're

asking," she responded before drinking the white wine in front of her.

"Harriet!" Adrian said. "Let's talk about you, as you're new. So, tell me more about yourself! Jax mentioned you went to university."

Harriet looked up, clearing her throat. "Um, yes. I went to University of Auckland and studied social work with a minor in English lit."

The man hummed. "Why social work?"

"She is an orphan," Dory quipped, sipping her martini.

"Really," he mused, "and you're from New Zealand? Jax was born there and was in the system for seventeen years," he told her.

Jax stayed still, and then it hit her. Did he forgot to mention about them? His hand dropped from her thigh as he took a sip of his whiskey.

"Yes, Jax and I-"

"Dad, the Paris settlement is going really well. Clifford took it, and we are ready to take action when we want," Jax cut her off.

Harriet blinked aimlessly as she turned her eyes to her boyfriend.

"Enough about work and business, son. I am very curious about this woman. After all, she did ruin your marriage. A perfectly good marriage might I add," he pointed out. Claudia scoffed as she drank her wine.

There it goes again, the lack of acceptance from his family. Adrian still cheered for Claudia and him.

"Where did the two of you meet?" The older man asked, fork in hand, as he glared at the couple.

"She was our nanny," Claudia cut Jax off as he was about

to speak. Harriet was in the middle of all of this, watching this unfolded.

"You had an affair with your house worker? Jaxon Fletcher, I raised you better than that! You mess with the prestige ones not the bloody work!"

Harriet had enough. Downing her whole glass of wine, she wiped her mouth roughly. The anger that flowed through her was unbearable. Was he embarrassed of her? The little white lie rolled off his lips like nobody's business. He said he didn't care about their thoughts, but this showed otherwise.

"No, you didn't," she scoffed, looking at Adrian. "You didn't raise him, so don't flatter yourself. *I raised him*. We met when I was four, and he was seven in the same orphanage. We fell in love in our teen years for *you to take him away* from *me*. Thirteen years later, Jax found me and brought me back to him, as *I am the love of his life*. I cannot stand this bullshit of a family right now. Lies are rolling off your lips. You say that reputation needs to be kept when you had no idea how dysfunctional your own son's marriage was. The two of them were having affairs left, right, and centre!" she yelled.

Jax gripped her arm, trying to pull her back down, but she shrugged it off.

"You call yourself parents, and I may not have them, but I know shit load more about good parenting than you. I love Jax, I really do, but I truly could never love this lying, so called family. I raised Jax, you didn't. So don't take credit. You fucked everything up, you changed him to be part of this toxic family and I am done. I have tried to be kind to you and tried to be part of this family, but I can't," Harriet got up, throwing the napkin that was on her lap onto the table as she left the room.

Jax watched her leave, however she turned on her heels and came back. All eyes were on her.

"Oh, Dory, back to what we were talking about before I called you a cunt. You wanted to know about my parents. My mother was crack addict, and my father is in jail for selling my mother the crack she died from. I am the definition of white trash, so thanks for reminding me," she retorted with a smirk. Her gaze turned to Jax who had his jaw clenched and fists balled up. "I need the keys, Jax."

He shook his head, getting up and gripping her arm, yanking her to the other room. Jax was furious, seeing red as he pushed her onto the chair in the kitchen. He was pacing, hands in his hair and dragging them down his face. Harriet tried to get up.

"*Sit* your fucking ass down, Miss," he roared, pointing at her.

Harriet swallowed the lump in her throat, realizing what she had done. Jax placed his hands on the counter, leaning on it as he looked directly at her. He let out a very heavy breath before he slammed his hand on the counter.

Harriet jumped a little, waiting for the wrath that was about to be heard.

"You're a menace," he spat.

"You *really* didn't tell your family-"

"Does not give you the right to tell all my secrets to my family. They are secrets for a reason, Harriet. My dad doesn't know that Claudia and I had affairs. The way you behaved is unacceptable," he belittled, taking a step to her.

"They treat me like I'm trash!" she screamed at him.

"Well, it doesn't help that you come from it, Harriet. Family is everything-"

"Your mother was a whore, Jax! She fucked your father for cash!"

"And your mother fucked your father to pay off a drug deal. We are from trash, but I have reinvented myself from that. You should try it!" he screamed at her. Harriet rolled her eyes. "Don't fucking roll your eyes at me, and don't give me that look. You're going to call it quits, huh?" She clenched her teeth. "You know what, I call it. *We are done*," he spat through his teeth, walking out of the room.

"Disinheritance my ass, Jax! You told me don't care about the opinions. Fuck you, you lying bastard!" she screamed, slamming her fist and running a hand through her hair tugging at it.

28

The two of them got in the car. An awkward silence arose as he drove back to London. Harriet let out a loud sigh looking back over to him.

"You don't mean it, do you?" she whispered.

Jax clenched his jaw a small groan escaping from his lips as he focused his attention back on the road. He knew the minute he looked over at her, he would be smitten all over again. The man would pull the car over and give her his love but punish her for her actions. However, he clenched the wheel harder. She watched his Adam's apple bob from him swallowing the lump in his throat.

"No," he eventually responded, "but you just fucked shit up."

Harriet reached over for his hand, but he pulled away from her reach.

"Jax-"

"*Harriet*," he sneered, "you just embarrassed me in front of my whole family."

"I feel like the minute we get close to being good

together, something happens. One of us then gets mad, and we 'end'." She did air quotations.

He groaned, "You drive me fucking insane, woman."

The car ride was silent after that.

JAX SLAMMED the door to their flat and was hot on her trail as she made her way to the fridge for something to drink. Once close enough, he grabbed her bicep and turned her around.

Harriet spun around her back hitting the counter as he pushed her against it. His lips hungrily attacked her, nipping and biting the pink flesh as his hands gripped her ass. Harriet released a loud yelp.

"Jax-"

He attacked her lips again as he pushed her dress up. His hand cupped her heat as he bit her flesh. Harriet gripped his hair, arms around his neck as he devoured her. She felt her arousal, but he was rougher than normal.

When they did have aggressive sex, he made sure to check up on her, to ask her if she was ok in that moment, and always held love in his eyes. Not a single word was spoken from him now, and his eyes held darkness.

Jax's hand was still on her heat, cupping it before moving her panties to the side and slipping in a finger. She clenched around it, walls tightening around his digits. The minute he felt her wetness, he pulled out.

Harriet whined from the emptiness, gripping his curls harder to pull his face away from her. What she was met with weren't the gentle eyes of Jax. There was something much more sinister and darker. Anger. He was angry at her, and she didn't recognise who he was at that moment.

Jax turned her, pushing her back down onto the counter as he shoved her dress up. His hands went to his zipper, undoing it, and pushing his boxers down. His hand jerked his cock, applying a few pumps before slipping Harriet's underwear to the side and slamming in.

Jax's hands went to her hair, gripping it as he fucked her, thrusting hard with all his might into her wetness.

Harriet was stunned, swaying with his motions with every pump. The man was fucking her from behind like she was some slut and Harriet despised it. Harriet hated every second.

"Jax," she yelled.

He pulled her hair harder and pushed further instead. She whimpered from his roughness. Jax continued, thrusting with anger into her.

"Purple," she muttered. However, he didn't listen. "Purple!" she yelled. Jax didn't flinch. "Purple, Jax, fucking purple!" She slapped his side repeatedly.

He heard it, dropping the clump of hair in his hand and removing himself.

Harriet turned around with tears on her cheeks as she pushed her dress around fixing it. The woman felt like a slut, a cheap whore that a man paid a little penny for. She wiped hot tears off her face, glaring at him.

Jax placed his manhood back into his trousers before grabbing his keys and leaving. The sound of the door slamming echoed through the penthouse. Harriet was left there shocked and shaking from what had occurred.

CHEAP BOOZE WAS the first thing Harriet smelt before she heard the banging echoing through the flat. She heard his swears as he slammed the door.

Harriet was lying on the couch with a blanket wrapped around her body as she heard his entrance. Jax threw his keys on the counter banging it with his fist before walking to the cabinet to grab more alcohol.

Her feet hit the cold hardwood floor as she wrapped the blanket closer around her. She waddled over to him slowly wary of his anger. Her shoulder touched the wall as she leaned against it. Jax poured himself another glass of whiskey downing it in one swift motion.

She noticed how his buttons were undone to the midpoint and his chest hair was prominent as he gripped the glass harder. He let out a loud sigh, fingers in his hair pushing the curls back. His hair was a mess, more messy than normal. The curls were going in every direction. His eyes looked up spotting her in the corner. The woman swallowed as his eyes were still filled with anger.

"Where were you?" she whispered.

"With an old friend," he muttered, throwing the glass in the sink. It smashed making her jerk.

He took a step to her, but she shook her head. "Stay away," she warned.

"Harriet, can we talk?" he asked again taking another step.

The stench wafted to her, the smell of cheap perfume, smoke and booze. She shuttered.

"You're mad. We can talk when you're not mad," she whispered, before moving away from him to go to the sink. The glass was scattered in the stainless-steel box.

She got a paper towel and picked up the pieces with it,

walking to the trash, and dropping it in. He watched her clean his mess.

"I am not mad."

"You are," she mumbled back. "I am sorry that I fucked shit up today, but you lied about me. I will always be the other woman in your parents' eyes. I will always be white trash and a cheap whore," she whispered hissing when she cut herself. Her eyes were locked on the sink, gripping her hand. She watched the blood coming from the small cut sighing as she went back to his mess.

He was quick on his feet. "Good grief, woman, you are bloody hurting yourself," he told her, taking her hand in his.

Jax took a paper towel and pressed it on the cut applying pressure. "I don't care what they think," he whispered back. "I am done conforming to their beliefs of how I should live," he told her kissing her hand. "I am proud you stuck up for yourself. You're right, disinheritance my ass. I don't need to be the star child in their eyes."

"I am glad you have come to your goddamn sense, Jax, but you *fucked* me like a whore," she whispered, watching as he removed the paper towel to see if it was still bleeding.

He grimaced from her choice of words. "Don't call yourself that."

"Jax."

"I am sorry. I really am, Kit."

"Do you want to be with me?" she whispered the dreaded words that were circling in her head for a while now. "We keep fucking us up, Jax. We keep destroying our relationship repeatedly, so I am asking you, do you want us to be together?" she pleaded, wiping her eyes.

"Yes," he said almost offended by her words.

"I fucked up with your family today."

"They were never really my family in the first place, Kit. You have always been my family. I want you and my kids to be a family. I want to marry you and see you grow with my child. I want *you*," he responded, tucking her hair behind her ear.

Harriet bit her lip removing her hand from his grip and dropping it to the side.

"Don't ever disrespect me like that again," she warned, "I will leave you if you do."

He nodded at her words kissing the side of her head. It pained him to hear those words.

"You're right," he mumbled against her hair, "my family are stuck up pieces of shit." His hands cupped her cheeks looking into her eyes. "You and me, Kit, forever and a day. I promise I will never disrespect you ever again."

Harriet nodded. "You better not. Now let's go to bed. The couch wasn't comfortable."

JAX WOKE up at six in the morning. He rolled over in the bed to grab his phone that was going off. He let out a loud groan as he reached towards the ringing device on the bedside table. Harriet stirred a little in her sleep but still was snuggled up against his side.

"Hello," he grumbled.

"Jax, it's Dorothy. I need you to come in. Clifford is throwing a fit right now," his PA told him. He let out another groan as he pushed the covers off.

"Ok, on my way."

He got up looking behind him at the sleeping angel. She

looked so peaceful in that moment. He leant over and placed a kiss on her lips.

Her hand cupped his cheek and her eyes gently fluttering open. "Where are you going?" she whispered voice groggy with sleep. It was too early for her.

"Work, Kitten," he mumbled, kissing her lips again.

"Ok, when will you be back?" she asked, sleep laced in her voice and eyes closing again.

"Soon," he kissed her again. "Let's have a lazy night movie, take out, and wine," he smiled as he turned his head to kiss her palm.

"Ok, I love you."

He smiled kissing her lips again as he sauntered off to the closet grabbing his suit and tie. Then he headed off.

Harriet rolled back in the navy sheets letting sleep take over once again. However, that didn't last long.

After what felt like minutes, but truly was hours, there was a banging on the door. A loud echoing banging as a female voice began to yell. Harriet grimaced rolling over as she got up grabbed her robe and headed down to the door.

Who desperately wants Jax on a Saturday morning? What is all the racket? She was genuinely enjoying her sleep.

Harriet pulled the robe closer to her body, as she yanked the door open. She was met with an incredibly angry Claudia and two of her favourite kids in the world.

"Where's Jax?" she grumbled, raising her eyebrow at her.

"Work..." she trailed.

"Well, he is supposed to take the kids today, and you're here. So here!" She passed Harriet a very tired Caleb. Ember was already wrapped around her leg.

"Hey," she muttered, leaning against the doorframe, "Yesterday...was it a..."

"It was f-ing hilarious. I have never seen such disgust on Dory's face. Priceless. However, you did butcher your meeting, and I genuinely believe you won't ever come back from it," she exclaimed. "Go you for calling Dory the c word that was really good. The woman deserved it."

"Jax was so mad," she told the dirty blonde.

"Jax is always mad though, at everything. The only time I have ever seen him not clenching his jaw and yelling is when he looks at you. As much as I hated him for the longest time, we both deserve happiness, and he has that with you. He loves you, Harriet. He truly does."

"I love him a lot. He has always been my Jax since we were kids. Though now my Jax isn't running from the law and has a lot of money. I love him and it's hard to navigate our relationship because of our differences," she told her.

Claudia sighed, "You sound like you need a friend, a girl talk. Do you want to talk?" Harriet nodded.

"Will you give me weed and then kiss me?" she joked.

"No, but I know the new Jax, and you know the old one, so we let's chat."

"I would like that. Come in."

Harriet took a step forward letting the mother and her children come in before closing the door. She headed to the kitchen as Claudia followed.

"Coffee, tea?" she asked.

"Tea, please," Claudia replied.

Harriet walked around the dark kitchen turning the kettle on as she grabbed two juice boxes for the kids. Ember was still by Harriet's hip trying her best to help as she manoeuvred around the kitchen. Caleb was back in his mother's arms asleep as always.

"What is happening with Jax?" Claudia asked, sending her a small, sad smile.

"No matter how hard we try to be together, it is as if the world doesn't want us to. We fight, we fuck," she whispered the curse word, "then we forgive and forget. It's this cycle," she told to the woman sighing with a roll of her eyes as she placed the mug in front of her with some biscuits.

"It is Jax's way or the highway," she told her. "The man isn't used to someone not listening to him. You tend to not listen. You won't say, 'yes, sir' and do what he wants. That angers him."

Claudia pulled out an iPad from her bag, handing it to Ember who then ran into the living room. Claudia got up walking to the couch and setting her sleeping son on it draping a blanket across him.

"Do you know about Paris?" Harriet asked, sitting next to the blonde at the kitchen counter nursing her cup of tea.

"Did he take you to Paris?" Claudia questioned with a grimace. Harriet nodded. "Oh honey, Jax is the stupidest man I know. Look, Jax loves you. I remember when we first met, he told me that there is this woman named Kitten that will always be his number one in life and that he will find her and be with her eventually. I was too high to understand what that meant, but I know now. Jax wants to be with you and to love you. That man looks at you like you are the only thing he needs to survive. However, he just doesn't know the difference between right and wrong."

Claudia had a point. Jax had always been a handful since they were kids. The two had their fair shares of fights.

"He wasn't exactly like this as kids, but we did have issues. I was too young and naive to realize it."

"The man is going to marry you, Harriet. He loves you.

He just needs to figure out his bullshit before he does. The divorce is close to being done, just weeks away. I signed the papers after I saw the way he was with you. Him and I both deserve to be happy," she said, then muttered, "sorry for firing you, by the way."

Harriet laughed. "It is ok. Though, I did think that maybe he lied and you two didn't have an open marriage and that... it is ok though. I love my new job."

"He thinks with his dick, all men do. Just try to take away the control, and he will realize how fun it is."

Harriet let those words circle her brain: take away the control. Jax would go completely crazy over that. A smirk appeared.

"Yeah, ok," she mumbled more to herself.

Claudia snickered, "You're thinking sexual."

"Quite possibly."

"I like you. You're funny. You may have broken my family up, but we've always been broken whether we admitted it or not. He loves you and love conquers all." Harriet nodded at her.

Jax loved her, and that is all that mattered. He loved her and wanted to be with her.

"I should leave. I have a plane to catch. I am always here if you need a friend, Harriet. Jax is a complicated character." She placed her hand on her shoulder, making eye contact.

"See you around."

HARRIET WAS DANCING in the kitchen that night. A glass of wine was in her hand as she swayed her hips to the rhythm of the music. Jax had yet to arrive home, and the kids were still in her care, which she absolutely loved. The one thing that was burning on her mind was, they needed to tell the kids about their relationship. The two of them were getting serious.

Ember was giggling along as she ate a slice of cucumber. Harriet made mac and cheese for dinner. The kids were in love with her cooking, which she took it as a compliment. The woman wasn't a cook whatsoever. Caleb was smirking as she sang to him, dancing around and shaking her ass. The kids were in fits of laughter.

Her phone rang. She halted her actions, walking out the room to answer Jax's call.

"Hi, bub."

"Hey, sorry for leaving so early, Kit, work called. I am on my way home. So, you want me to pick something up for dinner?" he asked. She could hear the bustling of traffic.

"Um, sure. The Italian place you took me that one time was really good."

"Ok, I will be home in an hour or so. I love you."

"I love you too."

She hung up, pocketing her phone into her sweatpants and pushed her glasses up her nose. The kids watched some television in the kitchen when she returned, hearing the babbles from Caleb as he shoved his food in his mouth. She chuckled at the cheese sauce smeared on his face.

"Oh baby, come here," she mumbled, taking the cloth off the sink and wiping his face off.

"Harriet," Ember perked with her British accent, "do you live here with my daddy?" It was so innocent, the words coming from her mouth, but in this situation, it wasn't. Harriet did live with Jax. Well, she was moving in, but to a child, that doesn't seem like a big thing. She had to choose her words wisely.

"Yes, sort of," she grinned, poking her nose as she cleaned the kitchen up.

"How long have you and daddy been living together?"

"Not long, babe," she told her, washing the dishes and packing the dishwasher.

"Are you my nanny then?"

Harriet gasped a little. Taking a deep breath, she turned around. "No, your daddy and I are just very good friends, poppet."

"Oh, I see."

"Well, since you two are very much done with your dinner as it's more on your face than your tummy," she quipped walking back to wipe Ember's face now, "it is time for your bath."

"No," Caleb mumbled.

"Yes, mister," she sassed hands on her hips as she winked to the platinum blonde boy. With a chuckle, Harriet picked him up and walked up the stairs. Ember took hold of her hand as they headed to the master bedroom.

They entered the masculine bathroom. Harriet placed Caleb on the counter as Ember danced around the bathroom. She walked to the bathtub, sitting on the rim as she ran the water and throwing in some soap for a bubble bath. Ember took her clothes off, giddy to have a bath. Once warm enough, she helped Caleb undress.

"Ok, one, two, three!" She exclaimed, picking up Caleb and putting him in. Ember followed, hopping in as well.

The kids splashed around in the water, which made Harriet smile. It reminded her of the old days, taking care of them and spending every waking moment with them. It felt like yesterday when she spotted Jax for the first time in thirteen years in that kitchen. With a small smile, Harriet picked up their clothes and threw them into the laundry basket.

"Kit!" She heard the velvety, deep voice echo throughout the penthouse.

"Upstairs!" she called back, sitting down next to the kids and swirling the water with her finger.

Jax ran up the stairs, taking two at a time as he entered the bathroom. He was met with her kneeling over the bathtub and washing his two children.

"Shit, I totally forgot," he mumbled to himself.

However, it was a sight for sore eyes. Seeing the woman, he loved taking care of his children. Harriet was all wet, splashed water on her clothes as she scrubbed shampoo in the kids' hair. Her white tank top now was see-through, but she couldn't care at that moment. The room was filled with children's laughter and splashing of water.

"Daddy!" they both exclaimed once they saw him in the doorway.

He smiled, giving a kiss to both their heads and leaned down to capture his lover's lips. Harriet turned her head away.

"No, they don't know."

He nodded walking to the closet to remove his tie and jacket. Harriet followed him.

"Hi, baby," she whispered, snaking her hands around him and applying a kiss to his back. His muscles clenched under her touch as she littered kisses up his back.

"Hi," he responded, turning around and capturing her lips.

Harriet let their kiss linger for a while before pulling

away. Her hands dropped to his waist as she looked in his eyes.

"How was your day?" she asked, smiling with such adoration in her eyes.

Jax tucked a piece of her hair behind her ear. "Better now that I am home. Sorry about leaving so early and forgetting to tell you about the kids coming."

"It is ok. Claudia and I talked for a little bit. It is good to see them again, but we should probably sit them down soon and talk to them about us. Em has been asking questions lately," she told him.

"I agree," he responded. "Let me change into something comfortable, you finish washing the kiddos, and then we can put them to bed. After all that," he whispered the last part capturing her lips and whispering against them, "we can have grownup time."

Harriet chuckled, "I thought tonight was going to be movie and a-"

"What were you thinking about, Ms. Kensington? Get your head out of the gutter. Of course, I was talking about wining and dining you, missy. Wine and dine then bedding you. After all, I am a gentleman," he winked, walking to the racks of clothes and changing.

"Whatever you say," she chuckled, turning on her feet and heading back to the ensuite.

Jax smirked watching her leave. Her hips swayed. He bit his lip watching her ass. After a quick change into sweats and a tank, he went back to the bathroom.

She was on her knees hands soapy and tank top more wet. Her nipples were hard from the water splashing as she washed the kids' hair and sang songs with them. Jax was in love with this image. He could imagine her doing this pregnant with their baby and a diamond on her finger. He was in complete heaven seeing her so domestic.

"Daddy!" The two exclaimed as they splashed the bubbles around.

She turned her head around and sent him a smile before going back to brushing Ember's hair. Jax pushed off the wall kneeling beside his lover as he looked at his kids.

"I need tell you two something," he began. His eyes locked with their beautiful and innocent orbs large and cartoon-like as they looked at their real-life superhero. Caleb's attention was broken after a second. The little boy went back to playing with his car in the water. He made little 'vroom vroom' noises as he puckered his lips. Harriet smiled caressing Caleb's cheek and kissing his head.

"You know that mummy and daddy are not together, right?" he said. Harriet looked over knowing where this was going. "Mummy and daddy will always love each other, but we are no longer married?" Ember was nodding slowly but didn't know where this was going. "Well, I love Harriet, and her and I are together. We are in a relationship, and she is my girlfriend."

Ember gave him a puzzled look. "Is she my new mummy?"

Jax shook his head. "No, love. Mummy will always be your mummy, but Harriet is my girlfriend and one day will be my wife like mummy once was. You will probably get more sisters and brothers-"

"You kiss Harriet on the mouth?" she asked, grimacing.

"Yes, I do. We live together, sleep together, and-"

"Mummy and you never slept together. You had different rooms."

He grimaced. Ember really knew how to make things difficult.

"That was different," he mumbled.

"Em, baby, this means you will see me all the time. I will be your best friend forever and I am not leaving," Harriet said cupping her cheek and placing a kiss on it. "I love you, Caleb, and Daddy."

"Ok!" she exclaimed.

Jax sighed, looking at his girlfriend and mouthing, "That was painful." Harriet let out a light chuckle, her wet hand went against the nape of his neck before kissing his cheek lightly.

"It was fine. Now, let's get these monkeys dried and ready for bed!"

HARRIET WAS SAT on the leather black couch facing the fireplace as she read over emails and took a sip of her red wine. The TV noise was in the background as night settled in. Jax came walking down the stairs to the main floor.

His heart leaped a little when he saw her on the couch with her feet out on the ottoman and a blanket draped over her body. He could get use to this, seeing her in his home. A little smile crept on his face.

"Tucked in and asleep. I had to read that bear story like three times, but I got it eventually," he said as he stood behind her looking over her shoulder as she typed away. His lips went down and kissed her head. "I could recite every line now, Kit. Test me!" he exclaimed as his lips began to kiss down her neck.

"Jax," she chuckled from his tickling touch scrunching her neck up.

"I love you," he muttered.

"I know. Now, you promised me a movie, mister," she grinned, closing the laptop and turned her head to him.

"Yes," he said, pecking her lips, "I did, didn't I?" He kissed her again.

Jax jumped over the couch landing next to her. Harriet let out a loud squeal as he crashed his lips with hers again.

"Hello, spider-monkey!" she laughed as he snuggled into her side.

Her arm wrapped around him and landed on his pec as he took the blanket off her and placed it on himself. With that, she placed her laptop to the side and placed a firm kiss on the side of his head.

"What did you and Claud talk about?" he asked as she began to draw circles on his sculpted pectoral. She shrugged as he took the remote and changed the channel.

"Life, the universe, and everything," she mumbled bringing the glass of wine to her lips.

"Mhmm, I don't buy it, Kit."

"We just talked about the kids and divorce, Jax. Nothing too crazy."

He hummed, "What did she say?"

"That she wants you to be happy, that you deserve to be happy," she responded raking her fingers through his hair. He sighed from her touch.

"Mhmm, sure," he scoffed.

"Jax," she grumbled, "she is trying to be nice."

"Nah, Kit. She is just being classic passive aggressive Claudia."

"I wouldn't call it passive aggressive, Jax. She generally is being kind. You both deserve to be happy, babe."

He shrugged. His eyes were locked on some show on the television as she shook her head.

"Claudia loved my interaction with your family," Harriet mumbled, eyes still locked on him, whereas his attentions were on the flickering screen.

Jax let out a loud groan as he covered his eyes with his hand. "Please, don't remind me. I will never be forgiven because of that."

She chuckled, "I am sorry. Still, that was un-"

He turned his head up looking at her. "Kit, it is ok. You're my real family," he said. She pressed her kiss to his lips.

"I love you."

29

That week she officially moved in. She had her stuff in his penthouse, room in his closet, and her own toiletries in his bathroom. They were really beginning to be quite serious.

Harriet had a plan in place, a solid plan that made her simply smirk by thinking of it. She had to make sure that the kids were back at Claudia's before she would do anything. Ember walked in on them once. She didn't need that to happen again.

The kids got picked up a week later, the following Monday. The week was spent with laughter, giggles and fun. Harriet felt like she was back at the beginning when she was their nanny and simply falling in love with their faces. She was in heaven.

Not only that, but Jax was there the whole time. He accompanied her to the playground for coffee, shopping, etc. It was their little family, and she was completely in love with it. She did mourn for them when Claudia came back a week later to take them.

One week with Jax, and then she had the kiddos again, she reminded herself.

MONDAY NIGHT, the two of them came home from dinner out. Ever since the conversation a few weeks ago, Jax had truly put an effort into their relationship to treat her like his queen. To love her unconditionally and treat her like his partner rather than his competition.

He had his arm wrapped around her waist as she giggled to his story regarding his youthful days. Jax rambled on about a bet he did back in university about whether he could jump from the roof and land in the pool with over fifteen shots in his system, and who knew how many other drinks. She chuckled as he told her he really thought he could do it. Spoiler, he failed and did a belly flop.

The flat was filled with his roaring laughter and her small giggles as they went to the kitchen.

"Stay there," he said to her, kissing her cheek before walking to the amp and turning music on.

Soft jazz began to fill the apartment. Harriet was leaned against the counter as Jax bowed to her. A giggle left her lips.

"May I have this dance, m'lady?" He asked, hand out for her to grab.

Colour went to her cheeks as she placed her hand on top of his. He brought the back of it to his lips and placed a kiss on it. She bit her lip as he began to dance with her, swaying them to the music with her in his arms.

Jax had both his arms wrapped around Harriet's lower back. Her arms were around his neck. They swayed gently.

Her cheek was against his chest as he whispered words in her ear.

"I love you," he said gently.

The lights were dim, and the dark night covered the sky as they swayed to the beat. Trapped in the love they had for one another as they let their imperfections be perfect for each other and were enough for their love.

"I love you too," she mumbled.

He took her hand, twirling her, before going back to the gentle rocking.

"I am sorry we didn't get together sooner," he said.

Harriet sighed, shaking her head and looking into his ocean eyes. "Everything happens for a reason, Jax. Our life apart was a learning experience, but we found one another again and that is all that matters. I love our little family, Jax. Em, with her wittiness and cheekiness, will grow up to be the most independent and extraordinary woman. Caleb, even though dirt and grass is more exciting than a toy, I already know he will be brilliant, strong, and wonderful."

He nodded, kissing her head as they continued to sway to the music.

"If we found each other earlier, Jax, maybe they wouldn't exist. I couldn't imagine our life without them. We are the now," she said, looking up as he kissed her lips gently.

"Marry me," he mumbled.

She stopped following his lead with the light dancing as she registered those words. 'Marry me' it echoed in her brain.

"I don't have a ring, but I want to be with you forever and a day."

"You want to spend forever with me? All my flaws and imperfections?" she whispered.

He had such love in his eyes looking at her with pure adoration. As if she was the oxygen in his lungs or the blood in his veins. She was the reason he got up every day.

"You make me a better person, father, and lover. You inspire to be a better person, and I love you. I have loved you since I was seven, and you were four."

A smile grew on her face as a blush covered her cheeks.

"Are you blushing?" he chuckled. His hands were on her ass while her hands were splayed on his chest. She could feel the thin material of his button up against her palms as they had their little talk.

"I," she began, "yes, I am."

"Marry me then," he mumbled again capturing her lips. She didn't kiss back for a moment.

"What?"

Jax pulled away. "Marry me, Kitten."

Harriet nodded slowly. "Ok," she whispered, capturing his lips again.

They kissed long and hard, as he wrapped his arms around her tightly squeezing her.

"I don't ever want to be without you," he said.

"I don't want a wedding though," she responded. "I want something different."

He let out a breath. "Whatever you want, Kit, but I need my divorce to be finalized first."

She chucked, "Of course. No rush."

He kissed her jaw, littering the small pecks down her neck to her exposed collarbone. It was funny how one-minute Jax could go from the most loving creature on the planet to the horniest.

"Woah there, tiger," she chuckled, pulling away as she walked around to the kitchen.

"We just got engaged, Kitten! We need to celebrate!" he gushed, walking over to grab her hips and twirling her so she was looking directly at him.

"We just got engaged," she mumbled, shaking her head as she registered what just happened. "We just got engaged," she mumbled again.

"Yes, we are *engaged*. So, let's celebrate!"

"I need to tell Cameron," she responded, picking up her phone and walking to the other room. Jax blinked as he watched her go to the bedroom.

Harriet paced back and forth as she rung her friend. Seconds later, Cameron answered.

"Hi, you!"

"Jax proposed," she muttered too quickly slurring the words together.

"What? Say that again."

"Jax proposed," she said again, but slower.

"Oooo," she said, "that's quick."

Harriet had her fingers in her hair as she walked in circles. "I know, but he is almost divorced."

"What did you say?" she questioned.

Harriet sat down on the bed as she took a breath. "I said, ok."

"Just, ok?" her friend chuckled from her response.

"Cam, I was shocked. I just said 'ok' and then I went on saying I didn't want a typical wedding." Harriet ran her hands down her face. "What kind of person says shit like that?"

"Someone who has been married before to an asshole," her friend responded.

"Cam, I moved in with him. He wants me to be part of his life, with his kids and shit. I fucked up with his family and-"

"What? Spill," Cameron interrupted.

Harriet explained the whole story regarding the family meeting. Cameron was in pure shock from the explanation.

"You called his stepmother a cunt?" she laughed.

"Yes."

"You have never been much of a family person. There is only one mother who can stand your stupidness-"

"Kai's, I know. I haven't talked to her in forever. I should call her soon, Cam. Edith really helped me with shit, so I owe her this."

Harriet walked to the door opening it to see Jax standing there listening in to her conversation. He had his hands in his dress pants pockets as he stood there wide- eyed.

She shook her head as she continued to the living room and sat on the couch.

"I love you, Harriet. You're a smart woman, and you know what is right. You have loved Jax since the moment you met him. He is the love of your life. The way he looks at you is as if you're the stars in his universe. The man loves you. Marry the fucker and make sure I am your damn maid of honour."

Harriet nodded, mumbling a goodbye before turning to the man.

"We are engaged," she said with confidence and a large smile.

"Edith?" He narrowed his eyes.

"Kai's mum," she responded, walking up to him and placing her hands on his hips. "Now we have celebrating to do," she winked.

A large smirk appeared on his face from those words.

"No, no, no," she mumbled, noticing his look. "We are celebrating my way," she purred kissing his jaw as her hands dropped to his ass squeezing it.

"Kit," he warned.

She pulled away.

"If I am going to marry you, you need to understand that you can't control me, so we are going to do an exercise to practice that," she whispered in his ear.

Jax stood there giving her a puzzled look as she said those words. What could she possibly mean by that? His eyebrows scrunched as his eyes narrowed.

"Kit..."

"I am in control tonight, and you will do what I say," she hummed, taking his hand and leading him to their bedroom.

"What does that mean?" he whispered as they entered.

Harriet stood in front of him, the back of his knees touching the end of the bed as she looked up to his towering figure. She bit her lip as she imagined what that night would include.

"Sit," she said her finger poking his chest as she pushed him down. "Stay."

Jax sat watching her as she walked around the room and to the dresser. He knew instantly what she meant.

"Harriet," he said. She scoffed.

"Be good and stay."

He shook his head, snickering as she turned around with the bondage cuffs in hand.

"You don't like those," he said, raising his eyebrows.

"On me no, but on you..."

"You're not gonna..." he whispered.

"Shirt off," she demanded.

Jax began to unbutton the collared shirt. She watched foot tapping impatiently as she waited.

"You're a minx," he chuckled, throwing the shirt at her.

"Jax! Take this seriously!" she yelled, dodging it.

"My *fiancé* is trying to dominate me. How can I-"

"Jax!"

"Fine!" He put his hands up in surrender. She took the opportunity to place the cuffs on his wrists. He obliged scooting back till his back hit the headboard.

Harriet hooked them to the side of the bed. Jax was now laying on his back, looking up to the white ceiling. This was all new this controlling side of her. The man had never been controlled by a woman before. Being tied down, that was new. To not be demanding and controlling, that was hard to give up.

Jax knew within ten minutes he would be done and hate this, but he decided that he should play along for Harriet's sake. He felt his ankles being pulled and the cuffs going around them as she yanked them to the side. She was going full out with everything.

He wouldn't admit it, but he was beginning to enjoy this side of her.

"No whipping," he said, his eyes still locked to the ceiling and his body sprawled out.

"Wasn't planning on hitting you; that shit doesn't do anything for me," she responded.

Jax let out a heavy sigh as she climbed onto the bed, straddling his body as she ran her hands up his legs and inner thighs. He jerked a little from the touch. Harriet placed a kiss on his lower stomach, the happy trail to his hardening cock. Jax moaned a little as she continued the light pecks there.

Her hands went to his dress pants, undoing the belt as she unzipped the tightness that held his angry cock. He bit back a moan when she cupped his manhood, holding it as she delivered kisses up his body.

Jax panted, trying his best to hold the sound of pleasure. He didn't want to admit that he enjoyed the lack of control. Harriet straddled him, ass on his groin as she ran her hands up his chest, leaning down to capture his lips.

"All mine," she growled, littering more kisses down his jawline.

Jax fought against the cuffs, wanting to wrap his hands around her smaller figure, but he couldn't. He had no control and it drove him mad.

Harriet sat up, knees tight against his side as she crossed her arms and pulled her shirt off, throwing it somewhere in the room.

His cock was angry. He felt the throbbing and ache coming from it. Harriet was on top of him sitting there so innocently. She began to tease him with pulling the straps of her bra down her arm.

"Kit," he warned.

"Jax," she mumbled back, "patience, my dear." From his reaction, she placed the straps back on her shoulder with a smirk. It was her turn to be controlling, to be a tease.

"You menace," he whimpered as her hand went back to his cock grabbing it again.

She swung her leg from his body back to her side and pressed a kiss on his covered manhood. Harriet got off the bed eyes still in contact with his. Jax clenched his jaw, teeth grinding as she began to walk to the bathroom.

"I will be back in a minute," she smirked, swaying her hips as she left and closed the door.

"Harriet!" he yelled, trying his best to move his body, but he was stuck. Stuck there with a terribly angry and needy cock while his woman was in another room.

"You fucking-"

"Jax, be quiet or else you won't get what you want," she responded back through the doors.

"Fucking hell," he whispered as he laid looking up to the ceiling. "I love you!"

"Jax," she warned, "patience, please."

Seconds later, the door opened, and he looked back up to her. Harriet in all her glory was dressed in leather lingerie. A leather and high waisted strappy thong with a matching bra that barely covered her breasts cupping them and pushing them up perfectly.

Jax was lost of words as she sauntered over to him. Their eyes locked as she crawled on the bed.

"Fucking hell, Kit. You're gonna be the death of me," he growled.

She placed a finger to his lips, "Shhh."

Jax was just stunned. He watched her throw her hair up into a high pony. Then she kissed his collarbone and dragged her tongue down.

Shivers went up his body as she moved closer to his most sensitive part. Her fingers pushed down his pants and boxers flinging his pants to the other side of the room. Her hand gripped his cock. Jax jolted but was restricted by the cuffs. His back arched with her touch. She pushed his body back down.

"Down, Jax," she pushed him back down onto the mattress. Jax groaned as her hand began to pump his cock.

"I want to touch you, Kitten," he gasped as her lips touched the tip of the member.

"No," she mumbled. Harriet licked up the shaft, bobbing her head as she deep throated him.

Jax let out a loud groan as she gripped his hips, holding them down as she worked her magic on his cock.

"Quiet, did I tell you to speak?" she teased, looking up through her lashes to him.

Her tongue did wonders, swirling as she took him all in her mouth. Hand on his hip, holding it down as her other one went to his shaft, jerking him as she sucked.

Jax gripped the straps holding him down to the bed, knuckles turning white as he held tighter. Swears rolling off his lips as she applied such pleasure to him. Harriet stopped and removed her mouth. Jax looked down seeing her lick her lips and biting them.

"Why-"

"Shhh," she mumbled, crawling up to him.

Her leg swung over his broad body, hands splayed back on his chest, muscles underneath them as he flexed. Her lips met his.

"You're in so much trouble," he mumbled against them. "You have no idea what I am gonna do-"

"Shhh," she hushed him fighting for dominance in the kiss.

Harriet pulled away fingers moving to the top band of the thong playing with it as he shook his head to her actions.

"Minx," he mouthed. She sent him a wink as she began to pull the hem down exposing her stomach more to him. Jax was still just shaking his head watching every move.

"Down now, Kit. Don't be a tease," he growled with a small smirk.

She leaned to him mouth by his ear as she whispered, "I am in control, remember?"

He nodded.

Harriet rolled off him quickly removing the thong before going back to straddling him. Her pussy bare once again for him to see. The second she was back sitting on his chest he could feel her wetness between the hair and skin of his chest. He smirked. She was having her fun, and he would get her back later.

"What are you going to do next?" he cocked amused by everything.

"You really can't give up control, can you?" she chuckled. "I am trying my best."

"I can still speak, Kit."

"Do you have a gag?" she joked. Jax choked on those words coming from her pretty little lips.

"Filthy woman," he smirked.

She chuckled, "Be serious."

He rolled his eyes, and Harriet shook her head.

"Fine, be like that," she mumbled.

She crawled, hands clasping the headboard as she helped herself up and lowered herself on his face.

"Suck," she commanded.

Jax instantly licked her womanhood, tongue flat against the flesh as he licked up. She moaned holding onto the headboard harder as he began to lap his tongue and suck her swollen flesh. Her body rocked on his mouth as she gripped harder.

"Fuck," she mumbled, holding the board and adjusting her grip.

"Unhook me, so I can hold you."

Harriet was overcome with pleasure, taking the cuffs off him, and letting them hang on the bed. Instantly, his hands went to her waist holding her there as he licked and sucked.

"Jax, right there!" He sped up flicking his tongue and sucking her clit as she rolled her head back.

She let everything go. The orgasm took over her body.

The shockwaves pulsing through her as the knot in her stomach released.

Jax pulled away. "You had your fun, my turn now, Kit."

Harriet nodded, rolling off his face as she went to the side of the bed removing the cuffs from his ankles. Jax got up arms wrapping around her figure and pulling her close to him. A squeal left her lips as she sat back on him arms holding her close as he kissed her jaw.

"I will *always* be in control, Kitten," he growled.

He picked her up and lowered her onto his aching cock. She gasped as he thrust hard into her. Her head rolled back as he sucked the right spot on her neck.

"Jax," she moaned.

"I know, Kit, but that little act was not so fun for me," he grunted. Jax rolled them over, so he was on top now.

Her arms were pushed up as he pinned them with his. The other hand went to grasp the cuffs hooking them onto her wrists.

She moaned when she felt the fabric wrapping around her wrists. He pushed back in making her jolt. She couldn't move that much due to the restraints.

Jax thrusted all of him inside of her, feeling every clench and her dripping wetness. He brushed her cervix but kept on pumping fucking her as he kissed her neck down.

"That little act, tying me up..." he tsk, "didn't know you had that kind of confidence, Kitten."

Harriet moaned as his fingers began to play with her clit, rubbing circles, and applying pressure. She moaned his name from the bliss of pleasure.

Jax got cocky during sex, she knew that. Harriet knew that the man loves control. He loved to watch her whimper and moan from every action. He had control over her with just his fingers and cock, and he loved it.

Jax smirked watching her wither under his touch. With a wink, he applied a smack to her throbbing cunt. Harriet jerked back arching from the pain and pleasure. She groaned and yelped. The noises rolling off her tongue were a mix of everything. The woman didn't know how she felt about it.

"You like that?" he whispered. She groaned.

He was still fucking her pushing everything inside of her and he knew he was close. Harriet had her face nuzzled into his shoulder teeth clenching as he rubbed her most sensitive part while fucking her hard.

She was close to being undone feeling the shakes and shutters flooding her system. He was close too. Jax could feel the jerk in his cock, the need to spread his seed inside of her. Seconds later, she groaned feeling the high go through her system as she came for the second time. Her moans filled the room as her whole body shattered from her orgasm.

She was huffing, heavy breaths leaving her lips as Jax experienced his undoing. Holding her hips to his pelvis he jerked everything inside her.

"Fuck, Harriet," he moaned, "I love you."

Jax removed himself seeing the juices spilling out of her pussy and down her thighs. He smirked. Harriet was still riding her orgasm her legs shaking as she tried to catch her breath.

Jax got up, an idea in his head as he grabbed the black vibrator on the dresser.

"Holy fucking shit!" she yelled as the vibration was placed on her clit. Jax smirked as she held the straps tighter. She was huffing, panting, and moaning at the same time.

"Jax! It's too much!"

He chuckled turning up the speed. Her body jolted but was pulled back by the restraints. She was gone, head in cloud nine, as the pleasure vibrated through her body. Harriet could feel the specific sensation in her stomach. The knot began to form in her belly. He pushed her folds apart as his fingers found their way inside of her. He fingered her as the vibrator began to vibrate her clit. Harriet was groaning, moaning, and swears were rolling off her lips.

Jax thought she was art itself seeing her like this: bare and exposed with pleasure running through his system and it was all brought on by him. He felt like a God having control over her delivering the perfect forms of pleasure and he could control it.

Harriet was so close to orgasming again. Jax noticed that and pulled the vibrator away. For a second, she could breathe again trying her best to catch her breath. Jax watched her back arch as she tried catch her breath. With a smirk, he went down and licked her pussy, sucking and biting her clit.

"Fucking hell, Jax!"

Her legs wrapped around his head as he ate her out with the mix of fingering. This was going to be the best orgasm she ever had. She felt the knot growing bigger as it sat in her stomach ready to be released. She was out of breath, jerking and trembling from every swipe of his tongue and push of his finger.

"Jax," Harriet mumbled, "Jax," she tried again, but it was higher pitch close to a scream. Finally, she screamed, "Jaxon!"

The knot was gone, the shaking came back and suddenly, she felt like she couldn't move. Her pussy was clenching the walls pulsing as the fiery feeling ran through her whole body. Her stomach bobbed up and down from her heavy breathing. As she tried her best to ride out this orgasm. The woman was done for, she couldn't take anymore.

Jax removed his mouth and fingers, watching her eyes roll back as she let go of everything. He licked his fingers clean before applying a firm and final kiss to her thigh, getting up, and going to the bathroom.

He got a cloth wet and came back. Harriet was still shaking in the bed. Jax smirked, loving the view. He did this to her, and he enjoyed every second of it.

The cloth hit her thighs making her shudder again. Everything was overly sensitive now. Her arms came down, slumping beside her as he undid the cuffs. Jax moved the cloth up her thigh, cleaning all the juices from their joining.

"You did so well, Kit, so, so well. I am proud of you," he purred, kissing her cheek. "Do you want a bath?"

Harriet nodded. Jax was beside her standing next to the bed as she laid there. Her breath was now caught. The shaking was gone as she regained normal feeling of everything. She felt human again. She felt that she was back in reality from that out of body experience.

He scoped her up bridal style and walked to the bath room. Jax sat her down on the counter then walking to the stand-alone tub and turning it on. He tested the water and made sure it was hot enough.

"Did you like it?" she said, getting down and removing the bra.

He turned around; eyebrows raised. "Hmm?"

"The tying up."

Jax thought for a second, then chuckled. “I didn’t mind it, but it was hard not being able to touch you.”

“Now you know the feeling,” she retorted, getting into the tub and placing her back against the side.

“Funny.”

“Come in, Jax.” He shook his head walked to the closet and took out a pair of sweats.

Jax sauntered back a container of black stuff in his hand as he settled next to the bath, sitting on the tile as he propped his elbow on the rim of the tub. Her eyes watched as his muscles flexed and relaxed. He truly was beautiful.

“Face mask,” he told her before removing the top and beginning to paint her face with the clay substance.

“You spoil me.”

He chuckled, dipping his hands in the water and wiping the wetness off on his pants. “You’re my girl, Kit.”

Her arm was on the rim on the bath as she laid her head on it, smiling from his words as his fingers brushed her hair back.

“Go back blonde,” he said.

“Why?”

“Because that is your natural colour,” he said, watching as the mask dried on her face.

“I have been dying my hair since I was eighteen. I don’t know my natural colour anymore.”

“It is blonde,” he replied, watching as her eyes fluttered closed. The warmth of the bath calming her as she relaxed.

“Mhmm, maybe. I’ve had silver hair since I was nineteen. I am twenty-eight and now brunette.”

“Can you get it lifted?”

“There is so much dye in my hair, Jax, that it would be impossible. Let me be a brunette for a while,” she mumbled eyes closed as she felt the massaging of his fingers through her hair. Harriet moaned a little from the love. Jax took a hold of the elastic that held her pony and pulled it letting her hair fall. She smiled.

"Blondes have more fun though," he mumbled.

Her eyes shot open. "Calling me not fun? I just got tied up-"

"You're fun, Kit," he whispered. "Now wash this mask off so I can kiss you," he said.

She laughed sitting up and placed her hand in front of her. "Hand me the mask" she said, making a grabby motion.

Jax placed the container in her hand. She unscrewed it and took some in her fingers sliding it down his face.

"Oh, Kit," he snickered.

"Now you have to get in the bath with me," she winked rubbing it all over his clean-shaven face.

"Fine, scoot over."

30

Friday afternoon, she sat with the beaten-up envelope in her hand again. She thumbed it as she flipped the envelope repeatedly, debating whether or not to open it. Harriet knew what it would say, 'Please give me money'.

"What is it?" She was pulled from her trance, and she looked over. Atticus leaned against the doorway in jeans and a cable knit beige sweater, beard gone, and hair shorter.

"Got a hot date? You're all clean-shaven, and your hair is short now," she chuckled, placing the envelope down.

"No, thought to change my look. Now what is in the envelope?" he asked her, walking over and taking a seat in front of her desk.

"A letter from my dad, but I don't know if I am going to open it. He is probably going to ask for cash. I know he is asking me for money," she shook her head as she dropped it back into her drawer.

"Now, seriously, you got a hot date?" she questioned, smirking.

Atticus let out a loud chuckle as he crossed his arms. "No, no hot date. I just thought I'd change my look."

"Well, you look great!" she told him.

He rolled his eyes.

"I am serious! You can really scrub up. No longer Mr. Rough Rustic Man CEO Gentleman. If you showed up at a coffee shop wearing that with your cute little cable knit cardigan and blue jeans with your hair all combed back and clean-shaven, I would definitely give you my number."

He laughed. "Thank you, Harriet. Now hand me the letter. I will read it for you as you're so terrified of it."

Harriet shook her head and muttering, "No."

"Yes."

"Jax proposed."

He was taken aback, giving her a puzzled look as he processed her words. "One, that is very-"

"Soon? Yeah, it is."

"What did you say? I see no ring..." he trailed off.

"He didn't propose with a ring, we were dancing, and he just said, 'marry me'. I said, 'Ok'."

"Ok?" he chuckled.

"Just ok...then I tied him up and fucked him," she mumbled the rest.

"Lordly, woman, I do not need to know your sex life... give me the letter now." He raised his eyebrows at her.

Harriet rolled her eyes and handed him the envelope.

"Crash course...my father is in prison for drug dealing. He thinks he can win his case, so he needs a good lawyer. But he can't afford it, so he has been rotting there for the past twenty years or so. I will never help him get out as he killed my mother."

"Killed?" he sputtered with his arm resting on the top of the couch.

"Drug dealer father, junkie mother. I am the product of 'she couldn't pay cash anymore, so she paid him with her body'. My father always wanted me to be part of his life, but I met him once and I hate him. No remorse. He is just a good manipulator," she told him, leaning back in her sky-blue chair.

Atticus nodded, opening the envelope and taking the letter out. "Let's see what he has to say."

Dear Harriet,

I hope you are well. We haven't talked since you were nineteen, but I wish you all the best. I remember you came in with silver hair and a sad smile. I am sorry that you had to grow up without me or your mother, that is not fair to you. I wish I could have seen you grow up, but God chose otherwise.

I will make it short and sweet as I know you truly don't want to deal with me. A few days ago, I was in the TV room in a middle of a poker game when I heard your name spoken on the TV. You were pictured with a man named Jax Alderidge. The last time I saw you, you were engaged to Kai. I never really liked him, I'll tell ya, but I am happy to know that you two are now divorced. Jax seems uptight and spoiled, doll face. He will never know your life and understand where you come from.

That is what I thought, at least. I was curious, why are you in England, and why were you pictured with a lawyer? I hate them. They are unfair and never do their job well. Lawyers do what benefits them not their clients. I know that from first-hand experience.

I googled him. He was in the same orphanage as you did you know him? He has money, Harriet, a shitload of money.

I read online that you two were together. That man loves you. I hope. I am glad you are reinventing yourself since Arlo. I am sorry you had to go through that, doll face.

She shuddered. Atticus looked up from what he was reading, seeing if she was ok.

"Who's Arlo?" he asked.

She bit her lip. "I had a baby and..." she swallowed.

Atticus nodded. "Are you ok?"

"Keep reading."

You may be wondering about how I know that information. Rumours spread, doll face. There are men here that know Kai personally and deal with him. I am not sending this letter asking you for money, Harriet. I am sending a letter to warn you.

We all know Kai's problems, the drugs, the gambling, etc. I know a man in the prison who has direct contact with men on the outside regarding his situation. After several negotiations, I came across some information. Kai is in trouble. He needs cash. I know he will contact you soon for money.

If I know about Mr. Alderidge, he must also. The man is famous in England, so if a Kiwi is pictured with someone of that high status, word spreads. I am guessing Kai knows about him. Put two and two together, sweetheart, Kai needs money, and your 'rumoured' man has it.

I know you hate me. You blame me for your mother's death, but it wasn't me. I cut her off and she went to another dealer. I know you won't ever believe me, and I have to live with that, but as your father, I am warning you.

The only thing I would ask in return is to see you. It has been nearly ten years since I saw you. You're my daughter, Harriet. I know you have this life in England now with the rich lawyer, but please don't associate yourself too much with that lifestyle. At the end of the day, you're still a product of a drug deal gone wrong.

See you soon, doll face.
With love,
Frank

Atticus finished reading and placed the letter down.

"Asshole...'product of a drug deal gone wrong' at least he didn't ask for cash," she mumbled, arms crossed as she processed the letter.

"Kai?" Atticus reminded her.

"Will probably call me," she said. "That man can't do any harm."

Atticus nodded slowly. "If he calls you?"

"I say, go pound sand as I have nothing for you," she groaned. "I may be with a man with a net worth of... who knows, but I may be worth ten grand. Every penny extra went to Kai's debt. Once Jax paid that off, I was free to save again. I don't have money, so he can fuck off," she grumbled.

"Ok, but your dad wants you visit."

"I will visit him one day, but not right now. I am glad he felt like he needed to warn me, but Kai can't harm me. We are divorced-"

"Spousal support?" Atticus asked.

"I made fifty to sixty grand a year. He made thirty to fifty grand a year. We aren't rich, and the judge made it clear that neither of us had to pay each other anything. He took everything from me so here I am," she told him.

"He is just in debt?"

"We were in debt, five hundred thousand dollars. Jax paid it off, and then we were free. However, he is in debt again. How much? I don't know, but it has nothing to do with me," she concluded.

Atticus nodded again, looking out the window. "Will you tell Jax?"

"Jax is in New York City for a settlement or something. He doesn't need to know. I don't want to worry him. The man would drop everything for me if he thought I was in danger, which I am not," she told him, shrugging. "The question is... you didn't respond to my question this morning. Are you coming to the pub tonight with my friend and I? She is hot, established and exceptionally good looking."

He chuckled, getting up. "I got a hot date," he winked as he walked away.

"No, you don't!" she shouted at him.

Atticus turned around putting his hands up and shrugging. "What I do outside of work is my business, just like yours! I don't need to know that you tied up my ex best friend and fucked him!"

"Speaking of that," she called out as he sat in his seat in the other room, "he wants to be friends again!"

HARRIET LEFT THE BUILDING, pulling her coat closer as she headed to the pub that her, and Cameron had decided to meet at. She had changed from her work attire to her pub attire. Now she was wearing a graphic tee and a mini skirt with boots and stockings. Ready for a girl's night out. The brisk August air hit her skin as she walked down the stairs to the tube.

The bag that Jax bought for her, hung on her shoulder as she scanned her pass at the gates. Continuing her way down the several staircases to the station, she waited patiently for the train to Westminster station.

Her leg bounced as she sat on tube looking around the full train; people heading to their Friday night plans. The train gave her time to think. Her father's words haunted her, but now she was excited to see her best friend and get absolutely plastered. The woman just smiled from that thought. Cameron had been in the Ukraine for the last month and Harriet was in dire need to see her best friend.

She got off at Westminster station, heeled boots clicking as she exited the station and echoed down the street as she walked to the bar. Her eyes glanced down the street, seeing people heading to or leaving pubs to jump to the next one. A classic British Friday night.

Harriet pulled the door open, eyes glancing over the room until she spotted her brunette best friend at the bar chatting up some man. She giggled as she watched her long-time best friend send a wink to the man before he walked away, clearly uninterested.

"His loss," she mumbled as Harriet sat down, letting out a laugh at her friend's failed attempt of seducing a man. "I almost had him, maybe if I just propped myself like this," she changed her position, so her boobs were on display, "he'd hit it."

"Cam, you really want to hook up with some guy because he is just interested in your boobs?"

"At this point, I don't care. I haven't had sex in a week. I am in dire need of some dick," she told her friend. Harriet rolled her eyes as she looked at the bartender, trying to get his attention. "Like seriously, you probably get fucked everyday with Mr. Fiancé, while I am here dry like the Sahara Desert from the lack of banging. This bitch needs to get a ticket to Poundtown."

"Poundtown?" Harriet asked unimpressed.

"Yes, Poundtown."

Harriet rolled her head back letting the roaring laughter come from her mouth. That surely was one way to put it. The bartender walked over sending her a flirty smile.

"She's engaged, sir, move on," Cam mumbled, taking a sip from her drink while looking at the blonde man over the rim of her glass. "However, I am not...in fact, I am very single."

He took a step back, recalculating his moves for the night.

"Gin and tonic, please, with lime," Harriet interrupted her friend. The bartender didn't look at her friend, instead, kept his eyes on Harriet.

"There is no ring..." he mumbled, throwing the tea towel over his shoulder and pointing to her finger, palms on the counter and leaning on them.

"Gin and tonic with lime, please," she told him again, more slowly this time.

The bartender nodded turning to go fix her drink. Harriet rolled her eyes.

"Men," Cam made a gagging sound. "See," she pointed, "you need a ring."

Harriet groaned at her friend's words. However, she was right. She took her right hand where a simple thick dainty band was on her ring finger, removing it, and placing it on her left ring finger.

"There, a ring," she scoffed.

"That is our friendship ring," Cameron responded. "We made them in a welding course back in uni."

"It is a ring. I don't know if Jax is-"

"Har, the man is a *gazillionaire*. He is getting you a big ass diamond probably at this very moment."

"Jax is in New York not buying me a diamond," she retorted, thanking the bartender for the drink.

He stayed in his spot looking Harriet up and down. The women groaned at him.

"Engaged," Cam stressed.

"No ring..."

"Do I really need to wear giant ass diamond to prove I am claimed by a man? I don't need a ring. Rings tell men like you I am taken because you can't believe a lady's word," Harriet fired at him raising an eyebrow.

The blonde man raised his eyebrows, putting his hands up in surrender before walking away.

"Fucking men," Cameron grumbled, toasting their glasses before taking a sip.

The usual chaos echoed in the room as shitty music played and dramatic chatter floated around. Couples in the corner, sharing salvia, and entering a night of either terrible sex, STD sharing, or both.

The two of them lingered their eyes on the bartender as they chatted randomly. He was a nice picture to look at while the two talked. Firm biceps, short blonde hair, and kind blue eyes. The man gave her a vibe, a very boring vibe of '*I want to settle down, place our kids in Sunday school, and have awful, awful sex'*. Harriet just grimaced from that thought.

The two girls looked back at one another, and at the same time, both mumbling, "Church boy." Laughter erupted from that comment. It reminded them of the good old days where they sat at bars and judged the men that came in. Harriet smiled from that thought. It felt like a lifetime ago.

"Hot bartender who can't get the hint my girl is engaged!" Cameron called, waving at him to come over. He turned towards and looked at her weirdly. "Is it possible to get a full bottle of vodka just in front of me?" she asked. "We are celebrating!" Cameron yelled louder.

The man walked over, holding a bottle of Grey Goose.

"Celebrating what?" he smirked.

"This fucker's engagement to Mr. Jaxon Fucking Alderidge, woo woo!" Her friend said pointing to Harriet who lost it, throwing her head back as laughter erupted from her.

"Ignore her...get her something strong, not whiskey, she can't stomach it!" Harriet yelled over the loud, shitty music.

"Come on! It's Friday. Harry!" she rolled her eyes at her and gave in.

"Blondie...three rounds of shots, please! Then just give us the rest of the bottle," she told the bartender as they raised their drinks, hitting and taking a shot together. "To getting married for the second time!"

THREE HOURS LATER, multiple shooters and Harriet turning away five hot men who tried to steal her best friend. Harriet had her head on Cameron's shoulder talking nonsense or whatever came to her mind in that moment.

"I don't know if I could do it," she mumbled as she closed her eyes. The world was beginning to spin around her.

"Do what?"

"Marry Jax. His life is perfect, parties and cars and...I am Harriet Kensington from Auckland, New Zealand. I surf, hike, and have terrible credit. My life is going to be so much different. I am going to marry him look at my bank account and see too many zeros."

"Is it about the money?"

Harriet shook her head. "It's the lifestyle I am worried about. I already fucked up his family. I just-"

Her friend placed her hands on her shoulder, making her turn to look at her. "Jax and you are the greatest love story. Who cares about the materialistic things...the events, the people, and shit. He is your Jax at the end of the day. That doesn't change anything. Yes, you drive a Range Rover now and you live in ten million pound flat or something. He is still *Jax*, your Jax," her friend told her, sending her a comforting smile.

"Yeah, he is my Jax," Harriet mumbled.

"Exactly, don't worry. Now let's scour the room for me to have a male companion tonight that will rock my world, hopefully, but probably not." The two giggled.

Her phone vibrated. Cameron spotted a man in the corner who looked interesting so off she went. Harriet nursed her drink as she opened the new message.

New Message at 1:43 a.m.

From Jax:

I am lying in my bed thinking about how much I love and miss you right now, Kit.

Harriet smirked, biting her lip as she wrote out her reply.

To Jax:

I miss and love you more. Xoxo

What arc you doing, Kit?

I am out with Cameron right now, celebrating a certain engagement.

A certain engagement...I wonder who is getting married ;) Where are you celebrating?

At the pub, babe. Don't worry, it's just Cam and I. Talk to you later?

Phone sex later? My cock is aching right now, Kit. It misses you as much I miss you.

Sure, sex fiend.

She chuckled at his response. That man can't go a day without sex. A complete sex-a-holic! Her eyes glanced over the pub, seeing her best friend all cozied up to a man now. Harried smirked, sending her a wink as she grabbed her stuff to say goodbye to her.

"Cam, you're an absolute minx. Ugh...I could never live without you. You and your ambition and your crazy mind, getting me to do things I could never fathom. What would I do without you?" she said, sending her a wink. "Anyway, I am heading out, love you lots and thanks for tonight," she beamed to her, kissing her forehead and then leaving the pub.

Harriet stumbled out as she grabbed her phone to call Beckett. However, a taxi was parked right outside the bar. It was close to two a.m., and she decided not to annoy Beckett. Her eyes glanced over the street one more time, seeing people stumbling home and accompanying one another for some midnight shenanigans.

Her hand curled around the handle, opening it as she got in. She pressed Jax's name on her phone as she got into the car, quickly telling the driver the address to their flat.

"Hi, you," his voice purred.

"Don't you have a dinner meeting to go to?"

She heard his chuckle as he rolled in his bed. "It's nine, and I went for drinks, but I wanted to talk to my fiancée instead of discussing settlements and law. How was your night?"

"Wonderful, plastered right now, but heading home."

"Did you call Beckett?"

"It is two in the morning, Jax, I didn't want to bother him. The man has a life outside of driving us, so I am in a cab."

His groans were heard through the line. "Harriet," he grumbled.

"I will call you when I get home, ok? Then we can have our nightly chat," she smirked trying her best to sound flirty.

"Ok, I love you."

"I love you more."

She hung up letting her head hit the window as she watched the streets roll by.

"Hi, princess," the rustic Kiwi accent rang through the vehicle once he was sure her phone was away.

Harriet instantly recognised the voice, looking up to see his hazel eyes in the rear-view mirror. His blonde curls poking out of his hood as he drove down the street.

"Kai," she mumbled.

Her breaths were shallow as she held a firm glare to his eyes. Her body was frozen and tense. Her mind was boggled with what was happening. Kai was here, he was here, and he was here for money. She intuitively knew it.

"Princess," he smirked evilly as he continued to drive the car.

"What do you want, Kai?" Harriet asked sternly, sobering up fast and trying her best not to stumble over her words.

"I am going to pull the car over and we are going to have a civil conversation. Ok, princess?"

Harriet nodded.

"And don't call Jax," he said coldly.

Kai turned the car down an alleyway. She didn't recognize the area, especially since it was night. Everything was dark and mysterious. Lamp posts lit the streets dimly as distant yelling and honking were heard. She noticed the area was industrial. There were factories around her and rough looking homes.

The car came to a halt. She clutched her bag closer to her as Kai turned around in his seat. He removed his hood and his hazel eyes locked with her blue. Light stubble and his long curly hair were now on display as a Cheshire Cat grin appeared on his face.

"I heard about your new man," he said coldly.

"What about him?"

"Oh, Ettie, all defensive on me, huh? What happened to you being so," he hummed, "compliant."

"Kai, what do you want?" she sneered.

"Come on now, Ettie, what is happening? Where is the 'how are you' and 'what have you been up to' all those kinds of manners, eh?" he chuckled which resulted in Harriet rolling her eyes. "Now, we are going to get out of this car and go inside the warehouse and talk civilly."

"I am leaving," she responded, taking her phone out and trying to call Beckett.

Kai ripped the device out of her hands. "You will get this back after we talk."

"You do know it is quarter past two in the morning and I am in a dire need of sleep and some water. How about we do a rain check, and we go for lunch tomorrow?" Harriet said with a groan and a smirk.

"Get the *fuck* inside the building, Harriet!" he screamed at her, teeth bared as he pointed to the metal doors on the side of the warehouse.

She shuddered at his words, looking him dead in the eye as she opened the door. He followed, hand grasping her arm. He tugged her inside of the brick building.

"Let's talk about this politely, no need to grab my arm," she growled, trying her best to yank it out.

"Behave for goodness' sake, Et," he grumbled.

The two of them entered the old warehouse where pipes and boxes surrounded them. Bright light hit her eyes and she winced seeing a chair in the corner with a desk. Kai pushed her towards the old chair, wooden and creaky and she slumped down into it. He sat across from her, glaring and crossing his arms.

"Who the fuck are you? Where is the man I once loved?" she scoffed, rolling her eyes as he placed an iPad in front of her.

"Shut the fuck up, Harriet."

"Where is the man I met at the bar? Asked me to a game of poker and I destroyed his ass," she questioned.

His loving eyes were gone, she realised. The eyes she fell in love with at eighteen were gone and now there was fear in them. Kai feared something. The question was, what was he scared of? Why was he in London, in a warehouse with her? Her dad was correct, the man did need money, and there was something of a higher power holding him in fear. He owed money to someone dangerous, she concluded.

"How much?" she spat.

Kai swallowed his Adam's apple bobbing as he pursed his lips. Two dangerous looking men came from nowhere. Harriet was being held ransom, or she was about to be blackmailed.

"Let's get this started," Kai began sitting across from her.

She sat there, looking at him with an emotionless face as the two large men stood behind her ex-husband with their arms crossed. Kai leaned farther back in his chair; eyes linked with her blue ones. He smirked.

"My ex-wife left without a trace, no note, no address and her number wasn't working. I tried to contact your friends, nothing. Contacted the lawyers, and they refused to tell me where you ran off too," he told her, glaring at her. "Then, I was sitting at our house, morning coffee in hand as I turned the news on. You were papped with a rich lawyer, so that made me question...why was my Et in England?"

"You know the answer," she mumbled.

"Of course, I am upset over Arlo-"

"You weren't fucking there, Kai, you weren't fucking there when they cut me open to take our child out and to see the doctors walk away with him. Knowing something wasn't right. You weren't there when I knew that our baby was going to die, so you can't say shit. I carried him inside of me," she yelled at him, spitting the words with such fire.

"He was my baby as well," he yelled back, hands slamming on the table as he pushed towards her, spitting in her face. She jerked back.

"For fuck's sake, he was not. The minute you knocked me up you were done with me, off with your women, drugs, and poker games. So, you can't say shit about being sad over him. He was mine, and I lost him. I hate you."

He scoffed, pushing the iPad towards her.

"I need five million pounds, Ettie," he cursed.

"I don't have fucking five million, Kai. I paid off our fucking debt, and now I am worth possibly ten thousand pounds. I don't have money and you know that," she spat at him.

Kai let out a loud scoff. "Oh, I know but your *fiancé* does."

She stayed still, arms crossed over her chest as she let out a loud sigh. "My men overheard that at the bar... Mr. Bartender? He is part of this. Congratulations on the engagement, Et, didn't know you would be over us so quickly."

"We were over for a long time, Kai," she mumbled. "So, what are you going to do, blackmail me, hold me for ransom? Jax is a fucking lawyer, he knows people," she teased, kicking her feet up onto the wooden desk and crossing her arms.

"You have always been so cheeky, haven't you? Maybe you should keep your mouth shut or else someone is going to get hurt. He has kids. I know people too," he quipped, raising an eyebrow.

The minute he said that she was done playing games. Rule number one don't bring people's kids into deals. That would go south. Harriet was fuming, her blood boiling.

"Don't you go fucking threatening me now, bringing in the kids. What the fuck do you want?" she spat, ready to pick a fight.

Kai turned the iPad on. "You're an established woman in London. Good job, status, engaged to England's favourite socialite and now part of his family, etc. It would be a shame if people knew the truth about you, princess. London's sweetheart, Jax Alderidge's woman...an addict? Well, that won't go too well within the media. Plus, your criminal record," he said with a smirk.

"My criminal record doesn't exist. I didn't get prosecuted."

"I know people."

He turned the iPad on, and a series of images appeared. It was her, roughly about five years ago in a basement suite. She knew where she was at their old home. It was a shitty quality, possibly from a phone, showing her stabbing a needle into her vein.

"Does Jax know about your past addictions?" he teased. Her eyes were locked on the images. "Does Jax know his perfect little *Kitten* did heroin? How that would that affect his image..."

"Five million," she scoffed, "or else you will release these pictures of me doing hard drugs?"

"I also have a sex tape plus your record. You are starting your life here in England, hate to see it ruined by this."

"Why are you doing this, Kai?" she asked, jaw clenched as her eyes glanced over the iPad.

"We do shit in order to survive, you know that. A man's gotta do, what a man's gotta do, Ettie. You understand that, don't you? Five mill by tomorrow night, meet me back here and I will wipe the footage. Here is my number," he sent her a sly smile, handing her a piece of paper.

"I fucking hate you."

"If Jax gets involved, say goodbye to this life."

31

Harriet was pacing, she had barely slept that night as she paced back and forth. Her feet were bare on the wooden floors as she held her phone in one hand and Jax's debit card in the other. Five million, would he know if she took out five million? That man drops money like nobody's business.

Images of her doing hard drugs, she couldn't believe it. A year ago, she wouldn't have cared if it got realised but now, she did. Her present life required keeping a certain image. It was still out in the media about how she was a home wrecker and for it to get out that she was also an addict!

'The Druggie who ruined England's perfect family'.

She could hear the headlines already!

Jax would lose it. He would leave her. She had fucked up enough already. Harriet knew that this would be the icing on the goddamn cake. Jax didn't know about the drugs, and if he did, he would go mental. He quizzed her before about it, and she had lied right to his face.

How would she do this? Call the bank?

'Hi, can I get five million out? Yeah, it just for some shopping, yes shopping...personal care, you know?'

They would call Jax in a heartbeat.

Her phone went off, making her jump. She saw Jax's name appear on the screen, her heart dropped.

"Hello?" she said, trying her best to sound herself.

"You didn't call me when you got home from the pub, Kit. Had to deal with my situation by myself, wasn't too nice if you ask me," he snickered.

"Sorry about that, I came home and collapsed. You should be asleep right now," she lied, diverting the conversation. Harriet stopped pacing and sat on the couch. A heavy breath left her lips.

"It is six in the morning. I need to get up for a meeting in an hour. Just wanted to check on you as you didn't call me back," he told her. Harriet could hear the ruffling of his sheets as he got up. "Are you ok? You sound different, panicked and jumpy," he told her, concerned.

Harriet hummed. "M'fine, just nervous cause I have this project due for Atticus, and I am not good at presenting."

He didn't buy it, and she realized right away. "Well, ok," he said.

"I have to go. I am late for an appointment," she said, getting up on the couch and grabbing her coat.

"Oh, ok. What appointment?" he asked, trying his best to dig for information.

"Umm, I can't tell you. It is a," she trailed off, "a wedding thing."

Jax, across the world sat on his bed with his eyebrows frowned from her words "Wedding thing?"

"Yes."

"I thought you said you didn't want a wedding," he

reminded her. Harriet's eyes widened; she really did suck at lying.

"Well, I was out last night with Cameron, and she reminded me that my last wedding was at a City Hall and my honeymoon was in a car for a few minutes, so I might want a wedding now. Cam and I are going to go look at wedding stuff."

He scoffed, "Ok, well-"

"Cam is here, got to go, love you. Bye!" she hanged up the phone and groaned. That was absolutely pathetic. He didn't buy it, not for a second. Jax knew something was up and she was hours from being caught.

It was now or never. The brunette grabbed her coat and bag and the keys to the Maserati. On the way out, she grabbed duffle bags from the closet and Jax's cheque book. How many bags would be needed to hold 5 million pounds?

She drove to their designated private bank, HSBC. Her mind was going a mile a minute as she created some form of excuse for this behaviour. What did she need to tell their banker? How could she make this not sound suspicious? Questions flooded her mind as she stressed over the situation. Jax would understand when it was all dealt with. Jax would one hundred precent understand this behaviour. Her life wouldn't be destroyed by those videos, by *him*.

She was finally at a happy point in life. Harriet had Jax, a great job, step kids. Her life was picture perfect. She couldn't afford to fuck it up now.

The car parked. She grabbed the bags and her wallet before entering.

"Is Anthony Green in?" She hurried in as she went to the till.

The lady gave her a look.

"I am Jax Alderidge's partner, Harriet Kensington. Tell him I need an emergency meeting with him."

The Asian woman raised her eyebrow at her before making a call to the banker. Harriet stayed put, arms wrapping around her body as she waited. Jax would be called any minute now. He would know. He was in New York, so she had at least ten hours before he was here. Harriet had time, and she needed to use it wisely and proficiently.

"Ms. Kensington," the older man's voice echoed. She turned around, seeing a balding man in a suit. "This way," he pointed down the hallway.

She nodded, following him to his office. He stayed quiet as she sat down in the office, leg bouncing and breath heavy. Her eyes glanced across the small space with a few windows and pictures of his face. It was very bare, minimalistic and plain, just like the banker across from her.

"How can I help you today?" Anthony asked, his hands were together in front of him.

"I need five million pounds in cash," she muttered.

Anthony jerked back. "Does Mr. Alderidge know about this?" he asked. "It is his bank account, after all."

"He knows," she lied.

"Write out a cheque, and I will be back in a moment. I have to call someone," he told her. His hand was briefly placed on her shaking ones before he exited.

Harriet nodded, pulling out Jax's cheque book from her bag and writing out the amount. Seconds later, Anthony was back.

"Ms. Kensington, there seems to be a problem. Under the account Mr. Alderidge assigned to you, there is only three million in it."

The brunette nodded, leg bouncing as he told her those words. Fuck, what could she do now?

"Mr. Alderidge is also on the phone and would like to talk to you," he told her.

Harriet nodded slowly as he handed her the phone. She took it, hand shaking as she brought the device to her ear.

"Harriet? What the fuck is happening?" She could hear the pacing on the line coming from his side.

Jax ran his hand through his wet hair as he paced his hotel room. What was happening? Why had she asked for five million pounds in cash?

"Are you sending money to your father?" he asked.

Harriet stayed quiet, biting her lip as he rambled on.

"Are you leaving me?" he eventually said, but that was much quieter, almost a whimper. "We don't have to get married if it is too soon. We don't need to. It can just be us, Kit, please. If I have you, I'm happy."

Harriet sighed, looking up at Anthony in the doorway, who stood there patiently.

"Jax, I can't tell you, but I promise you that it is for the best. I love you, I really do, but I *need* this money."

She heard his groan as a jingle of keys were heard.

"Don't do shit till I am there-"

"Jax, I don't have time. I need it now," she said flatly.

"Harriet," he mumbled, "are you ok?"

Was she ok? She didn't feel ok. The idea of lying to Jax made her want to vomit. The whole situation now was fucked. Her ex-husband holding footage of her that she wasn't proud of and extorting her for money was just not fathomable.

"I will be."

"Are you leaving me?" he asked again, slowly saying with

each word. Emotion covered every syllable as he whispered such a pressing question. Was she leaving him for good?

"No," she muttered.

A sigh of relief came from his lips. "Why do you need the cash then?"

"I can't tell you, but it will be ok. Everything will be ok. Jax, I love you. This will soon be dealt with, and I'll see you on Monday when I pick you up from the airport," she told him.

"Give the phone back to Anthony, Harriet." It was stern, emotionless and to the point, but what really stung was the fact that he used her full name. He said, 'Harriet', and that made her more scared. Jax was beginning to know things, she believed.

Harriet looked at Anthony, giving him a curt nod as she handed him the phone.

"Do whatever she says," he told him, "Give her five mill and if she asks for more, give it to her." The line went dead.

Anthony placed the phone back on the desk, looking at her.

"I need to call some people as five million pounds is a lot of cash."

She nodded at his words.

New Message at 12:05 pm

From Jax:

What the hell is happening, Kit? Talk to me.

Seconds later, he texted again.

Tell me we are ok.

We are ok, Jax. I'll talk to you soon.

Harriet placed her phone back in her bag as she waited, leg bouncing. She looked over the white office. There was a dead plant in the corner and family pictures hanging on the walls.

"I am so fucked up," she whispered, as she glanced over the room, hands rubbing her face. "What the fuck am I doing?" Her leg bounced faster as she waited for the bags.

Her phone was beeping again, but she chose to ignore it. Jax would be home tonight. At that very moment, he was possibly getting on the jet and heading back. He could be here in less than eight hours, then she would have to come clean.

Jax would know everything about her. The lies about the drugs. It made her stomach churn. He wouldn't leave now, would he?

"Ms. Kensington, the bags are ready. Please show us to your car." She got up, throwing her handbag over her shoulder, and dusted off her hands on her pants.

"This way, gentlemen," she smiled to them as they exited the bank, went down the stairs and out onto the streets of London.

The Maserati lit up as she unlocked it. The trunk opened and the bags were placed in the car.

"Thank you for understanding, Mr. Green," she nodded to him, confidence sounding in her voice.

She was leaning against the car, arms crossed as she sent him a smile. He sent her a firm nod. Harriet got into the car, taking a deep breath before speeding off.

She took out the paper in her pocket and checked the number on it. This was the next step. Harriet typed in the number and then let the hands-free system call him.

"Princess," his voice echoed in the car.

"I have your money," she grumbled.

"I always knew you were a good girl," he told her smirking.

"Where do you want to meet?"

"Is Jax with you?"

"He is in New York."

"Warehouse then."

She hung up, her phone ringing again. She groaned, pressing accept.

"What else, Kai? I have your fucking money," she grumbled as she turned at the lights, going back to the industrial area of town.

"Harriet, what is happening? What the fuck does Kai want?" Jax yelled through clenched teeth.

"Shit," she mumbled. "I will explain when you are back," she brushed off.

"What is happening?" he said again, voice louder.

"Jax-"

"No excuses, *tell me now*," he growled. Harriet shuttered at his words. The anger laced in his voice made her shiver. She had to tell him. He had to understand. At least, she hoped he would.

"Kai has images of me and is holding it for ransom. He needs cash," she said too quickly.

"What are the images?" he grumbled.

"Jax," she mumbled.

"Harriet Camille Kensington, for fuck's sake, tell me. I am about to board a plane, and I need to know if you are ok. What the *hell* is happening? Tell me everything, now!"

She shuddered from his voice.

"I was doing heroin and he has a sex tape."

He groaned, it echoed throughout the car. "You told me you didn't do hard drugs," he spat in his phone.

"Not anymore!"

"Harriet... that shit is illegal," he mumbled, hand rubbing his eyebrows as he sat down in the jet.

"Don't you think I know that!" she screamed.

"I am calling the cops, give me the fucking address."

"Jax," she tried, "let me fix this."

"Extortion is illegal, Harriet. Let me fix your fucking mess once again. Pull over, I will call Everett and he will deal with this. He is a cop, a detective."

Harriet pulled the car over to the side of the road.

"I am not mad, ok. I just don't want to lose you," he told her, voice softer now. She could hear the noises coming from the engine of the plane.

"I know. I love you," she told him over the phone.

"Let me fix this. I gave your number to Everett, and he will deal with this," Jax pleaded. "I am tracking your phone now. Everett will be there soon. I love you."

Harriet, who stayed on the side of the road, sighed. Would Kai really delete the footage? That is million dollar question. The man was a sociopath! Deep inside of her, she knew that if she handed the cash to him, he would delete the footage. That file at least, but there were possibilities that there were copies of it elsewhere. Then three years later, he would call her up again and try to blackmail her again.

Harriet concluded that it would be best for her to hand over this case to the authorities.

"Get the authorities involved, please," she pleaded in the phone.

"I will call Everett. Stay where you are. I will send your location to him."

She nodded, hearing the line die as she hit her forehead on the wheel. A loud beeping noise echoed on the street, causing her to jerk back. This was absolutely fucked up.

Several minutes later, there was a knock on her window. Harriet looked up to see a man in his early forties with long curly dark brown hair and dark green eyes looking at her.

She rolled down the window. He was wearing a black long sleeve shirt and black jeans with a holster. This must be Everett.

"Hi, Harriet?" he asked, arms crossed over his chest.

"Yes," she mumbled.

The man nodded. "August Everett, detective. I just got off the phone with Jax, and he explained the situation. Can I get in?" he asked.

Harriet nodded, allowing him to enter the vehicle. She was intimidated by him. His tall and broad figure came with an uncompromising attitude and minimal amount of emotion on his face.

"Ok, tell me everything and I will see what my guys and I can do," he told her with his raspy Northern British accent. August was leaned back, arms crossed as he nodded to her story. The man was all business, no hint of emotion in him.

Harriet came clean, the images, the divorce, her father's warning. She just told him everything within those ten minutes. August didn't show a hint of emotion, all he did was listen.

"He knows I am on my way." He hummed to her words, nodding.

"Here is what's gonna happening. What he is doing is illegal, it is called extortion. I am going to radio in this case, backup is going to head to the warehouse. I am going to ride with you, but I will be in the back. He won't be able to see me. Ask for the images before you hand the cash over, the minute it is in your hands, the team will head in."

"Ok," she nodded.

"I will get out. You leave as fast as you can with the flash drive or whatever device it will be on. Go home. Jax will be back soon."

"Why are you helping me?" she whispered. "I did illegal things."

August sighed, "Jax was my lawyer for my very shitty divorce before he switched to corporate law. I owe him one. He is a good guy when he chooses to be. Now, let's get this tape back. Drive," he told her.

Harriet nodded. "Thank you."

THE CLOSER SHE got to the warehouse, the shakier she got. The anxiety and nervousness were settling in as she saw the old brick building appear. August was in the back, hiding on the floor with a gun in his hand as she pulled up in the alleyway.

Harriet let out a shaky breath. She called Kai again.

"What took you so long?" Anger filled his voice as it rang through the line.

"Traffic," she muttered. The line went dead, and she took deep breaths, trying her best to calm her own anxiety.

"You will be fine, Harriet. Just do what I told you."

Harriet nodded, hands on the wheel gripping the soft

leather as she saw Kai exit the building. His hood was up as he swaggered over, eyes burning into hers. He knocked on her window and she rolled it down.

"Cash," he muttered.

"That isn't how I do business, Fitzgerald. Give me the footage and you can have the cash," Harriet told him, confidence laced her voice as she glared at him. "I work with multimillion dollar deals. Business is my middle name."

Kai looked around the alley as if he was nervous and waiting for something to pop out. Little did he know.

"Fine," he muttered, putting his hands in his jacket pocket and pulling out the flash drive. "You know I never wanted to do this in the first place," he told her, handing the flash drive over.

"I don't care if you threaten me, but you don't threaten *my* kids. Burn in hell," she spat. Rolling the window up and placing the car in drive.

August busted the car door open, gun in hand, as he pointed the device to Kai. Kai instantly placed his hands up in surrender as he was backed in the corner.

"Go, Harriet!" She nodded, flooring the gas as she sped out of the alleyway. Cars, sirens, and lights were visible in the rear-view mirror as she left the scene.

She did it. Tears were flooding her eyes as she sped down the downtown streets, rushing home to hide. This was all too much. Officers were on scene and dealing with him, but she was alone now. The brunette was going to go home and wait for Jax to get back. The wait would be hours, six maybe, eight more likely.

In the corner of her eye, she saw the salon she went to at the beginning of this mess. An idea sparked in her.

"Do you have time for a walk-in, Toby?" She smiled at the man. He nodded.

"You look like hell, girl," he told her with a chuckle as they walked to his chair.

Once settled, she looked at her appearance. The blotchy tear-soaked face, dark undereye bags, and her hair a mess.

"I am marrying him," she muttered to the hairdresser.

Toby raked his fingers through her hair as she looked at his eyes through the mirror.

He laughed, "The man who likes blondes? What happened to 'fuck you, you don't own me,' sweetheart?"

"I realized that he was actually a good man and that we just had our differences. Get rid of the brown. I want to go back to my natural colour."

"Which is?"

"Blonde."

32

Harriet, ash blonde now, walked into the apartment. It was dark, the fire was on, and silence filled as she entered. She turned the corner. It was a little past eight at night now. After Toby, she headed to be with Cameron until she was sure Jax was home.

He was there, suit jacket gone, and collar shirt unbuttoned. His palms were on the counter as he leaned on them and looked down. A scotch was in front of him, half-empty as he waited for her.

"He is dealt with," he mumbled when he heard her footsteps.

Harriet hung up the keys of the Maserati on the wall and placed her bag down on the counter, coming around to him and wrapping her arms around him.

Instantly, he nuzzled himself into her, holding her close as he cried lightly. Harriet took a deep breath, rubbing circles on his back.

"When I got that call, I thought you were leaving me for real. I thought you were done and that you were going to go."

He pulled away, looking in her blue eyes.

"You're blonde." She brushed his curls away from his face as she planted a firm kiss on his lips.

Jax rubbed a strand of her hair between his finger pads as he stared at her.

"Why didn't you tell me?"

"I was scared that you would leave me for good. Jax, I," she sighed, thumbing her tears away, "I feel like every day something comes up that makes me feel like I am not good enough for you. That I am just trash, from the low life. I already fucked up so much here that I thought you would leave if you found out I did drugs. If that video went out, I knew I was done," she cried.

Jax shook his head, cupping her cheeks as he wiped the tears away with his thumb.

"No, I don't care," he told her, face scrunching up. "You're my girl, my lover, my soulmate. I knew everything, Harriet. I had a private investigator looking into Kai and I knew about his gambling and the fact he was in debt. I was watching him. I knew you did drugs. I knew you were arrested for running a ring, but never charged. I don't care about that stuff. I care about your safety. You're not an addict. You're independent, healthy, beautiful woman who is my girl."

Harriet shook her head, licking her lips as he wiped her tears.

"You hired a private investigator?"

"Yes."

"Why do we lie to one another?" she whispered.

"Because we both believe we are not good enough for the other person," he told her, caressing her cheeks and tilting her chin to look up at him.

"You're enough for me," she muttered, "more than enough," she cried.

"Likewise."

"What is going to happen to Kai?" Harriet asked, leaning against the counter and taking his drink from him. "He'll be arrested and charged with extortion. Everett told me he threatened the kids, so I am going to make sure the fucker is locked up."

Harriet nodded. "He did."

"Where's the cash?" Jax asked, hand on her hip as he looked in her eyes.

"I dropped it back to Anthony. It is in your account," she muttered, walking to the fridge to grab something to eat.

Jax watched her. She was perfect to him, no matter what. He loved her with every fibre of his being. He cried when she cried, he hurt when she hurt, and he was happy when she was happy. They were connected whether they knew it or not.

"I was so scared," he admitted as she came back.

"I know, I was too."

"Come here," he said, opening his arms up. She walked into them, letting him cradle her as they rocked back and forth. They held each other like it was their last time, rocking back and forth as they cried a little.

"I love you," she muttered, "every imperfection is a perfection to me and every flaw that you possess, I see it as flawless. I will love you forever, even if you threaten everyone or," she muttered, raking her fingers through his hair as she looked up, "if you do have control issues. You are perfect to me." She kissed his cheek. "Perfect man, father, and eventually," she took his left hand and kissed his ring finger, "husband."

"Kitten," he muttered, "I was not in New York for work."

She frowned. "What were you in New York for then?"

Jax walked to the bedroom, leaving her there with her arms crossed. He came back with a blue velvet box in his hand. She instantly knew what it was.

"I found this designer, well my PA did, but that doesn't matter," he told her with a light chuckle. "Anyway, she takes antique rings and redoes them to make them better. I thought of you right away with your retro yet modern style," he rambled on, eyes locked on the box.

"Jax, are you nervous?" she chuckled, cupping his light stubbled cheeks.

"Yes, because I really haven't proposed before." She laughed. "Anyway, I met with the designer, and I looked at all the antique rings, and we came up with a plan. She took this band and like did shit to it, anyway. I am obviously not a jeweller. I am a lawyer," he was still rambling on.

She chuckled as he got down on one knee, looking up to her.

"Harriet Camille Kensington, I have loved you since I met you when I was seven. You had a stuffed kitten and a very shy smile. I watched you grow up and become this confident woman who doesn't give two shits about anything. You're not scared to give someone a piece of your mind or to outdrink someone. I have also heard you are the ultimate poker champion, so it is on my list to beat you, but knowing you, you will beat me. You possess this aura that makes me want to be a better man for you. Kit, you're so badass and independent. I love you, I always have and seeing you thirteen years later, you still have the same effect on me as you always did. You're beautiful, intelligent, confident, and I want to spend the rest of my life with you.

So, will you do the honour of becoming my wife?" he asked.

Harriet blinked away the tears as she nodded.

"Yes," she mumbled, cupping his cheek and bringing him up for a kiss. It was messy, as she cried tears of happiness in the kiss. Her arms wrapped around his neck as she kissed him with passion.

He pulled away, taking the most beautiful ring she has ever seen and placing it on her left ring finger. It had an antique rose gold braided band accented with white diamonds. An oval diamond, large and perfect, sat in the middle. It was perfect, vintage mixed with chic and glamour. Harriet looked at her finger, staring at it as she cried.

"I love you," she mumbled through the tears, kissing him again.

"I love you too, Kit," he smirked as she looked between him and the ring.

The woman was in shock, letting the tears roll down her cheeks. He loved her, even with the teary eyes, swollen lips, red cheeks, and snotty nose. Jax chuckled, seeing her trying to connect the dots of what had just happened.

"Kai," she mumbled.

"Is in prison, waiting to be deported back to New Zealand for trial."

"We," she mumbled, "we, we are getting married," she eventually got out.

He nodded.

"Ok, mister. I need to take a powder break, and then we are going to make love. Not fuck, no...devices, just you and me in missionary," she mumbled, taking the box of tissues and walking to the bedroom.

He chuckled, nodding at her.

"Jax!" she called, turning around, nudging to the bedroom.

"Right, coming!" He was shaken out of his stare as he followed her.

EPILOGUE

1 YEAR LATER...

Harriet stood in front of the mirror, trying her best not to cry as she looked over her white gown. The vintage, floral lace A-line dress with the deep V-neck and flutter sleeves molded to her curvy body. The blonde fanned her face as she tried not to cry.

She looked like a princess. Her hair beautifully curled topped with a flower crown. She took one more look at herself.

"You look so pretty, Harry," Ember said, dressed in her own pastel lavender dress with her hair curled and a little flower tucked behind her ear.

Harriet smiled, sucking in her tears as she kneeled, eye to eye with her about-to-be stepdaughter.

"Not as beautiful as you, Miss. Em," she winked, kissing her cheek.

"Daddy is going to cry," she told her. Harriet laughed.

"We will see. He can't cry though or else I am going to cry."

She could hear Cameron laugh in the background, "What a," she paused, "...wimp."

"Yeah, we don't want to use the P word, Cameron," Harriet chuckled, sending a look to her friend.

She got up, turning around to look at herself one last time before she went outside and walked down the aisle. Harriet couldn't believe the day had come. She was marrying the love of her life.

"I am going to fucking cry any moment now," she whispered to herself.

Harriet combed her hair one last time before turning to her best friend and soon to be stepdaughter. They were in her old bedroom at the manor getting ready for the wedding.

The two of them had moved back here. Harriet loved the gardens and the memories she had made there. Jax and her decided it would be perfect for them to get married at home, as Harriet had fell in love with the meadow. The trees, pond, and flowers everything was perfect. Jax agreed, but he would be fine with anything.

The wedding was small, less than one hundred people, but nonetheless perfect. Themes of pastel purple was what she wanted. So, the bridesmaids were dressed in the gorgeous colour, and wildflowers covered everything.

"Alrighty, Mrs. Alderidge, time to marry the man," Cameron interrupted her, handing her a bouquet of flowers.

A knock came at the door. Harriet walked up to the door opening it. Atticus sent her a warm smile, dressed in a grey suit, clean-shaven with short blonde hair pushed back.

"Isn't the best man supposed to be with the groom?" she joked.

"Yeah, but Jax told me to come to see you and say hello

quickly before running back and telling him what you look like."

Harriet chuckled, "Of course he wanted you to do that."

She gave him a hug and a kiss to his cheek.

"Thank you for everything," she said to him, patting his chest.

"You deserve everything, Har," he told her, fixing her glasses on her nose and fingering a curl.

"I am trying my best to not cry." Atticus laughed, placing his hand on her hip and giving her a quick peck on the cheek.

"You're not particularly good at it. Jax is getting antsy. He didn't like spending the night without you."

Harriet chuckled, "Of course he didn't. That man can't go a second without me."

Atticus rolled his eyes.

"Ok, I need to go marry that fucker now. See you at the altar, Atticus."

She bid her farewells as she walked down the hallway with her bouquet of wildflowers in one hand and Ember's hand in the other. The little brunette had begged for months to be part of the wedding, and Harriet couldn't say no.

Cameron was her maid of honour standing proudly beside her since day one. It was her dream come true to marry Jax. It didn't feel real, but it was.

She walked out of the kitchen to the backyard, where she saw the altar in the distance. Her man was chatting to Atticus and two other male figures.

'Sebastian Prescott and Christopher Everston?" she wondered.

Jax looked devilishly handsome in his black suit and a

clean-shaven face with his curls gelled back. She could just imagine ripping that suit off later.

He spotted her, standing at the doorway metres away from him, ready to walk down the aisle and vow to be the best wife. Jax admired her in her dress. She looked absolutely beautiful. Harriet sent him a small smile, he reciprocated it. Then, she turned to Ember.

"Are you ready? You go first with the basket with flower petals, ok? Throw them on the floor and everywhere. Ok, sweets?" she told her step-daughter. Ember nodded proudly and began to walk down the aisle.

Harriet quickly pulled her back. "When the music begins, muppet."

Ember chuckled in Harriet's embrace. The violins began to play, and she let the little brunette go. She was the spitting image of her father.

Harriet collected herself, taking a deep breath as her best friend walked down the aisle next. Now it was her moment to shine.

She placed her one foot forward and walked down the meadow to her lover. Harriet saw him stand proudly and watched her with such love in his eyes. He was by the oak tree next to the pond. She spotted Caleb on Claudia's lap next to her new girlfriend. Harriet gave him a quick wave and a wink. Jax noticed she wasn't wearing shoes and he chuckled. Kiwis and their lack of shoes. Harriet smiled proudly at him.

Jax placed his hand out for her, which she took proudly.

"You're beautiful, so beautiful even with no shoes," he told her. She giggled.

"You still wanna marry my crazy ass?" Harriet teased.

Jax rolled his eyes. "I would still marry your crazy ass

even if you walked down naked, drunk, or in a sheet," he whispered to her.

The two of them turned to the officiant as he began to speak. Harriet blocked him out and just looked at her lover's ocean eyes. Even though they only had been together barely a year, she felt like she had been with him since the beginning of time. The love she had for him was unbeatable and incomparable to anything else in the world. Jax smirked at her. Their hands were entwined as he muttered, "I do". Harriet looked over to the older man.

"Harriet Camille Kensington, do you take Jax Fletcher Alderidge to be your wedded husband, to have and to hold from this day forward, for better, for worse, for richer, for poorer, in sickness and in health, to love and to cherish, till death do you part?"

"I do," she beamed, biting her lip as her grin grew.

"Jax, your vows now."

Jax nodded and dropped his hands from hers. He quickly, took out a piece of paper from his pocket then cleared his throat.

"I met this woman when I was seven, she was four, and we were both abandoned by the person who made us. She was scared, her blue eyes filled with tears as she clasped this stuffed cat. I swore to myself the minute I saw her to be her protector for life. She stood by me throughout my childhood, whether it was run-ins with the law or crazy girlfriends. She was my best friend. When she was thirteen, she was asked out by a boy whose name I do not remember. I realised I loved her. You may shutter," he told the crowd, "that we started a relationship when I was sixteen, and she was thirteen, but we didn't shag till she was legal."

Harriet laughed, hitting his arm. "Jax!"

"Back to what I was saying, I promised to get her out, and I didn't. I will always regret it, but at same time I don't. If I had gotten her out from the system, I wouldn't have my two babies. We both agree that shit happens, which led us here. This woman became my nanny thirteen years after I was adopted out. We've had our highs and lows when we first started our relationship again, as we learned we aren't the same people as before, but we figured it out, and here we are now!" he exclaimed.

"I love this woman more than I love my life, my job, and especially my car which says a lot." Laughter erupted. Then he looked at her. "I promised you when I was seven to always be by your side, to be your best friend, and protector. Here I am promising you this under the law. I promise to love you forever and a day, Kit. I will always be your man, and you will always be my Kitten."

"I love you," she mouthed.

"To forever and a day, Kit," he winked at her. His hand clasped her waist twirling and dipping her as he planted a firm kiss to her lips. A yelp escaped her lips as she was caught off guard.

"Jax, I haven't even said my vows," she told him off.

He shrugged. "I now pronounce us husband and wife!" he yelled.

"Jaxon!" she groaned taking a piece of paper from her bra. "Don't you want to hear how much I love you," she muttered.

He snickered, "Yeah, I do. Continue on, Mrs. Alderidge."

Harriet rolled her eyes. "Well, Jax explained how we met. Which is quite a love story. Two orphans falling in love, cliché, but it is our love story. Jax, thirteen years after you had broken your promise, I stood before you gobsmacked that you were in front of me in your kitchen. You were fighting with Claudia, and the first thing I noticed was your unhappiness. The minute our eyes met you made a move towards me, and I freaked out. You were married, and I was finalizing my divorce. Nevertheless, I said to you I had loved you, but not anymore. That was lie. I have loved you since I was four. I love everything about you including your anger issues, slight control problems, and that you are sex crazed."

Laughter erupted once again, and she looked over to the audience blushing a little.

"I love you. Your every imperfection is a perfection to me. Every flaw is just another reason why I love you. I love everything that comes with you. I love your kids. I don't absolutely love your family, but we are growing to a form of like. I love your stupid jokes that are highly inappropriate, but I still laugh as if I were twelve. I love that you look at me like I am the best thing since sliced bread. I love every single part of you and that says a lot, because you are *a lot*."

She gestured to his broad figure. Harriet set him a smile before finishing her speech.

"The world is our chessboard and I just called checkmate with you, babe. After many defeats from the universe, we won. It was all part of the game. The game of life."

Jax had a toothy grin on his face as he looked over to the officiator.

"I now pronounce you husband and wife. You may kiss the bride."

Jax cupped her cheeks planting a firm wet kiss on her lips. Harriet smiled as she gripped his biceps.

Caleb came to them with rings in hand. Harriet kneeled down to him taking the silver band and placing it on her husband's finger. He did the same to her. She gave her stepson a kiss on his cheek as he scurried away back to his mother. Jax beamed proudly at everything in front of him.

"Now, time to celebrate!" he yelled.

Her pulled her to the side where Atticus was holding a flute of champagne with the two other male figures. Jax stopped in front of them, hand around her waist.

"Harriet, meet my best mates from New York," he introduced.

She looked at the two strangers. One, tall and broad with shorter dark brown hair and smug smirk. He embellished a grey three-piece suit and sent a wink. Chiselled, tone with a flirty demeanour.

"Sebastian Prescott, sweetheart," Sebastian said, placing his hand out for her to shake.

"Harriet Alderidge," she beamed, taking it. He took her hand and brought it to her lips kissing it.

"Seb," Jax warned knowing his friend well enough.

"Just being kind," Sebastian winked. "Got to have a look at this new lady in your life. Leaving your smoking wife for the nanny. Good one, bud," he teased. "Might I say, what a looker," Sebastian cock, sending her a wink.

"Mhmm, you must be the womanizer," she hummed.

"Hey, I have a lot of love and respect for women. I was raised by a single mother and women are amazing. Best things in the world. My company is the most progressive when it comes to women," he stated, throwing his hands up in offence. "Plus, you married Jax, and he is a lot worse than me. We met through-"

"Shut the fuck up," Jax bit.

"Sod off, Seb. She is a married woman," Atticus snickered.

Sebastian chuckled, leaning into Harriet's ear. "He is the troublemaker here, doll. Done a lot of bad things..."

"Oh, I know," she whispered, winking. "Good thing I like the bad boys." Sebastian just smirked, raising his brows and looked over to Jax who sent him a scowl.

"Enjoy then, doll."

"Don't be an ass. It's my wedding day," Jax stated, rolling his eyes.

Harriet chuckled, looking over to Christopher who homed a small smile and sent her a curt nod.

"We've talked on the phone before. You work for Atticus. Christopher Everston," he introduced pressing a kiss to her cheek.

"Yes, Everston Media and Records, right?"

"That's me," he grinned. "Congrats on the day. I look forward to seeing you more, Harriet."

He was tall and broad too but had mousy curls and a softer face. Clean shaven with a sharp black suit. Harriet looked between the two males then to Atticus and Jax. Trouble that is all she could think. Sebastian, she believed, was the most mischievous and the flirt. Christopher, stern and dominant. Atticus, the gentleman and her Jax, the controlling alpha but absolute sweetheart.

Any girl crossing their paths would be in danger as trouble never looked so fine and she bid them luck if they ever had run in with these handsome men.

"It's great to meet you all. Finally nice to put faces to the names," she hummed, looking back up to her husband. "Now, where are you going to take me on my honeymoon, Mr. Alderidge?" she asked as he pivoted away from the fine men to the house.

"Oh, Mrs. Alderidge, where am I not taking you is the

question?" he winked, kissing her cheek as he twirled her around. "I love you, wife. And I'm going to make sweet, sweet love to you tonight," he winked.

She rolled her eyes and raising an eyebrow. "Sweet, sweet love?"

"Nah, I am going to rip this fucking dress off of you and fuck you senseless till you scream my name. The whole world is going to know you're mine. Then I will make sweet, sweet love to you," he whispered in her ear as they walked into the kitchen, the guests following them.

"Oh, Jaxon, what am I going to do with you?"

"Fuck me senseless," he teased.

"I love you too," she whispered kissing his cheek.

THE END

ATTICUS' TRIUMPH

COMING SOON...

Adeline sat at the round table. Laughter rolled off her red lips as she sipped her rum and coke. Madi, her best friend since youth, was raging on about her last dating experience. The woman with short brunette hair continued explaining how the minute she spoke of her undergrad, physics, the man was gone.

"I swear, I am no longer going to date men! They seriously don't know the difference between a lepton and a quark and don't even get me started on the double slit experiment," Madi complained, rolling her eyes and throwing frantic gestures. Adeline continued to rip the room with her light laughter.

"Maybe you shouldn't talk about physics. Men like to talk about how big their cocks are or the newest win for England in rugby. Physics is not on their go to topic of conversation, but I am glad that you are testing their intelligence," Adeline mused to her.

Madi shrugged. "I just don't want to date an idiot. Gotta test them for their IQ."

"Yes, but doesn't mean you have to talk about physics. Make sure they at least know the quadratic formula, but not quarks and photons."

Madi groaned. "Enough about me. You have an appointment in an hour to talk about your manuscript...exciting!" she exclaimed, applauding her best friend. Another round of drinks came to them.

"I know. I am excited. I am happy that someone finally took my manuscript," she beamed, finishing her drink and asking for the bill.

Adeline, or Della as her friends called her, was a young aspiring romance writer. Writing stories similar to the classics, she was in love with historical romance with a twist, strong feministic characters, and secret affairs. The AVA House had accepted her manuscript and she had an upcoming meeting with them. The woman was desperately excited for this acceptance. Her dream had come true.

When Adeline dropped out of university at the end of her first year, she had decided that she should pursue a writing career as she always had one or a dozen love stories in her head. Her mother cheered her on telling her that she could really do it. However, there was one thing that was clear, she would need to find a publishing company that wasn't connected or owned by her father. Which in theory might be quite difficult as he owned eighty percent of Europe's publishing houses. She wanted to make sure that she was not going to make money off his company.

"So, the AVA House, never heard of it?" Madi quipped, sipping her rum and coke.

"Because you aren't in publishing, *geek*. The AVA House is an international, mainly romance, publishing company."

"Ahhh, I see, I see. And good old dad doesn't own it?" Madi asked.

"Hopefully not. Huntington Enterprises and Media has nothing associated with the AVA House, as far as I know."

"Well, your dream is coming true, babe," Madi winked at her.

Della glowed smiling fully as a red blush hit her cheeks. She really was so close to fulfilling her dream as an author.

DELLA WALKED INTO THE MODERN, yet chic building. The entrance way was decorated with a chandelier and quartz walls.

The golden blonde with hazel eyes was dressed in a pink dress with ruffle sleeves, a floral corset around her waist, and her hair falling in its natural curls. She took a deep breath and walked up to the receptionist desk.

"Hi, I have appointment with Harris Montgomery."

The black-haired woman with several tattoos and a multitude of piercings looked up. She typed away on the Mac computer before nodding at her.

"Mr. Montgomery will be down in a minute, Miss. Wisteria," she said politely, sending her a classic customer service grin.

Della smiled and gave a quick nod before looking around the entrance, her hazel orbs glancing over the room. This was really it. She was *really* releasing her own novel and soon. The woman couldn't believe it.

"Miss. Wisteria?"

She turned around to the male voice. He had dark hair, a toothy grin, and was dressed in a black suit.

"Harris Montgomery," he placed his hand out for her to shake. She took it kindly. "Let's head to my office, come."

He nodded to the elevator.

Della followed him, her slip-on beige heels clicking as they walked towards the elevator. The doors closed behind them and then the man, in his late twenties, turned to her.

"Your story, I genuinely enjoyed it. We have a ton of covers drafted up for you to pick from and there will be a publishing event hosted soon. I honestly believe that there will be lots of interest in the novel," he explained to her excitement evident in his voice.

Della gleamed, her dimples on display. "You really think so?"

"I know so."

The doors opened as she walked onto the top floor of the building and towards his office. He waved to the receptionist and a few people before he closed the door.

"So, here is what we have," he stated pulling out a few examples as he sat down.

She sat across from him holding her shoulder bag on her lap as he pulled out the covers.

"We can do the dress piece, her classic ballgown on the grand staircase..." he trailed on as he showed the different ideas.

"I like the meadow. It was quite significant to him and her. Felix and Sofia met secretly there. It makes sense for the cover to be them there," she added.

A knock interrupted their discussion. Della had her legs crossed as she turned around. A man, late thirties with longer hair, but looked short, came in. He was clean shaven and sported a grey suit that was patterned. Instantly, a blush arose to her cheeks. The mysterious man looked exactly like Felix in her book.

Atticus Astor, thirty-nine and a bachelor. He had dirty blonde hair that was combed back and narrow green eyes with a boyish smile. The man had a baby face but was still chiselled.

“I didn’t realise you were busy,” he muttered. His eyes shifted down to Della and a friendly smile grew. “Atticus Astor,” he introduced himself to Della, placing his hand out in front of him.

She shook his hand with a firm grip as he sent her a kind smile. “Adeline Wisteria,” she responded.

“Miss. Wisteria wrote ‘Forbidden Desires’, Atticus, our newest romance-“

“Felix and Sofia, I read it. It is very well done, Miss. Wisteria. I very much enjoyed it. Can’t wait till it hits the shelves.”

She thanked him shyly. The boyish face gave her a firm grin before diverting his attention to Harris.

“I was just wondering if you got Mr. Rogers’ book event organised?” he asked, crossing his arms across his chest. Della watched the bulging of his muscles as the suit shaped to his body perfectly.

“Yes, finished this morning.”

“Perfect. Nice meeting you, Miss. Wisteria, hope to see you at the publishing event.” Atticus nodded to her.

Della mumbled a yes, nervousness instantly flooding her system. She had never had a man affect her in that way before to make her choke on her words, and blush from every syllable coming from his lips. She didn’t even know anything about him besides his name, he owned the company, and that he looked identical to her character Felix.

"Back to what I was saying. We are thinking of September twenty-third for the release. Show up, look gorgeous, give a speech, and talk to everyone. How does that sound, Adeline? I can call you Adeline, right?" he asked.

She nodded. "Just make sure that it is signed as Della Wisteria."

"Of course, nickname?"

"Yes."

"Well, that is all we have time for today. Thanks again, Miss. Wisteria." Harris pulled his chair out again, going over to shake her hand. "See you in two months."

Della sent him a smile as she gathered herself to head out the door. She gave a final wave to Harris before she exited his office.

"Miss. Wisteria," she turned her head seeing *him* behind her in the archway of his office. Adorned in his grey suit, a boyish smile, and with his kind eyes looking at her. His stare went straight to her cheeks and red began to flush across them.

He took a step towards her. "I am glad you picked us to publish with. See you around."

"Thank you, Mr. Astor," she responded.

"Atticus, please," he charmed, sending her his toothy grin.

"Della...call me Della," she mumbled, before turning way and walking to the elevator.

Atticus watched her. "Della," he mumbled. Atticus knew there was something different about her. She gave him this feeling he couldn't quite put his finger on. In her presence, he felt warm and safe and a need to hold her. However, he shook it off. She was young, it could just be that.

AFTERWORD

I personally want to thank you for taking the time to read my book. It truly means a lot and I can't express the amount of gratitude I have.

Several more books will be coming to "The Checkmate Series".

- Jax's Game
- Atticus' Triumph
- Sebastian's Gambit
- Christopher's Ploy

I cannot wait for the next three books to be available for all to read. Thank you so much for making my dream come true.

ABOUT THE AUTHOR

A.E. Calder, known as Ava to her close friends, has been a writer since she was young. She always had a dozen stories in her head and dreamed of making them come alive. Ava found her love of writing by starting a blog and posting short stories which is still up to this day.

At fourteen, she said to herself that she would like to publish a novel by the end of high school and Ava did. "Jax's Game" was published on the last day of her high school career. She wrote the book while balancing her final year of school and applying to university.

In all her novels, most of her characters are based off her close friends and family as a way to say thank you for their help and support.

She currently lives in British Columbia, Canada and is looking forward to write several more novels. In fact, she has a few in her drafts ready to published soon.

Follow her on social media for news about her next books coming soon.

facebook.com/aecalderauthor
instagram.com/aecalderauthor
pinterest.com/aecalder28

Manufactured by Amazon.ca
Bolton, ON

22594155R00219